DAEIOS

---

140 FEET DOWN

COLLEEN ECCLES PENOR

Copyright © 2019 by Colleen Penor

All rights reserved.

Library of Congress Control Number: 2019913267

No part of this book may be reproduced in any form or by any electronic or mechanical means, including information storage and retrieval systems, without written permission from the author, except for the use of brief quotations in a book review.

Printed in Casper, Wyoming in the United States of America. Cover design by 100Covers. Author photo by Clint Saunders.

ISBN 978-1-7340037-1-0 (paperback)

ISBN 978-1-7340037-0-3 (hardcover)

ISBN 978-1-7340037-3-4 (ebook)

ISBN 978-1-7340037-2-7 (audiobook)

For Rob, who loves and believes in me unconditionally.
You are my safe place.

"Tell me, what is it you plan to do with your one wild and precious life?" — Mary Oliver

DEFINITION

DAEIOS (DAY-yos): God

1

Music blares in my head, and I startle awake, accidentally doing a straight-leg sit-up. It's the ringtone I programmed for Mother. Pressing the bud embedded below my left ear, I growl at my phone, "Buzz, voicemail." Then I feel bad. It isn't Buzz's fault he woke me up.

I lie down to sleep off more alcohol.

The music again.

What reason can she have for waking me up at ... this whatever time on a Saturday? I think it's Saturday. "Buzz, voicemail." I'm gentler this time. It seems like Buzz has feelings, and we're very close. He's inside my head, after all.

Rolling over, I'm suddenly aware there's no man in my bed. It's a little hazy, but I specifically remember that a Jerry? Barry? Joe, or Bo —someone—climbed into bed with me after I met him at the club last night. And yes, I smell his woodsy aftershave and that musky man-smell they all seem to share. And sex. I definitely smell sex.

Yes, she calls again.

I emit something between a groan and a snarl. She'll keep calling if I don't talk to her. "Buzz, answer." I let out a sigh the neighbors probably hear. When Buzz advises me in his courteous manner that we're connected, I say, "Mother, it's Saturday, I—"

"We're going to Daeios."

I kick off the covers and sit on the edge of the bed. "You're going underground. Why?"

Last night's clothes lie in a heap next to the bed, reeking of stale cigarette smoke. My head feels like it wants to fall off. Hangover.

"Don't you watch the news? Killer thunderstorms? The collapse of society?" Her words are clipped.

"That's somewhere else, far away. Not in Arizona."

"If you were paying attention, you'd know that weather-related deaths are increasing here, too, not just 'far away.'" She expels a puff of air from her throat. "You should come. Make a good decision for once."

If my face gets stuck like the face I make for her benefit, I will be one crazy-looking broad.

"The people at church think the Second Coming is near," she adds.

Ugh. "I'm not going to Daeios with you, Mother."

"We spent two million dollars on your share, did you know that? You're going to let that money go to waste?"

My ears ache from this conversation, and heat is spreading across my face. "Mother, even if I wanted to go, I can't. Finals are next week."

"Right. For your gym classes." She sneers the last two words.

"I take other classes. And I like to keep fit." I glance at my naked reflection in my full-length mirror, and I don't like what I see, so I turn away. "You don't need to go underground yet. What does Dad say?"

She clears her throat, a sure tell she's embellishing the truth. "He says it's time. Brother Christian called a few minutes ago to let us know they'll be locking Daeios down soon. We leave at noon. Your dad's getting the RV and the ATV ready now."

I stretch and vocalize a yawn. "I don't think I could last a week down there without going batshit crazy. Besides, everything's fine up here." I get up and peek under the shade, blinding myself. It looks fine to me. "Let me talk to Dad." After a few seconds, the phone transfers without her saying another word to me.

"Princess! Are you on your way?" He sounds so stressed and hopeful that I don't want to tell him.

"No, Daddy. Finals, remember?" I bite off a hangnail. "Are you sure it's time to go underground? We've had some stormy weather, but—"

"There's a lightning death in the paper almost every day. Lightning or softball-sized hail. The dam's about to burst. They're evacuating the Hills right now due to mudslides—"

"Evacuating the Hills? That's right behind the house." I sit on the edge of the bed again and pull the covers around me.

"Yes, and people are starting to panic. None of the grocery stores in town has any food left. We have our short-term food and water storage, but ... Shea, you'll have to hurry, or you're going to be stuck in traffic." His voice is tight. If anyone can make me cave, it's him. Him, or my little sister, Maya.

"I'm not burying myself alive in Daeios. I'll be fine up here." I sigh. It's so much harder to say "no" to my good-natured dad than it is to my mother.

"You're an adult so I won't argue with you, but ... Shea? We can't find Jace. Help us find him so he can go with us. Please. Do whatever you want after we leave."

"Did you try tracking him on his phone?"

"We found his bud sitting on a swing at a neighbor's house. It's a mess. He might've dug it out with his fingernails."

Gross. "Dad—"

"He can't survive on his own, Shea. He's still using that gloss drug. We have to take him away from it. We can't leave him."

"I'm not feeling well. I need to stay in bed." I lie back, pulling the covers over my head.

"Please, Princess. It'll just take an hour out of your day, and I don't like it, but we'll say our goodbyes and we'll be on our way." His voice quavers.

It's an hour I could be resting my hangover, though. What if I'm still drunk? Why, I shouldn't be driving. "Dad, I—"

"Please. For Jace."

My brother. He still lives at home because he's a GLSS addict. Gloss. He's twenty-four, two years older than I am, so if he was clean, he could leave and live off his trust fund, as I do. Mine's my Mother-escape fund.

Jace rarely leaves his room in my parents' basement now. Y Chromo could still find him there, of course. It's a chromosomal disorder that afflicts males of all ages, but it rarely affects older men like my dad. Lately, the mortality rate for men in their twenties has skyrocketed. Y Chromo has baffled scientists and put a sense of dread in everyone since the first diagnosis almost a decade ago.

Earth's male population is dying off. Even if Jace lucks out on Y Chromo, he'll kill himself with gloss. Dad's right: Jace can't survive by himself.

"Shea? Are you there?"

I throw the covers off. "I'll be there as soon as I can, okay?"

"Thanks." It's a sob, and he's gone.

I brush away my dragon breath and furry teeth and take a quick shower, washing the beer from my pores and the cigarette smoke from my hair and fingertips. The scent of Jerry/Barry/Joe/Bo slides down the drain in a thick pink foam with the bouquet of a cheap berry sangria. My head pounds from too many tap beers and Marlboros last night.

I step out of the shower and gaze in the mirror at the dark circles under my eyes. What am I doing? I was born December 12, 2012. Mother used to say I was destined for great things because—12/12/12. But look at me. Other than having great skin, I'm a mess.

My red hair is long and thick and takes forever to blow dry, so I skip it. Swallowing two painkillers with half a glass of water, I pull on a mint green tank top and navy shorts with my favorite running shoes, and grab my keys to run out the door. I glance at the clock. It's 10:41.

I hesitate in the doorway, then go back and fetch my survival pack.

I run out to my car, which I unimaginatively call Smart. He's modeled after an old Smart car from the early 2000s. My dad had him custom-built for me for high school graduation, adding a little extra space to the hatch. Smart has a Kawasaki Ninja engine, so he's loud and fast. He's also a shade of purple that's so dark it's almost black, with a license plate saying SMART1.

My survival pack barely fits in the hatch, landing with a thud and a clank amidst books and empty food and drink containers, and yes, I mean beer cans. Smart smells of fast food and stale beer. I manipulate the heavy backpack until I can close the hatch, and jump into the driver's seat. It's 10:44.

My mini-computer bleeps from the passenger seat, telling me I have a message. Number unknown. I press my bud and say, "Buzz, play message."

Nothing for a moment. Someone must've bud-dialed me. Then "Babe," in a voice that makes my stomach feel like I'm doing backward somersaults in the air. "I can't stop thinking about you, and with the storms ... I ... we ... Call me, Babe."

Scott.

I can't believe I slept through his call. Activating my bud, I say, "Buzz, return call."

The phone doesn't ring. A robotic, semi-feminine voice says, "All circuits are down. Please try your call later."

Dammit. I have to know what Scott wants.

I turn the key and rev the engine. It responds with a satisfying, high horsepower whine. I screech away from my campus apartment building. The campus seems deserted. Everyone must be tucked away, studying for finals, or else left school already.

The bold black letters on the marquee in front of the library jump out at me: *CAMPUS CLOSED DUE TO STORMS*. Shit, are you kidding me? I guess I'd know that if I'd been attending class the past couple of weeks. I've been nocturnal and drunk since Scott broke up with me. Now I know why it's only been the hardcore partiers at the bars.

It's sunny, and the air is always fresh heading toward Sedona. I have the windows down, my hair drying in the breeze, my oversized sunglasses hiding my dark-circled, bloodshot, baby blues. I drive up the ramp to I-17 and realize traffic is backed up on the interstate. Dad was right: everyone's panicking.

I ease up the ramp and try to slip into traffic. Horns honk all around me, so I honk too. The blue-haired old lady I'm hoping will allow me to merge in front of her extends her arthritic middle finger. Somebody's sweet grandma. I flip her off in return.

Feeling trapped on the ramp, I take advantage of having a tiny car and pull onto the shoulder, barely missing the fender of the old biddy's pearlescent white convertible Mercedes. She glares at Smart as I maneuver past her, and flips me off again, this time with both hands. I can't believe she has the top up on this beautiful day.

Unless my parents are right.

The shoulder ahead is mostly clear, so I drive faster, honking like a crazy woman when I need someone to pull left so I can get by. Some people honk back, some yell at me that I'm breaking the law or call me a bitch, and some flip me off, but they let me by. The shoulder is my little piece of paradise.

11:01. I leave the bumper-to-bumper traffic when I enter Highway 89A. It's a two-lane road, and there's no traffic as far as I can see. Eerie.

I roll my window down and press Smart's gas pedal to the floor. He does zero to sixty in 3.2 seconds, and we're flying down the road. I turn the satellite radio on. My "all music, all the time" station is playing the news. The female newscaster is speaking rapidly and is short-winded.

"—canceled due to severe weather conditions all across the country. Automobile traffic is backed up on the interstates and in cities. Trains are stopping where they can safely offload passengers and crew, and they will remain there. Remember listeners, stay calm, and—"

The emergency weather alert sounds, and a mechanical male voice breaks in. "The National Weather Service has just issued a severe thunderstorm warning for Yavapai and Coconino Counties in Arizona. This is an active severe weather pattern that indicates long-term and increasing threats. Damaging winds gusting to 110 miles per hour and baseball-sized hail are anticipated. Excessive rainfall may cause flooding. The National Weather Service advises that these storms are extremely dangerous. If you're in Yavapai or Coconino Counties in Arizona, consider severe thunderstorms to be imminent, and take appropriate shelter."

Turning the radio down, I glance in my rearview mirror. The sky behind me is roiling in blacks and grays. I have traffic behind me now, others trying to keep ahead of the impending storms. Lightning spikes in fingers across the swelling clouds, lighting them up magnificently for a moment. After, they seem even darker than before, as if they're bearing down on me.

Peeling my eyes from my mirror, I floor the throttle for the last few miles to Sedona.

I guess Dad was right. I guess Mother was right, too, dammit.

I hope I find Jace in time for their noon departure. It's 11:26.

2

I try to call Dad as I near Sedona, but I get the same tinny response as before: no service. What good are phones if you can't use them in an emergency? It's 2034. You'd think we'd have better technology.

The clouds behind me are more ominous than they were only minutes ago, a parasomniac's night terrors in the making. I cringe, and my scalp crawls. I try to concentrate on the road, but the glistening gold and diamond sun pendant hanging from my rearview mirror catches my eye. Scott gave it to me days before he broke my heart. When my family leaves, I'll go to his house and see what he wants. Me, I hope.

The sight of red rocks intermixed with greenery always takes my breath away, but today I dismiss Sedona's beauty without a second glance. Other than a couple of vehicles heading north, ahead of the storm, the desert town is so quiet it's creepy. Residents are probably huddled together with their families in their homes. I hope I have time to find Jace. 11:29.

As I pull into my parents' circular driveway, my sister, Maya, hurdles a landscaped area and slips on the wet, perfectly manicured turf as she runs toward me. Panic shows in the round innocence of her face. I pull in behind the red and black Zipper ATV hitched behind the two-tone gray RV. The RV, which will give my family privacy in Daeios, still has dealer tags. Dad steps down from the RV, and they approach me as I get out of my car, Maya panting from running.

"You haven't found him?" I ask, even though the answer is plain on their faces. Maya's big blue eyes seem too large for her face, and Dad looks older than his sixty-five years. Maya shakes her head and bites her trembling lip.

"Mother won't consider leaving any later?" I ask Dad.

He shakes his head. "We can't. They've expanded the evacuation zone to include our home. They think the houses behind ours might slide into it. We have to get out of here." He stares over my shoulder, his eyes wide with strain, and I feel it before I turn to see it: the storm. The air feels heavy and charged and smells of rain. We have to find Jace by noon.

"What time is it?" I ask.

Maya glances at her watch. "11:31."

"Where have you looked?" I have to remind myself to focus on them so I hear what they're saying. In my mind, I'm already racing around, searching for Jace.

Dad speaks first. "I took the Zipper and talked to the Burlingames, the McDougalls, and the Crowes, but they can't remember the last time they saw Jace. I remember he dated that girl not long ago: Kelly something? So I went as far as her house, but no one answered the door." He's breathing hard. "Punkin, where did you check?"

Maya inhales, exhales. "Jace used to hang out with a group of guys, remember, when he started doing drugs?" Yes, I remember. Two of them are dead now, of overdoses, maybe suicide. "Roger's parents said they haven't seen Jace since Roger's funeral, Ryan's sister slammed the door in my face before I could ask about Jace, no one answered at David's, and I don't know where Tim lives. Lived." She starts to cry, and Dad takes her in his arms and kisses the top of her head. She sniffles and wipes her eyes, her dimples showing as she tries to force back the tears.

"I don't know where else to look. I'm worried he might be lying in a ditch, and the rains have been flooding the ditches. We don't even know if he's alive ..." His voice breaks. He smooths Maya's pixie cut, dyed black with white tips—her only act of teenage rebellion so far. A low rumble of thunder reminds us we don't have much time.

"Where's the swing you found his phone bud on?" Once Jace removed the bud, he probably hid somewhere nearby. Gloss addicts don't get around much.

"At the house with the Greek columns, about a half mile from here? They let us go in the backyard to get the bud. They said they hadn't seen anyone."

"Do they have a big yard, a pool house, places where he could hide?" I ask.

"Yes, of course," Dad says. "The house sits on several lots. Are you going over there?"

I'm already jumping in my car.

I drive to the house with the columns, going fortyish in a twenty zone. No traffic. No people outside their homes. Many houses are dark. Thunder crashes, louder this time, and I have the urge to hide. I pull into the imposing parking lot of a driveway and skid the car to a stop. The house is the size of Buckingham Palace. I'm only exaggerating a little.

Getting out of my car, I hit my head on the doorframe, and let loose a string of swear words that would make a stand-up comedian cringe. I run to the front door of the house and ring the bell. I wait a few seconds and press the bell several times. I have to find Jace and get him home in less than thirty minutes. Depending on the shape he's in, it may not be easy.

Still no answer at the door. I pound on it with the meaty side of my fist a couple of times in frustration and then sprint around the house to the backyard. It's like running around the freakin' block. My footsteps beat out a rhythm: I hope I find Jace, I hope I find Jace, please, Lord, help me find Jace. More thunder.

An eight-foot white vinyl privacy fence surrounds the yard. Its tall, curved gate has no visible handle. I follow the fence line a short way to make sure there isn't an easier route than climbing over. I don't see one, and I don't have time to complete a marathon looking for one.

I jog back to the gate. It takes three attempts, a screamed battle cry, and a lot of grunting to get over it. Now where to search for Jace?

I head to the swing set and see that the rain has made pink swirls around a splotch of red blood on one of the white plastic seats. I cast my eyes away because it makes my neck throb where Buzz is implanted. I'll work my way out from here. Thunder claps, not so distant anymore. A large raindrop skids down my cheek. I have to hurry.

"Jace? It's Shea." I race to a garden area with some shrubbery and can tell with a quick look that he isn't there.

"Jace?" I dash toward a metal toolshed but veer away when I see it's padlocked from the outside.

Next stop: the pool house. It's locked, but I can see inside its numerous windows. I rap on the windows every few feet and call his name as I circle the structure. No sign of any movement.

"Oh, my God, the pool!"

Breathless by now, my heart beating too fast, I stand at the edge of the pool. My aching throat can't swallow the barbed lump in my throat. I inhale a deep breath and squeeze my eyes shut then open. He isn't in the pool.

I concentrate on calming my breathing as I crouch to check under the poolside furniture. Nothing but an underinflated beach ball and a bedraggled doll with matted yellow hair.

"Jace, where are you?"

I hurry to the massive deck and look under the furniture and behind the ornamental shrubs and plants. I can't find any access under the deck. There's a bright flash of lightning and thunder crashes, close this time. The storm is almost on top of us, a giant beast growling a warning deep in its throat. More raindrops. People have been getting struck by lightning every day.

"Jace? Jace!"

I'm wasting my time at the house with the columns. I head to the gate and find a latch, release it, and return to my car, not minding to shut the gate behind me. Where do I go now? When I open the car door, the numbers on Smart's clock jump out at me: 11:45.

Clouds creep above me, small clouds merging into larger ones. I jam the throttle down, Smart leaps forward, and I don't know where I'm going. As I'm speeding out of the driveway, I notice the house across the street is for sale, a sign placed outside the scruffy hedges surrounding it. Even whacked out on gloss, Jace may have stumbled this far.

After pulling into the short driveway, I jog to the front door, leaving Smart's engine idling with the door open. The "open door" chime warns me of the passing time. I ring the doorbell and pound on the windowless door. Peering through the front bay window, I see through a crack in the curtains that the house is empty. As I start to run around to the back, I notice a pile of clothing lying in a darkened corner of a neglected flower garden, up against the house.

"Jace!" I start screaming again, louder this time, with more urgency.

"Jace!" I bend down and recognize my brother's soggy clothes. The blue and gold Lumberjacks sweatshirt I gave him for his birthday last month has a dark splotch of blood on the hood from removing his phone bud. The jeans beside it are threadbare, faded, and dirty. I move his graying underwear and socks aside with a stick and find his dingy white high tops. He's naked, wherever he is. I hope he didn't wander far.

"Jace, where are you?" I dart around the side of the house toward the back and see him lying in front of a gate, in the fetal position, naked.

"Oh my God, Jace." My brother doesn't respond. What if he's dead? Gloss shines in patches where dirt hasn't dulled its sheen. Deeply addicted, he's gone from smearing the drug, which is colorless and clear and has a texture like petroleum jelly, only on his lips, to spreading it all over his skin. He may have OD'd. Please let him be okay.

"Jace. Jace, it's Shea. Wake up," I yell, right by his ear, getting a sour sniff of his grubby blond hair. He stirs just enough for me to notice, and I blink away a tear of relief.

He's mouth breathing—he's been putting the oily drug up his nose. Some gloss addicts die because they forget to breathe through their mouths. If he's swallowed it, his throat will close up, and he'll die.

"Jace!" He's barely responsive, and I refuse to touch him. Gloss is highly addictive, and I don't want to get any on me. I couldn't drag or carry him to my car anyway, even if he's just a skeleton with skin now. He's over six feet tall, and I'm five-foot-six. "I'll be right back," I shout by his ear, even though I'm not sure he knows I'm here. I run to my car and throw it into gear, my breath stuck in my throat. I take off with a screech and the door slams shut. 11:48.

Raindrops speckle my windshield.

It only takes a minute to get to my parents' house.

"Dad!" I scream out my window as I speed up the driveway. "I found him, but I need your help getting him in the car. Bring a blanket."

He goes into the RV and pulls out a faded, floral comforter, then hurries to the car, arthritis in his knees slowing his progress. His tan, twill pants are belted high around his white, short-sleeve dress shirt. He's wearing bright white sneakers. Gingerly, he folds himself into the passenger side, his head touching the black headliner. Smarts aren't the best for tall people, and he's six-foot-four. He's trying to stuff the blanket into the compartment with his feet when I drive off.

"Shea, seatbelts."

We only have minutes left, but I stop the car and comply. Dad's hands are shaking too much to buckle his seatbelt. It makes me want to cry.

"Here, Daddy, I'll do it," I say, and he lets me fasten it. He tries to smile. I give his hand a quick squeeze before clutching the steering wheel and pushing the throttle to the floor. Dad holds on to the worn oh-shit bar and stares straight ahead.

When we get to the house where Jace is, I slow down and pull into the driveway, take a right onto the lawn, and drive to where I found him. He isn't there.

"He was just here," I say, slamming the steering wheel with the palm of my hand. Dad's struggling to hold it together, so I say, "We'll find him. He can't have gone far. He was barely conscious."

I drive along the hedge and see him as we turn toward the back of the house. He's in the fetal position again, facing us. His knees are grass-stained.

I hurry to him. Dad is slowly extricating himself and the comforter from Smart. I go take the blanket from Dad and start wrapping it around Jace the best I can, tucking it underneath him. A dried and smeared stream of blood runs down the right side of his neck from removing his phone bud. It looks like angry birds pecked out the jagged, quarter-size flesh an inch below the back of his earlobe.

"How are we going to do this?" Dad approaches, hands on hips.

"We're going to carry him to the car and put him in the passenger side. With his seatbelt on," I add for Dad's benefit.

"How is he going to fit, wrapped in that blanket? And where do I sit? Your car only holds two people."

I've actually had three people in the car, two of us in the seats and one curled up in the elongated hatchback when I was the designated drunk driver. Today my survival pack takes up space in the back. Jace couldn't fold up that much, anyway.

"We'll put him in the passenger seat, and you can drive the car back to the house. I'll run." I'm talking fast. Mother's probably revving up the RV now, and the raindrops are coming more steadily, the sky the color of a dark bruise.

"Okay, but he'll have to make the ride naked. I don't see how he's going to fit with the blanket around him." He starts to remove the comforter.

"Dad, stop. He's covered in gloss. We need the blanket to keep it from getting on us, not to protect his pride."

Understanding dawns on his face, and he tucks the comforter back around Jace.

"Are you ready?"

Dad nods, and we lift Jace. I doubt if he weighs more than I do, and I only weigh 130 pounds, which is to say my driver's license says 120. Jace moans.

"I've got him," Dad says. He lifts Jace's dead weight easily, grimacing at the pain in his knees, and carries him to the car. A sudden flash of lightning brightens the sky, followed by a loud grumble of thunder that lasts several seconds. Freezing rain starts to pour, and I feel a blaze of fear.

"Hurry, Dad."

Maneuvering Jace into the passenger seat isn't easy. He's not cooperating, the comforter is bulky and gets in the way, and he's so tall. I slide into the driver's seat and pull while Dad pushes from the passenger side until we have Jace sitting in an upright position. We only bang his head twice. Dad stretches the seatbelt to me and, straining, I click the buckle closed. Dad hurries around the car as fast as he can, moves the seat back, and struggles behind the steering wheel.

"See you at the house," he says as he buckles up and drives off, more slowly than I've ever driven in my life.

———

It's not far, but by the time I reach the RV, I'm soaked and winded, and my heart is beating like it will fly out of my chest. Mother, as expected, waits in the driver's seat with the engine running. Her lower lip is pushed out, and she's breathing heavily through her nose, a bull ready to charge.

Dad pulls around the front of the RV so the passenger door of Smart faces the RV's side door. He reaches across Jace and opens the passenger door before battling his way out of the driver's seat. A squall of rain enters the car, and Jace sputters in protest.

I bend in and release the seatbelt. Dad comes around and, groaning, takes Jace into his arms, a giant child, and carries him toward the RV. Maya steps down to watch. A breath hitches in her throat when she sees Jace. Dad lugs my brother up the three steps with some difficulty, his broad shoulders filling the doorway, turning my brother this way and that to get him through without banging him around any more than he has to. He lays Jace on the bench seat across from the door. We're all soaked now, except for Mother.

Maya jumps up the steps and turns to me. "Come on, Shea."

No one told her I'm not coming. Her small frame seems even smaller to me as I consider leaving her; she appears to shrink toward nothingness before my eyes. Her wet, yellow T-shirt clings to her developing body, and cold rain drips down her black shorts and pale legs.

"Close the door, we're leaving," Mother shrieks from the passenger seat. Dad's in the driver's seat, facing me, a plea on his face. Lightning flashes and thunder cracks overhead, emphasizing the severity of the storm. It doesn't seem possible, but it starts raining harder, the hint of ice pelting my skin.

I run to my car to escape the sting and sit in the driver's seat. I don't like goodbyes. Tears mix with raindrops on my cheeks as I finger the keys in the ignition. Maya, a blur in the downpour, is watching me. Small pellets of ice disintegrate on my windshield and melt into the rain.

My hands at ten and two, I lay my forehead on the steering wheel and try to catch my breath, but there's a pinch in my lungs. I try to call Scott, but the phones are still down.

I don't want to believe things are bad enough to drive us to live in Daeios, but a wall of mud and building materials might flatten our house, and we can't get food here. Daeios lies below the earth's surface, safe from the storms. Daeios has food. If we reach Daeios before they lock it down, we'll exist until we run out of food, and then we'll starve to death. It buys us about a year, assuming staying up here would be fatal.

But Scott ...

It's not a picture of Scott that springs to my mind. It's six-year-old Maya, crumpled on the grass after her first bee sting. Her heart stopped beating. When the paramedics placed her small body on a stretcher, I thought I'd never see her again.

"Dammit, dammit, dammit!" I yell as I sit up and smack the steering wheel with my palms. I can't let Maya leave me forever. Not even for Scott.

I get out of the car and open the hatchback, pull out my survival pack and take it to Maya. I can't look her in the eye or I'll burst into tears. I run back to close Smart and, impulsively, I pull the sun pendant off the rearview mirror and pull it over my head. I grab my mini-computer and lock Smart with the remote. He chirps at me, and it sounds like goodbye. I pat him on the roof a couple of times. I want to hug him, but that would be weird, even for me.

Maya sets my backpack down inside the RV and is back at the door. "Hurry, Shea."

I run up the steps, throw my keys on the table by the door, and wipe the tears and raindrops from my face with my hands. As I close the door behind me, I ask Maya, "What time is it?"

"12:02," Mother turns around and snaps. She's dressed in her Sunday best, a black maxi skirt and a frilly white blouse. She's wearing her black granny boots with the flat heel. Her deep auburn hair is pulled into a severe bun, intensifying the whiteness of her porcelain skin.

Regret fills me as Dad pulls out of the driveway and onto the street toward Daeios. I'll never know what Scott wanted. Living in close quarters with Mother will be painful. I'll hate calling everyone Brother and Sister. I look at Dad, Jace, and Maya, and resign myself to my fate. They're worth it.

I'm going underground.

3

Dad drives out of town and on to Highway 89 North. He handles the RV well, in spite of it being new. He's probably been practicing. As survivalists, we leave nothing to chance. Dad and I have been driving to Daeios on some weekends in the Beamer, using two alternate routes and memorizing the landmarks.

Daeios is an unincorporated locality, so its owners manage it, but Coconino County laws apply. As owners of shares in Daeios, we can go there anytime and hang out for as long as we want. Brother Christian, the head owner and director of Daeios, acts like everyone should be thrilled to hang out there just for fun, but I'd rather eat dirt. It smells like dirt, earthy and damp, even though the common areas are modern and pristine. The white walls and stainless steel gleam. The smell lingers in spite of it.

Brother Christian is always present, dressed in white from head to toe. It accentuates the shiny silver of his hair and brings out the bright blue of his eyes. I feel I might burst into flames when I'm around him. He seems too pure to be around someone like me.

Dad breaks me from my reverie. "Shea, have you heard all the hoopla on the news about the storms?"

"Of course she hasn't heard, Aidan. She doesn't pay attention to anything but herself," Mother says.

To prove I'm paying attention, I say, "What did they name this one, Dad?"

"Hell," he says, and Mother smacks him on the arm with the back of her hand and graces him with a frowning half smile.

Dad gives her an innocent look and continues with the hoopla. "It just goes to show that no one knows what's going on. One station blames the climate crisis. Another says so-called climate experts lost control of the technologies we have for controlling the weather. Some scientists say maybe something is distorting the electromagnetic fields of the earth."

"Aidan, that's ridiculous."

"I'm telling it like I heard it, dear. Different scientists are predicting a new ice age, claiming the earth is reversing its polarity."

"The news." Mother shakes her head. "I believe what they're preaching at church. The weather is a sign of God's wrath for the immorality in the world. Murders. Suicides. Abortions. When they started terminating pregnancies in teenagers to lower the teen birth rate ..." She clears her throat, indicating Maya.

Dad takes up the dropped baton. "It's like we're under siege. No mail service, no phones, no food. We've been sheltered from the worst, though. Some cities are in chaos. Store owners are staying home with their families, so people are breaking in and taking whatever they need. Or want. I don't think people realize this is the end."

"Shea?" It's Maya. She nods toward Jace, who's trying to untangle himself from the wet comforter. The deep wound on his neck has reopened, blood seeping from the thick black scab. I hurry to them, snatching a towel from a neat pile on the table and blot my dripping hair. Maya's pixie cut is almost dry.

"Jace, hold on, I'll help you." He starts to thrash and scream, afraid of the comforter, the wild animal that's holding him down. I put my hand on his blanketed shoulder to draw his attention from his raving mind. He startles and stares at me, wild-eyed. I can't help but think, again, that he seems like a child, and he's frightened out of his wits.

"Shea, what's going on back there? Do I need to stop?" Dad asks, turning his head just enough to direct his question back to me.

"You most certainly will not stop, Aidan," Mother says. "You wanted to bring him. Deal with his behavior as you drive." She didn't want to bring him? She crosses her arms and stares straight ahead as if she's willing the RV forward.

"Thay." Jace says my name, sort of. He recognizes me, at least. I notice his mouth breathing more now that he's alert. His face is pinched and blue-gray around his nose and lips. He isn't getting enough oxygen. Gloss makes users appear shiny and young when they first put it on, but it shrinks everything it touches, drying the skin and membranes when it sinks in. Jace's skin is starting to dry out and shrivel like fragile, dried leaves in autumn. He used so much.

"What should I do, Shea?" Maya asks.

I feel like I'm in command, which is something I've never felt before. "Get him some food, something soft such as a banana or pudding, and a bottle of water." Maya hops out of her seat and brings a small container of chocolate pudding and a bottle of water from the fridge. She hovers nearby, awaiting further instructions. "Wet a washcloth or sponge for me. I'm going to clean him up."

She disappears further back into the RV and returns in a few moments with a sponge, latex gloves, and a small basin of warm, soapy water. The rain is pattering on the roof of the RV, and it's tapping out a rhythm that doesn't sound too threatening. Maybe I'm getting used to it.

"You're good at this. Thank you," I tell her, trying to smile as we wriggle our hands into the gloves. "Let's sit him up. See if he'll eat or drink anything while I give him a sponge bath. Don't touch his skin with your skin."

We're able to get him into an upright position without much trouble. Jace acts calmer now, but his breathing is loud and raspy. He lets the wet comforter fall away from his bony shoulders and exposes himself to us. Maya turns away, blushing. She probably hasn't seen a grown man's genitals. I hope not; she's only fourteen. She clears her throat and spoons some pudding from the cup to Jace's waiting mouth as I cover the lower half of his body with the blanket.

"Shea? I don't know if it's true, but I heard the wind is so strong in some places that it's carrying pets and little kids away. Do you think it could be true? Every time I see a poster of a missing child, I wonder." Maya's eyes are wide. She's quiet for a moment, then, "We're never leaving Daeios, are we?"

Jace chokes on the pudding, and Maya wipes his chin with the towel and gives him a drink of water. He guzzles noisily and chokes again.

"Try giving him smaller bites of food and small sips of water," I suggest.

She nods and does as I say. She doesn't repeat the question I don't want to answer. Jace eats and drinks as a toddler does, his unblinking eyes following the food and water from Maya's hand to his mouth. His usually blue eyes, the color of my favorite jeans, are all pupil, and I shiver at their blackness. He doesn't look human.

"Let's not give him too much, or he might throw up," I say. She stops after one plastic cup of pudding and a half bottle of water, sets them aside, and fetches a dry towel to help with the sponge bath.

"I hate seeing him like this," Maya says. "But at least he's with us."

It is hard seeing Jace like this. I miss my real brother. A couple of years ago, he completed the Ironman in Tempe in fifth place. He was so happy and full of life. I admired him so much. He stood up for me when Mother was being Mother. Now he regards Maya and me as his salvation.

I plunge the sponge into the soapy water and start wiping the worst of the grime from his face, ears, and neck. He smells like a yeti vacationing at a pig farm, and I have to stifle my gag reflex. I wash the blood off his neck and shoulder and clean the wound the best I can with a sponge. It's an ugly wound. He leans his head back, closes those disturbing eyes, and looks peaceful, which calms me.

Jace's terror of Y Chromo drove him to drug addiction. Everyone dreads Y Chromo, its cruelty and disregard for male human life. The chromosomal disorder causes the failure of two or more organs or systems at once. Many males die painfully and soon after the first symptoms arise. Some survive for months or years in agony, fighting for breath, losing tissue to gangrene, weak and unable to resist infections. Some, perhaps the lucky ones, enter low levels of consciousness, even coma. They're the only ones who get relief from the misery. Most of the males affected by Y Chromo are infertile, even before showing symptoms of the disorder. If they do father male children, those children will likely have the disorder.

I'm afraid for my brother. I say a little prayer.

The RV drives over something large and yielding—tender?—on the road and slams to the right. I reach for Maya, but she falls to the floor. Dad takes a second to steer the unwieldy machine straight. Mother grips the dash and Dad's seat like she's being pulled down the drain. Some of the water in the basin splashes onto the floor, and Jace tips toward Maya, panicking again. He can't right himself. Maya gets up and sets him upright using the damp towel, hugging him for a moment through the towel. He calms down again.

We continue with the sponge bath down his chest and over his shoulders, me sponging, and Maya toweling, until the RV slows down. The rain cascades down the windshield, the wipers at top speed and not keeping up. It's not yet one o'clock, and it's dark outside, like the frightened sun has already set.

"What's wrong, Dad?" I ask, raising my voice over the noise of the rain on the roof and the slap-slap of the windshield wipers. Lightning tracks across the sky, giving us a show we didn't pay for and don't want. Thunder booms, following us—it has caught our tail.

"I can't see well, Princess. I didn't see what we hit back there, but another bump like that could damage the RV. It would be impossible to fix anything in this downpour, with the wind blowing debris. The radio went out a short time back, and with no phones or GPS, we're on our own. Better safe than sorry." Mother shoots him a look that could turn him to granite, but it doesn't work.

Maya changes the grayish-pink water and finds a clean sponge and towel, and we work on cleaning Jace again. He looks better with a clean face. The wound continues to bleed. We've established a rhythm and have almost finished the front of his torso when he shits himself.

"Oh, my God." I turn away, and Maya retches into the towel. Jace seems not to notice. But he notices that we've stopped bathing him and whimpers like a forgotten puppy.

I do not want children.

I go stand behind Dad's seat and yell over the rain and the frenzied wipers. A long, leafless, tree branch flies in front of the windshield. "Dad, you're going to have to stop and help us." He's driving almost thirty miles per hour. We'll never get to Daeios at this rate.

"Good Lord, what is that smell?" Mother asks. Dad pulls onto the narrow shoulder and turns on the hazard lights. At a standstill, the heavy RV shakes in the wind.

My face flushes; I feel protective of my brother. "Jace had an accident. Dad's going to have to prop him up in the shower and clean him."

"Oh," she says, without any of her usual fiery contempt. She faces front again and sits motionless, perhaps hypnotized by the rain. Dad shuts the wipers off before leaving his seat, and the rain comes down in a sheet across the windshield. It continues its tap dance on the roof, and I'm getting tired of hearing it.

Dad moves back to us, ducking his head and putting his arms out for balance to walk through the rocking RV. We help him wrap the damp blanket around Jace. Maya brings him a pair of yellow latex gloves. Dad puts them on and carries Jace, in the blanket, to the shower. After a few minutes, Dad brings Jace out, and he's clean and no longer shiny from gloss. Dad removes the gloves and holds Jace in a standing position, facing away from me, while I towel him off. I hurry so he doesn't shit on me.

I ask Mother if she brought any clothes for Jace. "Of course I packed for him," she barks at me like I'm stupid. "His bag is the navy blue one."

Swallowing hot words, I retrieve the bag and search for something Jace can wear that we can put on him without much difficulty. I find a pair of sweatpants, a zip-up sweatshirt, and a pair of boxer briefs. Unfortunately, there are no adult diapers. I return to Dad and Jace and start to help my wobbly brother get dressed.

"I'll do it, Shea," Dad says and takes over. Jace's clothes hang on his gaunt frame. Dad heads back to the cockpit after helping my brother sit. He hasn't said a word to Jace all day.

———

We approach Flagstaff—I can tell by the increased traffic—although it's not your usual Saturday afternoon traffic. No spooks clogging the road for once. Since the cars have no drivers, they have no reason to flee to safety. The rain has slowed. There's an occasional arc of lightning and burst of thunder. It's not as dark as it was earlier. Dad's still white-knuckling the steering wheel, but he's increased his speed to match that of the surrounding traffic. Jace appears to have melted into the bench seat and is snoring loudly, with Maya in close attendance. He's coming down from the drug, or he wouldn't be sleeping. The shower speeded up the detox process.

I go up to talk to Dad, peering through the windshield. Debris blows around, leaving litter and broken branches everywhere.

"How's it going, Dad?" It's almost two o'clock. This may be the longest trip of my life. "Are we there yet?"

"Very funny. It's not too bad, Princess, it seems to be letting up a bit." He gives me a halfhearted smile. "We have a little more than a buck-and-a-quarter to go."

"Let's see. At thirty miles per hour, we'll get there in—"

"Smart aleck. I'll have you know we're going sixty right now, and there's not much traffic. We should be there in a couple of hours, barring any other ... incidents."

Mother scoffs. I throw her a dirty look, and she tosses one back. I go sit next to Maya, and she lays her head on my shoulder. She smells like baby powder.

We get through Flagstaff without any trouble. Thank God, it's not backed up as it was when I left school. We can't steal around traffic on the shoulder in an RV.

Dad maneuvers the RV onto Highway 89 North again, and I start to relax. I finger the pendant around my neck, looking down at the yellow gold sun—its rays glisten with tiny diamonds. It summons the pain of the day Scott broke up with me. He said something I didn't understand and flashed me that adorable crooked smile of his. He stood up, tapped the end of my nose with his forefinger, and walked out of my apartment and out of my life. We were only together three months, but those three months meant everything to me. I loved that he called me "Babe." I think I loved him. Love him. Since then I've been going crazy: drinking too much, not eating enough, smoking, and sleeping with guys who don't care one heartbeat about me. They all leave in the night. Now I'll never know if I had Scott's love and left it behind. I rub my eyes to keep the tears in.

The radio lets out a gurgle of static, and Dad tries to tune in a station, but there's nothing more. Lightning lights up the sky and the whole interior of the RV. Jace turns over with a grumble and a loud snort. Thunder crashes so loud it sounds like it's ripping the top off the RV. Maya lets out a little scream and covers her ears, so I hug her and feel comforted by her warmth.

Something strikes the RV with a boom. We all cry out, and Jace sits bolt upright like he's spring-loaded. The RV shuts down, and Dad steers toward the shoulder. He's unable to make it off the road, and the hazard lights don't work.

We sit in tense silence for a moment, the wind shaking the RV, until Maya says in a shrill, shaky voice, "Did we just get struck by lightning?"

It feels like my waist-length hair is standing straight up and the electricity is coursing through me.

"Is everyone okay?" Dad asks.

Everyone is okay, and no one needs to change his pants. Jace lies down and starts snoring as loud as a bull elephant, and I don't think I'll ever be able to sleep again.

Dad gives the verbal command to start the RV, but it doesn't respond. He tries it again. It doesn't start. Mother screams a command, but she doesn't scare the RV into starting either.

"Helen, will you get me the key from the glove box?"

"Where did you put it?" she asks as she opens the compartment.

"I didn't put it anywhere. I thought you did," Dad says. "Did you put it in your purse?"

Mother growls in irritation and starts digging through her ugly black purse, which is about the same size as my car. "I don't know, Aidan. We did all this planning, and you didn't put a key in the glove box?" She throws her purse at her feet in a fit of temper. "I don't see one. What are we going to do?"

Maya goes to her. "Mom? You can't find anything in your purse digging through it that way. Let's dump it out on the table and go through it better."

Mother hands the bag to Maya. We empty the contents of the purse on the table, and Maya and I sort through it while Mother and Dad watch from their seats. No key.

I open the purse and find a bunch of inside pockets. After going through several pockets of useless crap, I finally find a large key and take it to Dad. The RV starts, and Dad lets out a long breath and revs the engine with satisfaction. "Thank God it didn't fry the electrical system, or we'd be driving the Zipper to Daeios."

I picture the Flintstones in their Stone Age car as I scrape the junk on the table back into Mother's gigantic purse and set it behind her seat.

About an hour later, Jace startles awake, sitting up and looking around him like he's been fired upon.

"Where'd you put my mask?" he asks, and he gets up and

stumbles around the RV. "Where'd you put my goddamned mask?" He's not looking at any of us, but at someone or something we can't see.

I clutch his shoulders and try to get him to sit. "What mask, Jace?" He starts at the realization that I'm there and throws my hands off.

"My mask, I need my mask. Everything depends on my mask!" He's shouting now, walking in a circle and picking at his neck wound, smearing fresh blood onto his face. I'm afraid of him. I push Maya behind me and back away from him. We may be in more immediate danger in the RV with a drug-addled Jace than we would be outside in this terrible storm.

"What's going on back there?" Dad says over his shoulder.

"I don't know, Dad, he keeps saying something about a mask."

Jace sits again, pulling his uneven blond hair, getting blood in it, and rocking. He repeats, "Mask. Mask. Mask. Mask," as he picks at his wound. I don't know what to do for him. I'm afraid he might attack me.

"Oh, for Pete's sake, he's having withdrawal symptoms," Mother says. She was a nurse before she married my father. Her bedside manner must've frightened patients into quick recoveries. She unbuckles her seatbelt and comes to us while Dad slows the RV to a crawl. Although an inch shorter than I am, she seems much taller because of her erect posture and imposing demeanor. "I was afraid of this, but no one listens to me."

I think she was going to leave him behind. His own mother.

She kneels at Jace's feet, wrestles his hands down, and holds them on his skinny thighs. Sweat's running down his face, and his sweatshirt is wet. A bloody blotch grows on the collar under his right ear.

"That wound is a problem. Girls, get me a cool rag, the first aid kit, and a bottle of water." Maya goes.

Jace pulls his hands from Mother's and holds his head again. "No, no, no, no, no!"

"Give me the water, Maya," Mother says, without taking her eyes off Jace. She tries to make him drink the water, but he spits it in her face.

"No use trying to bandage the wound with him acting that way. The doctor can deal with him when we get to Daeios."

She takes my towel and wipes her face and hands as she makes her way to her seat and buckles herself in. Dad speeds up again. She helped for five whole minutes before resuming her throne.

Maya tries to put the cool cloth on Jace's forehead, but he slaps it away. I see the hurt in her sweet face. He lies down on the bench seat and emits great sobs, easing to little whimpers, until he cries himself to sleep a few minutes later. Maya and I exchange worried glances. It's so hard to see him suffer.

I was naïve when I thought this was going to be the longest trip of my life. It may be the longest trip of my afterlife, too.

Not long after Jace has settled down, his lips rattling with snores, the rain picks up in earnest again. Dad turns the wipers up high, and they battle to keep the windshield clear, but he has to slow down to see the road. After a few minutes, he says, "Uh, oh."

I peer out the windshield and see red and blue flashing lights ahead. A police car. An accident? Dad approaches cautiously and stops where indicated by the orange and white barrier with the amber flashing light, lying on its side. "It could be a trick. He could be after the RV."

A First American highway patrol officer fights his way out of his vehicle and runs to the passenger side of the RV, his campaign hat held on by a strap around his chin, the brim blowing back.

A non-Elite. They hate us. Maya sucks in her breath and grabs my hand.

The officer gestures for my mother to roll the window down, and she looks at my dad, who nods his head once. I squeeze Maya's hand. The officer is dressed in raingear, but it's clinging to him, soaked through.

Mother places the towel on her blouse and lap and buzzes the window down halfway, her right arm held up to protect her eyes from the rain blowing in. The tension in the RV feels like a trigger right before the hammer drops.

The wind distorts the officer's words, making them loud and then soft like we have a bad phone connection. "Folks, we've had some flash flooding up ahead, and the last one took the road with it. You're going to have to detour onto the old Navajo Trail, Highway 160, about five miles ahead."

Mother is red with fury. "We have a sick man in the back. We can't take the detour. We have to get him to a doctor."

"There's a hospital in Tuba City, Ma'am, they'll fix him right up."

"We don't want a Tuba City doctor. We want our own doctor."

The officer looks like he wants to get out of the storm. More likely, he wants to get away from my mother. "Well, Ma'am, the only way you can go north is to go east first, so if you need a doctor, I suggest you stop in Tuba City. Good day." He pulls the front brim of his plastic-covered campaign hat down and jogs back to his cruiser.

The wind sucks some of the tension out the window when Mother rolls it up. "We're not stopping in Tuba City. He can make it until we get to Daeios and a real doctor."

Mother may have been called a bigot a few years ago, but races have segregated, and we're all balled up in bitter prejudice. Dark-skinned people against the whites, whites against the people with colored skin. We Elites have further segregated from whites with disabilities, deformities, or who are marked—with scars, tattoos, too many piercings or other body modifications—imperfect whites. The racial tension started when I was a toddler, and culminated in the Race Riots of 2025-2026. Then the people with color in their skin segregated from us, their various races united against the whites.

Dad said the Segregation happened slowly, over time, but day by day the gap widened until the dark-skinned people were living their lives completely separate from ours. They built new communities such as the one in Tuba City, new businesses, and started their own ways of life. Biracial families were torn apart as those with colored skin went with the Segregation. The hatred that lies between the two groups is comparable to that of the Yankees and Confederates of the Civil War. The highway patrol officer could be sending us into an ambush.

We pass through several small towns, debris blowing in our path and sometimes hitting the RV. They're ghost towns now, not even a stray dog in sight. It feels like we're the last ones on Earth. We're quiet now, tired from the strain that seems to be decreasing the size of the RV as though it will close in around us and obliterate us.

I never thought we'd make this final trip to Daeios, that we'd live our last days there. I thought my parents bought shares in Daeios because they could afford them, and it seemed cool at the time. Now I'm glad Dad made me take survival classes and trained me to fire a handgun and a rifle. I feel better knowing I'm fit, and that I took that unarmed self-defense class. It makes me feel like I have more control of an uncertain situation.

What matters now, up here, won't matter in Daeios, though.

As we exit the last small town on the way to Daeios, there's a section of white picket fence across the road, blocking our path. Dad brakes in front of the fence and braves the pouring rain, bracing against the wind, to move the fence off the road. I stand to watch.

A large First American man approaches Dad, the wind pushing him into a stumbling jog. The man is taller than Dad, but he's deathly thin, his ragged clothing tugging at his body in the wind. A gloss addict, or an unfortunate, homeless man looking for a handout? Maybe he'll help Dad move the fence out of the way for a twenty-dollar bill.

But no one is out in this storm. This doesn't feel right.

The handle jerks from my hand when I open the door of the RV. The door slams against the side of the RV, and the door holder catches it and holds it in place. I call to my dad to warn him about the man, but my words are snatched away by the wind.

I step out the side doorway, my hair swirling about my head and blocking my sight. I twist my hair into a messy ponytail using the hair tie that's always around my left wrist. Neither man looks at me. They walk toward the broken fence, shouting to one another, but I can't hear what they're saying. They each bend over to lift an end of the broken fence, and I think everything will be fine.

The First American man drops his end and charges at my dad, a loose fence picket raised above his head. His primitive roar reaches me on the wind. He's going to kill my dad, and then he'll come after us.

As I turn to run back inside the RV to get my 9mm out of my survival pack, I am almost knocked down by Mother. She's wielding her .44 Magnum, her square jaw set, every line of her rigid. She likes getting wet about as much as a cat does. I've never seen her shoot, but I wouldn't want to be on the other end of her gun right now.

"Get back inside, Shea!" she shouts without looking away from her target, her skirt thrashing violently around her legs. I run in and pull my gun from my backpack and hold it in shaking hands as I watch through the windshield at the action unfolding in front of me. I could be watching a widescreen TV, except for the rain blurring the images. I wish I could see my mother. She's beside the RV, ahead of the open door.

By the time Dad notices the enormous, emaciated man charging at him, it's too late to react. The man hits Dad over the head with the fence picket. Dad slumps to the ground, and Mother fires a shot as the man raises the slat over his head to hit Dad again. I don't know if she hit the man. He doesn't act like it.

Wait. He touches his side and either screams or laughs. He marches toward us, unafraid. I'm sure he's on gloss. A red blotch grows on his side. The round only glanced him, made him more dangerous.

He slows for a few steps and then lurches toward us again, his arms out in front of him, his mouth open wide. What if he doesn't go down? Why doesn't Mother shoot again? He's getting too close. What if he seizes Mother and her gun? I may have to use my gun. I'm afraid to go out there.

Mother fires. The man continues toward us.

The gun fires again as the man is only feet from the RV. His right eye explodes, chunks of matter flying from the back of his head as he falls backward to the ground.

I exhale a sigh of relief. I've been holding my breath, but oh, my God, we have to get out of here before someone comes and sees what Mother has done. Someone may have heard the shots. We'll leave, and the rain will cover our tracks, but we have to hurry. I lay my gun on the table and step down from the RV to help.

Mother faces me, and she's terrifying. She's all sharp angles and shadows and smeared mascara. I expect a thunderbolt and lightning and a bloodcurdling scream, but there's nothing but hammering rain. My mother is soaked, her skirt clinging to her slender legs, her white bra showing through her blouse, translucent with rain. Her wet hair looks black in the gloom. Loose tendrils hang from her previously tidy bun. If she's concerned about having killed a man, she doesn't show it. It makes me wonder if there's something in her past I don't know about.

I turn back inside to see Maya holding Jace. She's rocking him as they weep quietly.

"Maya, come help with Dad. Hurry." Jace lunges for Maya when she gets up, but she's too quick for him to reach her. He continues to sob, his shoulders jerking. I doubt if he even knows what happened. I despise his weakness.

Maya's still crying as we run toward Dad, and I want to cry, too, but I need to be strong for her if I can. We fight against the wind that pushes us toward Dad's attacker. I don't want to see him, but my eyes are fascinated by this abomination.

The man's remaining eye, wide open and all black, stares at us as raindrops fall in the pool of blood collecting around what's left of his head. I imagine evil spirits, their voices howling on the wind, are pulling us toward the man's reach, and I panic, tugging too hard at Maya's arm, but it breaks the spell, and we run to Dad.

Dad's conscious and groans as he tries to sit up. Mother comes up behind us, her skirt whipping in the wind. She's no longer holding the gun, and her edges have softened some.

"You probably have a concussion, Aidan. How do you feel?"

"Mother, we don't have much time before—" I begin.

"It'll be okay, girls," she says, her voice calm, and Maya wipes her eyes and sniffles. "Aidan?"

"Like I need to throw up. Dizzy," he says, holding his head as he tries to get up.

"Aidan, let us help you. Why do you think we're out here in this weather? We came to help you."

It's not easy maneuvering Dad to a standing position in the battering wind, our skin slick with rain, but we do, and he teeters there for a moment, gathering his balance. We need to hurry, but I know we're moving Dad as fast as he can go. Maya and I stand under his arms as short crutches. "Okay, girls, I can make it back this way. Shea, you'll have to drive."

Mother doesn't drive. Maya's too young, Jace is too stoned, and I am just right.

Mother stands near the dead body as we make our way to the RV, her flapping skirt hiding the man's mutilated head from Dad's view. No evil spirits dare reach through Mother to pull us toward the man. We get Dad to the door, where we can't be his crutches anymore. I go inside to take his hands, and Maya and Mother hold him from behind so he doesn't fall backward.

"No, girls, that won't work. I'll crawl." I back up, and he crawls up the steps and rolls over on his back across from Jace, breathing hard from the exertion. It hurts me to see him so helpless. Rain is blowing in on him through the side doorway.

"Girls, you'll have to move the fence out of the way," Mother says, holding her skirt against her legs and standing with her back to the open doorway to keep the rain from pelting Dad.

We move the fence a few feet and turn it sideways, then hurry back inside. Mother releases the door holder and the door slams shut.

I climb in the driver's seat, soaking the fine leather with my wet clothing and hair. The vehicle's been running the entire time. The fuel gauge shows less than a quarter tank. Will we have enough fuel to reach Daeios? This is the last place to get fuel, and we have to get out of here. Mother hasn't returned to her seat yet. "Mother, let's—"

"Just a minute, Shea," Mother says in a mild voice as she squats down to Dad and studies his wound. "You'll need a few stitches when we get to Daeios. Aidan? Look at me, Aidan. Look at me." She cups his face in her hands as she does when she kisses him. "I'll get you a pillow. Don't go to sleep. Maya, there's an ice pack in the freezer. Wrap it in a dry towel and ice the wound. Keep him awake. Help him dry off."

As soon as she makes him more comfortable, Mother assumes her position as non-driving copilot, buckling herself in. Tears beckon, and I shrug them away. I shift into drive, and we move toward Daeios again, leaving a dead man in our wake.

Maya dries off and brings the towel to Mother. Mother undoes her bun so she can dry her hair. She has a touch of silver at the temples that she calls "stress highlights." She hasn't worn her hair down since she joined her church two years ago—the church that runs Daeios.

I often wonder how old she is. Dad knows, but he's sworn to secrecy.

What other secrets make up my mother?

4

I recognize the entrance to Daeios immediately, once we get close enough to see it in the rain. Its metal doors look a part of the red sandstone, as they are painted the same rusty color as the rock, as are a large satellite dish and a radio antenna. A high chain-link fence surrounds it, with razor wire across the top, like a prison. You have to know how to get here, or you'd never find it. I want to turn and drive away, to jam the accelerator to the floor and go anywhere but here.

The fuel light comes on.

Daeios has a camera system that triggers an alert when a vehicle approaches the front gate. A sensor scans the front license plate and allows entrance only to vehicles registered with Daeios. Dad just bought the RV, so it's not registered. I step out the driver's door into the brutal rain and push a buzzer mounted to the fence, the wind pulling at my ponytail.

"Yes?" a female voice asks, her voice echoing like she's in a tunnel. The fence chinkles in the wind.

"We're the Donovans. We're registered owners. What do we need to do to gain access?" I shout above the rain, which pelts sideways and stings my skin. The drops are big and cold, and I suspect they may be turning into hail. Killer hail.

"We have an Aidan Donovan family registered with us. Is that you?" the voice asks.

"Yes, that's us."

"I need to speak to him."

"My dad's hurt and can't come out here," I yell into the intercom.

A pause. The rustle of paper, the turn of a page. "We gave him an access code when he registered with us. Can you get that for me?" the voice asks.

"Just a minute," I say, and return to the RV to ask Dad. I drip on him, and he wipes his face with his hands as though he's awakening from a deep sleep. He has one eye open and one closed. He doesn't say anything. "Dad?"

"Yes, Shea, I'm thinking. I don't ... I don't know," he mumbles, his speech fuzzy.

What do we do now? I run back to the intercom, squinting my eyes against the icy raindrops that hurt my head and face. "Hello?"

"Yes?"

"He doesn't know it. Is there some other way? We drove from Sedona, are almost out of fuel, and my dad and brother need medical care." I almost choke on the last words. I wait for a reply, but there is none. Did my voice blow away on the wind, drown out in the rain? "Hello?"

"Yes?" the voice says again.

"What about Brother Christian? Is he around? He knows us, we've been coming here on weekends for a while," I shout into the intercom, straining my voice around the lump in my throat.

"I'll check. One moment," the voice says and cuts off, and I want to scream. Hail pebbles start bouncing off the metal box of the intercom, so I face the ground and put my hands on my head to shield it. I can't stay out here much longer being beaten by the storm.

My gut twists with worry for Dad. For Jace, too, but I'm still irritated with him. At least he has the drug addict's excuse for being a coward. I hesitated, standing there holding my gun and afraid to use it. I hid behind Mother's skirt. I don't think I could've done what

Mother did. I imagine her squinting, nonchalantly blowing the smoke from the long barrel of the silver gun, and stuffing it in the front waistband of her skirt. Her legend is growing in my mind.

It seems like I stand in the pounding hail for a long time, the fuel in the RV burning away ounce by ounce before the intercom buzzes to life. When it does, it's Brother Christian on the other end. "Sister Shea, is that you?"

Thank God. "Yes, Brother Christian, it's my family and me. We've come to stay, but your gatekeeper won't let us in. Please, we've come all this way and we need help." Tears threaten to surface. The harrowing journey we've been through seems too much to bear if he turns us away.

"Of course, dear, I remember you well. Let's get you out of that storm. Come through the first door, and we'll verify your identities to the photos we have on file before letting you through the second. Everything will be fine, don't you worry." He's so kind it makes me want to cry.

I get behind the wheel and wait for the first blast doors to open as nickel-sized hailstones bounce off the windshield and batter the RV. The wide doors open quickly, I drive through, and they close behind us.

We're trapped.

I take deep breaths through my mouth. The absolute silence, except for the quiet humming of the RV, seems eerie after the constant drumming of rain and hail.

Brother Christian approaches us from a side door with an armed female guard at his side. They're both dressed all in white, except for her black holster and gun, the contrast ominous in its boldness. He's holding a folder. Mother rolls her window down and scowls at him.

"Hello, Sister Helen," he says, not waiting for a response. "Permission to come aboard, Sister Shea?" he calls to me, with raised black eyebrows and a smile. He's dressed in his usual long-sleeved sweater and wool slacks.

"Of course." I get up and open the side door for him. The air in the RV rushes out to fill the entrance, leaving me short of breath. He enters.

"Ah, yes, Sister Shea, you are surely you," he says with a grin. For a minute I'm afraid he might palm my cheek, so I look at my toes. He compares my mother and Maya to the photos he pulls from the folder and nods.

"Hello, Brother Aidan. It's good to see you again, although I wish it were under better circumstances." Dad mumbles something unintelligible as Brother Christian turns to Jace.

Jace looks nothing like the photo Brother Christian is holding. Gloss has aged him twenty years, and his face looks wasted. Surreal. His skin could be tanned, semitransparent leather. He has none of his usual features. He's colorless, except for the blood smeared on his face and hair and coagulating on his neck, and those disturbing black eyes with the dark bruises encircling them.

What if they won't let him in? Do we leave him outside in the storm?

Brother Christian clears his throat. "So, this is Brother Jace? Gloss, is it?" he asks me.

I nod as the jagged lump in my throat grows. Jace has to come inside with us; otherwise, it would have been better to leave him lying in that yard back home. There's nothing out here but rock and sand.

"Welcome, Donovans!" he says at last. "You understand, Brother Jace will be locked in Detention while he detoxes."

"He needs a doctor," Mother says. "You can lock him up, but he needs a sedative, restraints, and an IV while he comes down from the drug, plus any medication you have to speed the detox. That wound needs to be disinfected and stitched. My husband needs a doctor for a head injury."

Brother Christian doesn't sound so in charge anymore.

"Of course, of course, we'll take care of everyone. Now, go on in, Sister Shea, you know the way." He exits the RV and bows slightly as the tall double doors open, granting us access. A flash of panic fills me as the doors close behind us, and we start down the long, winding driveway into Daeios. I'm chilled, not just from being wet, or from the cold temperature down here. For the first time, I feel a sense of foreboding at entering this huge hole 140 feet below ground. We'll never leave here.

Daeios is now our home.

5

The driveway into Daeios is a small set of switchbacks. The ceiling is just high enough for the RV to clear it until we begin descending. It's wide enough for only one vehicle at a time unless they're small like Smart or the Zipper. I imagine the left tires of the RV sliding off the driveway and plummeting us into the darkness below. The sconces set every few feet in the red rock give off an amber glow; it's not the same as sunlight through windows or a lamp in a home. The light doesn't go far into the absolute darkness. The weight of the earth seems to be pressing down on me, knowing I'll be living underground for the rest of my shortened life, not visiting for a few hours and then leaving. It's hard to pull air into my lungs.

The driveway ends in the southeast section of Daeios. A white barricade stands at the opening of the brightly lit tunnel that will take us west, to our family site, where I will park the RV. Some white-clad, socks-and-sandals-wearing people, mostly women, are standing in the cavernous area outside of the barrier, surrounded by a few tables full of supplies.

The rock of the towering walls looks blood orange underneath the overhead lights, and the people in white appear to glow with an inner light. I stop the RV and call to a woman I recognize from a potluck Mother made us attend at her church.

Sister Ariel is tall and commanding, mature with a pewter-gray bun and a pasty complexion, and she makes me feel small and inadequate. Although a group of men called the Elders, led by Brother Christian, run Daeios, women team leaders, such as Sister Ariel, oversee the day-to-day operations of the shelter.

"Sister Ariel, what do we need to do here? We're trying to get my dad and brother to Medical."

"Sister Shea, how good to see you. Hello, Sister Helen. Welcome! This is where you offload your valuables for safekeeping and receive the supplies you need for living in Daeios. You'll get your vaccinations here, too. No one is allowed past this point without their Daeios supplies and an ID badge."

An ID badge? Who's going to get through Sister Yes and the blast doors?

"In addition to any bags you packed, you'll have to leave the following with us: computers, including personal mini-computers; jewelry, other than wedding bands; cash and credit cards; timepieces; and any other valuables."

Mother clears her throat. "We barely got away in time. We have only what was on our persons when we left," she says, her face a dare. I turn away to remove the sun pendant from around my neck and tuck it into my shorts pocket. It's the only way I'll see the sun down here. Behind us in the RV, Maya takes Mother's cue and stuffs our bags and Mother's purse under the queen-size bed in the back.

"It'll only take a minute. We have everything organized so we can bag your supplies in a jiffy. Who's come with you?" Sister Ariel asks, picking up a clipboard.

"Aidan, Jace, and Maya Donovan, plus us." She checks off the names as I speak.

Jace chokes and moans behind me.

"Oh, my! Let's get this show on the road. Put your valuables in the basket with your last name on it. Take your applications to each person behind the tables, and they'll put what you need in your bags. Start at that end." She points to the table farthest to my right as she hands me our applications. "By the time you reach the end of the tables, you'll have everything you need for your first week in Daeios. After that, supplies will be in the Storehouse. It's in the east w—"

"I know where it is. Can we get the bags for my dad and brother?"

"That's against the rules," she says, shaking her head, her wrinkled neck flapping.

"What do you do for babies?" I ask.

The gears grind behind her furrowed brow. "I'll verify their faces to their IDs and get their bags for them. Sister Helen, bring their valuables. Brother James will vaccinate them at Medical."

"We need to hurry. Jace is on gloss. Be careful when you check his face to his ID, he might freak out on you." I'm irritated, and wouldn't mind if he did freak out. Maybe I will, too. I get out and open the side door of the RV for her. The frigid air envelops me, giving me goosebumps.

Maya comes out, her eyes and mouth wide with awe, and Sister Ariel boards the RV, bowing her bowling ball head through the door. Mother steps down from the passenger door. The wildness has left her eyes, leaving her looking like a disheveled homeless woman, her makeup a smudge and her damp hair uncombed and unruly. Maya resembles a Dickens street urchin. My appearance could probably make Frankenstein's monster scream.

Sister Ariel emerges from the RV a few minutes later, holding my gun away from her like it might bite. Shit. I wish I'd stashed it back in my survival pack. "I'll lock this in the vault. You won't need it down here. Do you have any other guns on board?"

We answer with silence, except for Mother clearing her throat, but Sister Ariel doesn't wait for a reply.

Several ladies approach the RV. "We winterize all RVs so you won't have any water or waste in your tanks. We don't have any hookups, so you won't have water or electricity in your RV," Sister Ariel explains.

Next, she leads us to get our vaccinations. Mother rolls up her long sleeves, and we follow her through two lines of four nurses and receive eight shots each. I try not to flinch, but I hate needles.

Mother goes to the tables first, dropping her and Dad's wallets, her pearl earrings, and their mini-computers into the basket. She hands her application to a young woman in a heavyweight, full-length white dress, with her dark, shiny hair in a bun on top of her head. I scan down the tables, stacked with goods, and notice all the females have their hair in buns on top of their heads. I look terrible with my hair that way. And I look a fright in white: my skin is too pale, and it makes it look paler. If the lack of men at the tables is any indication, there won't be anyone to impress, anyway. The two men present are probably my dad's age, and the rest are all females. Enforced celibacy.

Maya follows Mother, and I bring up the rear. Maya looks at her watch before taking it off and taps on the crystal. It must've stopped working. We drop our mini-computers into the basket. Giving up our mini-computers means losing our music, our games, our cameras. Phones and internet don't work down here. The lady behind the table even makes me give up my hair tie.

Sister Ariel falls in behind us. "Your men don't look well. I'll make sure this goes quickly."

We move down the tables, and the people in white review our applications and stuff supplies in white bags with our names and *Daeios* printed on them, and then hand them to the next person to fill. I watch them pack my bag and see them check off my list: three wool dresses, a pair of sandals, three pairs of heavy socks, two towels, two washcloths, a baggie marked *Sister*, filled with women's toiletries, a box of tampons, and a water pack with shoulder straps that also says *Daeios* in black lettering. Everything's white except some bobby pins.

No razors or tweezers. I'll be Sasquatch's twin with a monobrow within a week. And no undergarments. Are the men freeballing it down here, too? The women with big or saggy boobs will have them flopping around or hanging to their waists—not an issue for me. We won't have to pull the underwear out of our butt cracks, that's one less thing to worry about.

"What do you mean you don't have any Xanadoxalate? You see it on my application. And it's on Shea's list. Look again." My mother is flailing her arms and shouting at an old man with salt-and-pepper hair on his head and sprouting from his ears and nose.

"I'm sorry, Sister Helen, I see it on your list, but it's not among our supplies. I'm certain of it." He does appear to be genuinely sorry, his face drooping like that of an old hound. His ID badge says his name is Brother Michael.

"Sorry?" Mother says with an ugly laugh. "Sorry? Shea and I have bipolar disorder. You can't hold us responsible for our actions without our X. You'll all be sorry." Mother's eyes flash as she holds her bipolar bracelet in Brother Michael's face to highlight her point. I have one, too. We've had to wear them since I was thirteen, when a man went on a shooting spree, killing dozens of people, and the media blamed it on his bipolar disorder. Along with wearing the bracelets on the wrists of our dominant hand, it's part of our public record. If Mother goes on a shooting spree, it won't be because she has bipolar—it'll be because someone crossed her.

Mother snatches her application from Brother Michael and throws it at the young woman at the next table. It flutters off the table and onto the ground. Everyone watches it fall.

We all stare at the frightened young woman, wondering how she'll react. She stands, a wax figure, only her fluttering eyelids showing her distress.

After a moment, she picks up Mother's ID badge off the table, comes around to her, and places the lanyard over her head. Maybe she'll strangle my mother with it. She doesn't. She kisses Mother on both cheeks, and says, "Welcome to Daeios. Welcome to your new home. My name is Sister Bethany, and I run the Storehouse. When you need anything, come to me, and I'll be sure you get it, provided we have it. Your bed linens and pillows will be at your site when you arrive." She returns to her place behind her table, her hands clasped in front of her, looking serene. "Please leave your bracelets, Sisters, and I'll put them in the basket with your valuables. You don't need those down here."

We remove our one-armed handcuffs and rub our wrists.

She turns and speaks to another old man. "Brother Matthew, please take two water bottles to the Donovan site." Brother Matthew is an old bodybuilder with a dark buzz cut. He jumps into an ATV, which is loaded down with five-gallon water bottles, and drives west toward our site. The sound of the engine is amplified and echoes off the walls, making it sound like the Indianapolis 500. It's been quiet as a crypt on our weekend visits.

I ask Brother Michael for my birth control in a low voice so Mother doesn't hear. It's on my list of medications. "Oh, you won't need birth control here, Sister Shea," he assures me in his booming voice. Mother turns and gives me the evil eye. Everyone in Daeios probably heard him, the way sound carries down here. He's probably right, though—with my monobrow and bun, and white muumuu and socks-with-sandals ensemble, who'd want me? All that's missing is the cape.

We receive our supplies, minus our medications. Sister Bethany repeats the hanging of the ID cards around my neck and Maya's, the way leis are placed, kisses us each on both cheeks, and welcomes us to Daeios. Jace is missing out—the blonde and statuesque Sister Bethany is stunning, and she's giving out kisses like they're made of chocolate.

Sister Ariel finishes collecting Dad and Jace's supplies and places them in the RV. "Please write your names inside your clothing so you don't mix them up. You're responsible for doing your own laundry. The supplies are in the Laundry Room. You must keep your home sites clean and tidy. Hygiene is important in Daeios; be sure to shower every day. The lights will go out when it's time to sleep, except the path to the restrooms will remain lit. Is there anything else? Do you have questions?"

"No," Mother almost spits at her. We pile our supplies in the RV and hop in as two women move the barricade from our path. We enter the wide tunnel, uneven red stone walls to the left and human-made white walls to the right. Although the tunnel is less than three blocks long, the cool white fluorescent lights above us make the dark exit appear to be a great distance away.

I pause for a moment after we exit from the tunnel into the west wing to allow my eyes to adjust to the dimmer lighting of D section. It's in the living areas that Daeios looks most like the cavern it is. Lights shine everywhere—from sconces on walls and lamps at each home site—but much of the light disappears into the open space above us. The rock ceiling is up there somewhere in the blackness. I was never able to envisage what this would look like with furniture and people—hundreds of people living communally, with no walls between sites. It's worse than I thought it would be, noisy and bustling. I feel Mother's eyes drilling a hole in the side of my head, so I drive to site 119. Our new address: WD119.

Sister Ariel blacked out the RV's mirrors to protect us from the sin of vanity. I maneuver the RV into its designated parking place, going forward and back, forward and back, trying to get within the lines the best I can without running into anything, like a red rock support wall.

"Stop!" Mother yells. "It's good enough. Now help me get the Zipper off the RV so we can take the men to Medical." I get out and slam the door, and I feel better because it makes Mother jump.

A shudder runs through me when I see the damage inflicted by the lightning strike. It hit in front of the driver's door on the fender, leaving a charred, ragged hole as big as my thigh. If it had hit back a little further, my dad would probably be dead. If it had hit forward a little, it might've irreparably damaged the engine. Fate brought us to Daeios.

Maya and I figure out how to release the Zipper. Mother has Dad in a sitting position on the floor of the RV, and she's poking at Jace to get him up.

"Daddy, are you okay?" I ask, my voice small and tears burning behind my eyes because we almost lost him twice today. His head wound is bleeding into his silver hair, and he's unsteady. Mother and I help him stand, and I hug him for a moment.

"I'll be okay once I see Brother James. Come, Punkin, I need my little crutches." He squeezes us both to him for a moment as Mother tries to get Jace to leave the bench seat.

Jace refuses to come at first, but when we tell him we're going for a ride in the Zipper, he practically gallops to it. Like a dog, he wants to go for a ride. I imagine him with his head over the side, barking. Who knows? On gloss, anything is possible. Maya stays at the site.

Medical is in the north wing. There are other rooms in the north section, but they were closed when we visited on the weekends. The north wall is composed of red rock, as all outer walls are. The red rock of the floor, left uncovered in all areas of Daeios but the individual rooms, has been worn smooth by the tires of military trucks using the shelter as a parking garage for decades. With rooms on both sides of the hallway, which is wide enough to be a two-lane road with generous shoulders, it looks like an insane asylum—the outside walls of the rooms are all white, and the doors are all white. There are no signs on the doors and no windows. If they're accessed by key cards, there are no tiny red lights to indicate they have scanners. I'm not sure how many doors there are. My curiosity about these closed doors runs deep.

I checked out Medical before, so I drive right to it. It's right off the Communal Gathering Area. The bright lights of the Gathering Area illuminate the door and scanner so we can see them. The section is otherwise dark. I pull over and stop in one of the parking spaces across from it. I run to the door and scan my ID badge to open it, holding it open for my family. Dad gets out of the Zipper obediently and allows Mother to walk him inside. Jace sits in the ATV and bawls. I try to coax him into Medical, and he jumps out of the Zipper and runs back the way we came, waving his arms in the air, howling, and shouting something unintelligible. It bounces off the red rock, making it sound like savages are overrunning us. I let him go and step in to see how Dad's doing.

The antiseptic smell and glaring whiteness of the Medical Room assault my senses. Brother James attends, along with my mother. He's been here a couple of times on our weekend visits. He's a doctor and goes to Mother's church, so she's happy to see him, although her smile doesn't reach her eyes. He considers himself a real ladies' man and dyes his hair a brassy blond, wearing it poufy, as my grandma wears hers. I experience an unexpected pang for her, despite the fact she has resided in a nursing home for the last ten years and hasn't recognized me for much of that time.

"Your dad's going to be fine," Brother James says as I step over to the examination table. "Your mother's a good nurse." He grins at me, a wolfish smile with lots of teeth. Is he flirting with us? Ugh.

"Shea, where's Jace?" Dad asks. "I heard him, or some wild animal, out there."

"Oh, he's running around down here somewhere. At least we know he's in Daeios. I'll find him." I turn to leave, but hear Jace's echo down the wide hallway, and realize his shouts are coming closer. I scan the door open and look out to see two men dragging Jace, thrashing, to Medical. One is an old man, but the other is close to my age, and, oh my, he's gorgeous.

I'm suddenly aware I must smell bad. And look bad. And that the white dress isn't going to flatter me even when I am clean. I don't stand a chance with him. Especially if I can't keep from panting when he's around.

The two men bring Jace to another examination table in Medical and strap him down with ease. He's screaming, crying, and making an ass out of himself. How embarrassing. I try to act like I don't know him. The doctor gives him a shot, and he quiets down.

The young man holds out his hand. "I'm Brother Julian. Welcome to Daeios. Whom do I have the pleasure of meeting?" He smiles, head tilted to the side. I thrust my hand into his; a magnetic force is pulling me to him. He squeezes it. His hand is warm. My heart is drumming in my ears. I hope he can't hear it.

"I'm Shea, uh, Sister Shea. Glad to meet you." Did that sound too breathy?

"Nice to meet you." His eyes crinkle when he smiles again. He looks radiant with his long golden hair, cobalt eyes, and glistening white smile. He's slender and not much taller than I am. His features are small and like that of a beautiful Tolkien elf, but he doesn't have pointy ears. He has very nice ears. He's not wearing a wedding band, something a single girl notices. There's no way I can think of him as a "Brother."

"Ahem. We'd better get back to Maya," Dad says, and I realize I'm staring into Julian's deep blue eyes like I'm stoned. I wipe my chin with the back of my hand in case I drooled. I didn't.

"Yes. Back to Maya. My sister. At our site. WD119," I prattle, and almost walk into the doorframe. I glance at Julian, who's smiling at me, enjoying my comedy routine.

"See you later," he says as I scan my badge.

"Yeah, see you." Too cool? Not cool enough? Just get into the Zipper without tripping all over yourself.

My parents finish with the doctor and join me in the ATV, Dad in front. "How do you feel, Dad? Is Jace going to be okay?"

"Seatbelts." He waits for us to buckle up. He forgot to bring it up when we set out for Medical, so I rebelled and didn't wear mine. "I'm fine, Shea, the doctor gave me some stitches. He's going to stitch Jace's neck and start the detox process. Our boy will be back to himself in a few days. We're not to visit him until the drug is out of his system. By then he should be fattened up and joking around the way he used to." I'm not convinced, and Mother's shaking her head like she has palsy. Jace is more than a few days from okay. He may have lost a part of himself he'll never get back.

We drive back toward our site and see Maya surrounded by men.

I step on it and then screech to a stop next to the group of old guys. Mother and Dad slam forward, and Dad gives me that Dad-look that says, "Knock it off." I try to look innocent. I figure we may as well make an entrance.

I try to jump out of the Zipper, but my seatbelt holds me back, adding to the impressive entrance. I free myself and push through the old men until I'm next to Maya, my arm draped over her shoulders. My parents stand by the ATV, talking.

"What's up?" I ask Maya. "Did they mistake your white tips for gray hair?"

Brother Christian steps into our space bubble, and I step back, pulling Maya with me. Brother Christian fills the space again, and the old men encircle us.

"Hello, Sister Shea. We came by to welcome the Donovan family here. Is Brother Jace at Medical?"

"Yep." The old guys are all dressed in white, and I haven't burst into flames. But them encircling us gives me the creeps.

"Great, then you've met Brother James. Let's get your folks over here, and I'll introduce you to this band of ruffians." They laugh like it's the funniest joke they've ever heard.

My parents hear what Brother Christian said, and join the group.

"Brother Aidan, Sister Helen, I want you to meet some of my old cronies who help me run Daeios. You know some of them from church, Sister Helen." The pack lines up so they're easier to point out. They all appear to be in their sixties, at least, some a decade or two older. No wedding bands.

We line up in a similar fashion like we're playing Red Rover and are seriously outmanned.

He starts on his left. "Meet the other Elders of Daeios. Brother Mark is our Minister." Brother Mark is tall and thin and has a completely bald, shiny head. He bows as if he's used to applause.

"Brother Eli is our Chief Incinerator—of garbage, of course," Brother Christian says and chuckles, and they all chuckle with him. "He's in charge of the Purity Room." Brother Eli dyes his full head of hair pitch-black, and he has a pronounced widow's peak. He reminds me of a vampire with yellowing veneers.

"Brother Thomas and Brother Nathanael." They step forward, bow, and step back into line. They're identical twins, both about my height and thick around the middle, with curly orange hair. "They work in Security."

Brother Christian turns to his right and introduces the four remaining old men. "Here we have Brother Luke on the end, then Brother John, Brother Aaron, and Brother Adam. Brothers Luke and

John are in charge of entertainment—you'll find them in the Entertainment Room, of course," another snicker from the old guys, "the Art Room, the Theater, and the Music Room. You'll find we have plenty of fun in Daeios. Brother Aaron is in charge of Housekeeping and Maintenance, and Brother Adam is in charge of the Kitchen and Dining Hall." They've lined up from Brother Luke, who's the tallest, but isn't as tall as Dad and Jace, to Brother Adam, so short and skinny that he may be smaller than me. Two fat guys, Brother John, with curly gray hair, and Brother Aaron, with a white bowl cut, are in the middle. The fat ones are also the oldest of the bunch. They all have bald spots, except for Brother Eli.

Brother Christian continues. "You'll have met Brother Michael, the Pharmacist, and Brother Matthew, our Water Curator, when you collected your supplies. Now is there anything we can get you at the moment to make you more comfortable?"

"Xanadoxalate," Mother says, loud and deadpan.

"Oh, dear. That is the one drug we were unable to obtain, I fear. Brother Michael and I called all the pharmacies that were still open when we came underground, and, no luck." He shakes his head and indicates he's sorry. He'd better not say it, or Mother may come unglued. "Anything else?" Brother Christian asks, lifting his black eyebrows in question. Except for Mother, who is glaring at him and might start him on fire, we shake our heads.

"No? You'll hear three chimes when it's time to have our daily Gathering in the Communal Gathering Area. Please join us. You'll get to know more members of Daeios and hear announcements that affect everyone. It's quite informative and fun. Most Daeiosians gather in the Dining Hall for a meal afterward. Our sisters are excellent cooks."

"We'll be there," Dad says, and the cronies shuffle off in different directions.

I pull Maya aside and whisper so Mother and Dad don't hear. "What did they say to you before we got here?"

"They came up to me like they knew me and started asking questions about Dad and Jace, and where you were, and how old I was, things like that," she whispers back with a shrug. "I was glad when you showed up, I felt weird talking to all those old guys."

The creepiness I felt earlier is tingling from my head to my toes. Everyone we've seen has blue eyes.

So does my family.

6

We're tired and don't speak as we set our site up the way we want it, hydrating from one of the five-gallon water bottles using Styrofoam cups from the RV's cupboards. The RV is for privacy, which will be hard to find otherwise. I wish we could use it for showers. We have a small living area up against the rock wall, with seating and two small tables with lamps, all white, behind where the RV's parked. The white furniture against the red rock wall creates a startling contrast, illuminated by the round, squatty lamps. The living area opens into the wide, main hallway, but our RV, parked in front of it, hides it from passersby. It's one of only a few prime sites in Daeios where we can have the rock wall behind us and the RV in front of us. Dad spent a fortune buying it.

Most families don't have RVs, so their sites have bunk beds and dressers too. Some families paid less, but enough to have white human-made walls behind their living areas, and they're allowed to park a smaller vehicle in front. Others paid even less, and their sites are completely in the open, each home presented to public view like a small stage. They are so evenly placed that they appear to have invisible walls around them. I would hate that. These sites are smaller than my studio apartment, which is smaller than the supersized bedroom I had at my parents' home.

We make up our beds in the RV, with Mother and Dad sleeping in the king-size bed and Maya and me in the queen-size bed. The bench seat that Jace got to know so well will be his bed. We remove from our white bags everything we don't need right now, and head for the showers.

The showers and restrooms are marked *Brothers* and *Sisters* instead of *Men* and *Women*, painted in black calligraphy over the open entryways. Of all places to not have doors.

I hate communal showers. These don't have any partitions between them, similar to our living areas. At least the toilets sit within stalls and have doors for privacy. Maybe a couple dozen women and girls are in different stages of personal hygiene when we get there. The white of the tiles brings out the colorlessness of their skin, untanned and pale as winter, as is the fashion among the wealthy. All whites want our skin to be as white as possible so we're not mistaken for having dark skin. As Elites, we consider freckles, scars, tattoos, and piercings to be attributes of imperfect whites, other than a single tiny piercing in the center of each earlobe for females. Your eye color doesn't matter as an Elite, but as a Daeiosian it obviously does.

We go to the dressing area, a large room with benches, lay out our toiletries and new garb, and undress. The sun pendant falls from my shorts pocket and several sets of blue eyes land on it before I cram it back in my shorts. I put my wet clothes into my white bag. With my towel wrapped around my nakedness and my shower supplies in hand, I choose the shower furthest from the door. Maya follows. Mother stays near the dressing room, with a warning that my hair had better be in a bun when I come back to the site.

I turn my shower as hot as I can stand it to release the deep chill from my body. I let the water run through my hair, my eyes closed, enjoying the feeling of getting clean. The shampoos and soaps smell of lavender and freesia, and the scent is intoxicating as it steams up around me. I tune out the feminine voices and laughter and take my time in the shower, thinking of today and of Julian. Julian in the shower. Can you burst into flames while under water? I hope I'll see him again before my monobrow sets in.

When I finish my shower, Mother's gone, but Maya is waiting for me in the dressing room. She looks like an angel in her white gown with the big bow at the neckline. I unfold my white gown and find that it's plain, no bow. "Why do you get a bow and I don't?"

"Do you want mine? You can have it," she says as she tugs at it.

"No, I'm teasing. So what do you think of this place?"

"Everyone seems really nice." She's such a little cherub, her scrubbed cheeks round and rosy. "I'm curious about the Gathering thing tonight. It sounds like it'll be fun down here."

I try to smile, but I'm sure it's crooked; there are no mirrors in Daeios for me to check. Nothing is reflective, including the stainless steel, which has a brushed finish, and the spoons, which look similar to pewter.

It takes both of us to put my hair in a lopsided bun.

Maya and I join Mother and Dad at our site just as the three chimes begin.

"Time to go, ladies. I want to sit down before I fall down," Dad says, joking, but there's truth in it. Maya and I put our bags in the RV and hang our towels and washcloths outside on a line Mother strung for this purpose.

Dad takes Mother's hand, as always, and we head in the direction of the Gathering. It's maybe a hundred yards away from our site. Hundreds of other white-clad people are moving toward the Communal Gathering Area, sandals slapping on the rock floor of the hallway, talking and laughing. The Gathering Area is in the center of Daeios, at its heart, and has circular human-made white walls. It has wide, open doorways from the north, south, east, and west. The floor is tiled in white. It's about the size of my university's rec center, and it has large overhead light fixtures. The stage is oversized, taking up about a third of the room's area.

Everyone looks refreshed, excited, and a little enchanted. We sit on the floor near the stage, crowding in front of a group of young ladies. Dad sits down a little hard with an "Oof!" and Mother makes a big production of sitting with her gown draped around her, huffing and mumbling under her breath.

Only a moment after we sit, Brother Christian steps up to the microphone on the stage and says in a hearty baritone, "Hello, Brothers and Sisters of Daeios!" He holds out his arms as if he will embrace us all.

"Hello, Brother Christian!" the crowd answers. As Mother would say: Good Lord.

"We gather here today, as we do every day, as a community and as God's children. We, the Elders, have been called by God to lead you in the paths of righteousness in Daeios. We welcome those of you who joined us today. Please hold your hands up when I call out your names: The Donovans," a pause as a spotlight shines on us; "The Logans," another pause and the spotlight moves to another family; "And the Schreibeises." The spotlight moves again and then swings back to Brother Christian. "You'll find we have all the comforts of home—and then some. Welcome, Brothers and Sisters. Welcome to Daeios, where we're nestled safely inside the heart of God."

"Welcome all," the crowd says.

"I encourage those of you who have been with us for a while to welcome these newcomers into your hearts, and to help them become familiar with Daeios and our Daeiosian ways." He beams again. "Now, as your news anchor," he says, chortling, and the crowd laughs, "I'm afraid I have little new to tell you. As most of you know, we have absolutely no contact with the world of Gehenna." He raises his face, so we understand he is referring to aboveground. "No phones, no radio, no internet. We really are isolated here and may be the only survivors." I expect this to set the crowd abuzz, but only we new folks are surprised to hear it. The rest of the group shows little reaction. "We also have no way of tracking time, since timepieces don't work down here, either," he says, and his dark eyebrows go up in emphasis. "The last we knew, the weather and riots were threatening all life. Although we aren't at capacity yet, we fear that many of those who purchased sites in Daeios will not be joining us."

A few in the crowd show concern and mutter with those close to them, but most people are smiling. Mother has her head bowed, her hands clasped in her lap, and I know she's praying.

"We fear that they have been overcome by the perils that have overtaken Gehenna. As of today, we have 814 Daeiosians, while we have supplies for 1,000. Some of you have come to me worried about the water supply. Don't worry: we have plenty for both drinking and hygiene. Wear your water packs at all times. And drink up!"

He salutes us with his Daeios water pack tube and takes a big, sucking gulp into the microphone. It echoes, sounding like Daeios is swallowing us whole. Everybody in the congregation drinks from their water tubes, except for us newbies who didn't know to bring our packs along. What a weird ritual.

"Now, I'll turn things over to Brother Mark."

Brother Mark goes to the microphone and raises it to his height. "Let us pray for those we left behind in Gehenna. Let us pray for those of us who are ill or infirm, or lack strength: Brother Jace, Sister Naomi, Sister Ruth, Brother Aidan, and any others. Let us pray for the health and happiness of each and every brother and sister of Daeios. Please bow your heads and pray with me." He watches the crowd a moment while everyone complies. Apparently, we all pray our own prayers after that, for no one speaks, not even a whisper. Someone coughs. I look around, and everyone's heads are bowed, their hands clasped in front of them, some with their lips moving. Mother looks serene now, calmed by her faith now that we're safe. I bow my head when Brother Mark raises his and looks at me.

After a moment Brother Mark says, "Amen," and the crowd chants "Amen" in unison.

Brother Christian steps up to the microphone again. "Brothers and Sisters, let's celebrate the little ones, shall we? Mothers, please bring your babies and your toddlers to the front. Sisters who are with child, please come forward as well. These little ones are our future. We must take extra special care of them. Brother Mark, if you would please bless all of our little ones and little ones-to-be." He stands, arms outspread, with a beatific smile.

Mother squeezes Dad's hand and looks up at him, cherishing him with a look she reserves only for him. I want that someday. Someday. My life is so short now. Someday has to be soon, and in Daeios.

The mothers and tiny tots file across the stage, which takes forever. I bet a third of the Daeios clan is up there. Daeiosians have large families. Brother Mark reaches out his right hand and touches each child on the head, and presses his hand against each pregnant woman's gown, against her baby bump. Brother Christian takes two of the babies in his arms and kisses them on the tops of their heads, dramatically, and beams at the crowd. Mother looks so happy watching this. I'm cringing, afraid Brother Christian will squat down and kiss one of the pregnant ladies on her belly. He doesn't. I hope nobody saw my expression; everyone else seems to think this ceremony is delightful.

Have I mentioned that I'm not having any babies?

"Thank you, Sisters. Thank you, little ones," Brother Christian says as the last of the mothers and children file off stage. "Now, Brother John, please lead us in our favorite song. You know the one," he says and winks at the crowd, and the crowd chuckles as Brother John, the fat, curly-haired Elder in charge of the Music Room, makes his way to the microphone. Please don't let it be "The Chicken Dance."

"All rise, please. Those of you who don't know it, sing along the best you can. You'll know it after a couple of days," Brother John says with a wink. "We sing it every day at our Gatherings. Please join hands with those around you, and we'll begin." Mother, Maya, and I help Dad get up, and he stands, swaying, making me nervous. Mother puts her arm around his waist to steady him.

The Elders, including those who were working when we met the others, stand in a circle on the stage with Brother John and hold hands, demonstrating. I reach for Maya's hand on my right and, on cue, Julian slides in beside me and takes my left hand, a shy grin on his handsome face. Brother John starts singing into the microphone in a beautiful tenor, and the throng joins in. I stare at Julian the whole time.

Daeios, Oh Daeios
We live in God's light.
Daeios, dear Daeios
Our strength is His might.
Clean and pure, united we are,
Devoted to God every day.
In Daeios, sweet Daeios—
We love, we laugh, we pray.

I hear only women's voices, except for Brother John with the microphone, and Julian beside me. Everyone is enraptured, tears of joy seeping from the eyes of some, including the men on the stage, Julian, and Mother.

Dad and Maya and I are looking at each other—we're not feeling it.

The crowd files out of the Communal Gathering Area toward the Dining Hall, which is next door to the south. There are a few men and boys scattered in the crowd, but mostly I see bobbing buns. The Kitchen is the other side of the Dining Hall, and a long buffet line divides the two rooms. Everything is white or stainless steel.

Several dozen ladies either stand ready to serve food as we pass through the line or hustle around in the background, preparing the meal. The food is dehydrated, freeze-dried or canned, except for hard beans and grains that will keep a while. Brother Christian said the women are great cooks, but I have a hard time imagining it considering what they have to work with.

The crowd is loud and animated. Julian comes with us, and everyone turns to gape at us when we enter the Dining Hall, like I'm accompanying a screen star on the red carpet. Except in Daeios, it would be the white carpet. I wonder if the other ladies are jealous. Other than Jace, Julian is the only male I've seen under age forty, except for babies and children. The other men are married, except for the Elders. Has Y Chromo depleted the Elite male population so much?

The Elders sit at a long, rectangular table in the back corner and face outward, like the Apostles in da Vinci's painting of *The Last Supper*.

Maybe you have to be a single old man to be called by God.

Females are of all ages, from babies to women older than my dad. Most females are teenaged to middle-aged. That's a whole lot of PMS. Women have never liked me, so I'm not looking forward to being in close quarters with so many of them. My strained relationship with Mother doesn't help. I've always hung out with the guys and have never felt the lack of female friendships. If only I could have Julian as a companion—but I'm dreaming. He has his choice of ladies down here. Jace is attractive too, so the women will treat him like a rock star after he recovers.

The long tables feature white silk floral arrangements—a mixture of roses, lilies, and daisies—in white baskets. Mother chooses a table and sends the rest of us to fetch our food.

Julian notices I'm not taking any vegetables—I hate them. "You need to eat something green, even if it isn't fresh. You need to start thinking of food as fuel now. Treat your body like a temple. Be sure to get some whole grains, too. I like the quinoa." The cooks slop the off-color food onto our trays, their blue eyes following Julian. He seems not to notice. Occasionally, one of the cooks glowers at me. Only Sister Bethany says hello.

At the end of the line, Julian picks up a pitcher of water, and I collect four plastic cups. Julian has his pack on his back, already filled. "In the future, you'll have your water packs on you at all times. There's nothing but water to drink in Daeios, and you must stay hydrated and healthy."

Maya and Dad are through the line now, and we head back to join

Mother at the table. "It looks disgusting," she says as we lay our trays down and she gets up to go through the line.

"So, that's my mother..."

Dad introduces himself and Maya to Julian. My dad's assessing Julian. Julian is the only male I've seen in Daeios with long hair; it almost touches his shoulders. The color reminds me of the sun. I could use that reminder every day down here.

We sit down, and Mother returns. She probably bullied them, so they got her through the line as fast as possible.

"Helen, this is Brother Julian," Dad says. Mother twitches the corners of her mouth up for a second in greeting. If Julian blinked, he missed it.

Mother reaches across the table for my hand, signaling that she'll bless the food before we begin eating. I can barely hear her in the clamor around us, but I know what she's saying.

As we release hands, Dad suggests, "Brother Julian, tell us about yourself."

Julian digs into some mashed potatoes and mud-colored gravy. He's left-handed, as Jace and Mother are. "There's not much to tell. I don't have any family—"

"No family?" Mother asks. "Or no family down here?"

"No family at all. I'm an only child, since my parents died in a car accident when I was eleven."

"Oh, I'm sorry to hear that, Brother Julian. You don't have any extended family?" Dad asks.

"No, nobody. I was in the foster care system until I went out on my own when I was sixteen. It hasn't been bad. Brother Christian took me under his wing and into his home after I started going to the church. That's why I have a site here. He bought it for me. He's the greatest man I know." His passionate smile shows pride in his father figure.

"So how old are you, Brother Julian?" Dad asks.

"Twenty-four."

"Are you worried about Y Chromo?" I ask. Even saying Y Chromo puts fear in my heart.

"I'm not worried about it. We all die, eventually, and I'm going to be with my Lord and Savior when I do. There's no reason to be afraid." He's smiling and doesn't appear to be feeling sorry for himself, which I find attractive. I hope Jace will recover from the harm gloss did to him and learn from Julian's example.

"What about the pain?" Mother asks. "Or never having children?"

"I believe God doesn't give us anything we can't handle. Including children," he says with an exaggerated wink and a smile. We all laugh, and I snort water out of my nose. I'm so sexy. "I've even come to enjoy the close quarters. It's home. Have you looked around, become familiar with Daeios?"

"Dad and I have been here on several weekends, so both of us know a lot of it, except for the north and northeast sections. Medical is the only place we've been in the north wing. Maybe you can show us around?" I hope I don't sound too obvious.

"No one's allowed in the north sector, except for Medical, which is open 24/7. The northeast is the Purity Room, where I work. I'm the garbage man, and my main duty is to shovel waste into the incinerator. Pretty glamorous, right?" He grins. "Only workers are allowed in the Purity Room. What positions are you hoping to get? Do you have any particular skills?"

"I'm in real estate," Dad says. "I don't know how that will be helpful in Daeios. Helen's a nurse. Shea, what do you think suits you?"

Mother rolls her eyes.

Before I can answer, Dad asks Julian, "Is Maya expected to work? She's only fourteen."

"They'll probably have her work in the Nursery. Most young girls seem to like it there." He winks at Maya, and Maya blushes to her toes. By this time, everyone's finished eating, and Julian volunteers to take our trays. "I have to go to work at six chimes, maybe I'll see you tomorrow?" he says to me.

I can't even talk; I nod my head and smile and watch him swagger away with the trays. I come back to reality to see my family staring at me.

"What?" I ask. "Do I have food on my face?"

We walk back to our site, hearing the six chimes along the way. I'm starting to recognize some of the people from the church's potluck. I also put some families together by their resemblance to one another, especially the redheaded family with the short bangs, mullets, and caterpillar eyebrows, and the family of seven with big frog mouths who all bellow at the same time. Inside voices, people.

I offer to show Mother and Maya around while Dad rests at our site. Mother goes to inquire after Jace's condition instead.

I take Maya on the same tour Brother Christian took Dad and me on the first time we came to Daeios, although now the shelter is alive with people moving about. Since she's seen part of the west wing, I tell her that there are restrooms and showers on the other end of the wing, too. As we walk to the south side, I explain the layout of Daeios, as Brother Christian explained it to Dad and me. I have to admit it's an amazing place.

"Daeios is the size of twelve city blocks: a rectangle with uneven, natural rock walls. The shelter is longer running north and south than it is wide." I move my arms like I'm a flight attendant pointing out exits, and she laughs. "The Communal Gathering Area divides the sections." I stop and make flight attendant motions again, spinning around and gesturing broadly, delighted by her laughter. "The sectors to the north and south of the Gathering Area are twice as wide as the west and east sections, which run the entire length of the shelter. These sections are often referred to as 'wings,' although they're within the rectangle that makes up the shelter." I flap my arms like wings, and she doubles over, trying to catch her breath. We move on. "Brother Christian said the east sector compares to a public works division. Daeios is one hundred percent self-sufficient, not relying on anything from the earth above."

I don't mention the north section, because, other than Medical, it's a mystery to me. I will solve that mystery. If I'm going to live in a dark hole in the ground, I want to know every inch of it.

We reach the south wing, which is the most exciting place in Daeios—if you can call it exciting. It's like the downtown area, and it's bustling with activity. I let Maya open the doors with her ID badge because she thinks it's fun to use it. We tour the Entertainment Room, where we can watch G-rated movies, play board games and Bible-themed video games; the Fitness Room; the Library; the Theater, which is for live productions and seats an audience of three hundred; the Art Room; the Music Room, for those who play instruments or want to learn; the Nursery, which is full of screaming midgets; and finally the not-so-interesting Chapel, Repair Shop, and Laundry Room. All the rooms are state of the art, white and stainless steel, their floors carpeted or tiled in white. There are windows in the doors. You gain entry, or exit, by scanning your ID badge. Each of the scanners has a tiny red light that turns to green when the lock opens.

Why lock the doors? It makes me wonder if they're tracking our movements.

"They'll probably assign us duties in this section, except Mother might work in Medical," I tell Maya. Several women are busy cleaning the common areas—they work shifts around the clock and keep everything spotless. I hope they don't assign me to Housekeeping. I don't want to break my record of not cleaning anything, ever.

Brother Christian told Dad and me that they lock everything up tight in the east sector, and there are no windows in the doors, for security reasons. They don't allow anyone inside without staff supervision because they don't want anyone to steal supplies from the Storehouse, or to poison the water supply. They don't allow anyone in the Purity Room, where the incinerator is, except for the workers, for safety reasons.

We go to the Storehouse first. It has supplies for at least one year for one thousand people. I press the bell outside the door. Someone rustles on the other end of the microphone.

"Sister Shea, Sister Maya. What can I get for you?" It's Sister

Bethany's melodic voice. There must be a camera for her to know who's at the door, but I don't see one. How many other cameras are there in Daeios?

"Can we take a quick tour?" I say into the small mic embedded in the white wall.

"Of course, come in," says Sister Bethany, and she buzzes us through.

Daeios is chilly everywhere, but it's coldest in the Storehouse. Apparently, no one gets a jacket in Daeios, though. Sister Bethany and her crew must be used to the cold. I hope they don't assign me here.

Sister Bethany smiles as she hands us white hardhats, and says, "Hop in, Sisters." We climb into a vehicle like those in the airport for the people who need help getting around. Sister Bethany drives us up and down, aisle after aisle, explaining their inventory system and how they arrange the goods. Shelves reach up to the ceiling, which is high as a gymnasium ceiling, and cast shadows on the lower shelves. The shelves hold food and water, the white water packs and bags, hygienic supplies, cleaning supplies, light bulbs, fuel, linens, garments and sandals, paper and pens—anything you can think of that you might need for the next year. Not everything you want, but everything you need. We ooh, and ahh, and ask a few questions, and Sister Bethany stops at each crew member and introduces us, except for the ones working high on the scaffolding to reach the top items. They're all women and are wearing hardhats, with headlamps, over their buns. The ones working on the scaffolding contort so as to not flash their naked lady parts.

"Although it seems to be a lot of supplies, remember when we run out of something, we run out for good, so be frugal," Sister Bethany says as we return our hardhats and leave. "Run out for good" echoes in my mind as we go to the Water Room.

Brother Matthew, the Water Curator, is happy to show us his work area. It's much smaller than the Storehouse and is all dark red rock: a large cave. It smells wet, and you can hear the constant drip and trickle of water. "Daeios has several deep wells," he explains, "which will provide enough water to supply all of Daeios for our lifetime. Plus," he adds, his muscular chest puffed out, "I've devised a system to catch rainwater from above, run it through several filters, and have it collect in these cisterns. We do the same with our recycled water. It's all purified." Too bad Brother Matthew's not in charge of food: he'd probably have cows and chickens, a vegetable garden, and fruit trees.

The cisterns are the same color as the red rock that surrounds us. They have spigots at different heights for releasing the water into different sized vessels.

"Let's have a drink, shall we?" Brother Matthew pours us each a glassful from the nearest cistern. We each get a real glass. Classy place, I think, in my best Brooklyn accent.

"To Daeios," he says as he raises his glass, and we tap our glasses to his and drink. "Drink up, Sisters—I'm afraid you can't take those glasses with you." He laughs and watches us drain them. Church bells begin to ring. "Three bells, time to close up for the night. May I escort you to your site, Sisters?"

We decline. As we approach our site, it's clear something's wrong. Our parents are standing, waiting for us. We jog to them.

"It's Jace," Mother says, her arms crossed. Dad's head is bowed. "You know that mask he was carrying on about on the trip here? He tried to take it off. With his fingernails. He's covered in blood. Brother James doesn't think he has much skin left on his face."

7

"They've sedated him again. There's nothing to do but keep him under until that horrible drug releases its grip on him," Mother says, her face grim. Dad's breathing hard, like he might explode if he doesn't do something about it soon. I'm trying not to think of Jace's destroyed face, hoping it doesn't look as bad as I imagine it does.

"We can't let him go through this by himself, Mom," Maya says. "Jace isn't strong. He needs us. Can't we see if they'll let us visit him? After what's happened, maybe they'll change their minds about keeping us away." She's on the verge of tears. I know if she cries, I'll cry, too.

Mother's voice is shaking. "I told them he needed to be in restraints until he detoxed. He flirted with some googly-eyed nurse, and she undid the restraints. He lunged for her, and she ran off, leaving him to rip his face off." She closes her eyes and shakes her head, breathing out through her nose. "I blame myself. I should've insisted on being with him while he comes down. I am a nurse, and I am his mother."

"Helen, this is not your fault. I'll see what I can do. Brother James may say this doesn't change the rules, but it does. I'm going to speak to Brother Christian about letting us visit him. Brother James is just covering his fat ass. Please excuse my language." Dad would never say this if he wasn't about to boil over. He heads for the Zipper, wincing in pain with each step that jars his aching head.

"I'm coming too, Dad. I'll drive," I say, taking the driver's seat and buckling up without being asked, a good little chauffeur.

Brother Christian, although the head of Daeios, doesn't have an office as you might expect. He could be anywhere, helping where he's needed most. We check first with the women in the Kitchen. They suggest we may find Brother Christian in the Nursery.

"He just loves babies," a girl with a bow on her gown says. She's blonde, and is so petite she reminds me of Tinkerbell.

Tinkerbell's right. Brother Christian is sitting in the middle of the Nursery on the white carpet, holding a baby. A little girl shows him the doll she's playing with, and a little boy runs circles around him. Other children are playing near him, seeking his attention and approval.

He looks up and sees us enter. "Brother Aidan, Sister Shea! What brings you here? I would've bet you'd all be sleeping by now. You've had a long day."

Dad explains why we've come, and Brother Christian says, "Oh, dear Lord. I agree: a man needs his family at a time like this. I'll speak to Brother James about it. I'll have a solution for you by breakfast."

We thank him and drive back to our site.

None of us sleeps well—we're all restless and worried, acutely aware of Jace's empty bed.

I feel strange when I wake up—stranger than usual. A hymn is playing, increasing in volume with each stanza. I smell food cooking. The lights are coming up gradually like the sun is rising. I can't remember the last time I was awake to see a sunrise. Strangest of all, I now know what it feels like to wake up without a hangover.

Brother Christian's word is good. He comes to our table at breakfast and tells us we can visit Jace. The room is much quieter than at dinner last night, and his voice carries. "He'll be restrained and sedated until the gloss wears off. I've arranged for some sensible nurses to take care of his medication and hygienic needs, and to change the ban—"

"I'm his mother, I'll do the nursing," Mother says.

"Sister Helen, you can't nurse around the clock." He raises his bristly dark eyebrows in challenge.

"We'll help," Maya says, looking to me for agreement.

I hope it doesn't entail changing diapers. "We'll help, Mother. Show us what to do."

"I assume this means we won't be taking on any other assignments in Daeios until Jace has healed," Mother says, her head back as if her bun is heavy.

"Ah, yes." Brother Christian thinks for a moment, tapping his chin with two fingers. "I'll run it by my two most senior Elders. I'll let you know either way." He turns and leaves us, going first in one direction, and then turning and heading in the opposite direction. He seems lost.

Mother sighs heavily as she gets up from the table. "I dread seeing him," she says as she drifts past us.

"I'll meet you at home." Dad groans as he stands and fights to keep his balance.

Yep, home sweet home.

———

Mother is restless, waiting for Brother Christian's decision, so she seeks sanctuary in the Chapel. Dad lies down in the RV—his head's killing him, he says—and Maya goes to the Library. I decide to see how it is running on a treadmill, commando, in a bulky white muumuu and sandals.

The Fitness Room is spacious and holds a lot of equipment. Several women and teenage girls are working out, and they're wearing white sweatshirts and sweatpants, with white athletic shoes. I'm so happy to learn this I think about doing a cartwheel, which wouldn't be pretty in my current attire. It's not shorts and a tank top, but I'll take it. I change in the locker room and find we get to wear sports bras, too.

I'm familiar with the Fitness Room from our visits. It has weight machines, free weights, equipment for working your core, plus various types of aerobic equipment. It's nicer than the gym I use at home, except it doesn't have mirrors for watching your form.

I commence my weightlifting routine first. My arms hurt from the vaccinations, but I push through the pain. The other women don't lift weights. They watch me with curiosity, a monkey in a zoo. I consider scratching my underarms and ass for them. They'd just watch me do it. No one speaks to me, so I don't say anything to them, either.

After finishing my sets, I step onto the treadmill at the far end of the room. I have never been one for making conversation while I work out, anyway. I'm building up to running speed when Julian walks in. I can make an exception.

He scans the room, his face lighting up when he sees me. I smile so wide my cheeks hurt. He strides confidently down the row of treadmills toward me and seems to have eyes only for me. It could be a scene from a romantic comedy: Julian walks toward me in slow motion, running his hand through his blond hair, his smile radiant. The other ladies gawk at him, and one trips on her treadmill and flies off the back, hitting the wall. Ladies near her stop their exercise to help, exclaiming and fluttering about. He reaches me and motions to the treadmill beside me, acting as if nothing had happened.

"May I?"

"Of course." If I sound breathy now, I have an excuse.

We run in uncomfortable silence for a couple of minutes. I'm afraid to look at him, afraid that I'll trip or do something else embarrassing. At last, he clutches the rails, puts his feet beside the moving belt, and speaks, gasping for air. "How. Much. Longer. Will you. Be doing this?"

"A few more miles." This treadmill doesn't show your time, only distance.

"Oh," he says, and begins running again.

"Do you come here often?" I huff.

"No. Can you tell?"

"You're turning purple."

He pushes the stop button. "I give up." The treadmill comes to a stop, and he stands there, wiping his face and neck on his towel and panting. "Can I see you later?" he manages.

Yes, yes, yes, yes, yes! is what I'm thinking, but aloud I say, "Sure. Do you want to meet for lunch?"

He breathes out hard. "Just the two of us? Please?"

"Yes. Come by our site, WD—"

"119. I remember. See you then."

He walks away, and every female in the gym, including me, watches him walk out. When the door closes behind him, they give me the stink eye, and I flash them my sweetest smile.

I discover when I go to shower in the locker room that the dressing rooms and showers here have partitions. Aha! One problem solved. Still no mirrors.

My post-workout shower feels like a reward for exercising. I smell the ketones my body is releasing. I'm cleaning myself from the inside out.

I hate the idea of putting my sloppy gown back on, my white shroud, and of repinning my bun. I touch the area between my brows. No pesky monobrow yet. I sigh into the gown and fumble about with the bobby pins, not sure how crooked my bun is. It'll get easier. Won't it?

When I return to the site, no one's there. Brother Christian must have made a decision. I head to Medical, but my ID badge doesn't allow me access. I bang on the door, and no one answers. Where are Brother James and my family?

Oh, my God, something must've happened to Jace. My chest swells with panic the way it did when I looked for him the other day —was that only yesterday? I feel as helpless now as I did then.

I sneak down the wide, dark hallway to the rock wall of the forbidden north. Brother James emerges from a door halfway down the corridor and stares in my direction, lit from behind by the light of the room. My first instinct is to plaster myself to the rock wall in hiding. My brain quickly catches on and realizes that white on red is not hiding, even in the shadows. He can probably hear me breathing, too, the way sound travels down here.

"Sister Shea!" Busted. I try to arrange my face in lines that would indicate I'm lost, but I probably just look constipated. Brother James slams the door shut and approaches me, grumbling. "Sister Shea, please come with me." Shit.

He leads me down the hall past a closed door and scans a special key card in an unlit scanner. He throws the door open. It's the Detention Room. I didn't know they were so serious about not wandering into the north sector.

"We had to bring Brother Jace here because he doesn't stay under sedation. He's frightening all of my patients away, and he bit a nurse," Brother James says through clenched teeth. "You'll find your family in the room in the corner over there." He points and leaves, trailing too much spicy cologne, and slams the door behind him. The noise makes me jump.

I'm afraid to see what Jace has become.

I knock on the closed door, and Maya lets me in, her eyes red from crying. Mother and Dad have their backs to me, blocking my view of Jace. Dad's shoulders are shaking.

"Prepare yourself," Maya warns.

I step around to the other side, Maya right behind me. I have to stifle a gasp. My brother is strapped to a table from his forehead to his ankles, his arms imprisoned at his side, his clothes saturated with blood. He has an IV in each red-stained, destructive hand. His head and neck are wrapped in bloody bandages, with openings for his eyes and mouth. His eyes are wide open, and black, all pupil. He knows me instantly.

"Shea." It's not his voice; it's raspy from screaming or dehydration. "How nice of you to come," he murmurs, wincing in pain. His black eyes roll around in the bandages. The whites show for a second, and then back to black. I swallow hard.

"Brother James has given us permission to take care of Jace until he's better, and he left us some supplies," Mother says. "He's given me a key card to access the room. Brother James said your brother needs water, most of all, and clean bandages. He needs your prayers, girls. He's receiving painkillers, a sedative, a detox drug, and nourishment through his IVs. Be careful he doesn't bite you."

Jace lets out a gurgle that may be laughter.

"Mother, can I take the late shift?" I ask. I have to finagle it so I can keep my date with Julian.

"Yes, thank you, Shea. Aidan, you're not well. Why don't you let Brother James examine you? Girls, let me show you what you'll need to do for Jace."

After Dad totters out, Mother has us wash up and put on latex gloves. Maya holds Jace's chin down while Mother puts a bite guard in his mouth. Mother attaches a narrow tube to a plastic water bottle and snakes the tube down into his mouth. "Squeeze the water gently, so he can swallow it without choking."

Maya takes the bottle from her and looks for her approval.

"Yes, just like that. We'll let him finish the bottle, and then we'll change the bandages."

We have to release his forehead restraint to change the bandages. He starts shaking his head, screaming around the bite guard, trying to keep us from removing them.

"He has to make everything difficult," Mother says, the creases in her upper lip deepening. She gently pulls the blood-soaked bandages off and drops them into a stainless steel bucket. The wet, sticky sound of the bandages as they land on other bandages makes me queasy.

My brother's exposed face belongs in nightmares, not in waking life. It is a bloody mass of wounds, some deep, and some shallow, where he's torn the skin off. I smell the sour pus that's oozing from the neatly stitched neck wound, and I'm afraid I'll throw up.

He sees our expressions and starts to cry, sounding more animal than human.

8

I'm so relieved to be excused from the Detention Room that I almost sprint. After rebandaging his face, Mother showed us how to handle Jace's bedpan. Maya lingered; she will be a much better nurse than I will.

I stop by Medical, but Dad's not there, so I go to our site. I find him weeping at the table in the RV. He covers his eyes and then wipes his face when I come in.

"Your mother got rid of me so I wouldn't see the damage," he says and sniffs. "How bad is it?"

"As bad as you think," I answer, scooting in next to him.

"Oh, no," he says. "I can't stand to see what he's done to himself. Y Chromo or not, this is too much." He dries his tears again and blows his nose into a handful of tissues. I stand up and hug him from behind, snuggling my face into his warm neck. He's always been so tenderhearted. I don't know how he and Mother ended up together.

"Dad, are you going to be okay?" Two bells ring. Lunchtime. Lunchtime! "I'm going to have lunch with Brother Julian if that's okay?" I blurt out, one foot already out the door. Sensitive Shea, that's me.

"Sure, Princess. I'll just lie down for a while. You kids have a good time." I know he's hurting. He sounds like a sleepwalker, drained of emotion. He falls onto the bed, spent. I give him a quick kiss on the cheek and head for the Dining Hall. I have to remind myself not to run. But I can walk fast.

I step into the Dining Hall, seeking Julian.

"Boo!" He touches me on the shoulder from behind. I stop my scream just in time.

We laugh, my laugh shaky, the one I have after being scared silly at a horror movie.

"You scared me. Don't ever do that again," I say, holding my shaking hand to my chest to calm my heart.

"You're so cute. I won't, I promise. I don't want you to be afraid of me. Let's go sit over there." He points as he takes my hand and pulls me to a table for two. I'm so happy, I forget all about my brother. Julian and I are in our own little carefree bubble.

I don't notice if jealous blue eyes follow our every move. My senses take in only Julian.

When I left Jace, I thought I'd never eat again, even though I had only picked at my runny powdered eggs at breakfast. But after running five miles and having my heart race every moment I'm with Julian, I'm famished. Julian notices my heaped tray.

"Can you get any more on there?" he jokes. I blush, noticing that his tray is half as full as mine.

"I brought it to share," I say as I sit, which is not what I meant to do. I make the movement for flipping my long hair behind my shoulder, which must look pretty silly since my hair is in a bun. I swallow a nervous giggle.

"I'm kidding, eat up. You probably have the metabolism of a highly strung gazelle."

I dig in. We eat a moment in silence, except it seems that my chewing and swallowing is so loud it echoes throughout the Dining Hall.

"This is Sunday. Don't we have to go to church sometime today?" I ask.

"Is today Sunday? I had no idea. We don't have church services like they do in Gehenna. We have our nightly Gatherings instead. You're welcome to worship on your own. We have a Chapel." He scoops up some baked beans.

"Oh. What's Gehenna, anyway?"

"Hell. Up there." He points at the ceiling.

"Why do they call it that?"

"The Elders believe that we Daeiosians have been chosen by God. That they haven't. That's why they're perishing."

"Oh." I'm quite the conversationalist. I gobble my food the way I always do, leaving my peas, and notice Julian's only half done. He seems to savor every mediocre bite.

"No peas?" he taunts, tilting his head to the side, which I find irresistible.

"I ate one," I say, truthfully. It was stuck in my mashed potatoes.

He laughs. "Tell me something about yourself that no one else knows."

A challenge. He eats some peas from my tray and gives me a conspiratorial wink. I try to wink back, but I blink instead. I'm wink-challenged.

I look up, thinking. I lean forward on my arms to gaze into his eyes, but mine drift away as I say, "I've never been in love." I've dismissed Scott like a pair of old running shoes. I eventually return my gaze to Julian's eyes.

He leans forward, as I did, and eyes twinkling like the midnight sky, says, "Neither have I. Yet."

The blush reaches my bun, and a trickle of sweat runs down the back of my neck in spite of the chill in the air. My smile comes out a laugh, and he grins as he reaches for my hand and holds it as he finishes his lunch. Happy little hummingbirds flutter around in my stomach. Am I falling for Julian? Can he ever love me? I rest my chin on my fist and watch him eat. I hope I don't look too googly-eyed.

He stands when he's finished and gathers our trays in one hand.

He offers me his other hand, and I take it. My palms are sweaty. "Shall we move on to the next part of our date?" He acts mysterious and must know I'm dazzled by him. A giggle escapes me: now introducing Simple-Minded Shea.

We dawdle, walking so close that our hands press against the other's leg. We don't speak, but we glance at each other every few seconds and smile. My mind is whirling. The hummingbirds flap in a frenzy. My heart is pounding in my ears, and I even feel it beating in my ass. It's really going crazy.

We stop in front of the door to the Theater, and he scans us in with his ID badge. White velvet curtains hang floor to ceiling on the walls, and the three hundred seats are white. No one else is here unless their white clothing and skin is camouflaging them in this all-white room and I can't see them.

"There's a small room back here that nobody knows about. I snoop," he says with a double lift of his golden eyebrows. "It's a perfect place for a date." I'm so curious, I'm afraid I'll meow.

We reach a stack of white boxes against the wall in a large room full of colorful costumes. I'm surprised the colors aren't sinful. Julian releases my hand and unstacks the boxes.

A door.

He takes my hand and leads me inside, flipping on a dim light. It has only one bulb, where there should be three.

It's a big closet. A thick stack of forgotten, and probably taboo, crimson velvet stage curtains lay neatly folded at one end. It's a bed. I may not be the only one Julian has brought here. The hummingbirds land. I want so much more than this. I drop his hand and turn to leave. "I don't want to be one of your conquests, Brother Julian."

"Wait. What?" He reaches for my hand and pulls me back in. I point toward the bed. His other hand rushes to his chest. "Oh, my goodness, it's not like that. I'm not like that. No one else has been here, I promise. It's just that I need my privacy sometimes, so I check out a book from the Library and come in here to read." As if performing a magic trick, he pulls a reading lamp from behind the stack. "Please don't tell anyone about it. It'll be our little secret." He motions for me to get on the pile of curtains.

I sit, and he pushes the button lock in the door. A frisson tickles down my back. He sits next to me. He removes his water pack, sandals, and ID badge, so I follow suit. "Let's lie down. I want to hold you."

I've heard this many times before a one-night stand. I'm not on birth control pills anymore. But I don't seem to be able to resist when he lies down and gently pulls me to him, a magnet to steel. My misgivings recede as the hummingbirds take flight again.

We lie on our sides, facing each other, his right arm holding me close, his left hand caressing my right shoulder and arm. He looks dreamy. I feel dreamy. I'm tingling in my naked lady parts.

He moves his hand to cup my face and pulls me in for a kiss. He kisses me long and hard, letting out a soft moan. It feels like he's sucking the breath out of me. I have to break the kiss and take a deep breath.

"Did I do something wrong?"

"No. I'm … I'm just …"

"Don't worry." He strokes my cheek with the side of his finger. "I don't believe in sex before marriage, either. I do, however, believe in kissing," he says playfully, smiling, and swoops in for more kissing. I just about suck his lips off. My entire body is throbbing, wanting my skin to be touching his—wanting to make love to him.

He breaks the kiss this time. "I think I'm falling in love with you, Shea. I think God called us to Daeios to be together. Is that crazy?"

Yes. And it's crazy that you think I'm a virgin. "No, it's not crazy at all. I'm falling for you too, Julian." He may be the last chance I have for love before I die. He is my someday. I choose to love him.

We spend the rest of the afternoon in that closet: kissing, talking as I lie cradled in his arms, getting to know each other. It won't be difficult to love him. Those happy hummingbirds are fun. He's charismatic, positive, and romantic. I even admire his purity, in spite of the roadblocks it's putting up. Maybe some of his wholesomeness will rub off on me. He respects me, and I haven't experienced that for a while. I groan inwardly when three chimes ring.

"Dinner with the family tonight?" he asks, as he restacks the boxes in front of our secret chamber. "Can I come?"

I nod and grin at him. It's too good to be true. I hope my family likes him.

9

"Hello, Brothers and Sisters of Daeios!" Brother Christian begins, taking us in with a sweep of his hand. Welcome to the Kumbaya Show. The congregation is buzzing, and everyone is standing. Brother Christian must have some news for us tonight.

"Hello, Brother Christian!" the crowd answers. Oh, Brother. Maybe down here it should be Oh, Sister, considering that females outnumber the males by at least ten to one.

"We gather here today, as we do every day, as a community and as God's children. However, I'm afraid I have some bad news." He makes a moue. The crowd shuffles and mumbles around me. Julian and I look at each other and back at Brother Christian.

Brother Christian speaks in a funereal tone. "No new arrivals today. This is our sign from God to close our doors. As of this moment, Daeios is locked down. No one else will be joining us."

The woman next to Julian bursts into tears. There are other sobs in the crowd and a scream. Someone has fainted. People in the vicinity of these outbursts mutter and fuss, trying to bring comfort to the distressed. The rest of us stand in awkward silence, except for Mother, who is praying.

"God has chosen us to remain alive in Daeios. His reasons will become clear in time," Brother Christian says. "I hope you're all finding your way around and are getting to know each other. I've seen some friendships forming. Wonderful! We are, after all, brothers and sisters. I admonish you, however, to keep your friendships innocent."

Without warning, he and the other Elders look directly at Julian and me. The blue eyes of the crowd turn toward us. We face straight ahead, and Julian squeezes my clammy hand. My chest tightens, and my face flushes.

"While we're on the subject of finding our way in Daeios—a number of you brought ATVs to get around. We almost had a crash yesterday. So please reserve your usage of these vehicles for transporting large items, or for driving someone who is ailing to Medical. We can all use the exercise that walking provides. Okay?" The crowd murmurs an assent. "Let me remind you that we must treat our bodies as temples. You'll find no sugary treats, alcohol, or caffeine in Daeios. We encourage you to eat a healthy, balanced diet. Eat your veggies." He looks right at me. Busybody. "But most of all, remember to drink up. Cheers!"

We raise our tubes in salute and drink.

"Good, I'm glad to see everyone is wearing their water packs. It's imperative to stay hydrated."

Brother Mark leads us in prayer next, adding some names to the list of sick and injured. I pray for my family. I pray for Julian and me. I want to keep him.

"Amen," Brother Mark says. I wasn't finished praying. How rude.

I'm relieved when they finish the Blessing of the Little Ones, and the mothers and children file off stage. That ritual only reinforces my desire not to have rugrats.

We take the hands of those next to us. Brother John begins to sing that stupid song, which I'm already sick of, and it's only my second day. I would prefer "The Chicken Dance."

I glance around and see the emotional reactions of those around me and on stage. Sister Bethany catches my eye and waves as she wipes away a tear. Tears wet Julian's long, blond lashes as he sings at the top of his lungs. Mother has already learned the song, her thrilling soprano reaching me from Dad's other side.

I don't feel it, but I try to look emotionally unstable like everyone else so they won't notice I'm different.

———

Julian and I join Mother and Dad for dinner. The banter in the Dining Hall seems loud, jovial even, considering some families just learned they'll never see their loved ones again. Mother is staring at her tray like it might do something interesting. Dad's fiddling with his ID badge, preoccupied. He doesn't have a tray yet.

"Oh, hello," he says as he notices us, his voice flat. "Hi, Brother Julian."

"Let's get our food, Dad," I say, gesturing for him to join us in line.

"I'm not hungry. I came here to keep your mother company until you got here. I'm going back to the site." He gets up, kisses Mother on the cheek, and shuffles away with his head bowed, his shoulders rounded.

The last thing I want is to have my Mother interrogate Julian.

When we return with our trays, I notice Mother's eyes are dark-circled and glazed with fatigue, and her face is slack. She doesn't say anything, doesn't insist on saying grace. She pokes at her food and moves it around her tray, which I used to do when I was a kid. She used to yell at me for doing it.

"How's Brother Jace, Sister Helen?" Julian's making me look bad.

"He's resting now. Finally. I suggested Brother James try a different sedative, thinking the one they had him on was interacting negatively with the gloss or the detoxing drug. The new one knocked him out, thank God. He was muttering such awful things, about demons, and death, and killing." Her head shakes; I think a tremor ran down her spine. "I placed a catheter, Shea, so instead of helping with a bedpan, you'll need to check the bag and empty it when it's three-quarters full."

Please, Mother, we're eating.

The plan is for me to finish quickly to relieve Maya from her post with Jace so she can eat before the Dining Hall closes, but I'm not looking forward to nursing my brother. I hope Jace will be unconscious the whole time. I want to keep this light-as-air feeling I have when I'm with Julian, to not feel depressed the way my parents do. I peep at Julian to reassure myself he's real. He smiles and scoops up some peas from my tray with a wink. He must really love me. I don't want to be apart from him, even for a few hours. Or however many chimes and bells. Time passes so slowly down here without him.

I finish eating, not gobbling it down like I usually do. Mother notices that I'm lingering. "You need to relieve your sister, Shea. If you want it, eat it, otherwise, get going." She hands me the key card.

Julian squeezes my hand. "I'm off to work soon. See you in the morning? I hope Brother Jace is doing better." He gives me a peck on the cheek, and I watch him walk away.

I finish eating under Mother's wicked glare.

I fill my water pack as I leave the Dining Hall and head to Detention, ambling along like I'm enjoying springtime in twentieth-century Paris when Maya's waiting on me. Enter: Selfish Shea.

When I open the door to Jace's room, Maya is singing to him, probably a song she has on her playlist on her mini-computer. She holds my brother's hand. Jace is still, except for the rhythmic rise and fall of his chest.

"He's sleeping," she whispers as I come near. His empty eyes are closed, and he's clean. The bandages are fresh, with only two small blotches of blood on his face, and a hint of the grayish-yellow pus at his neck. "I just changed his bandages and IVs and emptied his catheter bag. He's been knocked out the whole time I've been here. You shouldn't have any trouble." She gives me a hug and kisses Jace on his restrained hand. "I hope he's getting better," she says.

I scan the key card to let her out. I won't be locked in here with Jace.

Taking off my water pack, I sit with him, doing nothing for a few minutes. I'm not good at doing nothing. Following Maya's example, I sing the song Scott and I called "our song," but I can't always find the right key, and today is one of those days. It's about as soothing as the shriek of a canned air horn. It feels like I'm cheating on Julian, singing that song, so I stop.

I massage Jace's icy feet and legs, the way Mother showed us, until my hands feel cramped. I'm afraid to give him a sponge bath after our history with that. I check to see if Maya or Mother left a book or puzzle. Nothing. I sit and hold Jace's hand the best I can with the restraints securing his hands to the table. I sit.

I am doing something, but it doesn't feel like I am. My restless mind makes a choice and says in a falsetto voice: "Let's go check out the north and northeast sections." No one should miss me if I leave for a short while. I pick up the key card and put on my water pack. If they bust me, at least they can't add a water pack transgression to my record.

The door between Medical and Detention is closed: no windows, no sign, as expected. A sliver of light lands on it from the Gathering Area. Finding the unlit scanner, I insert the special key card to see if it will open the door. It doesn't. I categorize it in my mind as Door 2, with Medical being Door 1.

The wide hallway darkens as I move toward the north, away from the bright lights of the Gathering Area. The next room is Detention, where Jace lies. Door 3. My hands tell me that Door 4 is the only other door on the west side, and it's inky dark at this end of the north wing. I feel my way along the north rock wall with my left hand, my right hand out in front of me, and count my steps to the east wall. Twenty-nine steps. I feel my way along the human-made east wall, finding a door, a narrow hallway to the northeast, and two more doors.

Door 5, Door 6, and Door 7. These must be larger rooms.

I return to where the hallway leads to the northeast section and peek around the corner down the hall. A faint light flickers in the distance. I'm sure the light wasn't there when I passed it a moment ago. The smell of burnt garbage is strong here and makes my eyes water.

I scream when Julian pops up out of nowhere.

"Shea, what are you doing here? You know this is off-limits. It's not a pleasant place to be." The outline of his face seems to glow, even in this dim light. He's wearing white coveralls, smudged in black, and he has soot on his face. Shiny black work boots have replaced his sandals.

"I wanted to see you," I say, trying to steady my voice. It's half true.

"Come, I'll take you to your site." He offers his hand, and I take it.

"I'm actually supposed to be watching my brother in Detention. You can walk me across the hall."

We walk, swinging our held hands as if they will take flight. "Why's he in Detention? I thought he was under medical care."

"He's eighty-sixed from Medical. It's okay. We have everything we need, and he gets a private room that way."

"How's he doing?"

"Better. He was sleeping when I left. I ... I wasn't gone for long."

"Can I come inside for a minute?" Julian asks.

I want to invite him in, but I feel protective of my brother. "Just family for now. Doctor's orders."

"Maybe someday I will be family." My heart skips a beat, and I'm warm all over. He grabs my face, passionately, and kisses me. He smells of smoke. "See you tomorrow, then."

When he lets go, my head is spinning, and I have to steady myself.

I watch him hasten down the hallway toward the flickering light, his footsteps echoing until he bangs a door closed and disappears into total darkness.

I enter Detention. I dread spending several more hours staring at my sleeping brother, and I hate the nursing part. Bodily fluids are not my forte.

He looks the same as before, although one of the blood spots may have grown. He's in the REM stage of sleep: his eyes move back and forth under his eyelids. At least I hope it's REM and not the evil that's lurking inside him.

I sit in the white plastic Detention chair, made for punishment, and try to make myself comfortable.

If I had to guess, I'd say we have been in Daeios for a week or two. With no sunlight and no human-made way to keep time, I don't try to track the days. It's pointless to do so, and keeping track would be placing a countdown timer on our lives. We mindlessly drift from one activity to another based on chimes, bells or hymns, and the intensity, or lack of, human-made light. I used to have a good sense of time before we came down here, but now it seems that some nights are longer than others, and that meals are sometimes too close or too far apart. Time is now abstract and undefined, and I feel the loss of knowing it, even as time goes too slowly down here. Religious zealots who don't have a weekly worship service seem incongruous to me. Perhaps the Elders are purposely keeping us off balance.

My days are monotonous, and I spend my nights with my sleeping brother. Only my time with Julian is enjoyable. My desire to work out has waned, although I continue to exercise, a rat with a monobrow running on its wire wheel and lifting tiny dumbbells. It's something to do.

I want to run outside. I want to see the sun. I want to breathe fresh air. I'm tired of the oppression of the red rock walls, which amplify the quietest of sounds and dampen the brightest of lights.

10

I'm dreaming that someone is calling me. "Ay. Ay." And something indistinguishable.

I jar awake. It's Jace.

My body is stiff and sore from sleeping in the Detention chair night after night. I stand, stretching, wary of his eyes like they might fly out of their sockets and attack me. I relax when I see they're his natural indigo blue with a dot of black pupil.

"Ay." The bite guard is keeping him from speaking clearly. He's trying to say my name. He tries to talk again, and I guess at what he's saying.

"You want water?"

"Uh-huh."

I get ready to snake the water tube into his mouth, but he seems okay now. "If I remove the bite guard, do you promise not to bite?"

"Uh-huh."

The bite guard's covered in slimy saliva, which drools down my hand, and I gag. More bodily fluids. The sooner my nursing days are over, the better.

"Thanks," he says hoarsely and flexes his jaws. "I see your

overactive gag reflex is still intact. How about that water?" He sucks on the tube, gulping the water.

"Slow down. You can have as much as you want." I wish I could see if he has any color in his face. I remember the wounds with a shudder and wonder what scars will remain.

He stops drinking and lies there, deep breathing. "How bad is it?"

"How bad is what?" I ask, wearing my poker face.

"My face. How bad is it?"

"I don't know," I lie, my cheeks hot. "I've only seen you with bandages on."

"Are you supposed to change them?"

I look at him and sigh. "Maybe. Mother and Maya have been doing it, but I know how."

"Let's do it. Is there a mirror so I can see?"

"We don't have mirrors down here. The Elders say it's supposed to discourage vanity."

"Down here? The Elders? Where are we?" he asks. He motions for another drink of water, and I put the tube in his mouth again and squeeze the bottle.

"We're in Daeios, an ultra-Elite underground shelter. The Elders run things down here, a board of directors. Supposedly, all of us in Daeios were called by God, and God called the Elders to lead us."

"God called me?" He laughs, a mocking laugh flavored with bitterness. "No way. They strapped me down so I don't hurt myself anymore?"

I tell him why they moved him from Medical to Detention. "You know you were high on gloss, don't you?"

"I hid so I wouldn't hurt anyone. Getting high isn't the group activity it used to be." I wish I could see his facial expression. His voice carries no emotion, the bitterness gone. "Shea. Bandages, please."

I take it back. I don't want to see his facial expression.

I remove the strap that's holding his head down so I can change the bandages.

"That feels better already. Thanks, Sis."

I cut the bandages where Mother showed us to cut, and start unraveling them, dreading seeing his once handsome face and the damage he did to it. I concentrate on wrapping the bandages around my hand in a perfect ball instead of looking at what I'm unwrapping. There isn't any blood or pus on the material.

I get to the end, steel myself, and look at him.

His eyes mirror my horror, and he winces when I clap my hand over my mouth to keep from crying out. He's missing strips of skin where his fingernails ripped the flesh, leaving black scabs in their place. The remaining skin is puffy, an angry pink. The area around his eyes, miraculously, is untouched. He got his mask, and his frightened blue eyes show through that grotesque mass of damage. I don't see any fresh blood, though. The neck wound is a rough-edged pink keloid now. He is healing.

"Would you mind removing the rest of the restraints? I promise to be good," he says. I imagine what he does with his face is supposed to be a smile. A scab breaks open, and he starts to bleed.

"I trust you." I hope I'm talking to the real Jace, that the gloss is out of his system and he doesn't relapse into the lunatic he was. That he doesn't have brain damage that has changed him into an animal. That my brother has come all the way back from where he's been.

I release him, and he sits up on the table he's been held captive to for days, weeks? He moves too quickly and becomes dizzy. "Oh, my God, I've never had such a headache. My whole body aches," he says, groaning.

"Maybe you should lie down again," I say, as I hold him to keep him from falling. He's so frail. I feel his brittle bones inside the leathery flesh of his arms.

"No, I'll be okay in a minute. Is there anything to eat?"

"I'll get you something as soon as it's okay to leave you. How do you feel?"

"Other than feeling ninety years old, with pain radiating from every pore, having no face, and no doubt being a jackass to everyone who cared for me? Pretty good." He tries to laugh, but it comes out wrong: raw and painful. "I would've probably been better off up there. Who found me?"

I stare at my hands folded in my lap.

"Dad asked you to, didn't he? Mom wouldn't have." The bitterness rises to the surface again.

"Jace, you've always been special to her because you're the only boy. At least she doesn't act like she hates you. The way she treats me …" I shake my head, not finding the words.

"Shea, I've never told you this, but right before Maya was born, Mom told me that you got all of the looks and all of the brains—"

"She did not," I say, laughing.

He doesn't join me. "She did. You don't know how beautiful you are. Or how smart. She said I'd have to work hard to make something of myself, that it would be easy for you."

"Only Mother would say that to you. And that was when she was nice."

"She's disappointed in your choices, but they're better than mine, obviously."

"Then Maya came along and made us both look bad," I say. This time he does laugh, and I do, too. It's so good to see him laughing. Well, to hear it. Seeing it is pretty gruesome.

My family needs to know Jace is awake. Our training was for a sedated Jace.

"Are you okay here while I get the family? Or I'll stay, and we can talk. If Mother shows up and finds you sitting, we're both dead."

"Bring it on. And bring me some food, I'm starving," says the grisly scarecrow sitting in front of me.

I don't know where I'll find food. The Dining Hall and Storehouse close at night, as most everyone is sleeping. Maybe Medical has access to food for their patients, and they're open twenty-four hours.

I need to get Mother first, though. She'll have a fit if I don't.

Mother's lying awake on the bed she shares with Dad. She springs to her feet when I come in.

"What are you doing here, young lady?" she says, loud enough to wake the dead in Cleveland. "You're supposed to wait until—"

"Jace is awake," I whisper, in case someone slept through my mother's outburst. "I don't know what to do now. He's hungry, and everything's closed, and ..." I stop because I'm rambling.

Mother slips her socked feet into her sandals and straps on her water pack. The good thing about living in shapeless white gowns is that you can wear them around the clock, awake and asleep, and no one knows the difference. They always look bad.

Dad and Maya haven't moved; either they slept through Mother's shrieking, or they were smart enough to pretend they did.

Mother is spryer than Dad; she sets a pace that I struggle to match. She scans the key card, and we hurry in. Jace is sitting in the chair now, touching his face.

"Keep your hands away from your face," Mother booms. He jumps, pulling his hands from his face. She moves around the table that held him prisoner and assesses his wounds without touching him. "Not as bad as I was expecting," she says.

What was she expecting?

"Shea, get him some water." Then to Jace, "You'll have to live with some pain for a while, as your body adjusts to living without gloss. The wounds will stop hurting and will itch as they heal. No scratching," she says, grasping his hands for a moment and staring into his eyes. "Drinking lots of water will help you recover. That reminds me, I need to remove that catheter. I want to talk to the doctor on duty to see what she thinks about the bandages. Do you need to have a bowel movement?"

Jace shakes his head. She leaves, and the key card leaves with her. I don't like the idea of being locked in here. Locked in anywhere, as we are in Daeios. I hope Jace can come home—to the site—with us. I want my nursing days to be behind me. We sit in silence as Jace gulps down a bottle of water.

Mother returns, bearing a heaped bowl of diced canned peaches and a small plastic spoon. Jace digs in, his mouth directly over the bowl, shoveling in the fruit like he's in an eating contest.

"Slow down," Mother says, slapping him on the shoulder. "It's time you started acting human again." Jace smiles at me like we share a funny secret about Mother.

Mother has some clean bandages in her other hand. "I'm afraid you'll have to wear these a bit longer. Sister Eve and I agree that we need to keep the wounds clean from infection. And safe from your hands," she says, frowning. "Lie down while I remove the catheter. Shea, step out while I do this."

I'm amazed, a few minutes later, when Mother and Jace walk out of the room arm in arm. I thought we'd bring the Zipper. "Shea, take Jace's other arm. He's not stable right now." In more ways than one.

We return to WD119, slowly this time, moving side to side as first Mother, and then I, take Jace's fragile weight as he stumbles. We help him to bed, and he winces as he lies down.

"Thanks," he says and closes his eyes, the only part of him that's still Jace.

11

I doze, on and off, and Mother flops around in bed as well. Jace snuffle-snores. Will he have flashbacks? I wonder how gloss has changed his life forever. Our lives.

The hymn announcing breakfast doesn't arouse me until it's at half-pitch; I was sleeping deeply when it started. Of course, I drifted off right before time to get up. I sit up and realize that Maya has climbed over me and everyone has left the RV. I check the living area. They let me sleep in.

Julian is with my family at breakfast. "Maybe someday, I will be family," echoes in my mind. I smile and crinkle my nose at him as he moves to make a spot for me. We hold hands under the table.

Jace and his bandaged head sit across from me. Only his eyes and mouth aren't covered. No blood stains. His tray is overflowing with food, and he's shoveling it down like it might vanish before he gets a chance to eat it. He smiles at me as he chews, his lips turned up at the corners and his eyes crinkling. Those around us throw furtive glances at him, and some children are gawking and pointing at my brother. Screw off.

"It's so nice to meet Brother Jace," Julian says. "You must all be relieved."

"As long as he doesn't relapse." Yep, that was Mother.

"I'm going to show him around," Maya says, grinning. "You're going to love the Entertainment section," she says to Jace.

"This place doesn't seem so bad. The food is great."

We all gape at him, puzzled. He must be more ravenous than we can imagine.

Julian and I sit with the family while they finish eating, then go to the gym to work out. He walks on the treadmill, looking at me every few minutes with chagrin as I run next to him. I laugh, breathing heavily. I stop after five miles. "How far did you walk?" I ask as we drink water.

"Almost three miles," he says with mock pride.

"That's good. You're much faster than when you started." I switch to a whisper as I towel off some sweat. "See you in our secret spot after showers?"

"Do you have to ask?" He tilts his head to the side, and I want to kiss him, but I don't since there are others around. I run my hand across my lips to remove the pucker.

As much as I enjoy my post-workout showers, I rush through this one, anxious to be with Julian. I hope to entice him into a little skin-on-skin action. Maybe we'll take our socks off and play footsie.

I'm glad to find that Maya and Jace aren't in the Theater when I get there. I go to our secret door, open it, and find the room lit with white candles, more than a dozen of them. They smell of vanilla. Julian is lying on his side on the stacked curtains—disappointingly, not naked. My hands rush to my cheeks, and I say, "Oh, how beautiful!" and I mean him as much as the candlelight. He grins with pleasure.

He pats the spot in front of him, and I join him. "In another life I would get you flowers, but here I'd have to steal them off the Dining Hall tables. I might get Detention." I laugh with delight. He removes my water pack and pulls the pins from my hair, stroking it. "I love your hair—it's shining like copper in the candlelight. It's so soft. It's a shame you can't wear it down." It feels good to be petted and to be free of the pins. I kiss him, hungrily, until he breaks away, holding my arms. "Shea, we can't touch each other that way. It's sinful. We must wait until we're married."

I didn't realize I was touching him "like that." Is he actually thinking of marriage?

"Yes, I'm actually thinking of marriage," he says, reading my mind. "I've never met anyone like you before. It was love at first sight. You told me you love me, too. It seems to be the next logical step."

Logical? We've known each other for a few chimes and bells. But I'd be an idiot to let him get away with all the competition here. "It's so sudden. I'll think about it," I murmur.

"Pray about it. I'm sure you'll get the same answer He gave me."

God said "Yes?" I'm suddenly feeling breathless.

He kisses me again. "I love you, Shea."

"I love you too, Julian." It's the first time I've said it to anyone. My ears feel hot.

"Unconditionally?"

"Of course."

He kisses my neck, right around the neckline of my sexy white muumuu. I don't know how people wait until they're married—I'm so turned on right now. My nipples must be poking him through our thick clothing. I feel him, hard, pressing against me, making the tingle in my lady parts worse. I let out a moan of longing.

He pulls away, holding me at arm's length. "I'm so sorry, Shea. I didn't mean to disrespect you. Nothing like this will happen again until we're married." A tear glistens in one eye.

"I understand. You didn't do anything wrong."

"We'll keep some space between us, okay? Room for Jesus." He holds me, but not too close to him.

How I wish he would disrespect me just a little bit more.

Julian shakes me awake. "Hurry. It's three chimes. We slept through lunch."

The candles have burnt out, leaving the room smelling of smoky vanilla. He turns the light on, finger-combs my hair, and helps me pin it up. "We don't want the Elders to think we haven't kept our innocence. It's good enough." He raises his eyebrows a couple of times, and I laugh. We leave the Theater holding hands and smiling. Julian may someday be my husband.

We return to the home site and walk as a family to the Gathering. Julian has become one of us.

"Hello, Brothers and Sisters of Daeios!"

"Hello, Brother Christian!"

"We gather here today, as we do every day, as a community and as God's children. I have some exciting news for you today." He beams down at us as though we were his children. "God has spoken to me, and the Elders and I are ready to impart his wisdom." The crowd hums with excitement. "However, we will convene with the rest of the Gathering first, as I want God's word to be the last thing you hear from us tonight." Mother clasps her hands in front of her chest.

"Let's welcome Brother Jace to the congregation. Brother Jace, please raise your hand."

Couldn't he just say, "Everyone stare at the guy that looks like a giant Q-tip?" Bright spotlights fall on my sibling.

"Brother Jace has been through a particularly difficult time, but God has healed him, and he's back with his brothers and sisters. Please make him feel welcome. Please introduce yourselves."

"Welcome!"

Jace waves around the room, enjoying his new celebrity status.

"I'm afraid I have bad news about Sister Ruth. She has succumbed to her illness. We will miss her, but she is with God. We will include her in our prayers tonight. Please remember her in your private prayers as well. Her family will hold a memorial service at their home site, WA139, directly after dinner. Please join them and pay your respects. Brother Mark, please lead us in prayer."

As usual, the Blessing of the Little Ones follows the prayer. It's starting to seem silly to me, all those kids waiting for their blessings, Brother Christian kissing the babies, the mothers watching and smiling proudly. Mother and Dad smile like they want grandchildren. A new mother-to-be walked up there this time, younger than me. She's a single woman. Has someone lost her innocence? Maybe the Elders were glaring at her the other night, and she was standing behind me.

We join in the song, and the faces around me are just ... goofy. Even Julian's, and of course I can't see most of Jace's, but I can tell he's smiling and he seems to know the song, pumping his left arm like he's holding a beer and singing an Irish drinking song. Maya must've taught him the words. Mother sings joyfully, her hands clasped in front of her heart. Mother's full heart smiles from her eyes as she looks at Jace, and I wonder who she really is.

"Now, Brothers and Sisters, we get to what we've all been waiting for: God's instructions for Daeios. Please listen carefully and hold your comments and questions until the end. I hope no one will question God's law."

He smirks, and the audience laughs. Julian grins at me and squeezes my hand.

Brother Christian's baritone reverberates off the walls. "God has spoken. We are, indeed, Earth's last survivors."

I expect mournful cries and tears, but the crowd is silent. I picture my fragile grandmother, with dementia, in the nursing home. Scott flashes in my mind, but I replace his picture with Julian's face.

"God has instructed us to procreate. I quote Genesis 9:7: 'As for you, be fruitful and multiply; populate the earth abundantly and multiply in it.' Daeiosians are the hope for the future of planet Earth. He will heal the earth and restore it to us in time. We'll create a new, Greatest Race, and we will live in God's ways. I see in your faces that you have questions. Let's see if I can answer them." Hands shoot up, but he continues. "We have so many beautiful, unmarried, vessels here to bring God's children into the world."

Mother pales and grabs Maya's hand.

"Women who are in menopause, or otherwise can't have children are, of course, exempt. We have that information from your applications. In addition, females must be sixteen or older to be breeders. That means no one with a bow on her gown, Elders."

The old men look at each other and laugh. Mother gives Maya a tight squeeze and glances at me, her mouth a straight line, before facing the stage again.

Brother Christian turns to the Elders, who step forward and stand on either side of him. "We have an exceptional group of men to father the world's children. They do not have Y Chromo, so there's no risk of your baby boys inheriting it. These Elders are enthusiastic to comply with God's will, to give Daeios more lovely children. God will assign each breeder to an Elder. One thing you can be certain of: your babies will have blue eyes."

Rather than questioning this terrifying vision, the crowd roars with laughter.

"Quiet, now. Quiet, please," he says, holding his hands up until the crowd subdues. "God doesn't want the nonbreeding sisters to feel left out. Breeders must eat balanced meals, drink plenty of water, and get adequate rest. Nonbreeders will assure this happens. They'll check your vitals every morning before breakfast. They'll help raise the children."

I realize I'm standing with my mouth open, shaking my head, so I stop.

"Before each consummation, the nonbreeders will treat our breeders to a day of beauty, so you will be at your most lovely and fragrant for the bearers of your seed. There are mirrors in the spas, Sisters."

Breeding-age females squeal and clap, hugging those around them. I can't believe their reaction—how can this excite them? I'm an outsider, an intruder observing. I couldn't pretend to be happy about this even if threatened by torture. Which this is.

"Sisters, please. I know you're excited, but let me finish. We have a special Breeding Room with a spa attached. Please be patient as you see others going to their breedings. Your time will come," he says, and

I remember thinking he was going to palm my cheek when we arrived. Maybe he will someday.

Ladies fall all over each other. It doesn't make sense to me. Everyone is so changed. Maybe I'm still sleeping in the Theater closet with Julian. No, he just squeezed my hand. I stare at him, and he smiles and says, "Isn't it exciting? You'll be a vessel for God."

"But ... But ... I thought we were going to be married? I don't want to get pregnant by one of them."

"You will want to. You will!" Julian's eyes and mouth are wide with excitement.

Why is he okay with this? More than okay, he's happy about it. I'm his fiancée, shouldn't he want to keep me for himself? "But I—"

Brother Christian interrupts. "And our young girls, those fifteen and under, remember to live in God's ways so you can breed on your sixteenth birthday. Won't that be a wonderful way to celebrate your sweet sixteen?"

Unbelievably, the girls in the gowns with bows clap, blushing, feeding into the excitement. Many of them probably don't understand what this means. Mother is clasping Maya's shoulders protectively. My sister, who is grinning at me—she's grinning at me!—looks so young. Dad's patting her arm, tapping out a rhythm, smiling serenely. Jace is smiling, too. Only Mother, the most devout among us, seems to be herself. What is happening here? Why is no one questioning this madness? Why is my family accepting Brother Christian's words?

"Are there any questions?" Our leader searches the crowd.

A young brunette raises her hand.

"Yes, Sister Eden?"

"I volunteer to breed first."

"God always likes volunteers, but I'm sorry. God is to give us a daily list, a breeding schedule if you will. Pray that you will be first. Believe me, the Elders and I are as excited as you are. Who will be first among us? We don't know. It adds to the thrill, doesn't it?" He smiles and bobs his head like a talk show host.

He calls on another young woman. She doesn't look sixteen, but she doesn't have a bow on her gown. "So ... we will raise our babies?" she asks.

"Of course you will. But you'll need help. Once you have a baby, it will be time to have another one. The nonbreeders will help you when you're tired, when you're healing. We want the births of our children to be as joyous as possible. How loved the little ones will be. Imagine our Blessing of the Little Ones, how wonderful it will be to have so many more youngsters and pregnant mothers on stage."

Mother raises her hand, speaking before he calls on her. "You say Earth will be restored, yet you make it sound like we're going to live the rest of our lives down here. You said we only have supplies for one thousand people for one year. The babies will barely be born by then. Did you stock enough diapers and other baby supplies for all these 'little ones'? What about the strain on our other supplies?" She talks like she's in a political debate. Except she's making sense.

"Sister Helen, those are all good questions. However, we must not question God's will. He'll take care of the details." He half smiles and turns away, dismissing her. "Any other questions?" He doesn't even scan the room. "No?" He raises his water tube. "Drink up, everyone, and rejoice. We are the chosen people of God."

Everyone drinks and starts moving toward the Dining Hall. The group is vibrant with elation, women of all ages and fertility levels tripping over each other, chattering like squirrels. How has our little world and its inhabitants changed so much in so short a time? I thought living out my days in Daeios would be comfortable, until the end, which I've tried not to think about.

Now I'm afraid of what my life down here will become.

12

Sick to my stomach, I'm unable to eat much at dinner. Sister Bethany stops by to welcome Jace. She's the only one who does. Jace ogles her as she walks away like he's invisible underneath the bandages.

My family and Julian discuss the "exciting" news we received at the Gathering. Only Mother and I are silent. The entire crowd seems delirious about it. Even our men are excited, saying they're proud to have me, and eventually, Maya, help repopulate the earth. Mother changes the subject by picking on Jace.

He makes quite a display of himself. A blob of brown gravy stands out on his bandaged chin. Mother watches him, jumping on him any time she thinks he's "eating like an animal," which is every few seconds. He pulls his elbow off the table, or sits up, but keeps shoveling. At this rate, he'll go from scarecrow to fatso in a week. It's rather entertaining and quiets my unease.

Six chimes sound and Julian springs off the bench. "I didn't realize how late it was. I'll take your trays." He notices mine is hardly touched. "Sister Shea, you have to start taking better care of yourself. You need to have a healthy body to do your work and to have strong babies." I blush to the top of my bun.

"Don't touch Jace's tray, you're likely to lose a finger," Mother says, glaring at Jace. "I'll get the trays. You go to work, Brother Julian."

Julian squeezes my shoulder and off he goes.

"I wonder if Shea can have Brother Julian's baby?" Maya says dreamily.

Mother's eyes bug out, and I'm so shocked, I almost scoop up peas instead of potatoes.

"Brother Julian could have Y Chromo. That's why the Elders are doing it. God thinks of everything," Dad says, smiling and shaking his head like he only has half a brain. What has happened to him? He's always questioned leadership and has stood up for those who needed a powerful, or wealthy, man behind them. His family is his greatest pride, and he has done everything to provide for us and protect us. Why isn't he protecting me from this? The man sitting before me is a passive stranger.

In my confusion, I hastily decide I must tempt Julian into making love to me. We've been so close—I'm sure I can wear him down if only my "call from God" doesn't come for a few days. Even if we have a boy with Y Chromo, it will delay my time before I have to have sex with one of those old men. Or maybe keep it from happening at all.

Mother pulls me aside as we leave the Dining Hall, asking in hushed tones to meet in the Library. I promise to see her there, and then take my time getting there. I never like what she has to say to me.

I stall as long as I can. Mother's standing outside one of the quiet rooms inside the busy Library. I go in, and she closes the door behind us. She speaks, pacing, before I sit down.

"How does this seem to you? Your dad doesn't think there's a problem, but I don't believe the orders came from God. They came from the Elders. They want to get their hands on you pretty girls, and they're willing to tell us anything in order to do so. How will God restore the earth to us when it's been so damaged?" She stops pacing and looks at me from across the table, her arms held tight across her stomach. "They planned this all along. They have a breeding room and spa that no one else knew about? Everyone has blue eyes? I bet they have plenty of supplies for new babies, but what's the point of new babies down here when our food will run out eventually? It's about the sex, not about the babies." Her anger is making her breathless.

"Why is everyone so accepting of this, other than the two of us? They act like it's a huge honor. I don't think I could feel that kind of zeal about anything."

"Me neither, and I'm a born-again Christian," Mother says.

"They're making us sex slaves, Mother. Even if the other women are willing to have children by the Elders, I'm not. What am I going to do?"

"They can't force you. You'll join a long line of people who have disobeyed God. What are they going to do, put you in Detention?"

Our eyes meet. Maybe there's something worse than Detention that we don't know about.

We return to our site to find Dad, Maya, and Jace talking animatedly and laughing.

"You missed it, girls," Dad says. "Brother Christian came by with our job assignments. Helen, you'll be in Medical, as we thought. They have Maya in the Nursery. I get to work in Security." He thrusts out his chest and pretends to be important. "Guess what you get to do, Shea? Three guesses."

Get pregnant? "What? Tell me, Dad. I can't guess." I never so much as fried a French fry or greeted a Walmart shopper before this.

"They have you in the Fitness Room. Brother Christian thought you would be a great personal trainer. Sister Bethany recommended you." He's smiling like a child who's found a shiny coin. "Until God calls you to breed. He said things might change for you then."

I ignore the nausea. "What about you, Jace?" I ask.

"That's the greatest news of all," Jace says. "I get to be in the Theater. I'm the Phantom of the Opera, hiding my ruined face from the world. Maybe a beautiful girl will fall in love with me, scars and all." He lets out a teenage giggle and then winces in pain.

"When is my first shift?" I ask.

"Six chimes. You start tomorrow," Dad says.

I get my time with Julian. "When do the rest of you work?"

"That's the bad news. We're all working different shifts, except for you and Jace. We won't be seeing a lot of each other, except at meals and Gatherings. They could've scheduled it better than that. Families are important."

"Maybe that's God's plan, too," I say, my voice cutting, but these aren't the people I want to cut.

"Shea," Dad warns.

"Sorry." My heart rejoices that I'll be able to spend time with Julian. Maybe by this time tomorrow, I'll be pregnant with his child. A dimly lit bulb comes on in my head. What if we just get married? The single women are the vessels. He said he wanted to marry me. If I must have a baby, it will be with Julian.

When we go to bed, I lie awake, dreaming of living my lifetime with Julian.

13

The music and increasing light don't wake me the next morning; Mother shakes me awake. It seems too early to get up. She searches my face as she takes my vitals.

"They don't have us charting your fertility windows, which would make sense if this was truly about procreating," she explains. "The thermometers they've given us aren't sensitive enough to check basal temperature. They could call you at any time, so be alert to your surroundings. You've got to be prepared to fight this."

I nod, my stomach clenched. She records my results on a chart that she brings with her to breakfast. Although each breeder only has one line of stats, there are several pages of names on the clipboard.

The powdered eggs are runny, the dried potatoes too salty, and the caffeine-free crap they pass off as coffee is watery. I try to flavor it with powdered creamer but can barely stomach it. Worst of all, Julian doesn't join us for breakfast, the one time our family can be together.

Mother gulps her food and heads to Medical. She's wearing a white coat over her gown. I wonder if she'll take part in birthing the new babies.

"Where's Jace?" I ask, finally pushing my concern about Julian's absence away and noting that my brother is missing from breakfast as well. "I can't imagine he'd miss a meal. Did he gobble it down and go off to haunt the Theater?"

They don't know.

I finish breakfast and head to the gym in search of a workout and Julian. He's not there, so I soothe my aching heart by running six miles and really pumping the weights. I'd rather be body sore than heart sore. I try to keep from thinking what this might mean, that he may have found someone new to lie with on the red velvet curtains. My heart aches as if it's being squeezed in cruel hands.

By the time I finish my workout, shower, and the pinning-of-the-bun, two bells ring. I'm getting good at the bun business. It feels even, centered. I wish I did.

I go to lunch hoping Julian will come up behind me and grasp my hand, or say "Boo!" He doesn't. He isn't at lunch, either. My eyes search for him, trying not to be too obvious, to see if he has defected to another table. I don't see him. Am I imagining that the other women are whispering about his absence? Has my monobrow set in and scared him away?

Jace isn't there either. "Does anyone know where Jace is?" I ask.

"Maybe he's at the Theater," Maya offers. "He's really excited about working there. Maybe he went to introduce himself and find his way around." She's eating quickly so she doesn't hold up the shift change at the Nursery.

Dad has no idea. Mother's picking at her tray again. The vertical wrinkle between her eyebrows is longer and deeper than usual. She must've had one hell of a shift. Dad notices it, too.

"Helen, anything wrong? You're awfully quiet, dear."

"Sister Naomi died in the night. I read her chart. She didn't have a life-threatening illness. She had a broken leg. I don't know why she hasn't been up and around on crutches. Brother James snapped at me for reading her chart." This offense would've usually caused Mother to get louder, not quieter. "He said she contracted an infection they couldn't cure, but no one made any notations about it on the chart. Something isn't right, Aidan. With this whole place. Something terrible is happening."

"Now, Helen, you're being silly. It's just first-day jitters. After all, you haven't worked as a nurse for a few years."

"Are you saying I don't know what I'm doing, Aidan? I can read a chart. Even Shea could read the chart." She waves her hand dismissively at me.

Thanks for your vote of confidence, Mother.

"We must trust in God's ways," Dad says, leaving the matter closed. I'm shocked that Mother doesn't jump all over him. Instead, she reaches across and squeezes my shoulder as she gets up from the table with her barely touched tray.

I'm lost without Julian. He's been my entertainment since I came here. I need him. Hopeful, I go to the Theater. Maybe I'll find Jace there, too.

By the time I reach the door to the Theater, I'm convinced that Jace and Julian will be standing in the Theater, talking. Or maybe Julian will be showing Jace around. Or maybe Julian is waiting for me inside our spot, with another romantic gesture like the candles. I find the Theater quiet and empty. The boxes are stacked in front of our closet door. I am bereft.

Not knowing what to do with myself, I decide to snoop some more in the north section. Brother James pops out just as I pass Medical. Did he see me slink past? "Sister Shea? You're looking for Brother Jace, aren't you?"

"Yes." My scalp starts tingling, and I break out in a sweat. "Where is he?"

"I'm sorry to tell you this." He checks his perfect nails and then meets my eyes. "Brother Jace is in the Suicide Room."

"Suicide Room?" The lump in my throat constricts my voice. It comes out small. "He ... he committed suicide?"

"I'm afraid so. He was so overcome by depression that we decided, as Elders, that it was the best way to go." He gazes into my eyes, his head tilted to the side, waiting for my response.

"What do you mean?" I stiffen, afraid of the answer. Jace was as happy as a dog in the back of a pickup. Why would he take his own life?

"We can't have anyone bringing the happiness of Daeios down like Brother Jace was with his depression, can we?" He tilts his head slowly to the other side, his neck appearing to be mechanical. "It could start an epidemic in our close quarters. We developed the Suicide Room, where people who feel that they are at the end of their ropes, pardon the pun," he shudders with silent laughter, "can end their lives. It's quite humane. Brother Jace chose to shoot himself in the head with a handgun. It happened so fast, he wouldn't have felt a thing."

My stomach starts to churn. "I thought you meant you put him in the Suicide Room because he committed suicide. You put him there so he could commit suicide?"

"It gives a person with suicidal thoughts a quiet and private place to do it. It's totally contained. No one has to discover the body. Plus, we stocked it with all the items one would need to commit suicide, many of which you can't obtain in Daeios. Take the handgun, for instance. We locked them all in the vault. He chose a pretty little Ruger with silver plating."

I turn away from him and throw up. That was my gun.

He continues speaking as I retch and dry heave and hate him. "He could've chosen pills, or hanging, or poison; any number of means. I imagine he was blowing his face off because he scarred it so badly. Suicides can leave notes, but he chose not to leave one. I suppose it's too hard to explain to the living why one would take his own life." He acts downright cheerful as I stand and run the back of my hand across my mouth.

"Can I see him?"

"I wouldn't recommend it. He made quite a mess."

"I want to see him. I'll tell my family before word gets out at the Gathering," I say, my heartbeat funny like my heart is trying to hide.

He leers at me and holds his arm out as if to escort me to a ball.

"Lead the way," I say, ignoring his gesture and fending off my need to slap his arm away. I don't want him to touch me.

He takes me to the last door on the left. Door 4. Door 4 equals Suicide Room. He scans me through, staying in the hallway, and closes the door behind me.

I can barely stand to look, and the smell of blood and spent gunpowder makes me woozy. A white couch stands in the middle of the room. Jace's body is slumped over on it, and the couch is covered in blood. He has no head. It's splattered all over the room: blood, bone, flesh, blond hair, brain. The bandages, covered in gore, are curled next to him on the couch. I know it's him because he's so tall and thin. Was.

My gun is in his right hand. Jace was left-handed.

14

I run to the door to leave. It's locked. I scan my ID badge twice, my hands shaking, but it doesn't work. Terror constricts my throat, and I'm breathing in short, rapid pants. I pound on the door, screaming for someone to let me out.

Brother James appears almost instantly. He swipes his card and holds the door open, bowing me through, an honored guest. He's smiling that wolfish smile. Without a word, I run past him, toward the home site.

Home? This place will never be home.

What's behind the other doors?

Mother was right. Something terrible is happening here. We're locked in with a bunch of religious maniacs. I wish with all my heart that I hadn't found Jace in that yard.

It's so much worse than that. Despite what they say about bringing life into the world, they have no regard for life. What actually happened to Sisters Ruth and Naomi?

By the time I reach our site, I'm crying uncontrollably. Maya's at work, but Mother and Dad are both at the site.

"Shea, what is it?" Mother asks as they rush to me.

"Princess, what's happened?"

I fall into Dad's open arms and cry until I can talk. Mother stands at his side with her hand on my shoulder.

"It's Jace. He's dead. He ... committed suicide," I manage to get out between sobs.

"Oh, dear Lord!" Mother says, her hands springing into white-knuckled fists.

Dad keeps holding me, rubbing my back, and says in a tranquil voice, "That's wonderful. He's with God now."

What the hell? Dumb with astonishment, I pull back and look at him. This isn't my dad. Has he lost his mind?

Mother's shaking with anger. "Suicides don't go to Heaven, Aidan. It's one of God's commandments, 'Thou shalt not kill.' That includes suicide."

Dad looks at her with a stupid smile on his face like she's talking through glass. He goes to his seat in the sitting area, opens a Bible, and reads with his lips moving.

"How did you find out?" Mother asks, pulling my lowered chin up to look into my eyes.

"I was worried about Jace, so I tried to find him. When I got to Medical, Brother James told me—and he took me to see him. Don't go, Mother. It's better to remember him when he was healthy and strong, before gloss and Daeios."

"How did he do it?" she asks, head held high. No tears. I once would've thought her cold, but now I think maybe it's great strength that fills her.

I tell her everything I remember: about the Suicide Room, about my gun being in the wrong hand, about how Brother James treated the matter as a big joke. It seems a vivid nightmare to me now. If only it were.

"What about Maya? We can't let her find out at the Gathering," I say.

She looks into the distance like she's looking down the long, hard road ahead of us. "I'll go tell her now. She'll be devastated. We were all so happy about Jace's progress. I don't understand your father's reaction at all. I'm sorry I brought you all to this godless place." She shakes her head as though awakening, and faces me. "We have to find a way out. We're better off aboveground, no matter what it's like. Maybe Brother Julian will help us when he hears what happened. Brother Christian considers him to be his son."

"I haven't seen Julian since dinner last night," I say, suddenly worried sick that he's met a fate similar to that of my brother. That the Elders may be getting rid of our men.

"We'll see him at the Gathering. We'll talk to him after dinner. I don't want anyone else to know what we're up to until we figure something out."

She clasps her hands and goes to tell Maya about Jace.

Three chimes come shortly after. I pull Dad away from his Bible to go to the Gathering. I'm dreading seeing what the news about Jace has done to Maya. I'm worried that Julian will be hanging onto another woman's hand, or worse, that he's dead, too. I'm dreading the public announcement of my brother's death. My feet and shoulders feel heavy as we move toward the Gathering Area. I may puke again.

Julian falls into stride with Dad and me, squeezing my hand for an instant like nothing's different. "Hello, Beautiful. How was your day?"

"Awful. Jace ..." My voice catches in my throat, and I stop walking. Dad doesn't notice that we've stopped and continues toward the Gathering Area. "Julian, I've been lost without you. I thought we'd spend some time together today. I was worried something awful had happened to you."

"Why were you worried? What could happen to me?"

I tell him about Jace's suicide, how I had been searching for both of them. His jaw drops. I don't tell him about the gun. I can't bear to say it again. It feels too much like a confession.

"That's terrible. I'm so sorry, Shea." He pulls me into his arms, and I burst into tears. He holds me for a long time. He kisses me on my forehead before pulling away to look at me. Cupping my face in his hands, he wipes my tears from my cheeks with his thumbs. "Are you going to be okay?"

"No. I don't know. I'm worried about how Maya's taking it."

Maya and Mother approach us from the left. Maya gushes, "I love working in the Nursery. All those babies! I can't wait to have one when I'm sixteen." She's starry-eyed, not sad at all. I look at Mother, who shakes her head, her brow furrowed.

"What about Jace?" I ask Maya.

"We'll miss him, but he's with God now."

"That's right, Sister Maya," Julian says. "He—"

"Hello, Brothers and Sisters of Daeios!" Brother Christian calls out. We filter through the crowd to Dad.

"Hello, Brother Christian!" the congregation answers.

"We gather here today, as we do every day, as a community and as God's children. I'm happy to tell you that we have more instructions from God." He smiles down upon us. The crowd heaves a collective sigh like lovelorn rock band groupies. Their excitement makes it feel like the walls and floor are alive, undulating. I'm dizzy. "Let's take care of our other matters of business, leaving God's word for last once again.

"Unfortunately, Sister Naomi and Brother Jace have gone to be with God. We'll miss them, but let us rejoice that they are with Him." He gestures above us, which sometimes means Gehenna. "The families will hold commemorative services at their home sites after dinner: WD119 for Jace and WA42 for Naomi. Please stop by and pay your respects."

We are? My parents are as surprised as I am.

Brother Christian drones on about housekeeping issues as I remember my brother when he was alive and healthy. Brother Mark leads us in prayer, and then we have the Blessing of the Little Ones. I can barely stand it tonight.

Then we sing the damn song, and everyone around me is so emotional. Happy. Julian, Maya, Dad, and everyone else except Mother and me. I feel the pain of losing Jace, remembering how he had sung so heartily the day before. We just got him back, and he's gone again, this time for good.

Brother Christian booms into the microphone, "Now for the glorious word of God." The people cheer and clap like we've scored a touchdown. "Brother Mark?"

Brother Mark takes the microphone. "God has spoken: no marriages are to be recognized as such in Daeios. We need all the breeders we can get to repopulate the world with God's Greatest Race. This allows more sisters to move into the breeding category. Isn't that wonderful?" Brother Mark says. Amazingly, both men and women are clapping, and the men in the crowd all have wives in Daeios, except for Julian. I've never seen her cry, but as Dad claps, Mother looks like she'll burst into tears.

"Quiet, please. Quiet. God views not only marriages, but any monogamous relationships, as unclean. Does everyone understand?" He leers at Julian and me. Julian puts some distance between us. I stare at him for a moment, but he doesn't meet my eyes. He's too caught up in all the excitement.

"Now, Brothers and Sisters, let me assure you that the family unit is still intact. We are all a family, isn't that true?" More applause. "We are merely to disregard the family units you came to Daeios with. It's important that we, as Daeiosians and brothers and sisters, love one another and comply with God's law. Please do your best to bond with your brothers and sisters around you, and not with your old family units. Back to Brother Christian."

Brother Mark tosses the microphone to Brother Christian, who catches it and says, "Brothers and Sisters, isn't God wonderful? We live in some exciting times, don't we? And now ..." he holds his water tube near his mouth.

"Drink up!" the crowd choruses, drinking from their tubes.

It's like they're suckling the Elders.

My family files out to dinner, but I stay behind to talk to Julian. I grab his arm, and he flinches and pulls away from me.

"Julian? Is everything okay between us? Even with the new law, we can be friends, can't we?" My heart is breaking, and I know what I want: to spend the rest of my life with him. To spend my afterlife with him, too.

Julian pushes me near a wall so we are out of the moving crowd. His voice is so low I barely hear him over the crowd noise. "Everything's fine. We have to be careful. I don't want anyone to suspect we're more than friends."

I breathe out and try not to seem too relieved, but his eyes tell me he knows. He smiles and his eyes crinkle, his head tilted to the side. "I'm sorry you were worried. Brother Eli called me into work early—I pulled a double. They had problems with the incinerator, and they needed everyone in the department's help to get it back online. Without it, Daeios would become a garbage pit." He makes a sour face. "We fixed it and had to catch up. Are we okay?"

I nod. "I wish we had some way of communicating things like that, you know?"

"I know." After a beat, "Let's get some food, my friend, shall we?"

"Yes, my friend." We don't hold hands, but we're together, so I'm happy.

Julian sits next to Dad, so I sit with Maya and Mother. He winks at me from across the table.

"I'm so sorry to hear about Brother Jace," Julian says to my family. "If there's anything I can do, please let me know."

"It's okay," Dad and Maya say in unison, without looking up from their trays.

"Thank you, Brother Julian," Mother says, her voice strained. "It's a comfort to have you with us."

Mother and I pick at our food. I'm thinking of Jace's voracious appetite and the gravy on his bandaged chin. I'm sorry I ever felt irritated with him, and for the time I didn't spend with him that I could have.

Julian scoops up some of my peas, dropping one on the table

between us. "Peaballs. My favorite." He pours them off the spoon into his mouth. "Mmm. Delicious."

Maya and Dad laugh with Julian. Mother and I manage wan smiles.

I'm starting to feel ... daughterly toward her.

After dinner, Mother and I corner Julian and ask him if anyone has left Daeios since he came here.

"I don't think so. Definitely not since lockdown. Why?"

"It's not what we thought it would be and after Jace ... We'd like to bury him in our family plot if that's possible ... now. Could you check around without anyone knowing who's asking?" Mother's face is inscrutable. "We just learned we're hosting a service for Jace. Come, Shea."

"Julian, are you coming?" I ask.

"I'm sorry, I have to work. Don't you also work at six chimes?"

"Surely, they will allow her to attend her brother's memorial service." Mother grabs my hand and leads me off like I'm an unruly child. I look back at Julian, but he's walking away.

Jace's service isn't widely attended; there are maybe thirty visitors. Sister Bethany's the only one I know. She's brought each of us a small pack of tissues from the Storehouse, and she gives us each a hug. She seems like someone I could be friends with.

Someone has taken the picture Brother Christian had in Jace's file and placed it on a seat in our sitting area. The Donovans are the only ones who knew Jace that way. People file by and say a short prayer, toast the photo with their drinking tubes, and drink. They file past the family and speak words of condolence, some stopping to introduce themselves and grasp our hands. Jace got the short end of the stick in life, and now he's getting it at his memorial service. He didn't belong to either world he lived in.

Brother Christian stops by to pay his respects. "Sister Shea, what are you doing here? Aren't you supposed to be at work in the Fitness Room?"

"She's paying her respects to her brother," Mother says, biting the words. "Where's Jace's body?"

Brother Christian puts his arms up, surrendering to Mother, but addresses me first. "Please keep it brief, Sister Shea. Sister Grace is waiting for you to relieve her. Sister Helen, I'm sorry to tell you this but ... Jace's body has been cremated."

"Without our consent?" Mother asks, her hackles up.

"You gave your consent when you signed the contract to live in Daeios. It's necessary. We don't have the chemicals we need to embalm the bodies, so it's imperative that we cremate them as soon as possible. I hope you understand."

"No. I don't." Mother's glare should've knocked him dead, but he lives and gets in the dwindling line of Jace's visitors. I'm starting to despise that man.

"You'll stay until Brother Christian goes through the receiving line," Mother commands, loud enough for everyone in Daeios to hear. "He could've been more prompt."

As soon as he grips my hand and gleams his rapturous smile at me like he's congratulating me on something, I head to the Fitness Room. Sister Grace, a tall woman with fine blonde hair, is happy to be relieved of duty and doesn't show any impatience at my lateness.

A few females come and go during my shift, chatting about work, and which Elder they hope breeds them. The consensus seems to want Brother James, the doctor and ladies' man, or Brother Christian. Will women never stop fawning after doctors and those in powerful positions? I'm in love with a garbage man.

Sister Johanna, who came to Daeios as a married woman, is catching up on the breeders' gossip. "Has anyone been called to breed yet? Do any of you know when this is supposed to start? I can hardly wait. My husband—former husband—never wanted children, and it's something I've wanted all my life."

It irks me when people use gyms as a social venue. These broads are just taking up space. Treadmills only go so slow. Most of the ladies are just standing around talking. Their jabbering and laughter grate on my nerves like a silver fork scraping across my teeth. I wish real music wasn't a sin down here. I would crank up some hard rock and blast them out of here. I consider sticking my fingers in my ears and saying, "LaLaLaLaLaLa" as loud as I can, but think better of it. Someday I may need a favor from one of these simpering fools.

I jump on a stair climber at level nine, trying to step away from my anger. It doesn't work.

15

Mother has to shake me awake again this morning, although the damn Daeios song is practically blaring from the speakers and the lights are up to full brightness. She pulls me out of bed. I'm sore and stiff from my double workout yesterday. I don't know if I could breed now if I had to. Unless it's with Julian.

Mother takes and records my vitals as I wake up enough to function.

Today will be a yoga day. Will Julian join me in the gym today? Men doing yoga is always good for a laugh. If I can make it there myself. Dining Hall first.

I'm glad Julian joins us for breakfast. He comments, laughing, on the depth of the food on my tray as he sits down next to Dad. Mother's trying to slow down my eating as she did with Jace. Jace. I try not to think about Jace's head blown all over the Suicide Room, but it's too late. My appetite gone, I stare at my tray, willing the hot tears to stay behind my eyes. It doesn't work. I cover my face with my hands and cry in deep, aching sobs that won't release me. I imagine everyone in the Dining Hall is staring at me. Maya puts her arm around me and lays her head on my shoulder. The Dining Hall falls quiet except for my bawling and some banging sounds from the Kitchen.

When I get my tears under control, I squeak, "Excuse me," and leave. All I want to do is lie down and go to sleep. I wish there was something I could take to blot out my memories. But that's why people get into drugs like gloss, isn't it?

Light footsteps run to catch up to me. Julian reaches my side. "Going to the gym today? Or are you getting your workout in during your shift?"

"I'd rather be alone right now," I say.

"Okay, we'll go to the Theater now instead of later."

I meant alone, without Julian. It might not be bad lying in his arms, though.

"Give me a few minutes?" He smiles and heads in the direction of our rendezvous spot. I want to wash my face and blow my nose first. I hate that he saw me this way. I'm an ugly crier.

I head to the southwest restrooms and clean up, thankful for the lack of mirrors today. I hope Julian will want the lights off. As I'm leaving the restroom, two young women hurry in.

"Did you hear that Sister Zemira was called to breed today? She's the first," says one, whispering loudly when she's barely through the doorway. I stop around the corner and listen. The voices carry to me as though I were standing with them.

"No! I wonder why God picked her first. Did you hear who's breeding her?" asks the other.

"That's all I know. Let's go to the gym and see if the other sisters have heard anything." They walk toward the exit, giggling, and I hurry away so they don't catch me eavesdropping.

Julian is waiting for me in our room. He's fashioned a peony out of toilet paper. It's so beautiful, the white flower lying on the crimson curtain. I hope I don't blubber all over it and ruin it. He pats the spot next to him and hands me the peony as I sit, a shy grin on his face. I sniff it, disappointed that it smells like paper.

"Use it as a tissue if you need to," he offers, rubbing my cheek with his finger.

"Oh, it's much too pretty to get snot on it. I learned something from my grandma." I sniff and smile the best I can as I pull a tissue out of my sleeve, swirling it around in the air like a magician. "Pretty hot, huh?"

His smile is radiant. "Yes, you are. You are beautiful, and you're hot, and I can't help loving you more every day. I'm so sorry about yesterday. How can I make it up to you?"

"Hold me, please. Unless you can get us out of this place?" He looks puzzled. "Not the closet. Daeios." My laugh comes out jittery.

He lets out a sigh. "I can't get you out of here, honey. I verified that Daeios is locked down without exception. But I will hold you, and kiss you, and love you ..." He starts kissing me, taking my mind off leaving Daeios and losing Jace, and drawing me into the sweet bubble that surrounds just the two of us.

I wake up to two bells and find Julian sitting and playing with my hair, which he has released from its pins.

"We'll have to hurry and put my hair back up. We don't want to get in trouble with the Elders," I say, rushing. He helps me, and it goes better than last time. We're becoming experts at doubles bun-making.

"Why don't you leave now? I'll follow in a few minutes so it doesn't look suspicious. When we get there, remember, we haven't seen each other since breakfast. What's your alibi?" Julian asks.

"The gym. Everyone knows I'm a fitness freak."

"I have a few minutes. That way, even you'll be surprised when I say what I've been doing." He winks and gives me a kiss. I'm relieved that everything's okay with us.

Our lunch is the same as usual; the chef doesn't change the menu every day. Today it has more flavor, though, as I'm both happy and hungry. I've managed to push the memory of my brother's corpse into the deep recesses of my mind to think of later, when the images aren't so sharp, when they don't conjure the smell of spent gunpowder and blood. Mother has already eaten and has gone to our site. I doubt she ate much.

"So what have you been up to today, Shea?" Dad asks jovially, acting like himself again. Maybe he is okay. "Not up to no good, I hope?" He wiggles his eyebrows, and I laugh.

"No, I've been working out. I ran, lifted weights, and did yoga today. I'm famished." I am truly famished, though.

"I came by the gym earlier to see if you wanted to watch a movie or something, and no one had seen you."

"I ... must've been in the shower when you came by," I say, just as Julian arrives.

"Hi, Brothers and Sisters. Beautiful day, isn't it?"

Usually, a beautiful day means the sun is shining, there's a soft breeze, and it's not too hot outside. All we have is rock, human-made walls, and stainless steel, and the constant smell of damp and dirt.

"Every day's a beautiful day in Daeios," Maya says. "I have to go— can't keep my children waiting."

"Her children?" I say after she leaves. "That's funny."

"It's all she talks about these days: this little guy took his first step, this baby smiled at her. She doesn't even seem to mind changing diapers." Dad chuckles.

She got broke in real good on the poop thing.

"Kids," Dad says, smiling at Julian and me. "I'm proud of you for taking God's instructions seriously. I know you had a little romance. Friendships can be just as rewarding." He pats Julian on the shoulder, and Julian smiles across the table at me. "It's nice to have a young man with us, Brother Julian. No one can replace Jace, but at least we can have a young man's thoughts and opinions. Too many women fluttering around down here if you ask me." He does something like jazz hands. "Now, if you'll excuse me, I'm going to spend some time with my wife—my friend—Sister Helen. She's not been herself lately. Will you come by later and see her?"

"I will, Dad," I say around a mouthful of food. My manners around Julian suggest we're an old married couple.

This leaves Julian and me sitting alone together, which we were trying to avoid. No way I'm walking away from a half tray of food, though. "You didn't have to use your alibi. What was it?"

"I was going to say I was watching a movie, good thing I didn't." He clears his throat. "I ... think ... I'm ... going to ..." He looks perplexed. "See you later?"

I nod my head and wave, my mouth full again. But that leaves no one to eat my peas, and they're policing us on eating healthy.

Should I call him back?

I'm at a loss as to what to do again. What would I be doing back home?

It would be five o'clock somewhere.

I wander around the south wing for a while. Read in the Library? Don't feel like it. Art's out, I suck. Music Room? Just hymns. If they used drums in hymns, I might be able to learn those. I could go to the Fitness Room, but since I used that as an alibi, I'll do my workout tonight on my shift. Not in a laundry mood, even though I should probably take a turn at it. Mother always does it.

I end up in the north section again, spying, trying to figure out what's behind those locked, windowless doors. I know what three out of four doors on the west side are, so I start across the broad hallway toward the east side, where I don't know what lies behind any of the doors. Door 5, near the north wall, Door 6, and Door 7. I'm planning to do my best to skulk without being seen in my white dress in the darkness.

I hear female voices. Turning, I see a group of women making a trail through the Gathering Area toward the north sector. They're mostly older women, and they're prattling on the way the young women in the gym did the other day. They must be getting a breeder ready for her breeding, to give her the spa day the Elders promised. Is it Sister Zemira? Or have I missed the first breeding? In spite of not wanting to be a part of the ritual myself, I'm as inquisitive as a child on Christmas Day. I back toward a dark corner, trying to make myself invisible.

"Shea, what are you doing here?" Mother asks as she approaches me. She saw me with the eyes in the back of her head as she did when I was a naughty little girl. Did she have to announce it to everyone?

"I'm just curious. Is this the first one?" The matrons in the front are moving through the door. I strain my neck to get a peek inside the room.

Mother comes close enough to whisper. "I don't know, but this is the first time they've called me to prep." A woman stands in the doorway, holding the door for Mother. She's doing her best to use her body to shield the room from my prying eyes. If she were a couple of inches taller, she would be perfectly round, so I only see over her head. The room's bright. That's all I know.

"We'll discuss it later. I'll find out as much as I can." She turns and leaves, running a couple of steps since Sister Sumo is holding the door for her.

Now I wish I'd created some female friendships here. Being able to gossip about this would be nice. Maybe it would stop the cold dread I'm feeling, knowing my time will come soon. I worry about what will happen when I refuse to breed. A picture of the Elders standing on the stage naked rushes into my mind and I suppress it. I don't want to think about having sex with the old men.

Door 7, the door on the east side of the north section nearest the Gathering Area, is no longer a mystery. It holds the Spa where the breeders are primped and pampered to meet their elderly one-night stands. I hope Mother finds out where the Breeding Room is. Is it behind Door 6?

It's too dangerous for me to be in the forbidden north wing with that going on, so I head to the Entertainment Room.

I wake up on a comfy couch to the sound of three chimes. The movie

I was watching put me to sleep. Some old Hallmark gibberish. I try to get up off the couch and find I can't move my legs. They're bound together.

I've been restrained.

Panicking, I thrash around, throwing myself off the couch and landing on the white-carpeted hard ground. I catch myself with my hands and look at my legs. It's my gown that's holding me captive—it wrapped around my legs in my sleep. I stand up and unravel my opponent.

"Nicely done, Sister Shea," Julian says as he gives me a standing ovation. "I was getting a kick out of the snoring, but that was too much." He bends over and puts his hands on his thighs, laughing so hard he can barely catch his breath.

"I'm glad you enjoyed it," I snap, sitting on the white couch, my face flushing. My bun is lopsided and threatening to roll off my head. "How long have you been here?"

"For a few minutes. I saw you through the window and had to stop and watch you sleep. You're extra cute when you're snoring, you know." His smile is irresistible.

"Off to the Gathering, then?" I finish straightening my bun and hold out my hand.

"Let's meet there. We need to be careful. I heard some women gossiping about us still being lovers." He leaves, throwing a smile over his shoulder. "You're awake, right?"

I stand up to prove it, my wrinkled gown billowing around me.

What new instructions will the Elders bring us tonight?

I find my family. Julian hasn't arrived yet.

"Hello, Brothers and Sister of Daeios!"

"Hello, Brother Christian!"

"We gather here today, as we do every day, as a community and as God's children. I'm happy to announce that our first breeding has taken place."

The crowd goes wild, as sports announcers say.

"We won't know for several days whether the seed has planted itself correctly," he says, beaming. "I won't announce the breeder and father until then. It's all quite exciting, isn't it?"

"Yes, Brother Christian!" Everyone except Mother seems about to jump right out of their clothes and start dancing with joy. Mother's head is bowed, her eyes blinking rapidly. She isn't praying.

"We don't have any housekeeping issues to cover tonight, and there are no sick and injured to announce."

Mother raises her head and glowers at him.

"We have more instructions from God. Let's cover those tonight before the prayer, and before the Blessing of the Little Ones, shall we?" Smirk.

"Yes, Brother Christian."

"God reminds us that, if you were married, your marriages have been dissolved. That means that having carnal knowledge of one another is sinful, correct?"

Old guys breeding young women, married to others or unmarried, isn't, apparently. Mother's right about the Elders; God can't have changed the rules so much.

"If you're still sleeping in the same bed as your former spouse, you need to make alternative arrangements."

"Yes, Brother Christian."

"God has also commanded that we banish anyone who does not obey God's laws in Daeios. No exceptions." He looks at my family. Julian isn't with us, and Maya is between Mother and Dad. What the hell?

The rest of the crowd stares at us. I hope I shrink until I disappear. Does he know about Julian and me?

One of the twins steps forward, and he and Brother Christian wrestle with the microphone. It goes back and forth several times as they grunt. The twin wins the skirmish by pushing when Brother Christian pulls, causing Brother Christian to lose his balance. He sticks his chin out at Brother Christian before turning to the crowd, and Brother Christian stands behind him with his arms folded, tapping his foot as the twin speaks.

"Banishments, as needed, will begin after the Gathering today. Security officers will escort the banished out of Daeios. Banishment is certain to end in suffering and death, as Gehenna is now a wasteland. Do not test God's word. His word is law."

Dad's face shows surprise, and he's a Security Officer. But he pipes along with everyone: "Yes, Brother ...?"

So that's what's worse than Detention.

Brother Mark takes the microphone from the twin without a struggle, and Brother Christian backs away to stand with the other Elders. "God has instructed us to include an oath to Him and Daeios in our prayers. That begins today. Please bow your heads and pray with me."

"God, our Father, please bless Your children, Your chosen few, Your people of Daeios. Please help us to live in Your ways and to obey Your laws. Please help us to repopulate the world with Your Greatest Race as You have commanded. Please help us to love one another, our brothers and sisters. We swear our devotion to You, dear Lord, and to the community of Daeios. Amen."

"Amen."

Brother Christian goes to Brother Mark and holds his hand out for the microphone, his other hand on his hip. Brother Mark scowls at him a moment before smacking the microphone into Brother Christian's hand, which reverberates over the speakers like a well-timed slap. Brother Christian says, "Now, let's enjoy the Blessing of the Little Ones, shall we? We hope in the near future to have many more pregnant women up here on stage to receive the Blessing, don't we?" He holds the microphone out to the congregation like rock stars do.

"Yes, Brother Christian!"

This time all of the Elders come out on stage while Brother Mark is blessing the children. They all hold and kiss babies, as Brother Christian has done at every Gathering. It's quite a melee. I'm glad they don't play tug-of-war with the babies like they did with the microphone.

I don't want anything to do with the Blessing. Ever.

One of the mothers onstage is bald. Sister Zemira. They must have shaved her head after breeding her. That's a good way to not announce the breeder. I hold my bun protectively the way women hold their baby bumps.

Instead of filing off stage to be with their families, the children stay up there, and the Elders hold their little hands, and the hands of the pregnant women, and start leading us in the Daeios song.

They're showing us where we breeders are supposed to end up—on that stage.

16

After dinner, Mother and I find a quiet corner in which to talk, keeping our voices low.

"Shea, they said no one is sick or injured, but we're turning patients away. Brother James only came in for a short while today. He informed me he has more important things to do than to listen to female complaints."

"What about the female doctors?"

"All but one of them are breeders, and the breeders think they're goddesses these days. None of them is working anymore, which means more work for the rest of us. One elderly woman is bleeding heavily, and she shouldn't be bleeding at all. She needs a doctor's attention. Something isn't right."

"What about the breeding today? Did you find anything out?" I lean in and whisper as two young breeders pass by.

"We pampered her, all right. She left looking like a prostitute and smelling like a perfume factory. You should've seen her admiring herself in the mirror. Miss America. The Spa is all we nonbreeders get to see. We escorted her to the Breeding Room, and she went in naked. It's another room with no windows."

"Oh, the mirrors—did you see your reflection?"

"No. Sisters Abigail and Mercy held a mandatory training session before we went to get the breeder. They informed us that the mirrors are for the breeders only and that we were not to look into them."

"I don't know how you resisted. Where is the Breeding Room?"

"It's right behind the Spa. To the east of it."

Door 7 solved: it holds two rooms. Maybe other doors contain two or more rooms.

Six chimes. Time to go to work. I've coasted through life until coming to Daeios, but I won't shirk like the other breeders. I'm developing my first ethic: a work ethic. I tell Mother goodbye, noting that the lines on her face are more pronounced, like she's becoming my grandmother. She leaves with a nod of her head, walking toward our site.

The Fitness Room is full of bantering females, and most of them are exercising. Now that they know the breedings have begun, they want to look their best. Sister Johanna asks me to demonstrate how to lift weights. Others watch as I show the correct way to perform upper body lifts. Then I get on the treadmill and try to picture myself running through my parents' affluent neighborhood with the sun shining golden in the pale blue sky, birdsong in the air. The image dissolves before I can add the fresh pine scent of the conifers and the sweet and spicy smell of sagebrush.

I'm about halfway through my run when an older woman comes in and hurries to a young breeder on a stair climber. The woman motions for her to stop, and whispers something in the girl's ear. The breeder exclaims, "Thank you, Lord!" and rushes out the door after the nonbreeder. The door closes behind them, and the gym becomes cacophonic with female excitement.

"Is she the second?"

"I think she's the third. Didn't Sister Diana get called from her sleep?"

"She doesn't have her head shaved. Doesn't Sister Zemira look beautiful and radiant without her hair?" one gushes, sounding daft. Sister Zemira looks pallid and unhealthy, as do the rest of them. The baldness and dark circles around her eyes make her resemble a cancer patient.

"She does. Oh, it's happening, Sisters. It's really happening. One of us could be called before breakfast." They're all hugging each other, laughing, crying. Again, I feel the lack of female friendship, but I'd feel weird going over and giving the whole group a hug. In spite of training some of them, I don't even know if they know my name, and it's on my ID badge.

"Come, Sisters, we need to work on our figures," a strawberry blonde coaches, and all of the women jump on machines as if they were going to take them somewhere.

When I get off work, most of Daeios is sleeping. Worried about my breeding—not knowing when it will be—I won't be able to sleep. I decide to do another recon of the north section, and I hope the northeast. I'm tired of mysteries.

The wide hallway in the north sector is much darker now than the last time I was here since the Gathering Area is dark. Starting on the west side, I skim my left hand along the wall and identify each door as I come to it. I wonder how many Daeiosians know what lies behind each door?

Door 1: Medical. No crack of light under the door, but it's supposed to be open 24/7. Mother's right, something is wrong.

Door 2: Unknown.

Door 3: Detention.

Door 4: The Suicide Room. This makes me think of Jace. I hurry across the hall, my left hand skimming along the rock wall and counting out twenty-nine steps. I turn and slide my left hand along the east wall.

Door 5: Unknown.

The narrow hallway to the northeast section. No flicker of light at the other end tonight.

Door 6: Unknown.

Door 7: The Spa and the Breeding Room. The only door that I know holds two rooms.

As I look back on the north section, I hear someone moving stealthily toward me, up against the east wall. I turn and run, grabbing up my skirt, hoping the darkness has concealed my identity. My sandals slap on the floor, leaving a noise trail.

I run to the restrooms furthest from our site and slam the stall door behind me. No one comes in. I flush the toilet and wash my hands, taking enough time to calm my breathing and quiet my heart.

Eventually, I emerge and return to our site, unable to shake the feeling that someone is following me. I don't see or hear anyone.

17

I don't sleep at all that night. Mother's sleeping on Jace's bench seat now, worried the Elders will find her in bed with Dad during inspections. They called Dad to work. The banishments have begun. I'm worried they'll pull me from my bed and banish me for spying, or take me to my breeding. I don't feel safe.

A knock on the door sends me into a seated position. "Shh," Mother says and gets up. "Yes? What do you want?" she says through the door.

A female voice answers; I can barely hear her. "My son is sick, and no one's at Medical. Will you help us, please?"

Mother hesitates a moment, then, "Yes. Of course." She slips from the RV and closes the door quietly behind her. I lie still, thinking about her words today, and my own fears. Maya is sleeping peacefully; I hear the quiet rhythm of her breathing.

I remain in bed after the Daeios song starts playing until Maya rouses me from sleep. The song starts again, rising in volume. They haven't turned any lights on. Even the lights to the restrooms are off.

"Where's Mom?" Maya asks.

"She went to Medical."

"When?"

"While everyone was sleeping. Someone needed her there."

She's silent for a moment, and the Daeios song begins playing again, louder than before. "What are we supposed to do? I'm hungry, but how do we get to the Dining Hall in the dark?" she shouts over the music.

I step from the RV into complete darkness. It's as though we've been buried alive in a massive underground tomb. My lungs feel like they'll implode. Maya finds my hand with hers and inches to my side. I'm so glad for her presence. I can't imagine facing this alone. All I hear is the stupid song, all I see is blackness, and I don't smell breakfast. Fear coats my stomach in ice.

The song stops mid-note. Others whisper in confusion nearby. People call names, trying to find loved ones in the dark.

"Let's get some flashlights from the cupboards. Maybe we have food left," I say, pulling Maya behind me.

The cupboards are bare. How is that possible? Sure, we may have eaten the food, but what about the flashlights, batteries, candles, and lighters we brought? We had dishes and silverware, towels, cleaning supplies. Where has everything gone?

I sit in the driver's seat and switch on the headlights—nothing. We check the Zipper. No lights. Whatever this is, it was carefully planned.

I lead Maya to the rock wall of our sitting area, feeling my way between chairs and end tables, knocking a lamp over. Maya jumps, jerking at my hand when it crashes to the floor.

"Let's fill our water packs and make a pit stop before heading to the Dining Hall."

"I don't smell food."

"Maybe we'll find out what's going on."

We feel our way to the water dispenser and fill our water packs. The glug-glugging of the water as it flows from the bottle into our packs is reassuring. We put them on, shamble to the opposite wall, and feel our way toward the women's restroom nearest our site. A flushing toilet tells us we're almost there.

The Daeios song comes on again, so loud that Maya and I scream and hug each other before our minds have time to tell us it's only music assaulting us.

We feel our way to the doorway of the restroom, and I slam into someone on her way out. I reach for her to keep her from falling. She slaps my hands away and scurries off. I couldn't hear her scream, but I know I frightened her. There are much scarier things in the darkness than me.

We manage to use the toilets and find each other at the sinks to wash our hands. The restroom already smells dirty, and the ladies who keep it clean can't work in total darkness. Thoughts fly at me, crashing into me like birds hitting a windshield. What happens if this total darkness continues? Will food be available, and more water? How do we communicate and sleep if the music continues to blare from the speakers?

Where are Mother, Dad, and Julian?

Maya touches my arm, and we find each other's hands. We are blind and, with the music blasting us, we are deaf. I can't hear my voice, let alone Maya's.

The Dining Hall is close to our site, so we locate it without much trouble. I was hoping someone would be there with flashlights or candles, but the Dining Hall is in total darkness, too. I pull Maya behind me, feeling for tables, and I keep touching people. They put their hands up to stop me from poking their eyes out, I suppose, or pat me as I pass by to let me know they're there. We can't speak to each other, but I feel better knowing Maya and I are not alone.

If our parents and Julian are here, how will we find them? Should we have stayed at the site? I don't know how to find our family table in the dark, so I find an empty table, and we sit. I put my arm around Maya's shoulders and try to untie the knot in my stomach. It keeps getting tighter.

The Daeios song continues to resound, repeating over and over and over until I think I'll go insane.

Time is alien when you can't see or hear—when you can't work, or sleep, or talk, or do anything at all to pass it. We sit, we stand, we stretch, we sit, again and again. We drink water, we breathe, we suffer. For hours? For a day? I don't know.

Maya tugs at my hand. I'm stiff and sore from sitting on the hard bench. We make our way back the way we came. Fewer hands touch us as we go by. People must be giving up on food, and news, and light, and have gone back to their sites if they can find them.

We attend to the only physical need, other than drinking water, that we're able to attend to right now. It's as we're using the toilets that the music stops. Maya is singing at the top of her lungs, "Ooh, ooh, baby, yeah-eah," tapering off when she hears herself. She giggles, as only a fourteen-year-old girl can. I try to laugh, but it comes out a grunt like someone punched me in the stomach. I'll laugh later when I'm not so scared. I hope there will be such a time.

"Shea, are you okay?" she asks as she flushes the toilet. Her voice and the flush sound far away.

I don't want her to know how serious this could be until—until my fears are realized, and she sees for herself.

"Yep," I say as I flush. My voice catches in my throat, and it's all that comes out.

———

The walk back to the site without the music deafening us is disconcerting. I want the brutal music back. People are calling out names, wailing, moaning, screaming. The pounding of flesh on flesh. Someone's being beaten, someone's being slapped, is someone being raped? More screaming. Every sound echoes, bouncing off the walls and hitting us again. Maya's holding onto my arm with both hands, and I hear her sniffling and feel the shuddering of her shoulders.

I feel nothing except stifling terror.

We reach our site and feel our way to the side RV door. It's open. Anyone could be inside.

I stand to the side of the door, as a police officer would, and push Maya behind me. "Mother? Dad?"

A woman screams like a wild animal from inside the RV. She runs out the door, clearing the steps and landing with a thud and a grunt a few feet from us.

"What are you doing?" I yell at her, keeping my distance, protecting Maya.

She runs away, sandals slapping until I hear another thud and a grunt. She ran into a wall. I hope she knocked her crazy ass out.

I go up the RV steps cautiously, Maya on my heels.

"Hello?"

I find the cupboards are open by banging my head on one of the doors. Sister Crazy Ass hunted for food and light, as we did.

"Let's lock up," I say to Maya amidst the sounds of depravity swirling around us.

"What if Mom and Dad come back and the music is playing again? We won't hear them." Her voice is shaky.

We need to lock everyone else out. "Mother's screech can wake the dead in New York, and Dad's the biggest person down here. It'll be all right. Lock the cockpit doors, Copilot Maya." I lock the other doors.

The closed RV offers us little protection from the madness outside.

We lie on our bed and hold each other, listening to the nightmare unfold around us, the screaming and wailing and gnashing of teeth that is Hell. Someone tries to open the doors once, and several fists hammer their way around our haven. I want to scream and cry, but I don't. I squeeze Maya tighter to me, and she shivers and cries until she can't cry any longer. We lie like that, for hours, unable to sleep, until three chimes sounds and the lights come up full. The sounds of depravity silence as if sucked into a vacuum.

It makes me think of descending in a spaceship and landing on a distant, red rock planet in deep space. We don't know what we'll find when we open our doors. We don't know if we'll be met by friends or foes. We don't know.

My knees are weak and shaking, my body stiff as we fill our water packs, rubbing our eyes against the brightness. We stop to use the restroom on the way to the Gathering, and it's disgusting. An overflowing toilet has left an inch of dirty water on the floor that dampens our socks. Our scarce toilet paper is gone or wet, and the white surfaces are smeared with excrement. I gag as we clean ourselves the best we can without paper towels. The common areas have always been spotless, day and night, and this filth further unsettles me. My stomach recoils and I splash to the nearest toilet to vomit. My empty gut purges bile until I don't have any left to expel. The fear lurks inside me, filling my stomach and lungs and throat.

"Are you okay, Shea?" Maya asks when I straighten up and face her, my eyes watering.

"Let's go find Mother and Dad and Julian," I say, grasping her hand.

I dread what comes next.

The crowd filters into the Gathering Area, sleepwalking ghosts. We're a disheveled and dirty bunch, smelling of body odor and sewage, guarding our eyes against the overhead lighting until we can stand the illumination. The foul smell increases as more people enter the room. We're silent except for the squishing shuffle of our damp sandals on the floor.

Excitement and enchantment no longer show in the eyes of those around me. Instead, I see skin too pale to be healthy on faces tight with strain. Some have bruises, scratches, both. Bloodshot, red-rimmed eyes are fearful and unsettled, flitting around the room seeking loved ones who've been swallowed by the darkness.

I don't see Mother and Dad yet, and it feels like a family of bats is flapping around in my stomach as I wonder what has become of my parents. Where's Julian? I squeeze Maya's hand and pull her to the area in front of the stage where my family and Julian meet for

Gatherings. The rest of the crowd stays back from the stage a few feet. Fear must be holding them back.

Dad sees us and pushes his way through the crowd to our sides. He clasps each of us in an arm and holds us to him.

"Where's Mom?" Maya whispers, and he shakes his head. He releases us and looks toward the stage with tears in his eyes, and the bats in my stomach try to flap their way right out of my throat.

"Hello, Brothers and Sisters of Daeios!" Brother Christian shouts into the microphone, hurting my tender, ringing ears. He seems especially jovial today. The other Elders stand in a half-circle behind him on the stage, their arms relaxed, their hands grasped in front of them. They seem awfully cheerful. Awful may be the key word.

A handful of Daeiosians, including Dad, answer Brother Christian in meek voices, "Hello, Brother Christian."

"I can't hear you," Brother Christian singsongs into the mic. He points the silver phallus to the crowd, engaging his elderly rock star persona.

"Hello, Brother Christian," the crowd responds, but without feeling.

"Approach the stage. Speak up!" Brother Christian booms into the mic. He stabs the microphone toward us, and his smile is gone, his heavy black eyebrows bearing down on us. The crowd surges forward, a small army of beaten-down zombies.

"Hello, Brother Christian!" we all shout, similar to being at a pep rally, but we don't give a damn about football and bouncing cheerleaders.

"Much better." He graces us with his smile again. "We gather here today, as we do every day, as a community and as God's children." He sighs heavily into the microphone. "We had quite an ordeal, didn't we? Would anyone like to speculate why God punished us today? Anyone?"

Mother enters the Gathering Hall from the north and stumbles toward us as if pushed from behind, her usual backboard-straight posture gone. Everyone, on stage and off, turns to watch her as she approaches. Her eyes catch sight of Dad, Maya, and me, and then she lowers them to the ground. She comes to stand nearby, but doesn't appear to be one of us. She doesn't even look at us.

Brother Christian leans in to the microphone. "There have been so many sins that have gone unpunished, so many sinners. As is His will, God commanded us to punish the entire community of Daeios. We've taken all the worldly goods you were supposed to relinquish when you entered Daeios. We've banished some of the congregation to Gehenna." He casts his eyes up, and members of the crowd seem to freeze in place. "Look around you. You'll see some faces are missing. Go on. Look." He pauses as we obey.

The congregation is noticeably smaller. I didn't take the time to build relationships down here, except with Julian, but I recognize that some faces are missing. There are fewer males. The frog-mouthed family of seven is now a family of five, mute now, with the father and oldest boy missing. The mother holds onto the rest of her silent brood, tears streaming down her face. Sister Grace from the Fitness Room isn't hanging at the back of the crowd as she usually does. Many more are missing, but I can't summon the faces that should be there.

Julian is one of the missing. I'm so desperate to see him that I imagine his smile in every shattered face I see. My heart feels like it's holding onto my blood, not pumping it out for my body to use it.

"Let's keep this in mind whenever we feel weak-willed or selfish, shall we?" Brother Christian takes his time scanning the crowd, making quick eye contact with each of us. I follow Mother's lead and stare at my soggy feet.

"We need some joy. Let's have the Blessing of the Little Ones, shall we? Come on up, mothers, come on up children," he says, beaming at us again. I'd like to slap that smile right off his face. Brother Mark steps forward to do the blessings, smiling broadly. I'd like to butt their heads together. That would bring me some joy.

The mothers and children file across the stage, as before, but those that manage bleak smiles do so tentatively. The children are scared, tired, and cranky. Mothers clasp their babies tighter to them than usual. Toddlers hide behind their mothers' skirts.

The angst at handing her baby to Brother Christian is evident in the first mother's eyes, but she allows him to hold and kiss her baby while she wrings her hands. The other Elders step forward, take babies, and kiss them. It doesn't seem silly now. It seems serious, and wrong. They're taking ownership of our children—of all of us.

Brother Mark blesses all of the baby bumps and the flat tummies of the three bald breeders. One woman flinches when Brother Mark touches her abdomen, and the crowd simultaneously holds its breath. Is that a punishable sin? Will we all be mistreated for this one tiny, involuntary action? We don't know what sins we've committed, what will trigger punishment. She recovers, taking Brother Mark's hand and holding it on her pregnant belly. The crowd shuffles and murmurs as people begin to relax.

"Aren't they lovely?" Brother Christian says as the newly blessed file off the stage. "Just lovely. Brother Mark, will you please lead us in prayer? Join hands, everyone."

An oily-faced young woman takes my hand. Not Julian. Did they banish him? Brother Christian wouldn't banish him; Julian's like his own son. Then I hear in my mind, from a story I heard long ago, that God sacrificed His only son. I'm sick with fear, the bats beating me up from the inside.

Brother Mark steps to the microphone. "God, our Father, please bless Your children, Your chosen few, Your people of Daeios. Please help us to live in Your ways and to obey Your laws. Please help us to repopulate the world with Your Greatest Race as You have commanded. Please help us to love one another, our brothers and sisters. We swear our devotion to You, dear Lord, and to the community of Daeios. Amen."

"Amen." We don't sound cheerful, but we share a voice.

The next part of the meeting is about housekeeping. Brother Christian assigns team leaders to section heads, and Daeiosians to team leaders, to assure we return all areas of Daeios to spotless purity. We will restore the well-oiled machine that was Daeios to working order. We're to fix anything that's broken, such as the overflowing toilet, and replenish supplies that are running low or missing, starting with the five-gallon water bottles. We will wash all dirty clothing, linens, towels, and cleaning rags.

"If you complete the task assigned to you, check with team leaders or section heads at other areas for further assignments. Only after everything else in Daeios is pure and clean can you attend to your personal hygiene. I'd better not see anyone in the showers before I've heard from those in charge that all cleaning and stocking in their areas is finished." His eyes rest on me. "No one will use the Fitness Room showers. You'll work together and shower together."

The Elders are watching us shower.

Brother Christian instructs all kitchen shifts to shower first and then get to work preparing the meal we'll get to eat sometime this century, adding, "In spite of the decrease in Daeiosians, add ten percent to the menu, as folks will be extra hungry. Who knows when the next meal might be? It depends on the righteousness of each person in Daeios." This threat halts the shuffling and murmuring that started when he was giving job assignments. The crowd holds its breath once again as Brother Christian's dark eyebrows descend.

And then he smiles. The man has multiple personalities, and I don't like any of them. "All hands on deck in the Nursery. You're going to have your hands full, Sisters. We will supply you with snacks for the little ones, to help with the crankiness from hunger and the separation anxiety from The Ordeal. Do not—I repeat—do not indulge yourselves with even a single bite of these snacks. They're for the children. Understood?"

A few heads nod.

"Now, let's rejoice. We're the chosen people of God. Brother John, please lead us in our favorite song." Brother Christian hands the microphone over.

I'll die right here, right now, if I hear that song again, but it starts up, and people begin to sing, hesitant at first. I don't die, but I wish I was dead. Mother lifts her head, and my family sings the damn song. I look at my toes and move my mouth, but they can't make me sing the words.

Daeios, Oh Daeios

We live in God's light.
Daeios, dear Daeios
Our strength is His might.

The voices gain purchase, and the energy and spark from previous Gatherings reignite the fervor.

Clean and pure, united we are,
Devoted to God every day.
In Daeios, sweet Daeios—
We love, we laugh, we pray.

When the song ends, I look up to see the glistening of tears, the rapture again, in everyone's eyes but Mother's. Sister Bethany catches my eye with a wave and holds her hand to her chest in relief. I return the gesture, and she smiles through her tears. My eyes are dry until I turn around and see Julian approaching me through the crowd. His beautiful face is scratched and bruised, but he's smiling at me, radiant as always, and looking every bit as crazy as the rest of them. Oh, yes, I love him, crazy or not. I start toward him, but Mother grips my arm. I'm afraid I'm seeing him in others' faces again—I want to touch him and know for certain that he's here. But I understand my doing so could put us all in jeopardy.

Brother Christian makes a big production of drying his eyes and says, "Such a beautiful song. It sure gets your heart pumping, doesn't it?"

"Yes, Brother Christian!"

"And now," he says holding his drinking tube up.

"Drink up!" the crowd yells, and we drink.

As we file out of the Gathering Hall to our cleaning duties, I try to pull Julian aside to see how he is, but Mother keeps us separated with a glance and a shake of her head.

"Everyone, go to your assignments and work hard so we can eat," Dad says as he puts his arm around Julian's shoulders, and they head to the Storehouse. Easy for him to say, they assigned Dad and Julian to stock supplies. I have shit detail, cleaning the dirty women's restrooms. I mourn the end of my record of not cleaning anything. Maya goes to the Nursery, singing a nursery rhyme, her spirits so high her soggy sandals barely touch the red rock floor. It's like The Ordeal never happened.

"Don't talk to anyone," Mother says as she heads to her duties in Laundry.

She doesn't have to tell me they're listening to us.

I tuck my ID badge in my dress to keep it from floating in the filth of the toilets. I don't know how long we work at cleaning the restrooms, but it seems to be hours before we wipe off the last bit of grime and mop up the last of the stinking water. Brother Aaron, the fat Elder with the white bowl cut who's in charge of Housekeeping, comes by and tells us it's okay to shower, then to take our dirty clothes and towels to Laundry. We'll take over at Laundry while they shower, and once showered, they'll come back with their dirty laundry. We'll finish up together.

I go to the site and fill my white bag with clean clothes and toiletries, careful not to touch my soiled gown to anything. It's smudged with grime, and its hem has been soaking in the water from the overflowing toilet. I wrung it out the best I could when I was wearing rubber gloves, but I'm afraid I'm dripping sewage in the RV. How clean can Daeios be, considering we scrubbed it while we were so filthy? I can hardly stand to smell myself. I don't know if I'll ever feel clean after today.

I join the long line of ladies waiting to shower. They've been passing it down the line, like in the old kid's game, "Telephone," that they're sharing showerheads to get all of the females through the shower more quickly. They seem excited about it and are laughing like a bunch of teenagers about the hardships of the darkness and the loud music as if it happened long ago to someone else. As though the missing Daeiosians were still here. I'm trying not to think about it, to keep the fear it ignited in me at bay.

I shower with three strangers. We take turns cleaning our sandals in the spray.

When I relieve Mother in Laundry, I take advantage of the noise and chance a whisper in her ear, asking her where she was during The Ordeal.

"Solitary confinement. Go back to work," she says in my ear and leaves before I can ask her why they punished her in that way. Did others endure solitary confinement?

I work in Laundry until the last of it is clean and folded. Sister Ariel goes to find Brother Aaron to see if we need to help elsewhere and comes back bearing good tidings of great joy: it's time to eat.

Once outside the Laundry Room I sniff the air, and cooking smells reach me from the Kitchen. I could sprint there in less than a minute, but I contain myself and walk to the Donovan table for our meal plus ten percent. My family and Julian are already there. Many Daeiosians are sitting, but no one has food yet. Now they're going to make us wait until everyone's here before we go through the line. I'm so hungry I could eat a freeze-dried horse.

It's more apparent, as the last people file in and sit at their regular tables, how much they depleted our population. We're lucky to have our family unit intact—intact as it can be since we lost Jace. It's as if we're at war, and the enemy was picking us off one by one, until now. This last attack took an entire platoon.

The Elders arrive and make up the front of the line—they've never gone through the line before—and Brother Christian addresses us, shouting to the back of the Dining Hall. "Brothers and Sisters of Daeios, listen up," he says as the crowd quiets. He pauses until it's so quiet, everyone within a four-table radius stares at me when my stomach growls. "Let's remember the lessons we learned today, shall we?"

"Yes, Brother Christian!"

Is anyone else as clueless as I am as to what lessons we learned today? I'm afraid to do anything. I'm afraid to not do anything.

"All right. Please join us in line, and eat as much as you like," he says. He doesn't say it again, but it echoes in my head, "And who knows when the next meal might be? It depends on the righteousness of each person in Daeios."

I don't want to be near the Elders, who are all chummy again. Maybe they took their animosity for each other out on the Daeiosians in the darkness. I allow a few people to get in line first. Once in line, though, God help anyone who tries to cut in front of me.

I'm so single-minded in my pursuit of food that the sounds of the Dining Hall become static in my ears. I see no one; I talk to no one except the cooks scooping up my food. I have them pile my tray so high that I have to glide like I have a book balanced on my head so I don't spill anything. Not a peaball falls from my tray. When I get to the silverware, I take an extra fork for Mother, in case she refuses to get a tray of her own. Her face is so thin now. She has to eat while we have the chance.

I'm not pleased to find Brother Christian sitting at our table, eating. Everyone else is in line. Will Julian be able to eat my peas with Brother Christian here?

"Sister Shea, put that tray down before you drop it," he says, chuckling. "Were you getting food for your entire table?" he asks, his steely blue eyes wide.

I put the extra fork in the center of the table and sit across from Brother Christian. The other Elders sit at other tables, spread throughout the Dining Hall. They're slumming it tonight. "I brought enough to share, in case someone wasn't in line yet. We're starving."

He guffaws and scoops some peas from my tray and eats them with a wink.

18

The days return to normal, for the most part. Normal for Daeios. I eat meals and attend Gatherings with my family and Julian, although we never hold hands and say grace now. Julian has given up on the gym, but I run five miles and lift weights or practice yoga during my daily shift. I train females to be fitter breeders. Except for Sister Bethany, they act like they don't know me, like they learned from a workout video.

The Gatherings have returned to pure rapture for everyone but Mother and me. We do our best to act like we're caught up in it all, making faces like we've just won a zillion dollars.

More bald mothers appear on the stage during the Gatherings. One embarrassed young woman appeared in Medical during Mother's shift, and they diagnosed her with a pulled groin muscle. What did she do in her breeding to pull a groin muscle? Who'd she breed with?

Julian and I continue our trysts in the closet in the Theater. He didn't want to at first, saying it was too dangerous; I said I couldn't bear Daeios without him. "Our room is secret, isn't it?" I asked, and he caved in. We meet there instead of going together now, varying our arrivals so we don't set up a pattern that might arouse suspicion. The fear we felt at our first meeting after The Ordeal was palpable. It has lessened now, although I still insist we keep the light on if he hasn't brought any candles. He agrees. He tells me once, in a quavering voice and with tears in his eyes, that his experience during The Ordeal was too horrific to share with me, so I let it be.

Every day I'm sure we'll make love, but it doesn't happen. I know he loves me as much as I love him; the fever in his eyes when he looks at me, and the heart in his voice when he speaks to me, tell me so. His body responds to mine, and then he puts more distance between us. It's a frustrating never-ending cycle, but I want to consummate our love. And I refuse to give up on this last effort to avoid breeding with an Elder.

They took our bags and Mother's purse from under the bed in the back of the RV. I think Mother suffered solitary confinement because we kept them. When I question her, she tells me she doesn't know why they took her there, and to drop the subject.

Sometimes they close the entertainment areas and the Storehouse to punish us for a small infraction, which keeps Julian and me from meeting in our spot, from being romantic. I don't like it, but I don't complain.

The nights terrify me. I no longer wander the perimeter of the north wing, searching for answers. I'm afraid of the dark now, afraid one of my loved ones will vanish in the night, as others do. No one makes a big deal out of it anymore, but as our numbers dwindle, a missing face is more noticeable. There are only a few men left. I'm anxious that one day my dad won't show up for a meal or a Gathering. I hug him every time I see him. I worry about Julian too, but not as much, due to his relationship with Brother Christian.

I have nightmares. I'm afraid they'll call me to my breeding from out of the darkness. I'm exhausted, I'm in and out of sleep, and I wake at the smallest sound and listen for the snores and breathing of my family.

Mother sleeps less than I do. When I wake up and can't hear her breathing, I whisper, "Mother?" and she answers from the darkness, "I'm here, Shea. Go to sleep." And I do.

19

I oversleep one morning, and Maya shakes me awake. "Come on, Shea, you're going to miss breakfast. Hurry, I'm starving," she says, pulling me to my feet.

I get up, rubbing my eyes the way a sleepy child does.

"Wait, your hairpins are coming out, let me fix your bun." Maya's not very good at it; she's always had short hair, and the little girls wear their hair down, but she smiles as she finishes, proud of the results. She'll be a good mom someday, I think, and then stop, horrified—she's only fourteen. I don't want it to happen down here. I hug her for a good long time, then pull away and peer into her eyes, smoothing her hair, which is no longer a pixie cut and now has auburn roots. It's almost long enough to fashion into a tiny bun. The beautiful roses that once colored her cheeks have faded until they're an almost imperceptible pink.

"Don't grow up too fast, okay? You should be a kid as long as you can."

"O—kay," she says like I'm a crazy person. Sometimes I wonder about that.

We head down the hallway toward the Dining Hall, and just as I spot Julian waiting for us, two older women seize my arms, one on either side of me, and pluck me away from Maya.

"It's your time, Sister Shea. Start working on that smile. The Elders like them smiling, don't they, Sister Leah?" the thin woman on my left says in a honeyed voice.

"They certainly do, Sister Victoria," the stout woman on my right replies in a Minnie Mouse-on-helium voice. "You'll have plenty to smile about. You're going to be as beautiful and fragrant as a whole garden of flowers. To be a vessel for God. You girls are so lucky. So, so lucky."

I look to Julian for help. I know he loves me. Why won't he publicly profess his love for me and fight for me? His misty eyes tell me, his bright smile tells me, the relaxed lines of his body tell me that he won't try to stop my breeding. My devout Julian believes this is my calling from God.

Everyone around me is smiling and clapping. Some try to touch me as if I'm valuable and they would steal me away if they could.

"Tell Mother I've been called by God," I shout to Maya as they pull us apart. She's squealing and jumping up and down as she always does when she's cheering someone on. I hope she heard me. I need Mother.

As we move toward the Spa more middle-aged women fall into step with the group, an avalanche picking up snow. They jabber like they're going to the most prestigious affair, and I'm nothing more than the flowers they're bringing to the host. Or the vase. I'm the vessel. I'm queasy and have a headache coming on. Is that a good excuse to get out of sex down here?

We reach Door 7. Mother hasn't arrived yet. Did Maya ask her to come? They won't let her in once the door closes behind us. Hurry, Mother! Please hurry!

I'm afraid to comply with the breeding, but I fear refusal more, knowing the danger it could bring all of us. The Ordeal made my decision to breed for me.

"What about breakfast?" I stall at the door. I come to an abrupt halt, and an overweight woman behind me runs into me, pushing me a step further. "It'll be easier for me to smile if I have something in my stomach. We don't want my stomach growling during the breeding, do we? That would be a turnoff for anyone. I'll just ..." I turn to go the other way, but the sisters surround me.

"We have delicacies for you to eat, sweetheart: chocolates and luscious frozen berries," Sister Victoria says, touching the corners of her mouth like she's drooling. "And wine. You'll be absolutely swooning with pleasure before you meet the father of your first child." She pats my hand, and I think she's going to pinch my cheeks.

Just as the group is turning me around to face the door again, Mother runs around the corner, breathing hard. I make my body an X, my hands and feet holding me in the doorway. Some sisters push, some pull me through, and the door slams shut. I glance over my shoulder and see Mother. I'll be okay with Mother here, exuding strength and calmness. Having her here will remind me why I'm doing this—I cannot have my family vanish in the night.

The Spa is a spacious room, everything stark white except for stainless steel and mirrors in brilliant silver. It's balmy. The light isn't harsh here as it is in other rooms in Daeios. The Spa seems to twinkle with stars as light bounces off the mirrors and stainless steel. A large Jacuzzi tub sits in the center, a halo of soft golden light shimmering above. The water is bubbling and steaming and fragrant, the scent drawing me into the room like a field of bewitched red poppies.

I'm trying to get a sense of the rest of the room when four sisters remove my water pack and ID badge and then pick up the bottom of my dress. My arms lift automatically as they pull the dress over my head. I'm naked, except for my socks and sandals. Sisters on each side bend down and bare my feet as I balance on one back, and then another.

As two tall women escort me to a seat in the Jacuzzi, their eyes downcast, I see in the mirrors on the wall that the curves of my body have disappeared. My muscles are too defined. The sisters turn me to face the hottub. "Careful, Sister Shea, it's slippery getting into the tub," they say in unison as they help me to sit down.

Ah, it's heavenly. I hadn't realized how much I miss a good bath.

The water bubbles around me, not too hot, and they leave me to soak up the heady fragrance: lavender, with something green like eucalyptus. The lights are low, the light gleaming off the mirrors and projecting a pastel rainbow over the tub. The jets hit my body, and the steam opens my sinuses. I picture all of the dirt and rock around me crumbling away, leaving me to bathe in the outdoors as the golden sun sets. The chattering is absent. I hope the sisters left and forgot about me. This is as far as I need to go.

I'm relaxed for the first time in a long time as if I were drugged with a magic potion.

When my fingers have begun to prune, a woman kneels behind me and removes the pins from my hair. She shampoos my hair with a lilac-scented shampoo. Her fingers feel amazing on my scalp. She pulls a hose from the floor near the Jacuzzi and rinses my hair with lukewarm water, adding more bubbles to my bath. She rubs in a creamy conditioner and leaves it in.

"We'll be shaving this off soon, hmmm?"

I touch my hair as if I can protect it.

The other women move as a group toward me. The sisters who seated me each take an arm and help me up, leading me up the steps of the Jacuzzi. Cold air assaults me, but two other matrons hurry in and dry me with two warm and thirsty white towels. Another nonbreeder brings a thin towel and wraps my head in a turban. Another sister flutters over with a comfy, white robe, helping to place my arms through the holes, and shooing my hands away when I try to tie the belt. She ties it for me. My ensemble wouldn't be complete without a pair of fuzzy, white slippers, which yet another sister places on my feet as I hold on to other ladies for support. How many of them are there? I sense my Mother is here, calming me. I imagine her caressing my shoulders, but I don't see her. She's hanging back so the others don't notice her. She wasn't in the training class.

The sisters coax me to a white manicure/pedicure station, where they poke, prod and trim all twenty nails to perfection. One paints my nails, fingers and toes, a ruby red, and then covers the top half of the nails with a sparkly midnight blue. I don't usually go for this kind of thing, but I have to admit I like the way the polish looks. Not white, for one thing.

The matrons bustle me to a massage table covered in white flannel sheets. The woman who encased me in the robe removes it and indicates I should lie face down on the table. I comply. Four razors deftly shave my entire backside, except for my head. I never thought of shaving my butt before. They have me roll over on my back and shave my entire front, including all of my pubic hair. The only hair I have left is on my head. It's becoming more precious to me by the minute.

Once shaven, they exfoliate my skin with lavender oil and sea salt, the excess removed with hot towels. My skin retains a light sheen; I hope I'm too slippery to stay on top of. Robe Lady swoops in and replaces the robe, and then the gaggle takes me over to a barber's chair with a large, round mirror in front of it, encircled in bright, clear light bulbs.

I haven't seen my face in so long that it's like an awkward meeting with a stranger. The light acts as a filter, softening the lines of my square jaw, but I can still see that my cheeks are too thin. The circles under my eyes are darker than before, the hollows beneath my eyes too deep to reflect the light. The glow doesn't touch my hair, which once had sunny highlights from being outdoors. It no longer has any sheen to it. And my monobrow is flourishing.

A sister comes forward and places a small silver bowl of chocolates and frozen blueberries in my lap. She hands me a generous crystal goblet of full-bodied red wine, which matches the ruby color of my nails. I guzzle it down and hand the goblet back for more. I need a lot more wine. I catch sight of my Mother for a brief second in the mirror, but she disappears in bun-heads and blue eyes before I can make eye contact. They shape my monobrow into two eyebrows—thank you, Lord! I finish all of the treats as they trim, blow dry, and curl my hair, letting it fall across my shoulders, and spray it with a shiny spray that makes my hair glimmer rose gold in the brilliant light.

Now the makeup, which I've also been dreading. I've never bothered with it and don't think I need it. They start gooping it on. First, one bad-breathed sister spackles on foundation; another applies powder; another makes my cheeks flushed and rosy. A woman with striking features seems to be in charge of the overall effect, as she gives instructions and moves my head from side to side to assure my makeup is even. She darkens my brows until they look heavy and ogreish to me. She shadows, lines, smudges, and wings my eyeliner until my eyes are lupine, and adds several coats of black mascara as I try not to blink. One last woman rushes in and expertly applies my crimson lipstick.

The sisters assemble behind me to observe the results in the mirror, looking only at me, as if their reflections weren't showing in the looking glass. They exclaim at my beauty and declare my makeover a success. I see a deranged Barbie doll with small boobs. Maybe they're too flat to be called boobs. They turn me in the chair with a small mirror in my hands so I can see the back of my hair—it's pretty in curls, and has grown a few inches since we came here. They beam at me, they caress me, they play with my hair, they gloat over the results. All except Mother. I catch one glimpse of her face in the mirror. She's not elated or disapproving of my appearance—her face is etched with angst. She disappears again behind the bevy of women, but I'm reassured that she's here.

The women seat me in a plush, high-backed white chair that reminds me of a throne. I'm facing a mirrored door opposite the one through which we arrived. It surely contains the Breeding Room. Has my seed-bearer, or perhaps all of the Elders, been watching the entire time? The sisters form a ring around me, holding hands, their eyes closed, with peaceful smiles on their faces. I wish I could see Mother.

The ladies begin a prayer, in unison, that I'll be fruitful, that my womb will be accepting of the seed-bearer's sperm, that I may have many babies in the name of God and Daeios. That I'll maintain my health and that of my children. They repeat themselves and repeat themselves, and after a while, the prayer becomes more of a musical chant filled with resonant voices. The sisters sway from side to side, and it's as though they will transport me from the throne to the other side of the door with their voices alone.

The chanting stops abruptly, and two women drop from the circle to take my hands and help me rise from the throne. Robe Lady slips in to remove the robe. The women get behind me and drive me toward the door, giving me a moment to admire my lithe body in the full-length mirror one last time before it becomes distorted with pregnancy. I look prepubescent with my labia shaved and my almost nonexistent boobs. I drink up every line of my face and body. When will I see my reflection again?

"Off you go," Sister Leah says as she scans a key card to open the mirrored door. As she holds it open for me, the women exclaim, "Bless you, Sister Shea! Bless you!"

They push me through the door with soft hands on my back and ease the door closed behind me.

20

I stand, shivering, in a large round stainless steel and white room that shines under bright overhead lights and smells disinfected. Bleached. My feet are icy on white tile, the walls are white, and there's a short, white-sheeted, narrow bed isolated in the center of the room. Goosebumps ripple my flesh, not only because of the freezing temperature but also because of why I'm here—waiting for one of the old guys to have sex with me. I don't know who it will be. I don't know from which direction he will come.

My body tenses and my lungs feel empty. I take in big gulps of frigid, sterilized air. I don't want to have children. I don't want this to happen.

A door slams behind me, and I whirl around to see Brother Christian approaching me, naked except for a white tented loincloth, a lusty grin on his finely lined face.

"Sister Shea, welcome to your breeding. You look lovely, my dear, just lovely. Quite tantalizing. You know, you caught my eye the first time I saw you, so this is a special day indeed. For both of us. We'll make beautiful memories and have a wonderful child together. I hope we will have many children together, Sister Shea. Is there anything I can get you before we begin? More wine, perhaps?"

A chastity belt?

"No, thank you," I manage to say, my voice shaky, my body trembling. I don't want to do this. I have to do this.

"Don't worry about the chill; you'll be nice and warm once we begin. This way, my dear," he says as he takes my hand and leads me to the small bed. "Please, lie down on your back. Relax. You're going to enjoy this. I'm very good in bed." He winks at me with a salacious smile.

I lie down on the short bed, see the deranged Barbie reflection in the mirror on the ceiling, and want to cover my nakedness. My legs dangle off the end; there's no place to put them. Brother Christian bends down, and I think he's going to dive in with his face. Instead, he pulls two shiny metal gynecological stirrups up and extends them with a clank. You have got to be kidding. This is a baby-making clinic; there's nothing beautiful about it.

"Give me your feet. Yes, dear. Oh, they're cold. I'll place them like so ..." He puts my feet in the uncomfortable stirrups. They didn't even put socks on them like they do at the gynecologist's office. "I have some wonderful lubricants down here, so don't be worried about being tense, or dry; it won't be painful in the least. In fact, I'm sure you'll want another go of it later. I have to tell you, the other Elders are as jealous as can be that God chose me to breed you. They're hissing like old cats vying for a warm lap." He cackles.

Please, no.

"You're welcome to watch in the mirror, and I'll even pose for you." He snatches the loincloth away to reveal a penis hard enough to put my eye out. "Would you like to hold it?" he asks, stepping to my side and thrusting it toward me so I can.

"No, just ..." Get it over with, is what I think. "Go," is what I say, my eyes closed. He doesn't waste any time, tweaking first at my nipples for a moment. He uses his thumbnails like guitar picks. Not it.

He stands between my legs, and I hear the lubricant squirt from the bottle, and then listen to the slapping of his hand against his penis as he lubes up. He grabs hold of my ass, pulling me to the right level for easy entry by his old dick.

"No!" I scream. I can't do it. I pull a foot from the stirrup to close my legs before he enters me, defiles me.

"Sister Shea, you're being quite unreasonable. This is a joyous day for both of us, and for God. We're following God's word. You must cooperate, or be damned in His eyes. You'll be banished."

The word "banished" echoes in my mind. Brother Christian's face is close to mine, his eyes monstrous. They have a glint that makes them appear darker instead of lighter.

"Now put your foot—"

"No! I won't do it! You can't make me!" I thrash as I scream, kicking Brother Christian away from the bed and trying to sit up so I can run away from this bed of horrors, this chamber of nightmares realized.

More Elders run into the room to restrain me. I try to scratch them, but my nails are too short, and then they strap my hands down. One of the twins holds my feet in the stirrups and keeps my legs from closing as Brother Eli binds my feet to them. They open my legs wider. Brother Adam holds my forehead with one hand and covers my mouth with the other. I bite him, drawing blood. He yowls and jerks his hand back as I scream. Brother Luke, the tallest Elder, expertly places a wadded cloth in my mouth.

"The bitch bit me!" Brother Adam yells and pulls his other hand off my forehead to assess the damage. "Does this need medical attention, Brother James? Damn, it's going to leave a scar."

"Don't worry about it now, let's get this breeding done, and I'll disinfect it. Female bite wounds can be nasty. Blindfold, please," Brother James says. The other twin stretches a wide headband around my head to cover my eyes. No light escapes through it. I scream around the gag, the darkness sending me over the edge into complete terror.

"This'll take care of the problem," Brother James says by my ear, as I feel a sting in my neck. I cry out around the cloth in my mouth and black out.

21

I awaken with a splitting headache, the sun shining in my eyes. I'm lying on my back on a hard, cool surface. I move to cover my eyes with my hand and find that my arms are bound at my side. My chest swells with a scream. I wiggle my arms and breathe out with a shudder when I find it's an emergency survival blanket wrapped securely around me. I sit up enough to loosen the crinkly blanket from around my shoulders and just about take the top of my head off. It hurts that much. I hurt all over. I lie back and shield my eyes from the sun.

My sluggish brain comes suddenly alert. The sun? The sun, shining straight down on me! Oh, my God, I've been banished! I'll die up here! I sit bolt upright, contorting in pain, and find that I'm just inside an alcove in red rock, where the sun can peek inside.

A coiled snake watches me from a few feet away.

I freeze. I'm terrified of snakes. It slithers toward me, ash brown and cream scales, a triangular head that tells me it's venomous. A rattlesnake. It flicks its tongue in and out, sensing me. As it draws near, my pounding heart shrieks for me to roll away from it, but my mind shouts at me not to move. It stops inches away. I fear the emergency blanket may be giving off the sun's rays in a manner enticing to the snake, luring its cold flesh to the heat radiating from the blanket. At what point will the snake find me dangerous and bite me in self-defense?

I close my eyes and hold as still as I can. I'm unable to block the fear from my mind. I imagine the snake sensing I'm a warm-blooded mammal, biting me, and slinking off to curl up on a warm rock. Leaving me to die in agony.

I hold my breath and tense my muscles while my heart slams against my chest. I hope I'm doing the right thing. Will the snake mistake me for that warm rock and curl up on me? I couldn't hold still for long with a snake resting on my chest. I wait, thoughts of my certain, painful death twirling in my mind like vultures circling overhead.

When I don't feel the bite of the snake or its body slithering next to mine, and I can't hold my breath any longer, I open my eyes to find it gone. It left no trace that it was here. Breathing out slowly, I release some tension from my muscles. My body aches as though I've completed a triathlon, my head pounds, and I thirst as if I drank acid last night. It feels like fire searing inside me, burning its way out to consume my flesh.

I lift the blanket. I'm naked. Blackness between my thighs. I was raped.

Exhausted and woozy, I lie back again and breathe the fresh air. I smell the heat in it. The sun is too hot. I remember the day I drove to Sedona to find Jace, with the clouds festering into darkness behind me. The killer storms will come, and I have only this open cavern and a flimsy blanket for protection. Or the storms have ravaged the earth and gone, leaving a barren landscape that won't support life.

I can't remember anything after seeing the naked, deranged Barbie in the mirror on the ceiling of the Breeding Room. Brother Christian was there, and I was so afraid. I move my hands to touch my face, arms, chest, hips. Slow, gentle movements. Every inch of my skin hurts.

I sit up again, which wracks my body with pain and I cry out. I lift the blanket. My skin is bruised and swollen, every inch discolored and taut and radiating pain. My wrists and ankles show signs of restraints. My painted nails are ludicrous. My hands reveal that one eye is puffy, but not sealed shut. They didn't shave my head—I think it's there in its entirety—although my scalp feels like someone tried to pull my hair out by the roots. I try to see my face in the emergency blanket, but it doesn't offer my reflection. It's probably better that way.

I put my hands on the rough red sandstone and twist onto my hip to get up. It hurts so much I don't know if I can. I don't know if I can walk.

I muster all of my courage to withstand the pain. Screaming. Moaning. Crying. First, I kneel, and then I squat, shaking like I'll fall apart. I unfold into a standing position, my head reeling and threatening to take me down. Vertigo. My stomach heaves and I fall to the ground on my hands and knees, vomiting a red that's almost black. I stay that way until my hurling becomes dry heaves, and another minute, spitting. When I swipe my arm across my lips to clean off the bloody spittle, I blanch at the pain it causes my mouth. My mouth is full of sores where my teeth broke the skin. My lips are swollen and cut, and my face is sunburned. I've never had a sunburn. I'm hotter than I've ever felt before, but I'm not sweating.

I have to venture into this wasteland to find water, or lie down and accept a painful death here. I'm half dead already. I reach for the blanket to cover my nakedness and stand up again, moaning. I'm shaking with the pain. So this is what it feels like to be banished.

I wrap the bloodstained blanket around my shoulders like a cape and tie it in a knot at my neck. It reminds me of a shiny hospital gown with the slit open in the front. Slow, steady tears course down my cheeks; frustrating, hurtful tears that offer me no release from my pain. I turn and face out of the alcove, my blurry eyes scanning for water, my most urgent need. A few white clouds surround the sun. Desert, sagebrush, red and yellow rock formations, and sand. No water. A shimmer of heat rises off the sand in the distance.

I feel eyes on the back of my head. I spin around, alert enough now to check the space for other occupants.

"Hello?" I say into the semidarkness, and chide myself for being silly. It does feel like I'm standing in a room, though, a small room with three walls. I can stand up straight here but will have to stoop around the rock walls.

I drag my hand along the rock as I did in Daeios. Stooping causes more pain than standing, so I hurry. I sniff in the darker corners, fearful that something will attack me. No odor of shit or urine. No sign of an animal using this as a den.

As I move along the back wall, I find a small nook with an entrance just big enough to crawl through. I get down on my hands and knees to investigate, grimacing at the pain. It's too dark to see, so I use my least-important left hand and feel around warily inside the nook. My hand lands on a large bundle standing up against the rock wall. I crouch, wincing, to get a feel with both hands.

Can it be? The bundle is heavy, and I exert myself pulling it out, straining my injuries, gasping like an old woman until it pops from its nook. Sitting before me on the rock floor is my survival backpack.

I wasn't banished. I was rescued.

22

I'm so happy to see my survival pack that I have to remind myself not to smile. It would be too painful. Without this pack, I doubt I'd survive. It may give me a fighting chance if the earth has healed enough. It may save my life.

It's heavier than when I first packed it and practically bursting with its contents. I kept the pack at forty pounds so I could carry it for a distance, but this must weigh at least fifty. I pull the blue aluminum water bottle from the webbing on the outside of the pack. It's full. Gulping the lukewarm water in a few swallows, I lean against the wall of the cavern to close my battered eyes a moment, giving thanks for this small miracle.

Now to see what I have in my arsenal against death.

Wincing and groaning, I sit cross-legged. I face outward, the pack in front of me, my back against the wall of the alcove so I can see anyone—or anything—approach me. I pull my emergency blanket down to sit on it and wrap it around me the best I can. I finally have a cape, now that I don't have an ensemble to go with it.

I'm thrilled to find that the clothing I had originally packed is there: an olive green baseball cap; two pastel green polypropylene shirts, one short-sleeved and the other a long-sleeved mock turtleneck; moisture-wicking underwear and socks, two pairs each; a sports bra; some khaki hiking pants that have cargo pockets and zip-off legs; and my favorite Merrell hiking boots.

Some things I hadn't packed: the running clothes I went to Daeios in, including my beloved running shoes. My awareness of being naked is almost paranoia. I resist looking at my battered body as I pull on the running clothes, sans underwear, to keep everything but the running clothes clean. If I find an adequate water source, I'll clean up and wash these clothes.

I locate the food: beef jerky, dried pinto beans, chocolate, peanut butter, and almonds. I wish I had packed some of those dehydrated meals, but I never thought I'd actually use this survival pack. Will there even be any water for cooking the beans? I scarf down a piece of peppery beef jerky and ten almonds, rationing myself in spite of my hunger. The salt burns the open wounds in my mouth, and I reproach myself for not keeping some of the water.

I unload the rest of the pack and inventory my supplies, creating three lists in my head: protection, tools, and fire/water/food. Although I packed extra equipment for making fire, obtaining clean water, and hunting food, my arsenal seems meager. It seemed a lot when I packed it.

At the bottom of the pack, a surprise. Mother's care package: her .44 Magnum pistol and the gold and diamond sun pendant.

I tear up when I see them. She does love me.

Thinking back, I realize she was always there when I needed her. Always. I have been mistaking her sharp words for meanness when they came from worry; her stern, painful silences for dismissal when they stemmed from hurt that I caused; and her lack of emotion for coldness when she was being strong for the rest of us. I was immature. My chilled heart warms with the thought of her. She's such a beautiful woman, inside and out, but I haven't been able to see it until now.

She's a good mother. A good woman. Please, Lord, let me see her again.

Wiping away my tears, I inspect the gun. It's loaded with six rounds and has been cleaned and oiled. The heavy weight feels reassuring in my hands. I hope I can handle the kick; I'm used to a 9mm. With only six rounds, I can't spare any for target shooting. Every round must count toward my survival. I can't imagine how she managed to keep it from the Daeiosians. How did she hide my survival pack so they didn't confiscate it during The Ordeal? My respect for her inches up another notch. I'd give her a hug right now if I could. I don't know if I'd ever let go.

I put on the olive drab survival bracelets, one on each tender wrist, snapping the black plastic buckles together. The bracelets are woven of sixteen feet of mil-spec 550 paracord. Woven into each is a small, foldable knife with a one-inch blade. A small compass sits on top of each of my wrists now.

I pull the pendant over my head, its sun resting on my chest. Putting on my cap, I pull my hair through the back elastic. I bend to put on socks and hiking boots. It hurts so much to lean forward that I feel lightheaded. I lie down until the sickening spinning stops. It takes several attempts to tie the boots. By then, I'm shuddering with pain and exhaustion.

I have so much more to do.

I pack what I think I need in the drypack, which I had included in the larger survival pack because it doubles as a daypack. I need to keep it lightweight, considering my physical condition, and also allow some room for firewood and kindling. My most urgent need is a water source, so I bring the two water bottles, the aluminum one, and a one-liter collapsible water bottle, water purification tablets, my mess kit in case I need to boil water, and some coffee filters for filtering chunks out of the water. I bring tampons, which I packed to use as tinder, to keep the blood from ruining my pants. I bring all of my fire-starting supplies, and all of the food, in case I don't make it back here. I pack small waterproof binoculars; a hatchet multitool; my compact multitool; two bandanas; a signaling mirror; a first aid kit; a fifty-gallon garbage bag; some one-gallon plastic bags that seal; a lightweight, super absorbent towel; my toothbrush; and clothing. I also bring the hunting knife and the gun. No telling what I might run up against, but I hope it has four legs and I can make food out of it before it makes food out of me.

I think of my crippling fear of the dark, courtesy of The Ordeal, and throw in the running headlamp.

I clean up my puke the best I can with the bloody emergency blanket. Having sealed it in a plastic bag, I cram the blanket into the bottom of the large pack. Tucking the remaining supplies back in the survival pack in an orderly fashion, I shove it, pain wracking my body, back in its cranny, straps facing the wall. I leave no other trace that I was here, except for my scent and the dark spot where my puke was. I can't do anything about that.

I shrug into the smaller daypack, wincing at the pain even this light pack causes my injuries. Taking a deep breath, I survey the edge of the alcove for the easiest way down and find a gently sloping trail to my left. It's wheelchair accessible. I take jarring baby steps down the ramp, and suddenly have a distinct feeling that someone is watching me. Goosebumps prickle my arms in spite of the desert heat and my fever. A quick scan with the binoculars doesn't reveal anything with eyeballs. It's probably that damn snake, spying on me.

I look at the sand and find no trace of tracks. No human tracks. No tire tracks. No signs of my rescue in the sand.

The compass on my left wrist says the opening to my new home faces south. I use the binoculars to survey my surroundings. The sky has no menacing clouds. There's a small stand of trees to the southeast, a good two hundred yards away. Trees mean water.

It's not easy trudging through the sand. Every step hurts. It feels like my insides are coming out. My whole body is a bruise and my head booms with pain. My throat is parched and raw, and that's what pushes me toward the trees. I keep looking back to assure myself the shelter is in view, and to see if that unnerving feeling is the result of someone, or something, following me in the tracks I'm leaving in the sand. Following the scent of blood, of semen, of inhumanity.

Nothing's there.

23

It feels like I've walked a mile when I get to the trees. I'm disappointed in the amount of water. The trees have pretty much sucked it up, the bastards. But I can fill my water bottles from one of the small puddles and sponge off with a bandana in the large puddle.

I place water purification tablets in the bottles. I strain the water through a coffee filter, pouring with my mess kit cup. Once the bottles are full, I shake them to disperse the tablets and set them aside to purify while I clean up. Getting water ready when you're burning with thirst is maddeningly slow. Not even the slightest breeze stirs the hot air.

I'm thankful for the trees as I undress, for they provide shade and some protection. Laying my olive drab towel beside me, I soak a red and white bandana in the cloudy water. I cringe at having to remove the blood and filth from my body. At what it means. My skin is so tender that I can't help but inhale deeply when I touch the wounds, no matter how gently. I have bruises, burn marks, scrape and scratch marks. A bite mark on my shoulder that hurts me on the inside. I painstakingly bathe each wound individually, using the signaling mirror to help me see parts of my body I can't see without it. I'm unable to reach multiple wounds on my back. I avoid looking at my face for now. I'm afraid to see it.

Bathing away the evidence of the rape, the penetration part, is particularly painful. Clotted blood. Human waste—its smell assaults me once I wet it—is difficult to remove with a wet bandana. I can't leave any on me, or I'll go insane. I ease myself into a sitting position in the large puddle to soak first. I'm sitting in the mud, but there's nothing else to do. The water turns dark, with a red tint, and smells of bloody sewage. I won't be able to use this as a drinking source in the future. I'm contaminating it with blood, urine, semen, and shit. I don't trust my tablets to purify that away. Will I ever feel clean again?

The water cools my raw skin and provides some relief. Sitting in the puddle, I scrub the filth away until I have to stand to get to the areas I can't reach while seated. Every movement is painful. Every touch of the wet cloth makes me want to jump out of my skin, which might not be such a bad idea, considering its condition.

I finish cleaning my body and hesitate. I need to clean my face. Summoning all of my strength, I hold the mirror, shaking, in front of my face. I gasp, and my eyes fill with tears.

I knew my left eye was puffy, but I didn't realize how black the skin around it would be. Blood vessels have broken in my eyes, the red burning out of the whites in my reflection. My nose is broken, and there's a cut on the bridge. It may be a little crooked. Dried blood streaks from my nose, and there's fresh blood where my lips are cut. I don't need to see the cuts in my mouth. I feel them, taste them. I won't be brushing my teeth today. My hair is intact but dirty. There isn't enough water to wash it. At least the garish makeup is gone.

Moving to another small puddle, I use a fresh blue and white bandana to clean my face as gently as possible. I daub on antiseptic from the first aid kit with my ring finger. It stings like a son-of-a-bitch.

A sudden boom of thunder cracks behind me. The nerves in my brain scream for me to run away. I turn to see that the once wispy white clouds are now swollen and dark, like my eye.

I towel off as quickly as I can, smearing my towel with grime. The water is a mess now, so I stuff the bloody clothes and towel into plastic bags and into my pack dirty. The sky lights up behind me as lightning flashes. Another thunderclap, closer this time. It's cooling off. I have to get to my shelter soon.

I apply the stinging antiseptic sparingly to the open wounds on my body that are within reach and bandage the worst of them. I take two painkillers with water. I insert a tampon and almost pass out from the pain. I take two more painkillers with water. I dress in the T-shirt and pants with the legs zipped off, wearing underwear and socks, but forego the tight running bra. I feel better being cleaner. Not clean, but cleaner.

It starts to sprinkle. I pull the large trash bag from the pack and, using the compact multitool's scissors, cut out the neck and armholes where I had marked them in white marker. I pull it over my head, a long poncho.

I shove everything else into the pack. I find a few dried branches in the copse and stuff them into the pack, along with some twigs. Everything fits so I can cinch the pack up and maintain its waterproofness. It will be nice to have a fire tonight, for heat, cooking beans, and keeping wild animals from approaching. For keeping the terrifying darkness away. I hang the wet blue and white bandana from the mesh on the outside of the pack to dry. I leave the other one. The defiled one.

The journey back is excruciating, and the rain bites harder and colder as I near my alcove. It's growing dark with storm clouds, and my fear of the dark is crouching in the back of my throat, ready to strangle me. I've removed my cap, so the rain is washing my hair. I'll eat. I hope I'll be able to sleep, to heal my aching body and my sick heart.

I drink water as I head back to my shelter. "Drink up!" rattles in my mind, and I shudder at the thought of Brother Christian, my savage rapist.

When I'm almost at my shelter, I spot movement on the ledge. My ledge. I pull my binoculars from the mesh on my pack—it's a thin St. Bernard, taking shelter in my alcove. It's probably gone wild. Maybe his eyes are the eyes I felt watching me.

The lightning and thunder increase, reminding me of our torturous trip from Sedona. Bile rises in my throat as I taste the fear that drove us to Daeios. Lightning struck the RV and almost killed Dad. Dad's friend was struck by lightning while playing golf. I have to get out of this electrical storm, and the only shelter I know of is my alcove. I have to get rid of that dog. I trudge forward in the cold rain to meet my enemy.

I have the gun, but with only six rounds, I want to save it as my last option. The knife is for close contact, which I'm trying to avoid. The hatchet tool? The chances of me throwing it far enough and hitting an animal with the ability to flee are close to none. What about a flaming torch? Yeah, right, a flaming torch in a downpour. Maybe. If I go under the ledge, I'll have a bit of an overhang to protect me. But the dog could leap on me as I approach.

I have no choice—become a meal for a hungry St. Bernard, or die in a lightning storm.

Not after what I've survived. I continue toward the rock formation to claim it as my own. I approach the dog with only my cap in my hands, and the hope of scaring him away in my heart.

The rain is coming down hard enough that it's running downhill across the sand. I remember the heavy rainfall warnings on the radio on my trip to Sedona, the mudslide we evacuated from, the flash flood that washed away the road we'd planned to take to Daeios. The rain will provide life-giving water or will wash my life away. I start to run and my body shrieks in protest, so I settle into what normally would be a nice, easy walk. Instead, it's an excruciating, stumbling walk.

I see the giant dog clearly now without the binoculars, although the downpour dulls my vision. It seems less dangerous with its outline blurring into the rock around it. I have to assume it's dangerous and will kill me if given a chance.

I try to swallow my fear, and it joins the fear burning in my lungs.

I bend over like I'm going to tackle a running back, positioning my insignificant daypack to protect my back. I put the cap on and cover my head with my hands, knowing this isn't enough to protect me if the huge dog attacks.

I don't have to ask myself if I'm crazy. I don't have to ask myself if I'm worth fighting for, either.

Running the last few feet to get under the ledge, I picture that hulk of a dog landing on me, his teeth tearing my flesh. I stifle a scream and ignore the pain that's blaring through me. The dog barks as I run underneath the ledge. The ledge overhangs enough to keep me out of the rain, except for my boots.

As I calm my breathing, I realize it's more than one dog barking. Shit. A pack. And they know I'm here. They could run down the wheelchair ramp and pounce on me, destroy me in a few painful minutes. Fight, flight or fright? I don't have the strength to fight them. But if I flee, they will surely come after me, a running, meaty, target. I'm frightened, but not catatonic, and my fear screams for me to act. My only choice is to fight, fight for my shelter. Fight for my life.

They're leaving, one way or another.

I set the drypack and cap down on a dry patch of ground and pull out my largest branch, about six inches in diameter at the widest part. It's completely dry, no sap or dampness to keep it from igniting. One end is narrower and fits my hand better than the other one does. I pull out my other fire-starting materials and squirt petroleum jelly on the wider end of the branch. My fire starter sets it alight instantly. I have a flaming torch, less than three feet long. I've always wanted a flaming torch, like in the old Frankenstein movies. I let it burn for a couple of minutes to build a good, solid flame. Feeling the heat emboldens me.

I run up my wheelchair ramp as fast as I can, ignoring the pain that shoots through me, and roaring as loud as my raw throat will allow. Adrenaline and fear race through my veins as I brandish the torch in front of me, moving it back and forth to make the threat—little old me—appear larger than it is. The torch swooshes and crackles and impresses me.

Two small, spotted terriers, a golden retriever, and a big, black mutt come from behind the St. Bernard. They lunge at me, snarling and growling, just short of the burning torch. My heart is slamming around in my chest and I squelch the urge to run.

I take a deep breath and move along the back wall of the alcove toward the dogs, stooping as before and facing my back to the wall so they can't come around and attack me from behind. They back into a corner, barking, their eyes snapping golden. I don't want them to go back. I want them to flee across the ledge and down the wheelchair ramp. They crouch and growl at me, their lips pulled back to bare their teeth, their wet lips convulsing savagely. The terriers creep toward me, ahead of the larger dogs, their hackles up and their teeth bared.

I approach from my right, swinging the torch toward the slavering dogs. The terriers pounce at me and then run down the wheelchair ramp to avoid the dancing flames of the torch, and the big dogs follow. As they scurry down the ramp, a terrier turns and barks at me twice. A warning. They won't be far away.

Shea Donovan: 2. A snake and a pack of wild dogs: 0.

I lay the torch down and get my pack, put on my cap. Then I remove the poncho and unload my drypack. I'm trembling with exhaustion. The painkillers barely touched the pain, but I need to make them last. I build a fire near the wheelchair ramp, but far enough inside to protect it should the wind force the rain in. As I set the wood aflame using the torch and toss the torch on top, I know it won't burn through the night. I'll have to bear the total darkness. I'm not sure I can do it without losing my mind. Lightning is slicing through the sky, highlighting the crashing thunder.

I use my tiny sleeping bag as a cushion, protecting my sore butt from the hard rock floor of my shelter. The ability to get dry is imperative to stave off hypothermia. I dry my hair and the socks to dampness in front of the small fire. My soaked hiking boots sit on the other side of the fire. I doubt they'll be dry by morning.

I boil pinto beans for dinner. Tomorrow I'll set snares and hope for some meat to go with them. I sip water. My loaded gun is right behind me, where I can reach it in one quick movement. I still have the nagging feeling that someone is watching me. I snap my neck around, feeling that it's coming from behind me. I'm alone.

But something is out there. Something that knows I'm here.

I throw the last of the wood on the fire, lay out my mummy-style sleeping bag, and unzip it. Chilled, I pull on the mock turtleneck and my dry socks. I zip the legs back on the pants. I get in the sleeping bag fully clothed, including my lovely survival bracelets, and leave the zipper undone in case I need to get up in a hurry. Lying on my back, I arrange the top section of the bag around my head, with the soothing weight of the gun on my chest. Exhaustion lulls me to sleep in spite of the thunder crashing and the wild dogs howling, amplified and echoing in my alcove. In spite of my fears.

My sleep isn't peaceful. I'm uncomfortable from the inside out. I'm bleeding internally.

I have nightmares about the rape. It's not just Brother Christian— it's all of the Elders. Their faces in mine, their rank breath. Their laughter. Pain. They fight over who goes next. Then I'm face down, my hair held like tight reins. I'm screaming throughout the dream, and the only response is their continual hooting laughter, the fighting, the pounding of their flesh on my flesh, shouts of pleasure and goading each other on, echoing throughout the dream.

Animal sounds. Brutality.

24

I wake up to the sun rising. It's beautiful: the color of pink grapefruit and tangerines shot through with golden rays. It's quiet except for some birds and running water. Running water?

I get up, moaning and groaning about my aches and pains like an old woman. I bled in the night: it soaked through the tampon and left a large dark spot on my pants. I wish, for the first time, that it's from one of my infrequent periods, but I know it's not. It's from the rape. I hope to God that the rape wasn't as bad as the dream. My injuries tell me it was.

Did I really see my attackers, or is my subconscious trying to fill in the blanks of what turned the deranged Barbie reflected in the ceiling mirror into this suffering woman?

Scorching shame fills me. I'm bewildered about the rape. Why did it happen to me? I lie down on the sleeping bag, wishing for death. What do I have to live for? Why should I even try? I'm broken. Defiled. Alone. I cry out in agony and weep uncontrollably, the tears wetting my hair. My shoulders shake with sobs, hurting me until my tears dry up and I can't cry anymore.

I sit up and hold the gun so I'm looking down the barrel, my thumbs caressing the trigger. If I pulled the trigger, would I feel the round enter my skull and take off the back of my head? For seconds, for a minute? I sit there, rubbing the trigger with my thumbs, letting my eyes go out of focus. Fearing death. Wanting it.

Eventually, the gun comes back into focus, and I pull my thumbs from the trigger. I survived what happened to me, and I survived yesterday. I am a survivor, after years of being a sheltered and spoiled child.

Get up, Shea, you've got work to do.

I peer over the ledge to the desert floor and find a small, clear stream running across it. I stumble to it, jerking on my wounds and forgetting to bring anything with me, including the gun that's on the sleeping bag and my supplies for collecting water. I'll have to think more clearly if I'm going to survive.

I go back to get my drypack, inserting the gun in the outer strapwork. I drink all of the remaining water and take two pain pills. I slip on my running shoes. It's easier to put them on than the hiking boots, and the boots are still damp. I go down the ramp to follow the stream, every step hurting.

The stream flows southeast, running down the incline that leads up to my alcove. It heads in the direction of the trees. The rain waters the trees every night and then evaporates in the sun. Maybe I'll get an actual bath today, after filling my water bottles. The thought of it makes me smile, which makes my face hurt. But the sun, the glorious sun! I thought I'd never see it again.

It's drying out the stream, and I hurry, jarring and tearing at my wounds, to the copse of trees, my oasis, to find the trees all standing in water.

It's miraculous to see that the earth is healing itself—or this small area is healing. I saw the destruction the storms were making on our way to Daeios, and now I'm seeing that the rains are helping to heal the earth.

How long was I in Daeios? How long has it taken for the earth to heal so much?

Avoiding the tainted puddle from yesterday, I find the deepest, clearest pool and lay my pack beside it. I fill my water bottles first, performing the purifying ritual. I recoil in pain as I undress, pulling the cloth away from wounds that have stuck to it. The burn marks ooze clear liquid tinged an ugly yellowish-pink. They're my most severe injuries, other than those inside my body.

I step into the cool water. It comes almost to my knees in the deepest part, near the tallest tree. I glance back at the gun. It's a few feet away, but I need to risk being away from it.

Cleaning my wounds thoroughly to ward off infection is vital. An infection out here will kill me. Easing my throbbing body into the pool, I squeeze the bandana in the water, allowing the hardened blood on my nether regions and legs to soften before I start scrubbing. Closing my eyes, I lean back, savoring the coolness.

I sit up with a start, certain that someone is standing right over me. There's no one there. I lie back again but keep my eyes open this time. I startle and glance over my shoulder—no one.

I clean my wounds, shocked as I touch each one, recognize each one. I'm actually getting clean this time, not just bathing in muddy water. The water turns a brownish-pink.

Moving to another small pool to clean my hair, I get the oil and grime out the best I can without shampoo. As I get out of the pool, five deer approach and watch me, their noses and ears twitching. Always something watching me. It's their watering hole, too.

I consider shooting one, but each shot is one bullet gone, and the deer perhaps missed. I'd have to process it, and it's more than I can eat. Maybe I could cut off what I need and leave the rest for the wild dogs and other predators. I've no doubt not an ounce of meat would go to waste. My body convinces me I'm in no condition to do that right now—maybe in a few days if I'm not too weak from hunger or dehydration. Or feeling too sorry for myself to care.

Tucking the towel around me, I turn in a circle with the binoculars. Nothing.

I dry off on the filthy towel and pull on the T-shirt. I can't shrug off the feeling of eyes on me.

I zip the legs off the pants, leaving just the cargo shorts, and stoop to wash them, the running clothes and the towel in a third pool, getting everything reasonably clean except the pants. The pants are stained, so I pull on the running shorts. They'll be dry soon. I pack the rest of the wet clothing in the plastic bags and shove everything into the pack. I'll have to come back for firewood later when some wood has dried out. I leave so the deer can have some water before it evaporates.

My head is so full of plans that I almost forget to insert the tampon.

I return to my shelter, the physical pain lessened a fraction by more painkillers. If only the pills could dull the pain of my troubled mind and aching heart. I stop often to view my surroundings with my binoculars. Always the same, I don't see anything with eyes on me. I wish I could shake this feeling.

The stream that led me to the trees gets gradually smaller until it no longer exists a few feet from the alcove. I've always wanted to stay at the Ritz-Carlton, so name my shelter the Ritz-Carlton, Room 2323. It's a pretty snazzy place, I think in my Brooklyn accent.

My room at the Ritz-Carlton is empty, but after pulling out my survival pack, I know that someone's been there. My pack is in its nook, but with the straps facing me.

Those eyes that have been watching me are human.

I pull everything from my pack, breathing hard. Setting everything down in the same order as before, I run the inventory through my head twice and find that nothing is missing. Not a thief. A spy who wanted to see what I have.

Friend or foe?

I piece the pack back together and place it with the left side facing out this time. Going to the edge of the ledge, I scan as far as I can see with the binoculars, including the tops of the rock formations. I hang the wet laundry from the pack off the ledge of the alcove to dry. Putting on my drypack, I limp around the rest of the rock formation that is the Ritz-Carlton, stopping every few feet to peer through the binoculars. Nothing.

I'm tired, sore, thirsty, and hungry. I return to Room 2323 and cook a handful of beans for breakfast. My stomach declares them the best beans it's ever had. My brain says I need meat, so I eat a piece of jerky, down a bottle of water, and head out to set a snare.

I walk to the oasis, knowing that small animals probably use it, too. Watching for tracks or scat along the way, I'm surprised to see a rabbit run in front of me a few yards away. I advance to where I saw the rabbit and search for a trail. No trail. It wasn't moving along a familiar path.

I don't find any trails or scat until I get to the familiar trees. Going to where I saw the deer this morning, I see that they came in on a well-traveled trail. Probably many types of animals use it. I try to remember the survival camps I attended. (Last year or the year before? How strange to not know what year it is.) Arizona has such varied terrain, from its deserts to alpine tundra, that I took a one-week course in Scottsdale learning desert and urban survival, and a three-day winter survival course in Flagstaff.

My thoughts begin whirling in my mind, scattering like leaves in a windstorm so I can't properly recall my instructor's lesson on setting small game snares. Frames of a film, but they're out of order, some are blurry, and some are missing. My instructor's name was Cody; I see his long blond braids and his strong hands building snares, showing me how to build them, watching me build them, but I'm running them all together in my mind, his hands are empty, and I only see his mouth moving, his hands moving, creating nothing. My sweat turns cold. I'll die if I can't pull myself together. Sitting, I try to piece together what it is I need to do.

Breathing in and out, I inhale the hot sun and the scent of the still water, the musky odor of the animals that have been here, until my mind grasps hold of a picture of the trigger spring snare. It's a page from a book and looks cartoonish. Cody's hands are busy with a noose. He's sitting by a sapling. What did he call the sapling? The engine.

I unravel the bracelet from my right hand and release the small knife it holds. My hands start telling my erratic brain what to do. Cutting off two pieces of the cord, each about two feet long, I place them on the ground before me. Fusing the ends of the remainder of the cord with my fire starter, I coil it and stuff it in my shorts pocket.

Closing my eyes, I try to picture Cody's hands working with the short pieces of cord, but my mind keeps traveling back to his face. His hands. His face. His hands. My brain lights on a thought, and I pull one of the paracord strands apart, forming the inner strands into the noose for my snare, trying to remember how to knot it. I tie the only knot I can think of, a granny knot, knowing it's not right.

I tuck the noose and the other piece of cord into my other shorts pocket and look for wood to use as a base and hook. They need to fit together, the base in the ground and the hook attached to the sapling with the piece of cord. I find two branches with Y shapes that will fit together, and chop away what I don't need with the hatchet.

I try to picture Cody's finished snare and the trap I constructed with his help, but I can't make them look like the snares in my mind. I remember the hook had both the noose and the piece of cord attached to it, one at each end, and tie two more knots that I know aren't right. I find a sapling. The engine. A sapling that stands next to a small pool right in front of the game trail. I pound the base into the ground in front of the water, which will serve as bait for my snare. I tie the loose end of the cord to the sapling. When I set the hook into the base, it bends the sapling over. That part's right.

I hope this snare works.

I follow the game trail to see if it leads off in other directions, or if I find a rabbit den. Nothing.

I go back and set another snare at the watering hole, and a third snare further away from the water on the game trail, baiting it with a dab of peanut butter. By now the merciless sun is high overhead; it feels like I'm in a dry sauna at the gym, the temperature so hot that it's difficult to breathe. I'm sweating hard, but I don't care, I'm too tired to care. I'm too tired to wipe the sweat off until it runs into my eyes and stings them, which brings me back to reality.

I finish the other bottle of water. Filling both bottles, I add the tablets and place them in my bag. They'll be fit to drink by the time I get back to the Ritz-Carlton. The pools have shrunk, and some wood has dried out, so I gather firewood for later, wincing in pain each time I bend or squat to pick it up.

"Hello?" I say as I charge up the wheelchair ramp to my room, making my injuries blare with pain. "Hello?"

No one's there. Whoever it is knows where I'm at and what I'm doing at all times. Knows what I look like naked. Knows I'm injured. Easy prey. I know nothing about him. Or her.

I settle in to prepare something to eat from my dwindling food supplies. It sucks to be hungry with a hollow ache that may have no end except death. I can't remember ever being painfully hungry before, except during The Ordeal. That hunger was nothing compared to this. I hope my snares capture something juicy to eat.

It seems to take forever to build a small fire and to boil the beans. The chocolate from my pack is a melted mess, so I lick it off the wrapper. I may die from this simple pleasure. So many ways to die in the desert.

As the water comes to a boil, I notice the sky is turning dark, the fresh air cooling. If it's like yesterday, I won't be able to leave the Ritz-Carlton until tomorrow. I gather the dried clothing from the ledge and put it and the poncho in my drypack. No thunder yet, but I keep my ears peeled for it.

The fire gives off a loud pop, almost getting me on my feet to run.

By the time my beans are tender, thunder and lightning play in the sky amidst the blurry stars. The stars seem fewer now than before the storms. Watching the lightning show for entertainment, I add a soundtrack by singing some songs I know the words to. Not the Daeios song. I hate that song. I hate Daeios. I ponder Julian's reaction to my being marched away to my breeding, and I just don't get it. How does he feel now that I've disappeared from Daeios? Does he give a shit?

I hope Maya and Mother and Dad are doing okay. I hope rescuing me didn't put them in danger.

Maybe it wasn't all of them. Because of the gun, I know Mother helped me. I can't imagine anyone else would've kept my pack hidden. Someone had to carry me because I was unconscious, so I think my dad was there. If it was all of them, why didn't they stay with me? If it was just my parents, they would've gone back to Maya.

Suddenly my heart feels heavy—they were already in danger. Mother was singled out for punishment in Solitary Confinement during The Ordeal. My sister will reach physical maturity soon. Much too soon. Other than the Elders, Dad and Julian were two of the last men left, and they were getting rid of our men. My heart squelches my anger at Julian. I do still love him and hope Brother Christian is protecting him.

All there is to do at the Ritz-Carlton is eat (very little), sleep (very little), and keep the fire burning once it's dark. The nights are so much longer than the days. Drink water. Dab antiseptic on my wounds. Smear petroleum jelly on my scabby lips. Survive.

I take the gun from the netting on the pack and remove the rounds from the cylinder. Standing the rounds up in a small semicircle in front of me like little sentinels, I dry fire the gun, holding it in both hands. I practice holding it steady as I squeeze the trigger again and again. I practice my aim, blowing my breath out in a slow, steady stream and squeezing the trigger. I hope my aim will be true if I need to use it. Sliding the rounds back into the gun, I close the cylinder and lay the gun next to me.

I'm sleepy but afraid to drift off into nightmares, to be a target of a wild animal, to be a target of that person who is watching me. What if it's more than one? A pack of wild animals. Persons. My mind whirls as I contemplate the danger I'm in: attack, infection, poison, starvation, dehydration, hypothermia. I'll run out of water purification tablets soon and will have to drink unclean water. What if someone steals my supplies? What if I cripple or blind myself? What if my mind unravels like the bracelet?

I feel small in my little alcove, the darkness watching and touching me as I sit behind the flickering, diminishing fire.

25

My nightmares awaken me, screaming. I jolt upright, hurting myself, breathing hard, ready to run, the gun in my hand. It's so dark it's stifling, the air heavy and brooding. My fire is out. I shiver, but not from the cold. It's pouring, with an occasional flash of lightning and a distant grumble of thunder butting in from time to time. What lurks in the midnight darkness below the ledge of my alcove?

As far as I can tell, I'm safe. Safer than I was in Daeios. The raucous laughter and the slapping of their bodies against mine ring in my ears. It's hard to close my eyes again. I try to sort out the voices. Who was there? Were they all there, the Elders? Did they all rape me?

I lie back and try to think of happy thoughts. Santa Claus sliding down the chimney used to help when I was little, but it's not doing anything for me now. Jace crossing the finish line at the triathlon, how happy he was, how excited we all were for him. Maya was jumping up and down and squealing with excitement. This image is replaced by the image of Jace's head blown off. Of Maya jumping up and down and squealing when I was taken to my breeding.

Grasping for another thought, I find a memory of Mother rubbing sunscreen on me as I squirmed and complained, excited to swim in my new red one-piece swimsuit with the ruffles around the waist. I remember her braiding my hair for school, a braid on each side, looping the braids under and tying them with a bow at each ear, telling me how pretty I looked. We always ate home-cooked meals together when I lived at home. Will I ever see her again? Thoughts of my mother, good thoughts, lull me into a fitful sleep until the sun comes streaming in my window at the Ritz-Carlton hotel, middle of nowhere.

I awaken to the sounds of running water again. If the storms have taken up a pattern, I can follow it and survive. Rain means water. As long as the rain continues to provide water, and the land provides food, I have hope of surviving up here. Wherever here is. Unless a storm is too violent and takes my life. I try not to let my mind wander to everything that can go wrong. I have to think positive thoughts.

I failed to save any wood for my morning beans, so intent was I on keeping the fire burning to allay my fears. I eat a piece of beef jerky and take a painkiller with water. Adding the gun to the mesh on my drypack, I set off toward the oasis for water, and, I hope, food. Today's special may be a nice fat rabbit or squirrel. Even a skinny one would be good.

I move faster today, in spite of the jolting pain. I feel raw on the inside. My heart aches at my separation from my family, and my angst about their welfare makes it hard to swallow. I miss Julian too, but I'm not as worried about him. I'm sick with the thought of what someone did to me; something that no one should ever have to endure—brutality of any kind. My thoughts keep circling, making me dizzy. The rape—think of something else—the rape—think of something else. Someone is watching me. My nerves are as raw as my wounds.

I reach the trees and startle some antelope that are drinking there. Well, they look up, they're not exactly startled. I continue toward them, thinking they'll run away, but they don't do so until I'm almost at the water's edge. Finally, one gives a secret signal, and they all turn and run away at once.

I check the snares first. Nothing triggered them. No meat to go with my beans, to expand my food supply for another day. I'll run out of food today. My stomach complains loudly at the thought.

And I'm not going to eat bugs like Cody said we should in survival training. I'll starve first.

I settle into my routine: water bottles, body, face, hair, interrupted by frequent starting and looking around me. I don't see anything but sand, rocks, and the trees and water immediately around me. A bird twitters and then breaks off abruptly.

I'm exposed. I need to take shelter. The eyes know everything about me. My thoughts, my fears.

I scold myself again for not saving some firewood, for the wood here is wet. No boiling water means no beans. My breakfast today will be the last of my beef jerky and some nuts, leaving the peanut butter for bait for as long as I can. My stomach's not going to like that.

I gather everything and place it in my drypack, leaving the gun and the aluminum water bottle in the webbing. I'll come back later to check my snares and fetch firewood and more water. I sure do have to work hard in my new world.

———

As I approach my shelter, I again have the sense that someone, or something, has been there. I feel eyes on the back of my head. When I spin around to face them, I still feel eyes on the back of my head. I'm surrounded by eyes I can't see. My flesh is bumpy with gooseflesh, a chill running up and down from the top of my head to the bottom of my feet.

My supplies. Without thinking of my safety or my injuries, I throw off my daypack and run up the wheelchair ramp with my gun drawn. No one there.

My survival pack is in the same position I left it in. I pull it out and find that everything is on top in the same order as before, and everything that was in the netting is still there. I sit down hard, huffing a big sigh of relief. I need to check my surroundings with the binoculars to see if I spot anyone.

I pull on my daypack, which is a part of me now, a part of my uniform, like my cap, and travel to the side of the Ritz-Carlton opposite my shelter, searching for tracks as I go. No tracks except my own. You would think this area completely deserted, but for the clandestine activity with my pack.

Returning to the Ritz-Carlton, I settle in for the last of my jerky and almonds. The eyes watch me eat. The wounds in my mouth are healing; the pepper of the beef jerky and the salt on the almonds don't burn as they did when I first woke up aboveground. I inspect the sores on my body, the edges pulling together, the thick scabs held to my limbs by red, raised skin. Seeing them makes me long to scratch them to relieve the itch.

I know that I should look for another shelter. Perhaps the eyes belong to other Daeiosians who were sent to find me. They're coming after me to return me to Daeios so the Elders can punish me. Perhaps the gun on my pack is fending them off for now. But my injured body isn't up to walking around in the desert looking for anything suitable that's near a water supply. And the storms limit the amount of time I'll have to return to the Ritz-Carlton for my large pack. Right now my body is too damaged and tender to carry such a heavy pack. I'm stuck here for a while.

Once I do heal, I'll look for Daeios and rescue my family. My bond with them keeps calling to me. I'm incomplete without them. I ache for them. I worry that I'm already too late to save them. Or maybe they found a way to escape and I'm merely returning into the Elders' evil hands.

Julian, are you safe? Will you let me take you away from Daeios so we can be together?

The Elders. I want them not just dead but ripped from the earth in pieces. Unidentifiable chunks of flesh and bone burned to gray ash and then scattered in the wind until they no longer exist. I imagine myself carrying out their implausible fates, a different one for each Elder, with tools I'll never possess: a mace; an auger; a guillotine; a wood-chipper. Each Elder dying a more hideous death than the one before.

Fearing I'll morph into madness, I force the hatred and revenge from my thoughts, my mind swirling with questions. How long was I unconscious before awakening? How many days have I been up here? How many days before I can physically look for Daeios?

And, in the middle of the questions for which I have no answers, I remember the kind of knot to tie for my snares.

26

In spite of the storms rolling in soon, I head back to the pools a second time to set my snares correctly. Perhaps I'll have meat for breakfast tomorrow.

The pools are barely puddles now, too low to fill the water bottle I drained heading back to the shelter and then coming here again. It doesn't leave enough for cooking my beans and drinking too. I'll have to sleep on an empty stomach, and I already have enough trouble sleeping. My body needs food for healing. I'm using energy to survive that I need to restore myself to good health. These snares, actual snares, must pay off soon or I'll perish.

The granny knots I used on the snares are impossible to get out, so I cut off more of the cord from my shorts pocket, tying overhand knots, running the other end of the cords through the loops to create the nooses. I have to place another small blob of peanut butter on the snare that doesn't use water as bait, for the peanut butter that was there this morning is gone. I can't resist eating a small glob of it before returning it to my pack.

The snares should work now.

A grumble of thunder sounds in the far distance. The clouds are coming in like sheep from a field. Dark grey sheep. I pack up some dry wood and put on my garbage bag rain poncho and head for the Ritz-Carlton. Another night of monotony and fear is on the agenda.

I reach my shelter just as the rain starts, and by the time I'm up the ramp it's pouring, the temperature dropping. My muscles and insides are aching as I change into my long-sleeved turtleneck and long pants. It's as I'm stacking the branches for my fire that I notice my fingernails again. They're ragged, the tips broken and uneven, with crescents of my natural nails peeking through the nail polish near my cuticles. I don't want it on me, so I chip away at it with my fingernails, getting most of it off. My toenails are a different story; I'll have to live with the polish there until it wears off.

My days continue wearisomely the same as one another. My snares are catching small game now, jackrabbits and squirrels, although occasionally I'll have a day without meat. I've eaten all of the food from my pack except the peanut butter. I build spits behind my shelter and cook my meals on them, spinning the spits every so often to keep the meat from burning, and scanning the horizon with my binoculars for predators.

I visit the oasis twice a day getting water and wood, retrieving the animals and resetting the snares. Sometimes a rabbit or squirrel is alive in the trap and I have to kill it with my hunting knife. Only a few water purification tablets remain. I work around the storms. My body continues to heal as I have more to eat, which helps me to sleep. The nightmares occur less frequently but haven't loosened their grip on me completely.

My mind is occupied by the future rescue. My main obstacle is not knowing where Daeios is. It has to be within the range of fuel for a vehicle to come and return to Daeios, but I don't know how far that is. How will I gain access? The Daeiosians may protect the Elders from me. The Elders may imprison me. Rape me. Kill me.

It frustrates me to sit and plan the break-in and not be able to do anything about it. I practice dry-firing the gun every night. I hone my hunting knife so the blade stays razor sharp. When I'm healed, I'll work my way around the directions of the compass, seeking new shelters and water supplies and Daeios. In spite of my fear of heights, I'll climb up high so I can search the landscape for a longer distance. I must force myself to be brave.

I increase my exercise from my daily walks to and from the copse to incorporate running, earning stitches in my side. Wearing my large pack, I do squats, increasing the supplies it holds each day. I do pushups until I'm shaking.

In my mind, I hunt each Elder down and destroy him, finishing each one slowly and painfully. Getting vengeance for my rape, retribution for Jace. It adrenalizes my workouts.

I no longer find the pack disturbed. But the eyes still watch me.

27

The day finally arrives that I can start putting my plan into action for finding Daeios. For rescuing my family and taking the Elders from power, for annihilating them for what they did to me and Jace. Surely Julian will help me when I tell him what the Elders did to me. My insides no longer feel raw and my outer wounds are raised shadows of what they once were. I have healed enough to go out seeking what my sick heart requires: my loved ones and my revenge.

I change into my running clothes, stuff my hiking boots into the survival pack, and put the pack in its nook, the straps facing out. Leaving the alcove with my drypack on, my binoculars in hand, I head south according to the compass on my wrist. I have a full stomach and I'm well-rested. I need to keep in mind that the storm clouds roll in in the late afternoon, and I only have so much water for today's trek if I don't find another source. The odds of finding water lessen as the day heats up.

Will I find Daeios? Will seeing its entrance splinter my mind and leave me to wander the desert, delirious, until I die?

My travel is slow. I scan frequently with the binoculars, looking for landmarks to memorize. I don't find a new water source or anything that would work as a shelter.

After a while, I approach an area of tumbled limestone boulders that resemble a pileup on I-17. I circle them, searching for an easy way up to the top rock for a better view. The eyes bore through my back and I feel uneasy.

This isn't especially high, but I have to picture Mother, calm and steady, encouraging me to climb it. I place my hand flat on the sun pendant on my chest to center me and stand atop the rock formation. Making sure I'm nowhere near the edge, I turn in circles looking through the binoculars, my ponytail blowing in the breeze, noting a few landmarks that I'll check out on future searches. Warm-hued layers of sandstone in shades from salmon to brick, shaped and smoothed by the wind. Pillars and eyes of needles. No satellite dish or radio antenna. I climb down to continue my journey.

When I look up from stepping down to the ground, I freeze. A woman is drawing back a bow, an arrow pointed at my head. My gun's in the netting on my daypack.

A blood-freezing yowl behind me makes my hair rise to the point that it has to be shooting off my body.

I spin around to face a bristling mountain lion above me on the highest boulder. I was just there.

Throwing off my pack, I release the .44 Magnum from its webbing. I point my gun wildly in its direction. It issues another yowl of warning, its mouth wide and filled with razor-sharp teeth. The lion crouches, muscles twitching, and appears ready to attack, only feet from where I stand.

My heart is beating so hard I'm afraid it will burst from my chest.

The woman rushes up to stand beside me as the lion squalls. The arrow aimed up at the lion. The arrow released. The arrow hits the lion's front leg and sticks, making it fiercer.

Aiming at its chest, I try to calm my breathing. Air bursts from my lungs and I'm lightheaded. I shoot one of my precious six rounds at the animal. The gun kicks out of my control, and the bullet goes wild.

The lion launches toward us, screaming. The woman beside me pulls the bow as I aim again, focusing all my strength and wits on holding the gun steady. I shoot twice as I run from its path, hoping a bullet hits my target. The woman releases another arrow and runs the opposite direction from me.

The big cat pounces on the spot I vacated, just feet away from me, making my mind go blank for one terrifying moment. Shaking myself from my stupor, I turn and shoot it in the head as it crouches and hisses at me. Its head explodes into blood and gore, a warm splatter landing on my arm.

I turn around to face the woman who fought next to me. She's now stretching the bowstring back again, an arrow pointing at my chest.

Adrenaline surges through my veins, telling me I have two more bullets. Telling me to shoot again. The gun is shaking in my hand. My hand comes into focus—I'm pointing it at her. I lower it to my side. Gaining control of my voice, I say, "I won't hurt you. Please lower your bow."

She eases the tension on the bowstring, the arrow still pointed at me, feeling me with her eyes. After a moment she lowers it to her side. Her muscles are tense and ready to spring to action if I flinch the wrong way.

We stand assessing each other for a moment. She fidgets as she looks at me, her head turned slightly away.

Trying to shake off the fear, my mind racing in circles, her pale blue eyes. Her baby-fine blonde hair, bleached almost white from the sun, is only a couple of inches long. She's deeply tanned. She's dirty and smells sour and looks wild. But there's no mistaking that this is Sister Grace.

She's the one they sent after me. To bring me back to Daeios. The Elders. My gun feels itchy in my hand.

I'm compelled to look over my shoulder, imagining others are creeping up behind me.

"No one's there." She speaks slowly, in the lower register of her voice. After searching my face a moment with her unreadable eyes, she pulls a quiver off her shoulder and places the arrow in it, her bow lying benignly near her foot. Her moves are meticulous as she seeks the perfect place for the lone arrow to join the others.

As she's absorbed by her task, I study her. Any roundness has left her cheeks. She's ripped and looks much fitter than I am. She's dressed in fitness wear, a too-short black tank top and skirt. Her sneakers have the fronts cut off to release her toes. She wears them with white Daeios socks scrunched around her ankles. Both are covered in red dirt. She has a tan leather belt with a sheathed hunting knife around her waist. Attached to the belt are a coiled climbing rope and a small chamois pouch. She wears an Army-issue canteen across her body.

She stands, pulling back her lips and showing her teeth. Her eyes crinkle. An unsteady smile. Feral. I'd say she's been up here for a while. Banished. The Elders didn't send her but she may be just as dangerous if she's lost her mind.

"Sister Shea?"

"Sister Grace."

She shoulders the quiver and bow and reaches down for my pack, her eyes on me. She holds it at arm's length. "You were rescued. You have survival gear."

So it was her crystalline blue eyes I felt on me. She went through my pack. She knows where I live.

"So do you. Were you rescued too?" I lay my pack beside me, my gaze holding hers.

I'd forgotten how tall she is, probably about six foot. She gives me that untamed smile again. My smile is fighting to the surface when she speaks.

"Banished. They brought me to the desert and left me to die." She swallows, the muscles in her neck working.

"In your Daeios clothes? Where did you get what you have now?" It comes out harsh, an accusation.

She draws back and speaks defensively. "They took me from my breeding. I was naked. They left me out here with nothing. I found a woman at the bottom of a cliff. Over there." She points southeast. "I took everything she had. She didn't need it anymore." She narrows her eyes. "Your head's not shaved. Were you bred?"

I want to scream at her that I wasn't bred. I was raped. But she's not the one I'm mad at. I say nothing.

"I almost died." Her voice is lifeless, her lucent eyes as cold and sharp as cracked ice.

It seems we stand like that for a long time, not talking, looking for answers in each other's eyes. Flies buzz around the lion carcass. The sky gives a warning growl.

"The storms will come soon," she says as I don my pack. "Your shelter's too far away. Come with me." She turns on her heel and heads toward the cliffs.

28

I turn to face the direction of the Ritz-Carlton. The sun is behind clouds, and a chill breeze that smells of rain rustles my hair. There's no way I can make it to my shelter before the storms come in. I'll have to take a chance with Sister Grace.

When I look behind me, Sister Grace has put a lot of distance between the two of us. I run to catch up and fall into step beside her. As we trudge toward her shelter, gray clouds are rapidly overtaking any white clouds left in the sky.

"Run!" Sister Grace shouts after a while, so I start to run, my pack jostling on my back, wondering what we're running from.

I'm out of breath when the wind picks up, kicking up the dry sand, which stings my skin and eyes. By the time we reach the shelter, the clouds loom dark overhead, and the air is thick and moist, charged with electricity.

Sister Grace disappears while my eyes are scrunched closed against the sand, my hands on my thighs, trying to catch my breath. When I open them I see a cave entrance and dig my running headlamp from my pack. Tamping down my claustrophobia and fear of the darkness as best I can, I enter with the light switched on.

"Hello? Sister Grace?" No answer.

I shine my light around the cave and recoil in shock. Seven white wool Daeios gowns are placed around the cave, like sisters in a prayer circle. Sister Grace has hunted down other banished women and is collecting their gowns like pelts. I crouch down to pick up a gown and look at the inside of the neckline, where the name is written in laundry marker: *Sister Evangeline*.

An odor fills the space and I almost gag. "So you've met the other sisters," Sister Grace says as she enters the cave from behind me, a tiny flashlight in her hand adding light to the small space.

I stand up, my heart racing in my chest. She's blocking the cave entrance. "They keep me company at night," she says, taking Sister Evangeline's gown from my hands and laying it down carefully with the others, straightening it into place, patting it. "Stop looking at me like I'm crazy. I didn't kill them. They don't need the gowns anymore. So I took them," she says, her eyes in shadow so I can't see their expression.

Are Mother and Maya's gowns among this collection? "My family?" A sick twist in my stomach.

"I would tell you if I'd seen them." Sister Grace runs her hands through her stringy hair, smoothing it back and off her forehead.

"The woman you said you found at the bottom of the cliff?"

"I didn't kill her—she fell. And I won't kill you, Sister Shea. We need each other. We kill lions together." A savage grin twitches to the surface of her face.

I swallow several times, trying to swallow the fear that's threatening to choke me. I'm breathless when I say, my voice small and shaking, "Where are the bodies? Will you show me the bodies when the storm passes?" I want to see how they died, to see if they were punctured by arrows or gutted by her knife.

"Predators got to them." Tender, naked women with buns, pulled apart by sharp teeth and carried away piece by piece, leaving nothing.

She watches me walk to each gown, as if I'm introducing myself, checking the necklines to make sure Mother and Maya's gowns aren't among them. I didn't know any of these women.

She looks me in the eye, that animal grin on her face. "I haven't seen any banished for a while, now."

The Elders must be done with banishing.

We won't have a fire to warm us tonight because a fire would smoke us out in this enclosed space. I don't have my long sleeves and long pants or my sleeping bag. Sister Grace gathers up the seven Daeios gowns and offers four to me for making up a bed, showing how she wears one and places one on the ground and one over her as covers. I place two on the ground and use two as covers. No way I'm slipping a Daeios gown over my head.

Daeios gowns encasing me may keep me warm, but the feel of the wool against my skin ignites my paranoia. I lie back with the gun on my chest, wearing my running headlamp switched on, hoping for sleep and trying to ignore Sister Grace's fetid smell. To ignore the fact she may have lured me here to take my daypack and my gun. To ignore the fact she may have gone insane up here by herself. The closeness of the cave stokes my claustrophobia. My skin crawls within the Daeios gowns.

"Afraid of the dark?"

"Yep." I can't hide it. "There was a night of darkness in Daeios, and—"

"The night I was banished."

I lie there for a bit, then sit up, shrugging gowns into my lap.

Sister Grace sits up too. She covers her eyes. "Your light is blinding me."

I take the headlamp off and light up our faces. It reminds me of summer camp when we used to distort the scary faces we made with a flashlight beam held underneath our chins. It's creepier than I remember. I lay the light on the ground between us, facing sideways.

"Why were you banished? Do you know?"

"I guess I'm not good in bed." The left side of her mouth tilts up.

A grimace or a smile? Something human. I favor her with the frowning half smile I learned from my mother.

"Brother James, uh, couldn't do it. I think that's why," she says. "I was disappointed, although I'd been saving myself for marriage. Wanting the Elders to breed me was—"A crash of thunder drowns her out. " ... crazy. I look back now and can't believe I was excited to breed. With an old man. Outside of marriage. I would fight him off now." She accents this with a shake of her head, perhaps a shudder. She clenches her eyes closed and opens them again. "The nonbreeders cleaned me up. Shaved my head. Two women with guns took me to Security."

They have guns in Daeios, I file away. Obstacles.

"Where's Security?" I'm hungry for insider information that can help me in Daeios.

"It's in the north section. In the corner. Same side as the Spa."

Door 5. That leaves Door 2 and Door 6 unknown.

"So how'd they get you out?"

"In an ATV. They told the gate agent they were banishing me. She let us through the main gate."

"Did they leave you near Daeios?"

"No idea."

I scrutinize each facial expression, the timbre of her voice, looking for tells that she's lying to me. Her eyes shine in the light of the headlamp and she never wavers from looking into mine. It's unnerving, that steady stare, although she's becoming less wild before my eyes.

"I wandered around, my skin cooked by the sun and my feet blistered by the hot sand. I took the best shelter I could find when the storms started rolling in. Whenever I found water, I drank as much as I could. After a couple of days, I was lucky enough to find the dead woman. I was barely strong enough to get these clothes off her." She's looking through me now, gone with the memory.

Thunder booms overhead, bringing her back to me. For the first time, I notice the rain pounding on the ground outside the cave entrance.

"Why did you need to be rescued, Sister Shea?" She watches for the effect of her words on my face.

"I blacked out." My story tumbles out of me, lifting a burden from my shoulders in the telling. "I have no idea how far my rescuers brought me, or if someone might come after me. At first I thought they sent you after me, but you've been up here too long for that."

Her gaze is unwavering. "I have been up here for a while. Why did you need to be rescued?" she repeats, her words staccato. Her shadow on the cave wall behind her seems to grow.

"I fought Brother Christian off," I say, my voice defiant. The name slithers over me and down my back.

She looks stricken. "Why would you fight it? You didn't believe it was your calling from God?"

"Not my God. I think they gang-raped me." My voice is treacherously close to quivering. "I have nightmares, and it's all of them." I shrink from the image, my face burning, a lump in my stomach.

"Are you pregnant?" It's barely a whisper.

"I hope not. I don't want children. And I wouldn't want it to be one of theirs if I did."

"A baby out here would complicate things."

Babies always complicate things. When we leave Daeios, if I'm pregnant, I can have the pregnancy terminated, if I'm not too far along. I must hurry.

"I don't want to talk about this anymore." I stare at my hands in my lap.

"Sister Shea? I know I scare you. I can only imagine how I look. But I was joshing you about the gowns keeping me company. They keep me warm at night. That's all."

That's not the only thing about her that scares me. "Maybe we should get some sleep."

"Okay," she says through an enormous vocal yawn. She lies down and is almost instantly asleep. I lie there with my lit headlamp on my head—my new fashion statement—and listen to her soft snoring. Will she let me leave in the morning? Will she come after me if I do? I fight my fatigue for as long as I can, then fall into a troubled sleep.

A scream rises from my throat. A heavy weight presses on my shoulders, keeping me from moving. The Elders.

"I've got you," Sister Grace says, her voice quiet and even. "Stop struggling."

That brutish grin on her face, a slash of wild blue eyes in the light of my running headlamp, the sharp smell of her. I can't feel the gun on my chest.

"Get off me," I manage to say. It comes out little more than a terse suggestion.

"You were having a nightmare. I tried to wake you up and you started thrashing around. I was afraid you'd hurt yourself. Or me." She eases her hands off my shoulders.

I'm winded and my heart is beating so fast I can hear it. "Where's my gun?"

She reaches a distance, picks up the gun. Tonight is the night I'll die.

"Promise me you won't shoot me? This gun is the reason I didn't approach you sooner. I want us to trust each other. I want us to be friends." She places the gun near me. "I won't hurt you. You said that to me earlier." Her eyes look gentle now and the brutish grin is gone.

I open the chamber to check for rounds. They're both still there.

"We work together. We survive together," she says.

Even without the gun, it wouldn't take much for her to overpower me. I'm smaller than her. Less fit. But maybe, if she does have one shred of humanity left, she can help me find my loved ones. I'll take the risk for them.

I sit there another minute, reading her. The feral smile is gone—perhaps I imagined it. Her eyes stare back at me nonthreateningly. Have I been viewing her through a fear filter, or is she dangerous?

"I'm looking for Daeios. You can help me."

She holds her arms up, palms facing me. "I'm not going back there. We both almost died because of Daeios. Stay with me. I've been going crazy up here alone."

"I have to get my family out of Daeios. Help me. We can get your family too."

She sits for a moment, picking at the dirt under her broken nails. When she looks up, she asks, "How do you expect to get in?"

How will I get in? "I'll find a way."

She lies down with her back to me. Sleep comes fast for her.

She's not going to help me. She may try to keep me from leaving her. From finding Daeios.

I return to my bedding with the gun on my chest. If they're no longer banishing Daeiosians, what has become of them? What has become of my family and Julian?

It takes me a long time to get to sleep, enfolded in the arms of the woolen gowns.

I wake up to find Sister Grace gone. I have to return to my shelter for my survival pack, then find a shelter she doesn't know about. And leave no tracks for her to follow.

She has placed the three Daeios gowns she slept in in their allotted spaces around the cave. The four I used are in a pile at my feet. She pops in behind me and I shriek.

She frowns and shakes her head at me. She sorts the gowns by name and places each one in its proper spot while I contemplate making a run for it. Yeah, right.

"Water and food. I've got wood. Come help me."

I need water for returning to the Ritz-Carlton, so I follow her a few yards behind her shelter to a spring that I can't see the bottom of, though the water is clear.

"It's clean water." I fill my water bottles, drink from one and then fill it to the top again.

She leads me to a small pond where she has set up snares similar to mine using water as bait. I kneel down as she removes a jackrabbit from a snare. She made the noose and leader line from fibers and bark from green branches. Her survival training was better than mine.

Sister Grace takes me further east, to some bushes covered in red berries. She explains that the dark red berries are safe to eat but to avoid the bright red berries, which are poisonous. She goes back to the shelter to start roasting the jackrabbit and leaves me to pick berries. How long would it take her to notice if I left? How quickly could she catch up to me?

The berries draw me to them and I gobble a few, savoring their juice and their sweetness, sedating my fear of her for now. I resolve that she will help me find Daeios. I wrap a small pile of berries carefully in my bandana and return to the site to find the rabbit nearly done.

In spite of the pressing nature of finding my endangered family and rescuing them from religious maniacs, my biggest concern today is to get Sister Grace to bathe and wash her clothes. She may seem less dangerous to me if she smells human. "Where do we clean up?"

"There's a pond over there you can use," she says, gesturing in an ambiguous direction without looking up from her task.

"Let's go together. We work together and survive together, right?" I show her my most charming smile.

She looks at me like she's either trying to read my mind or has the sun in her eyes. "Okay. After we eat."

I eat at what I thought would be a comfortable distance from Sister Grace, but my gag reflex goes into overdrive and I put my food aside in spite of my hunger.

She finishes her meal and we go to the pond to clean up. At first, I'm self-conscious about bathing naked in front of Sister Grace, of her seeing the wreck of my skin, but she doesn't look at me. She comments that the water feels good, but balks at cleaning her clothing. "I don't want to walk around in wet clothes."

"They'll dry quickly in the heat. Animals can smell your scent on your clothes and might track you." Or they might invite her to join them since she smells as bad as them.

I'm right. When Sister Grace is clean, she seems less animal. Her eyes make me think of snow on the mountain at twilight.

"You're sure you want to find that hellhole?" she asks as she puts on her gear.

"It's not a choice for me. I miss my family and Julian more every day, not less. It's my one wound that isn't healing. And I have business with the Elders," I say, my molars tightening. I tell her about my plan to search around the directions of the compass.

"Let's go east today, then," she says and heads in that direction.

As we move east the land gradually becomes verdant with foliage. Swathes of grass leave dew on our shoes. As we pass under a deciduous tree, a drop of water trickles down my neck like a cold finger. I can't help but feel that eyes are on me—and they're not Sister Grace's. We're being followed. As I look behind me, I walk into a spider's web and perform a spider web dance, my skin crawling with tiny, eight-legged creatures that I hope are imaginary.

Sister Grace places her index finger to her lips to motion I be silent. I freeze in place. She begins walking, stealthily, and I follow suit.

Something crunches nearby while we're in an area with low-hanging branches. We stop moving, listening, holding our breath. Quiet footfalls approach us—human footfalls. We take cover behind a bush, my heart beating in my throat.

"We know you're there," a man says. "And we know where you live." Eyes.

We come out of hiding, Sister Grace with her knife held out in front of her. Four people stand in the clearing, holding an array of weapons pointed at us. A bow and arrow. A spear. A hatchet. A hunting knife. They're not flawless, alabaster-skinned, blue-eyed robots from Daeios.

A man and woman are First American. The other two are white women, but with tattoos and piercings. These people are not Elites, which means they hate us.

"We're looking for a place," Sister Grace says like she's standing in the mall asking for directions. Only the knife she grips, her knuckles white, betrays her unease. "Have you seen a rock formation surrounded by a fence with a satellite dish and radio antenna?"

"What I see," the man says, his teeth held together and his jaws strained tight, "is two people hunting on our grounds. This land won't support any more people. Leave." His hand clenches his knife.

"And if we don't?" Sister Grace takes a step toward them. They raise their weapons. A white woman's nostrils flare and a growl emanates from her throat.

"We'll go," I say to Sister Grace, struggling to hold my voice steady and pulling her back by the elbow. She allows me to pull her but glares at the man. "We'll go," I repeat, meeting the man's fierce dark eyes this time. They don't know we're Elites because we don't look like Elites anymore. We're merely a threat to their subsistence.

The man speaks, his voice low and threatening. "We'll be watching you."

"Come on, Sister Grace," I say. We back away from the non-Elites until they turn and leave us. In one quick motion, Sister Grace sheathes her knife and reaches for her bow. I stay her hand.

"We have just as much right to be here as they do. I don't see why—"

"We're heading in the wrong direction. Daeios can't be that way. Do you remember how barren it is around Daeios from when you arrived? It's pure desert, and no amount of the earth's healing would make it this green." It must be safe to live in the cities now. I bet people have been rebuilding while we were stuck in Daeios. We can go home.

We walk in silence to the shelter, our movements large in disagreement.

The sky is starting to cloud up. Large dark clouds crowding in small white clouds, wolves in a herd of sheep. We begin running to her shelter as freezing rain starts pelting us, collecting in our eyes. It could hail.

We're unable to check the snares or pick berries. Hostility and hunger fill our empty stomachs as we lie, cold and damp, in the Daeios gowns. Tension radiates from Sister Grace like heat from a fire. It fills the cave until I can barely breathe. She hasn't sunk into her usual quick deep sleep and I wonder if she'll cut my throat if I should fall asleep. I should've left today when I had the chance.

Soothe the savage beast, they say. "Sister Grace?" I sit up and put the running headlamp on the floor between us as before. "Can I ask you about your family? I never saw you with anyone."

She doesn't answer and I think she'll spend the rest of the night plotting numerous ways to kill me. After a long moment, she lets loose a heavy sigh and sits up, rearranging the Daeios gowns around her. I'm surprised at the mildness of her voice.

"I was supposed to meet my family at Daeios—my parents and my little brothers. I ran out of gas outside the gate into Daeios, so I walked the rest of the way. I was soaked, and bruised by the hail. They locked Daeios down before my parents could get there." She pauses, and a single tear traces down her cheek. She blinks a couple of times. Nothing more.

She has no reason to return to Daeios. She's all alone in this world.

"I know we didn't really talk, but I've always felt a bond with you, Sister Shea. The other sisters didn't include us. It made me feel like a woman on the outside looking in." She gives me a soft smile. "I went to Brother Jace's wake after you relieved me in the Fitness Room. He was really cute in his picture."

"He was really cute. He was a great guy." We sit in silence. I drop my eyes under the intensity of her luminous blue ones, not knowing what to do with my hands.

It's a long time before she speaks. "Tell me about the necklace. I saw it in Daeios when you dropped it in the dressing room."

I finger the sun, rubbing my fingers along the roughness of the diamonds on the rays. "My mother gave it to me. It reminds me how much she loves me. Whenever I feel it around my neck it reminds me of her." I have reinvented history, cutting Scott from my past and forging a bond with Mother. My eyes meet Sister Grace's as I say, "We have to find Daeios." It's eating me up inside that my family may be in danger and I can't find them. I yearn for Mother's arms. To be held by my dad as he calls me "Princess." To smell Maya's baby powder scent again when she lays her head on my shoulder. And Julian, how I long to see him again, to kiss him again.

Sister Grace pulls me away from my thoughts. "Brother Julian. What was he like?"

Julian. When I return to Daeios, what will happen when I see him? Will the hummingbirds take flight as before? Will he believe me when I tell him what Brother Christian and the other Elders did to me? Will he accept my scars? "Well, he's funny. He has a beautiful singing voice." He ate my peas.

"Did he ever try anything with you?"

"No," I say, covering my mouth after an outburst of laughter. She smiles uncertainly. "Julian was too devout. More so than I was. I tried having sex with him to get pregnant so I wouldn't have to breed. He wouldn't do it."

She frowns, shaking her head. "The rest of us are all gaga about breeding and you're trying to figure out how to avoid it. How come?"

"My mother didn't get it either. Maybe because we're both bipolar ..."

It hits me like a slap to the back of my head. The paranoia, the suicidal depression, being unable to think clearly when I was trying to set snares because my manic mind was racing. All bipolar symptoms. I started feeling this way almost immediately after awakening aboveground, but why? I was okay in Daeios without the Xanadoxalate.

Unless I was taking it without knowing it.

"Drink up!" Brother Christian says in my head, and I picture everyone obediently sucking water from their Daeios water pack tubes. We carried the packs around with us and sipped water all day long. It has to be in the water. Xanadoxalate. X.

That's why Mother and I didn't feel what everyone else felt—the enchantment of Daeios. The X kept us stable but made the others pliable, suggestible. It explains the change in my dad, Maya's lack of concern about Jace's death, Julian's unquestioning happiness about my breeding.

Oh, Julian, you are in danger. You've been in danger the entire time.

Mother was right. The Elders planned the breedings all along.

29

"Sister Shea? Hello?"

I tell Sister Grace my suspicion.

Her blue eyes widen as she thinks it over. "So ... you were clear-headed in Daeios and feel that your bipolar disorder is causing you problems up here ... and because of that, you think I was excited about being bred because I was drugged and brainwashed?"

I nod. "Am I crazy?"

Her frown deepens. "Well, from my experience? I didn't even question being bred by the Elders, when my first time was to be with my husband, whenever he came along. No. No, I don't think you're crazy." She shudders. "No wonder you fought off Brother Christian."

Do the Elders know the X doesn't brainwash bipolars? Do they know Mother has bipolar disorder, and if so, is she in more danger than Dad and Maya? My mind scrambles back to our hurried entrance to Daeios, when we were more concerned about Jace's gloss overdose and Dad's head injury than anything else. Brother Michael. Brother Michael knew ... and then Sister Bethany had us remove our bracelets. They know about Mother.

The next morning I'm irritable, having been awake half the night listening to the struggle between the wind and the rain. Fretting about not knowing how to find Daeios. Trying to fill in the blanks of what I'll do when I get there. I'll seek my family and Julian. I'll get irrevocable justice for what they did to Jace and me. Finding Daeios is only the first obstacle. Getting into Daeios may be just as difficult, if not more so.

As we prepare to leave the shelter, I explain to Sister Grace that we need to use the Ritz-Carlton as our shelter and search for Daeios from there.

"If your mother was able to get you out, she could get them all out. They're probably not even there."

"I have to find out. It's all I think about. Being with my family again. Being with Julian. Making sure they're alright." And making sure the Elders never hurt anyone again.

"I'm not going to Daeios," she says with a jut of her chin.

"It's not just those I love. Everyone in there is being held against their will because their will has been taken from them. There's no reason why any of them need to be there when the earth has healed. Once the X is out of their systems, we have hundreds of witnesses to what they've been doing to us in God's name."

"I consented," she says, her voice toneless.

"You were on a mind-altering drug. You were incapable of consenting to anything. Brother James planned to rape you. The Elders made choices about our bodies. I want to stop them. I'm only telling you this so you understand that I'll leave you if you don't go with me. It's not a choice for me." Will she try to stop me?

"There's no one there I care about." A rise and fall of her shoulders, sucking breath in and blowing it out.

"Don't you want to punish the Elders for what they did to you? They left you to die."

The cave is quiet; the wind outside has died away.

"But I didn't," she replies after a long silence. "And I won't. With you or without you." She ducks out of the cave.

I follow her out, tucking my headlamp into my pack.

"I think my shelter is closer to Daeios than this one is. The landscape is the same. Come with me, Sister Grace. Just help me find it, then do whatever you want to once I'm there." Dad said something similar to me when he asked me to help them find Jace. Perhaps I never should have. I would never have gone to live in Daeios then. Jace might be alive now. But Mother and Dad and Maya would have gone, and they would still be in danger. And I wouldn't know.

She's silent for a moment, her back straight, her eyes shiny and distant. Perhaps she's thinking of her family that never made it to Daeios.

I need to get on my way. I put on my pack. She's looking down now, her eyes hooded from mine. I hear her swallow.

She snaps her head up like she's afraid it won't move without momentum. Her eyes are wide with fright.

"I'll take you there, Sister Shea. I know where Daeios is."

30

"You've known where Daeios was all this time and didn't tell me? You looked me right in the eye and said you had no idea where it was!" My words increase in volume as the last sentence nears the end.

"Forgive me, Sister Shea. I was trying to protect you. And I'm not happy that you'll be leaving me. But it'll take you days, maybe weeks to find Daeios on your own, and I won't put you through that. I would do what you're doing if it were my family and my boyfriend in there. I'll take you to Daeios, Sister Shea, but that's as far as I go."

I was right, the Ritz-Carlton is closer to Daeios than we are at this shelter. I'm ready to go, and watching Sister Grace decide what to bring with her is grinding on me like I'm chewing pebbles. My patience is unraveling. She doesn't have much to consider. She finally settles on folding up three Daeios gowns, tying them in a bundle with a length of the climbing rope and tying it to her back over her gear.

"You're sure this is what you want to do? We can live well up here. We're free."

"I'm sure. Let's go," I say, drawing out the "o", and heading in the direction of the Ritz-Carlton. I feel a spike of anger and hold back hot words. It could be my bipolar brain having a temper tantrum and I can't let the mania take control. I can't risk alienating her now.

"How far is it to Daeios?" I ask when we've walked a few minutes.

"It'll take us a couple of days. I could see Daeios from where they left me in the desert. I've tried to purge the directions to Daeios from my mind. Now you're making me remember. My first few days up here were a nightmare."

"You do remember, don't you? We're not just heading in the general direction and hoping to stumble across it as we go? I could do that on my own."

"I can get you there in a couple of days. It would take you much longer to stumble upon it, I promise. I do remember."

She's draining her canteen and I'm drinking all of my water from one water bottle. There won't be enough water to fill them by the time we make it to the Ritz-Carlton, so we have just the one water bottle until morning. The snares aren't set, so we won't have any food. There should be some dried wood for a fire.

"Did you watch Daeios, Sister Grace? Did you see any other activity outside after you were banished?"

"I just walked away, Sister Shea. There was never anything in Daeios I needed but food, clothing, and shelter. I've got that here now."

"What about the banished sisters you found up here? Did you get a chance to talk to any of them before they died?"

"They were all dead when I found them," she snaps.

"Okay, okay. That's the first thing I'll do when we get to Daeios. I'll watch for a way to get in."

"And if you can't get in? Will you find me?"

"I'll find a way in if it destroys me." Saying it makes something scurry down my spine.

"It just might. If they see you out there, they'll come out and drag you back into Daeios and punish you for escaping. They won't banish you, so what will they do to you? They'll kill you."

A bird of prey soars soundlessly above us in the rippled sky.

I think of the cameras that were watching us. They were listening to us. Of course, they have security set up outside. I'll have to look for cameras and disable them. I don't know how to do that. I try not to think of all the horrific things they could do to me besides kill me. Solitary confinement? Torture? Will they rape me again?

"You can't just walk in there and drive out with your family and Brother Julian. The Daeiosians may try to stop you. They're brainwashed, if you're correct. They may protect the Elders."

I've been concentrating so hard on finding my family and getting them out of there that I haven't really thought of the other obstacles. In my mind, Daeios has been empty except for the Elders and my family and Julian. But the remaining Daeiosians will be there and may try to stop me. How will I handle them? I don't want to kill them, or even injure them.

"I used to explore the north end of Daeios, trying to find out why they forbade it to us. I can get around in that area in total darkness. The restrooms and the Dining Hall too, I've been to them in the dark. I think I can figure out the Activity Area in the dark if I have to."

"And you have your headlamp," she says, cheerfully.

"That might give my position away," I say, looking at her and trying to grin, but my face feels stretched thin, taut.

We arrive at the Ritz-Carlton. My survival pack is just as I left it. Sister Grace leaves her bundle of Daeios gowns behind her and we walk to the oasis, which is little more than some mud puddles surrounding the trees. It's after noon and hot right now, the sun beating down on us, the horizon shimmering on the desert sand. We set my snares and gather enough dry wood to burn through the night if one of us is awake to feed the fire. I'm afraid that will be me. My mind is racing with thoughts on what could go wrong. My body feels like it's vibrating.

We spend the evening going through my two packs. My plan was to travel light and allow myself to move freely to protect myself. But when I look at the supplies I have in the survival backpack for the first time in a while, I know that many of them could be useful to us both on the trip or to me once inside Daeios. The thought of carrying this large pack, too heavy for a long distance, overwhelms me for a moment. But I can leave the daypack behind. And the ultralight tent I brought. It will never withstand the fury of the storms.

"Is there a shelter close to Daeios, Sister Grace?" I'd stay outside Daeios all night and watch it, but the storms won't allow that. That means there are several hours I can't watch Daeios, so I don't want to spend much time walking back and forth from the shelter. "Is there a water supply near there?"

"A shelter, yes, but it's tight. You can find water first thing in the mornings after the rains. It pools on the tops of the rock formations where the sandstone has eroded."

I survey the supplies strewn around the floor of the cavern and sit back, breathing out a long breath. I'm beaten before I've even begun. I can't carry this stuff for miles and then move around inside Daeios with it on. This is a monstrous task and I'm already defeated.

"I'll carry the pack for you, Sister Shea. Pack as much as you want, I'll carry it to Daeios. We can bring it all if you want."

"Thank you." I manage a real smile this time. "I can see how just about everything could be useful."

Now that getting the supplies to Daeios isn't a problem, seeing them gives me some ideas for my task once there. "I've thought of a couple of possible ways to get through the fence. I have wire cutters on my pocket multi-tool, and I've got this foldable shovel and the leather work gloves. Maybe I can dig my way under the fence."

"I'm not helping you get in. I'm just taking you there." A spark in Sister Grace's eyes warns me to drop the subject. "Put what you need to get into Daeios in the big pack and what you need inside Daeios in the daypack."

Into the bottom of the large pack I stuff my running clothes, the zip-off legs from my cargo shorts, hiking boots, ultralight tent, and a small sewing kit. Next, I pack my daypack with the things I'll need inside of Daeios. Sister Grace's watchful eyes move from each item to the bag. To the next item, back to the bag.

I bring my first aid kit in case of injury. My compact multi-tool could be useful inside and outside of Daeios, so I place it in the strapwork.

The hunting knife also goes in the webbing, along with the gun and the aluminum water bottle, as before. I add back in those items I've kept in my daypack for my everyday survival: the hatchet multi-tool, which includes a pry bar and hammer in addition to the hatchet; the small mirror; the bandana; the three remaining gallon-size plastic bags; the fire starter; the tube of petroleum jelly; and the running headlamp. I add in the duct tape and a fifty-foot climbing rope.

Now to pack the large survival pack. The binoculars go in an outside pocket, as does my trash bag rain poncho. Inside I place a foldable shovel, a lightweight tarp, the mess kit, and heavy leather work gloves. The Daeios gowns will make the trip in this pack. I'll use my sleeping bag tonight and then it will travel in the survival pack. The remaining fire-starting materials go in a small outside pocket. The collapsible bottle and water purification tablets will also ride on the outside of her pack.

I'll wear the cap and the survival bracelet, my stained cargo shorts with their multiple pockets; short-sleeve T-shirt; and my running shoes. I place the remaining paracord from the survival bracelet I've taken apart into a pocket and hand its small compass to Sister Grace. She tucks it in her chamois pouch.

After cleaning up tomorrow I'll leave my towel and toothbrush behind.

That's it. That's all I have for getting to Daeios, breaking into Daeios, destroying the Elders, and rescuing my loved ones. Maybe I can find more useful items in Daeios. But I don't want to spend much time in that wicked abyss. In and out.

I lie awake most of the night worrying, the fire snapping and crackling a few feet away. I roll over on my side and close my eyes to the lightning. I listen to the rain falling, the thunder rumbling, and the howling of wild dogs dissolving into the wind. I have goosebumps, and I don't know if it's because I'm cold, or because I'm returning to Daeios. I get up several times to add wood to the fire, hoping to dispel my fears, until we run out.

I wonder how far it is to Daeios.

Sister Grace sleeps peacefully—she's not going in. I finally fall asleep with my hand gripping my necklace.

I wake before sunrise because I'm not feeling well. Struggling out of the sleeping bag, the gun sliding off my chest, I run toward the wheelchair ramp, hoping to be on the ground below the Ritz-Carlton before I throw up. I end up puking and coughing in the corner next to the ramp. Sister Grace comes up behind me when I'm dry heaving and choking, my guts emptied.

"Do you think you're pregnant?" she asks from behind me.

I stand up and whirl around to meet her concerned eyes, wiping my mouth with the back of my hand. "What?"

"The vomiting. It could be morning sickness."

"This is the only time I've been sick since I've been up here." I self-consciously put my hand on my belly. It doesn't feel pregnant to me, but a little voice in my head says it could be true. I think of the rape and shudder in the cool morning air.

31

Once the rain stops we head to the oasis to clean up, get water, and retrieve the game from the snares. It's as we near the water that I realize I used all of the wood in the night to assuage my fears, and the wood here is wet. We won't have a meal today. When I tell Sister Grace, she just nods. We're going to Daeios hungry. I don't know if I could face it this morning anyway, skinning the game, cooking it, eating it, with my stomach so unsettled. The possibility that I'm pregnant niggles in my mind.

As we head toward Daeios, my determination to get my family and Julian out of that terrible place strengthens. Mother's gun on my back makes me feel powerful. Touching the necklace fills me with her strength and love.

We stop along our journey to sit in the shade of a towering rock formation and drink water. We probably won't find any more until tomorrow morning, after tonight's rains. "How much further to the shelter?"

"Are we there yet?" Sister Grace says in a little kid's voice and grins before becoming serious. "It's still pretty far away. I hope we get there soon enough," she says, unable to keep the worry from her voice as she looks at the graying light of the sky. "We're not going to make it before it starts raining. The lightning is getting closer. If the wind picks up, we'll be fighting blowing sand. Let's go."

By the time we near the shelter, the sand is pelting us and the rain is starting to fall in fat, cold drops. Sister Grace doesn't have a rain poncho, so I forego donning mine. Fingers of lightning in the sky, thunder rolling overhead. But at least we might get to the shelter before the storm breaks loose.

The evil storm read my mind. The rain starts pummeling us, which at least wets the sand so it's not sandblasting our skin and threatening our sight and ability to breathe. We reach the shelter soaked, winded, and chilled. We need to get out of our wet clothes and in front of a fire. But there will be no fire tonight.

The shelter is off the ground about three feet, a small cave. I poke my head and shoulders in, shining my headlamp ahead of me. It opens up some after I get through the narrow opening. It's about the size of my three-man tent. No snakes, no animal poop, no standing water.

I pull myself through the narrow opening and Sister Grace shoves the bags through. They barely fit through the small opening. When she comes inside her teeth are chattering.

"We'll have to get into dry clothes so we don't get hypothermia," I say.

"It gets cold in here. If we hold each other we'll probably generate enough body heat in this small space to be reasonably warm." Sister Grace wriggles around on the cave floor, removing her wet clothing and pulling a Daeios gown over her head. As much as I don't want to wear a Daeios gown, I wiggle out of my wet clothes and slip one over my head to keep from getting hypothermia. I'm cold and wet, hungry and cranky. I'm having problems with my bipolar disorder. The depression is setting in, telling me I can't do this, that I shouldn't even try. After a few minutes, mania has chased depression away and has taken its place. My mind races with ugly thoughts.

The sounds of the storm are dulled by the small entrance. At least there's that.

"We're almost to Daeios. Phase one of your plan is almost

complete," Sister Grace says. The light from the headlamp shows her apprehension, and I try to smile.

I don't want to talk about it. My paranoia is kicking in.

"Are you cold?" she asks.

"Yes." But that's not why I shivered.

We settle in, spooning, with Sister Grace behind me. She could choke me, smother me, without breaking a sweat. But I'm not afraid of her anymore. I fear Daeios and the Elders. I want to crawl out of this cave and run back to the Ritz-Carlton, where I'll feel safe. My heartbeat is strange, fast and then slow, my brain manic and then depressive.

Soon I will enter Daeios and face my attackers. It's the last thing I want to do. My body remembers the fresh wounds from the rape, I see their monstrous faces in mine, I hear their wild laughter. No matter how hard I try to breathe deeply, to fill my lungs with air, my chest won't expand enough to let it in. I feel like I'm suffocating. The closeness of this small cave and its tight exit don't help.

I have to find my family and Julian in that labyrinth, and I have no idea where to look. What have the Elders done to my parents for rescuing me? Are they hurt? Are they still alive?

I finally fall into a fitful sleep, dreaming I'm alone in Daeios, without my pack, and can't find my way out. I can't find my family or Julian. It's pitch-black and silent as death.

I scream into the void, but no one can hear me.

I sit up in the morning, too fast. Head rush. The movement makes me dizzy; I'm going to puke. I put my hand to my mouth, gagging, not knowing what to do.

Sister Grace pushes me to the cave opening just in time for me to pop my head out and vomit to the side, my head and shoulders out of the cave and the rest of my body inside like a moray eel. When I stop shaking I pull myself the rest of the way through, kneel and vomit around the corner. As the retching subsides, I hold my hands on my abdomen. I feel the tenderness in my breasts.

I'm pregnant.

Tears beckon, and a lump fills my throat. I've never wanted children. But I want this baby more than I've ever wanted anything. No matter how I conceived it, it's a precious life, and I am its mother. A spark of warmth fills my chest.

"Are you okay out there?" Sister Grace calls, her voice muffled.

"Yes," I say, but I don't feel okay. The risk of my task has doubled.

She pushes the bags out and then wiggles her way out of the opening. The sun has been up for a while now and it's getting hot. It was so dark and cold inside the cave I thought it might not have come up yet.

"How much further is it?" I ask as we start today's journey.

"Not far. A couple of hours, maybe."

As we walk toward Daeios, it feels like something is stuck in my throat. I swallow hard, several times. I imagine my baby's heart is racing in its chest, trying to flee from danger while I take it nearer. The thought that eyes are watching me makes my skin crawl as if I were ringed in writhing, venomous snakes. Is it my bipolar, or is somebody—or something—watching us? As we walk toward Daeios, I stop frequently to scan with my binoculars to try to lessen my increasing paranoia.

As we follow the sun, birds circle overhead—giant, black crows in full cry, their cawing grating on my nerves.

We're going back to Daeios, and the closer we get, the colder my dread. I'm afraid that when I face my attackers, all the strength I have will leave me and I'll melt into a puddle of revulsion and despair.

How will I face my abusers, the men who almost tore me apart?

My armpits are sticky, and I smell bad. The sour taste in my mouth makes me want to puke again. I'm returning to Daeios. I'm risking the life of my baby, not just my own life.

Can I do this? What if I don't find my family or Julian? What if they rape me again? What if they hold me captive and take my baby when it's born? I want to run away, to keep running until I'm on the opposite side of the earth. I feel faint, as if hands are squeezing my throat and choking the life out of me.

I take a deep breath and square my shoulders, fingering the sun pendant around my neck. A glance at Sister Grace provides me with a reassuring smile. I can do this.

Soon the first signs of Daeios show in the distance: the satellite dish and the radio tower. Most people wouldn't see them until they were right in front of their faces. I wish I couldn't see them now, that I was anywhere but here.

"Do you see it?" Sister Grace points.

"Yes," I say, my tongue numb. A cold stone is tumbling around in my stomach, and my throat is closing up. Daeios. One hundred and forty feet underground. To face my attackers. To face the cold light that's only a filament away from absolute darkness. I envision my family and Julian, trapped in Daeios under the Elders' rule, and my resolve to find them builds. As does my fear.

"Sister Shea, I'm afraid for you. I can't believe you're so calm."

Me? Calm? I must have a better poker face than I thought. "I have to do this, Sister Grace. I'm the only one who can get my family out of there. I hope to rescue Julian too. I need to find a place to set up so I can watch it for a while, try to find a way in. Can you stay with me long enough to get set up?"

She stands silent for a long moment. She lets loose a heavy sigh, her shoulders rising and falling with the lost breath.

"I will. But only because you're my Spoon Sister." She sports an impish grin.

I give her a grateful smile. "Where would you set up?"

"I think our best bet is to climb up on a rock formation. Watch from a distance first. That one over there should give us a good angle." She points to a stand of rock that's twenty or thirty feet high, east of Daeios, with a good view of its entrance. My stomach does a flip-flop.

The rock pile I climbed wasn't far off the ground, so I sucked it up. This one is too high. Formidable. But it is the right location for us to spy without being seen if we crouch low on the rock. I do have climbing experience—the bare minimum to obtain my survivalist certificate.

Sister Grace notes my hesitation. "You don't know how to climb?"

"I do, it's just not my favorite pastime."

"Let's see what we've got to deal with."

We walk around the formation and find the easiest route up will be on the side that faces Daeios. Of course. The rock formation is made up of several small sandstone boulders leading up to larger boulders, which should be an easy climb, even without our climbing ropes. But I'm shaking so hard I don't know if I can keep my feet steady enough to keep from tumbling down. I take the binoculars off Sister Grace's pack and try to get a look at Daeios. The angle's not right from down here.

"I've done a lot of climbing. This looks pretty simple. I'll climb up first and then belay you. Just in case. I've got carabiners in my pouch and I can tie you into a harness."

I nod and swallow hard and we take off our packs. When she takes her rope off her belt, I notice that it's been used before, where mine is straight from the store. Uncoiling the rope, she cuts off about half of it with her hunting knife. She has me tuck in my shirt as she folds the rope in half. Placing the halfway point at my left hip, she wraps the rope around my body and ties it off. Then she runs the ropes between my legs and runs them underneath the waist rope.

"Squat down so I can pull this tight," she says. She has me squat two more times, each time pulling the rope tighter. She ties a square knot on my left side with a knot on either side of it. "And that's how you create a Swiss Seat harness," she says, holding her arms out like she performed an acrobatic feat.

I feel safe in this harness, but then again I'm standing on solid ground.

"I used to belay my little brothers like this." She clips a locking carabiner to the front of my harness. "Now I need your rope."

I bend down, the harness tugging at my thighs, and pull the rope from my drypack. She uncoils the rope and threads one end through the carabiner. "Hold on to these for a minute." Placing the ends of the rope in my hand, she squeezes it for a moment. "I'm good at this, don't worry. You won't even need me. It's a precaution so you feel safe. Now stand back a ways. I don't want to kick rock down on you."

She puts on the survival pack and takes the ends of the rope in her hand. She scales the rock in only a few minutes, kicking down a few small stones as she goes. When she disappears for a few minutes, the rope in the carabiner moves and twitches as she walks around on top of the formation. The eyes burrow into the back of my head and I turn to see if someone is approaching us from Daeios. When Sister Grace is at the edge of the rock, seating herself, with the ends of the rope on either side of her, I feel hot all over, a tingle in my scalp.

"Do you have it anchored on something besides you?" I call up.

"Yeah, I found a great rock to anchor it on. Come on up."

I put on my pack and begin climbing, following the path she took as I watched her ascend. She takes the slack out of the rope as I climb. My foot slips a couple of times and I pause to balance myself, taking several deep breaths before moving on. When I stop to even out my breathing, she asks if I'm alright.

"Just a little shaky."

"You've got this. You're almost here," she says, even though I'm not even halfway up the face.

I make it to the top, and she doesn't have to catch me or support my weight. She helps me out of the harness. We situate ourselves so no one from Daeios should be able to see us on top of the rock, trying to avoid large movements as much as possible because that's what will give us away—if they haven't already seen us. We take turns looking through the binoculars, switching off frequently as our eyes become tired.

The first obstacle I'll have to contend with is the fence. The razor wire flashes and glints in the sun, taunting me. "How do I get through that fence, Sister Grace?"

"Razor wire is nasty stuff. I helped my dad put ours up. Do you have wire cutters?"

"You have razor wire around your house? Or should I call it a compound?"

She rolls her eyes. "We were ready for shit to hit the fan. In the short term. Daeios was for the long term. Zombies would cut themselves to pieces trying to get over razor wire. Looters? They'll go to the neighbor next door. You have wire cutters on that multi-tool?"

"Wow. Your family was way more survivalist than mine. I do have wire cutters. But they won't cut through the chain-link or the wire. I was thinking I might have to dig under the fence."

"I doubt if you can dig a big enough hole to get under it. You'll probably run into caliche."

Caliche is nature's concrete; I'd forgotten about it. You need a jackhammer to get through it. "Okay, about the wire cutters?"

"You take your rope and cut it in two. Pull a section of the wire apart by pulling the ropes in the opposite direction. Then you clip the hog rings—the anchors—with the wire cutters. Wear your gloves to cut the anchors. Pull it down with the rope. Just a section wide enough to get over. I'll leave the survival pack with you. Put the tarp and Daeios gowns over the wire. It'll be less likely to cut you when it comes down. If you do get caught in it, stop moving and then back away from the barbs so they don't cut you as bad. Then climb over the fence."

That should be easy, my sarcastic inner voice says.

We're silent as Sister Grace watches Daeios. It's as she's handing the binoculars to me that she freezes like a pointer when it sees a pheasant. "There's an RV leaving Daeios. It's coming through the blast doors." She pauses, and my heart hammers in my chest. "The doors are closing. They're waiting for the gate to slide open."

"Can you see who's in it? Is there more than one person?"

She's silent for a moment. The hair is standing up on the back of my neck. "Okay, the gate is opening. Big hat and sunglasses. The windows are tinted. Here." She hands the binoculars to me and I watch as the person waits for the gate to open. I only see a driver.

Once the gate is open, the RV drives off and there's not much to see, just a vehicle driving down the same road my family came in on. I watch the gate close, studying it as it moves slowly toward the fence post. The gate pauses for a moment before the mechanism locks.

I hand the binoculars to Sister Grace.

"Look at the gate."

"It's closed. What am I looking at?"

"That's how I'm going to get inside the grounds of Daeios—I'm going over the gate where there's no razor wire."

32

Sister Grace guffaws, making me jump. My nerves are stretched to breaking point. "That would've been stupid. Taking razor wire down to climb over the fence when the gate has none. Next you can duct tape the lenses of security cameras if you can reach them."

"The cameras inside Daeios were hidden, so I imagine these are too. I don't think my entry is going to be a surprise."

We watch until we notice clouds coming in. There's no threat in them yet, but soon the storms will roll in and it will cool off. It's time for us to climb down and head back to our shelter before the wind finds its voice and the rain starts falling. We pack up and Sister Grace ties me into a harness again. She belays me to the bottom of the rock formation and then follows, climbing down as sure-footed as an ibex. I'm shaky, and it's from more than scaling down the height of the rock formation. I'm hungry.

We gather wood whenever we see it so we can build a fire. As we near our shelter, we hear an angry buzz. A rattlesnake is coiled up ahead of us, only a few feet away. I suck in a big breath. Sister Grace already has her bow stretched and an arrow pointed at it.

"Tell me, Sister Shea, is there anything you're not afraid of?" she asks coolly, not taking her eyes off her target.

"I'll have to get back to you on that," I say, letting air rush from my mouth.

"Don't move, Sister Shea. He can strike out a few feet. He's furious." I stay as still as I can, holding my breath and then breathing in and out through my nose as the snake coils and uncoils, rattling incessantly. Its black forked tongue darts in and out, moving up and down.

I want to scream and run away. The snake could lunge and strike. Sister Grace takes a deep breath and releases the arrow, shooting the serpent through the eye. It stops rattling, lying still.

She lays the survival pack on the sand and pulls out a tent pole, extending it. "Get your hatchet out. Hold this on the snake's head until I chop it off."

The distance the pole leaves me from the snake isn't enough, but it only takes a minute. She has me hold the head down a bit longer while she searches for a large rock and places it on the head. "It can still bite due to reflexes." She picks up the writhing snake body. "Now we have dinner."

"I don't think I can eat that. You couldn't have gotten a bird?" Sister Grace frowns a smile at me and shakes her head like I'm a picky child. Vegetables seem enticing right now.

She makes quick work of skinning the snake while I build the fire, ignoring her, trying not to see the snake. I have to use some cotton balls and tampons for tinder to get it going, and petroleum jelly to help it light. It won't last long but should burn long enough to cook her dinner. Sister Grace uses a tent pole to hold the meat over the fire.

"If not for you, you should eat for your baby. You sure you don't want some?" she says around a large bite of the snake and then spits out some small bones. "It—"

A lurch in my stomach. I'm off, running a short way before I puke in the sand, sick with fear and pregnancy.

Bending over, emptying my guts, reminds me of the Elders. A cold, hard truth thrums in my brain.

My solution for vengeance clicks into place.

33

"Show me how to restrain the Elders," I say when I return to Sister Grace.

She studies me for a minute or two. "You're not killing them? You're showing them mercy after what they did to you?" Her voice is brusque.

"It's not mercy. Show me."

She shrugs. "I'll show you how to tie them up, then," she says. "You could hog-tie them but they could asphyxiate. Put out your hands in front of you. Watch what I do. You'll tie their hands behind their backs, though."

She cuts off a few feet of her climbing rope. I watch as she wraps it around my hands, twisting it and looping it and eventually tying it off, talking it through as she goes. "Now try to get out." She grins at me, a gleam of white teeth in her tanned face.

My breath catches in my throat when I try to loosen my bindings. They get tighter. A bright slash of panic as she laughs deep in her throat. It feels like a steel band is crushing my chest, flattening my lungs. She reaches behind her and brings out her hunting knife and my head starts spinning and I see flashes of light.

"Put your head between your knees," she says. "You're white as a ghost. On second thought, I don't want to cut these ropes. I'll try to untie them and I'll leave them with you. You'll need them for the Elders."

When the spinning stops I hold my arms out to her and she works the bindings off, struggling with her teeth clenched. "You'll want to tie up their legs, too. Over the ankles. Now try it on me."

It takes three times for me to get her hands tied so she can't get loose, with her coaching me the first two times. Then she lets me tie her legs together at the ankles. She sits quietly this time, watching my movements and shaking her head when I start to ask a question. When I've finished she demonstrates that she can't get loose. "But I can warn the others. You'll want to duct tape their mouths. Wrap it around their heads a couple of times. They can't rip it off easily if they get their hands loose. Now untie me."

After I get the ropes off we stand and she shows me how I should hold a knife for self-defense. For cutting, for stabbing, for slashing. Many of the moves she teaches me are similar to what I learned in my unarmed self-defense class, but with the knife as an extension of my hand.

Before I know it, she's behind me with the knife at my throat. I have no air in my lungs, as though I had belly-flopped off a cliff.

She releases me. "Breathe." I stand there a moment, calming my breathing, trying to reconcile Assassin Sister Grace with Spoon Sister Grace. "You have to pull them off balance because they have a height advantage over you. Except for the short one. Get them in this position. It's hard for them to maneuver out of it without you slashing their throats."

"I don't want to kill them," I reiterate.

"I thought you wanted revenge."

"Let me worry about that."

"I'd kill them up close and personal. Your face would be the last one they'd see." The look on her face chills me. The fact that she may be unhinged enters my mind again.

"Sister Grace, this is my decision."

"Alright," she says after a brief pause. "You have to disable them first. They're not going to hold still for you. You'll have to knock them out."

"If I bash them on the head, I risk killing them."

She laughs, a guttural laugh with no mirth in it. "You'll feel differently when you're in the heat of the moment. Use a trip line, then. You'll have to man it and get to them before they can get back up and run away. Or come at you."

I'll have to be twelve places at one time before I even look for my family and Julian.

We're silent for a moment as thunder rumbles. A bright twist of lightning strikes in the distance behind Sister Grace's head, appearing to enter her crown.

I inspect the cave before it starts to rain, the air cooling off, the smell of moisture in the air. I switch on my running headlamp and make a cursory search of the cave before entering with the light on my head. The dank air closes in on me. Once Sister Grace is inside, we settle in.

"They know it's safe to be aboveground," I say. "Tomorrow, I think we need to get closer. I saw a pile of good-sized rocks we should be able to set up behind."

"Tomorrow, I leave you," she replies. "I'll carry the survival pack to the rocks so you'll have it. I'll be in the open shelter that night. You know where to find me after that." She's stroking the chamois pouch, already parting in her mind. "We'll need to get up earlier. I'm going to have to run back to the open shelter to make it before the storms roll in. It'll give you more time to watch too. Maybe all of the Elders come and go. We weren't there long enough to see the others. Or to see if the RV came back."

What if everyone has left Daeios already and only the Elders are there?

"The Elder who left was wearing a disguise. Or trying to avoid getting any sun on his face and neck. They probably haven't told the rest of the Daeiosians that it's safe to be up here. They need to keep their baby-making factory in working order." A shard of anger stabs me behind my eyes.

We fall silent for a moment.

"I'm going to keep the baby," I say, the warmth filling my chest again.

"No one will fault you if you don't keep it. You were—"

I break in before she can say the dreaded word. "I haven't done much with my life yet. I will now, with this child."

"You'll remember the rape every time you look at your child. They'll ask you about their father. You won't know what to tell them."

"Every time I look at my child, I'll feel love. I'll figure out the other thing later. I have a few months," I say, crinkling my eyes at her. "What if your family is still alive? Maybe they couldn't get to Daeios but they're still okay, waiting for you back in your fortress."

"Our home," she says, chastising me with a puckered brow. A bitter laugh. "Here I have that hope. It would hurt too much to know for certain that they're gone."

We lie together again to stay warm. The Spoon Sisters. Even with the light of the headlamp shining on the wall of the cave, I feel the darkness as it listens to my thoughts and dissects my fears.

The next morning we climb up and fill our water containers with my mess kit cup from the top of the rock formation we stayed in, gulping water and filling them again. We leave when the rain is still falling lightly, as the sun is flinging its first golden rays over the horizon. We use a combination of running and walking to get to the rock pile as early as possible. Although decked out in scars, I'm healed and fit. We dry off quickly in the simmering sun.

We stoop as we near the rocks and run the rest of the way to them.

Sister Grace removes the survival pack and pulls out the pieces of rope so I can stuff them in the daypack. She's given up her climbing rope for me. She's not taking the Daeios gowns with her, so she'll sleep on the hard rock floor, chilled, tonight. She leans the pack against a rock. "You're going to be okay, Sister Shea. I admire what you're doing. Your family is fortunate to have you. Julian's a lucky guy." She gives me a goodbye smile, running her hands over her tow-haired head, breathing out through her nose.

"Thank you, Sister Grace. I'll always remember what you've done for me."

She nods and I think her lip trembles. Then she turns and runs away, stooping at first. When she starts running upright, I stop watching.

I pull the binoculars out of the strapwork on the survival pack. I'll combine the two packs this afternoon before heading back to the shelter. Watching the front entrance through the binoculars, watching the area around Daeios, I formulate my plan for climbing over the gate.

Assuming I make it over the gate, how do I get in? If they see me through the cameras, I don't have the advantage of surprise. Say I make it that far. How do I get through the blast doors?

A puff of ocher shows in the distance to my right. I aim the binoculars at the trail of dust coming down the road toward Daeios, and then move them to see what's causing the dust to rise. It's the RV we saw yesterday. We didn't miss them. Whoever left Daeios yesterday is returning today.

I pull the gun out of the netting and struggle into my pack while staying low behind the rocks. I'm going in behind that RV. That's how I get through the blast doors.

34

The RV bumps along the road slowly, adding more dust to the trail.

A tremor runs through me. I'm going into Daeios. I thought this would be another day of watching, that I'd tramp back to the cave and here again. But I'm going into Daeios. Now. The watchful eyes size me up.

The RV pulls around the final bend and faces me. Much closer than we were from the top of the rock formation, I steal a glance at the driver through the binoculars. The same sunglasses, the same floppy hat. A bright, icy chill confirms it's an Elder. No one in the passenger seat.

I gaze longingly at the survival pack. It will have to stay here. I add the binoculars to the strapwork on the large pack. I won't need them now.

Holding the gun in my left hand, I crouch, ready to run. While he's sitting there, waiting for the gate to open, I'll sprint up behind the RV. If there's a ladder on the back, I'll ride it in. If not, I'll run in behind it.

The RV starts turning toward the gate.

They may have security personnel inside like they did when we arrived at Daeios. The security guard had a black holster and gun. She'll have more than two bullets.

The RV faces the gate and eases to a stop. It has a silver ladder from the bottom of the RV going over the top.

I straighten out and sprint for the ladder, my pack jouncing on my back, knowing the driver could see me approaching in his side view mirror. Propelling myself forward, I jump onto the bottom rung of the ladder on the side nearest the driver, grasping a rung above me with my right hand. I lean my body against the back of the RV to steady myself when the large vehicle starts moving.

Did anyone see me? Is there a security guard coming up beside the RV now, a gun held out in front of her, to take me prisoner? On both sides of the RV?

The RV starts forward with a hitch and then drives unhurriedly through the gate. I turn to watch the gate close.

Movement on the other side of the gate. Sister Grace is sprinting toward it, a few yards away, her arms pumping, her teeth clenched in determination. I'm so happy to see her that I have to suppress the urge to call encouragement to her.

When the vehicle stops, I know we're in front of the blast doors. The gate starts closing. Sister Grace is too far away to get through the gate.

A rattle of metal wire and the sound of the chain pulling. The gate moves toward the fence post. Sister Grace's eyes are locked on the shrinking gap between the gate and the fence. Still running, she shrugs off the survival pack and, holding it by one strap, heaves it between the gate and the fence to pause the gate for a moment. She steps one long leg across the pack and squeezes through sideways. Giving the pack a hard jerk, she pulls it free. The gate slams closed with a metallic clank as Sister Grace hops on the ladder beside me, the pack on her back and her hunting knife in her hand. There's an excited grin on her face. The outside blast doors will be opening now.

Panting, she says, "Will you give me a ride to Flagstaff when we're done, Sister Shea? I'd like to think my family is okay, and they're just waiting for me to come home."

"Sister Grace, I'll take you wherever you want to go." My voice is husky with tears.

The RV sits there a long moment, the exhaust fumes making me queasy. I look at Sister Grace. A lift of her shoulders, a mischievous smile of excitement. We're going into Daeios. The RV jerks forward and breath bursts from me like I was punched in the stomach. I grip the ladder harder to keep my body against the back of the vehicle.

Will someone see us inside the entryway between the blast doors? Brother Christian and the security woman came out of a door and he boarded our RV. Which way did they come from? The passenger side. If someone sees us, it will be on that side.

I turn to Sister Grace, and she has her back to me, watching for someone to come up on her side of the RV.

The outer blast doors thump closed behind us, a vacuum sucking the air out of the enclosed space, leaving me breathless. Exhaust fumes surround us. Nausea clutches at my stomach. Someone could come out to greet the driver of the RV and watch it descend into Daeios. Or they could do a cursory check around the RV. Perhaps cameras do that check. The eyes reach out and touch me, prod me.

I hear a rushing sound and know that the inner blast doors are open. The coldness of Daeios pricks my skin. The RV starts creeping down the twisty ramp into the dim light of Daeios. My heart ceases to beat and then takes up again at double speed.

The blast doors shut behind us with a thud. I think of Cerberus and the twelfth labor of Hercules. There's no going back.

35

My body presses against the back of the RV as we begin to spiral down the ramp. The large vehicle is geared down, the engine whining, to slow it on the decline. I peer down over the edge of the driveway and instantly regret it. Motion sickness plays with my brain and thrashes at my stomach. Even in the dim light, my fist looks chalky white from my death grip on the ladder.

I look over my shoulder at Sister Grace. She seems to sense my eyes on her and glances over her shoulder at me. The shadows on her eyes and nose make me think of a skull.

"I'll stay on this side and draw the driver's attention to me. You can take it from there," she says.

I nod at her like I know what I'm doing, and she faces away again.

The vehicle drives on. Goose pimples rise on my arms and legs.

The RV reaches the bottom of the driveway and we dip down as the back end of the vehicle reaches the level road. It makes a left turn toward the tunnel and the driver shifts out of low gear. The overhead lights are off, the sconces on the wall giving the only light in this cavernous room, making the rock walls the color of dried blood.

We enter the tunnel, as brightly lit as it was on the day we arrived, the human-made wall to our right reflecting the cold, white light back at us. I blink as my eyes adjust to the harshness of the light. I shrug off the shudder that runs through my body.

The RV continues on. The black exit into D section will be looming ahead of us. The southeast section we just left appears charcoal from this angle. It will soon be time to confront the driver. My feet feel superglued to the ladder, my hand soldered a few rungs higher. Sister Grace turns her head and begs the question in her eyes. When?

The RV slows to a crawl, reaching the ninety-degree angle that leads into the D section. No sounds of chatter and bustle from the living area. Daeios is deathly silent except for the drone of the vehicle's engine.

Giving Sister Grace an abrupt nod, I jump off the ladder, my jelly legs absorbing the shock of the drop, my gun in my left hand. She hits the ground behind me and we sprint toward the front of the RV on each side. I stay just behind the driver's door, ready to strike.

I hear the snap of the handle of the passenger door. "Get out now!" Sister Grace yells.

The vehicle is shifted into *PARK* and the driver's door pops open a few inches. The driver holds the door there, hesitant.

I spring up onto the running board, throwing the door open, the force of the action pulling the driver with it. Pulled to the side, his right ear is lying in front of me, tempting me. I grab hold of it and jump down from the running board, pulling him with me. He shrieks as he falls to the ground, pounding off the rock floor on his left shoulder and hip. I stand over him with the gun at his head. Sister Grace comes around the front of the RV, pulling a strand of rope from her belt. She didn't leave anything behind.

It's Brother Michael, his long jowls jiggling as he shakes off the fall. Jiggling as they did as his face hovered over me in my dreams, his caustic breath hot on my face, the tufts of hair growing from his ears and nose. He squints in the severe lighting to get a good look at me. He's dressed in scrubs and a white lab coat. He's been working as a pharmacist today. Bringing something back to Daeios?

"W-what are you d-doing in Daeios? Who are you?" he stammers, shrinking away from me when his eyes focus in on the gun pointed at his head.

I lift the bill of the cap so he can see my eyes. I hope they look as hard as the black ice in my heart feels. "Recognize me now?" He breathes in a quick breath of recognition and puts his hands above his head. I pull my cap back down. "Did you rape me? Did you torture me?" I don't need to ask them about Jace. The gun in my brother's right hand is confession enough for me.

"It wasn't rape, it was your breeding, your calling from God," he says, the high pitch of panic clear in his voice.

"Yes or no? Were you there?"

"Y-yes. Yes," he says, closing his eyes to ward off the round that he expects to travel through his brain. "Please don't shoot me."

"Where's your badge?" Sister Grace's voice vibrates with rage or adrenaline.

"My badge isn't here." His lips press together in obstinacy. His eyes dart back and forth between the two of us.

"Check his pockets, Sister Grace."

Sheathing her knife, she pulls the contents from his pockets and tosses them to the ground: a ballpoint pen, lip balm, some coins. She hands me a white plastic card, blank except for a black magnetic stripe on one side. A key card.

"What does the card give us access to?" she asks him. He turns his head to the side like a stubborn child. She gropes for his testicles and gives them a quick squeeze and he contracts his body with a sharp breath out. "What does this card give us access to?" Her voice is low and jagged, her hand at his crotch.

"Everything!" he shouts, his voice held tight, his face scrunched in agony. "Every door. It gives you access to every room in Daeios." Sister Grace stands up and steps back.

"Where do we find the other Elders?" I ask.

"I don't know where they are. I left Daeios yesterday."

"Roll over on your stomach. Is that how you liked me? On my stomach?" I say. As he rolls over on his side to obey I place the sole of my shoe on his back and shove him onto his front. His breath comes fast, in and out. He could hyperventilate.

"Don't shoot me, please don't shoot me," he says, sobbing with fear.

Sister Grace places her shin and her weight across the back of his legs and ties his hands behind his back as he snivels. She ties his legs together with another piece of rope. Taking hold of one arm, she forces him onto his back so the cruel white light glares in his eyes, then takes hold under his armpits and drags him to lie next to the icy, light-reflecting wall of the tunnel. I hand her the duct tape from my pack. She winds a few feet of tape around his head across his quavering mouth and jowls and slips the roll over her wrist.

Opening the side door of the RV, we take a look inside. It's stacked full of large boxes. Dozens of them. I pull one from the top of a pile and bring it into the light.

"Xanadoxalate," Sister Grace and I read at the same time. Restocking their brainwashing drug. We got here just in time. Placing the box back inside the RV, we walk into D section. The sconces are lit, the lamps are switched on. There's no one here.

We walk through D section, observing the clues. Beds are unmade, the sheets rumpled. White sandals are neatly lined up underneath beds. A pillow on the floor, a shattered lamp. The Daeiosians left their living areas in a hurry, probably during a period of darkness. Where are they?

We make brief checks of the RVs in the section, the restrooms and showers. The same story, all empty and disorderly. The restrooms and showers weren't cleaned as the majority of the Daeiosians slept. We investigate the other living area sections—C, then B, then A—in the same way. There's no one in the living areas. Where are they? Where are my family and Julian?

An icy claw traces down my spine.

36

"Where to next, boss?" Sister Grace asks, an eager grin on her face.

"The Activity Area. I don't have any hope of finding the Daeiosians there after what we just saw, but maybe the Elders are relaxing there. Waiting for Brother Michael to return with the drug. Let's take the hallway that leads to the Gathering Area, then head down the hallway to the south."

The lights are set on dim in the Gathering Area, but the Activity Area hallway is brightly lit.

"You stay to the right of the hallway and I'll stay to the left. We'll check through the windows for lights or any other indication there might be someone inside. After checking a room, give me a signal and we'll move to the next door," I say.

"Right. The first door is yours. The Chapel. Let's go."

I'm armed with the gun. Sister Grace has her bow in her hand. A mellow glow of light filters through the window of the Chapel door. I pull the key card from my pocket and insert it in the scanner. A click indicates the door is unlocked. Sister Grace pulls the door open and I sidle in, the gun out in front of me. She's on my heels, an arrow in her bow now.

My eyes adjust to the dim light. Burned-down white tapers flicker from candelabras around the room. Brother Mark is on his knees in supplication, his head bowed, his chin resting on his cupped fists. In my nightmares he slavered through gritted teeth, his eyes closed, his hips rocking between my legs. I swallow my revulsion.

"Can I have just a few minutes to myself, Brother Christian?" he says, his voice muffled.

I steal up behind him and place the muzzle of the gun on the back of his head, mobster-style.

"What are you praying for, Brother Mark?" I say, my voice irreverent in a place of God. "Are you praying for forgiveness for raping me?"

"Is that ... Sister Shea?" he asks, his voice peaceful, as always, in spite of having a gun to his head.

"How do you know it's me, Brother Mark? Am I the only one you forced yourself on?"

"It wasn't like that." He pulls his hands from his chin and tries to turn his face toward mine. I force the gun against his bald head so hard it feels like his skull gives a little. He cowers, breathing too hard and too fast. "We were obeying the word of God. He ordered that we produce the Chosen One, a child that could've been fathered by any of us. You have to believe me," he says, his voice clogged with tears.

"I believe in a different god than you do. Did you have sex with me when I was unconscious?" He doesn't respond. "Answer me." I cock the hammer of the gun with a click. "My god's impatient."

"Yes, yes," he says, shrinking from the gun. He begins muttering a prayer.

"Lie down on your stomach with your hands on the back of your head."

He moves into position, his prayer becoming louder, pleading. Not for mercy from me, but from his god. Sister Grace makes quick work of tying him up.

"Any last words?" I ask, the words slathered with contempt.

"I didn't hurt you the way the others did. I was gentle. God kept me from hurting you."

Sister Grace rifles through his pockets, pulls out his key card and stows it. She tears a piece of duct tape from the roll and slaps an end over his mouth, wrapping the rest of the tape around his head.

"You did hurt me. You offended my soul." I ease the hammer down on the .44 Magnum. We blow out the candles and leave him crying in the dark confessional, praying silently to his god.

Latching the door behind us, we sneak down the hallway to the next door. The Dining Hall, on my side. No lights. I motion Sister Grace forward with my hand.

Sister Grace motions me past the Art Room on her side.

Muted voices ahead of us, coming from the Kitchen. A trill of high-pitched laughter. Two men, their voices thin and aged. Brother Aaron and Brother John, the old, fat Elders. The ones who breathed heavily in my face in my nightmares, grunting and pumping away. Their sordid laughter more exultant than today.

Sister Grace crosses the hall and falls in behind me. They'll see us as soon as they open the door. We're on that side of the doorway.

When the door pops open a few inches, I kick it open with my foot and shove the gun in Brother Aaron's face. A small, wordless noise escapes his lips. Both men pull back, food falling from their hands. Forbidden candy bars, cookies that crumble when they hit the floor.

"Surprised to see me, Brothers? Take a good look at me. Don't be shy."

Sister Grace moves through the door, her bow stretched, an arrow pointing at their faces, smashing the cookies into tiny crumbs.

"Don't hurt us. Why are you doing this?" Brother John says as they back further into the Kitchen, and I follow.

"Don't you remember me? The breeder called to bear the Chosen One?"

Sister Grace forces Brother Aaron into a prone position on the floor with her arrow pressed into the back of his neck, indenting it.

"Sister Shea, you don't understand. We were only—"

"Doing God's will. I know. So you admit to being a part of it?" I motion with the gun for Brother John to take his position on the

Kitchen floor. He groans as he gets down first on one oversized knee then on the next and eases himself down with his quaking arms.

"Yes," Brother Aaron says.

I kick Brother John in the side and he cries out. "Yes, I was!"

Sister Grace takes their key cards and holds one out to me. We place them in our pockets and she ties them up as I hold them at gunpoint. Brother John is crying now, saliva stringing from his mouth. She slams his face into the tile floor before standing up and snatching the roll of duct tape. When she tapes their mouths, she gleefully wraps the tape around their heads, catching as much hair in the tape as possible.

"Onward?" she asks, her incandescent eyes shining.

We take our positions on each side of the hallway and move south. Past the Laundry Room. Past the Nursery, hushed and dark.

Sister Grace indicates there's a light on in the Fitness Room with a sideways tilt of her head. I cross the hallway and stand behind her, against the wall. She inserts a key card. The click of the latch. She pulls the door open and runs in.

I follow her in. No one in sight. Faint sounds of a shower spraying, off-key singing. I'd guess it's Brother Matthew, the muscular one. In my mind, a view of his fist as he punches me in the mouth and roars with laughter, the other Elders egging him on. My face burns hot with rage.

I pull the remnants of the survival bracelet from my shorts pocket and hand one end to Sister Grace. We squat down on either side of the open doorway that leads to the showers, the paracord held ankle high, and wait.

The shower stops, the singing cuts out. He'll be toweling off. He'll be putting on his Daeios whites, slipping his feet into his sandals. His sandals scuff as he approaches the doorway. My eyes meet Sister Grace's as we pull the tripwire tight.

A tug on the tripwire and Brother Matthew smashes to the ground. He utters a cry of surprise before his face hammers the hard rock floor. Blood issues from his broken nose and split lip. He puts his hands on the floor to lift himself up and Sister Grace lands on him, knees first, forcing the breath from his chest.

"Confess to Sister Shea what you did to her!" she yells, moving so she can pull his hands back and tie them together.

"I bred her, you crazy bitch!" he shouts, his voice thick from his broken nose. "We all did. Is that what you want to hear?" He struggles to get away from Sister Grace and she pulls her knife, holding it to his throat. He holds his hands up off the floor, gagging. She lets the pressure off and he says, "I'm done. I won't try to get up. Don't hurt me."

She finishes tying him up and tapes his mouth, pausing to press on his broken nose with her palm. There's a sickening crunch. He sucks in his breath but doesn't cry out against the tape. She puts his key card in her pocket and sheathes her knife, taking up her bow again.

We leave the Fitness Room and hustle to the Entertainment Room, also on Sister Grace's side of the hallway. Her eyes tell me that the light is on and I cross over to stand behind her. She opens the door and we run in. The TV is blaring but no one is in sight. I motion with my head to the couch, and we step around it with our weapons ready.

Brother Adam, the small Elder, is lying on the couch on his side. His eyes grow wide with astonishment and then he ogles me, sitting up. This is the one that rode me like a pony in my nightmares, almost pulling the hair from my head. If only I could throw him through a rock wall.

"The bitch that bit me. Welcome back, Sister Shea. And this breeder's head was shaved. Who's the father of your child, Breeder? Sister Shea's could be mine," Brother Adam says, smirking. I want to snip that smirk away with dull kitchen shears.

Sister Grace throws down her bow and arrow and pins him to the couch with the full weight of her body, her hands around his throat, thumbing his Adam's apple. She's much taller than he is and the primal grin I thought I saw before is on her face as she massages his throat with her thumbs. His Adam's apple bobs up and down as he struggles to swallow.

We've got our confession. "Get off, Sister Grace," I say.

She presses his voice box in, leaving him choking and gasping. I hand the gun to her and take hold of his sleeve and his pant leg and belly-flop him onto the floor. He expels all the air from his chest and fights to catch it again. Sister Grace hands me the rope and stands back as I tie him up, her eyes watchful, feral. I take his key card and put it in my cargo pocket.

The next room is the Music Room. Sister Grace moves to stand in front of the door and gazes in, gesturing to me to join her. Brother Luke is sitting with his back to the door, his tall frame sitting on a bench in front of a white baby grand piano. We watch him a moment as he reaches from side-to-side stroking the keys, evoking a sonata. Those long fingers squeezed my breasts. He hooted with pleasure.

Sister Grace opens the door and holds it for me. The music is delicate and then firm as his deft fingers work the keys. I pull the paracord from my pocket and hand it to her as I enter.

As the door slams shut I walk to the front of the piano and face him, the gun held down at my side where he can't see it. His face registers disbelief and he stops playing, mid-arpeggio, and starts to rise from the bench. Sister Grace wraps the cord first around one palm and then the other. Slipping the cord over his head, she forces him back down by pulling up and back on the cord. His hands clench the paracord, trying to pull it away from his neck. He drops his hands into his lap when I point the gun at his face.

"Remember me? Or do I have too many clothes on for you?" I tilt my head to the side, my voice loud and sharp under the acoustical tiles. Sister Grace eases the cord around his neck a fraction.

"It was ... was ... supposed to happen that way. God said your baby would be special. No one would know who fathered it so it would belong to all of us. To Daeios. I was honored to be a part of it," he wheezes. Sister Grace tightens the garrote around his neck until his face turns reddish-purple and his heavy-lidded eyes bulge. He opens his mouth wide, struggling for breath. When he blacks out, she shoves him off the bench. He lands in a heap next to the piano, a twist of arms and legs.

We lay our weapons aside and rearrange him facedown. Sister Grace holds his long arms behind his back and I bind them with the last of our rope. I pull off a length of duct tape to cover his mouth and Sister Grace presses his ankles together and rolls the duct tape around his ankles several times. She scrounges in his front pants pocket and finds his key card and hands it to me.

As we take up our weapons she asks, "What do we do now for restraining the other ones?"

"I think we've got enough paracord in my bracelet to hold one Elder," I say. "We'll have to do some scavenging for other restraints. Maybe in the Repair Shop."

We go out into the hallway and clear the Library and the Theater, which are dark and empty. We enter the Repair Shop and flip on the lights to look for restraints. No wire, no straps, no rope. But there's a full roll of white duct tape. I remove the packaging and stuff the tape into my daypack. It won't be enough to detain the five remaining Elders. We may have to get creative.

———

We walk back along the hallway of the Activity Area toward the north. As we pass each room containing prisoners, we look in to make sure they're still confined.

We stand in the dim light of the Gathering Area, facing the darkness of the forbidden north sector. The wing is obsidian black against the north wall.

"Ready?" I ask Sister Grace.

"You know I am, Sister Shea. Lead the way."

I angle toward Medical with my gun held down by my side and Sister Grace falls in behind me. We pass through the doorway between the Gathering Area and the north wing.

A sliver of light shows under the Medical Room door.

"Brother James," we murmur at the same time.

We hurry to Door 1. Sister Grace pulls out a key card. She uses the light from the Gathering Area to see the black stripe on the card and positions it to open the door. I wait on the opening side of the door, ready to enter. When I nod, Sister Grace scans the card and swings the door wide.

I step in with the gun held out in both hands. A woman is strapped to the table that held Jace when we first got here.

Mother.

37

I lower the weapon as Sister Grace enters the room and closes the door behind us. I try to ease the duct tape from Mother's mouth and then rip it off like a Band-Aid when it takes too long. It leaves an angry pink stripe across her face.

"Shea," she says, her eyes shining. "You came back. It's so good to see you. Get me out of these restraints, girls. Hello, Sister Grace."

We unbuckle the restraints on Mother's wrists and lower legs. "Mother, we've got to hurry. We've captured seven of the Elders, but—"

"Just a minute, girls. Help me sit. I'm stiff from being strapped down."

I take her hands and pull her up so she's sitting on the edge of the table. She's aged since I last saw her, more silver in her hair, the wrinkles around her eyes and mouth deeper. "Mother, where's Dad?" I ask, my heart in my throat.

"Just a minute, Shea. Are you okay? Let me look at you," she says, holding my face in her hands and gazing keenly into my eyes. "You look ... strong. I knew my little girl would be alright." She smiles at me and then turns to my companion. "I'm glad you're here, Sister Grace."

Sister Grace grins her acknowledgment.

"The Elders keep me locked up here to tend to their injuries. I think the Daeiosians started fighting back, girls. The Elders have done something to them, though, because they aren't coming in here with new injuries. Brother James brings me meals."

He could walk in any minute.

Hurrying, I tell Mother about the X being used as a brainwashing drug. That Brother Michael just brought a stockpile into Daeios. "I hadn't connected the X to their compliant behavior. It makes sense," she says with a brisk nod. "They ran out of X."

"Mother, where's Dad?"

"I've been praying he's in Solitary Confinement. It's in the corner over there, along with Security. I can't bear to think the worst." Her voice cracks and tears well in her eyes. "Shea, I don't know what's happened to Maya, either. Or your sweet Julian."

I feel off-balance; the world is spinning too quickly. She doesn't know if they're alive. They have to be okay. They have to be.

"We'll find Maya and Julian, don't worry. I'm sure Dad's okay," I lie. "How did you get Dad to help you if he was brainwashed?"

"I held his face in my hands like I do and I brainwashed him myself," she says, triumph in her voice, reminding me of my grandmother telling her stories. "The prep ladies had come to me because you needed a nurse. You were ..." Her voice falters, and she swallows. "We loaded you in an ATV from Security and drove you out. You would've been so proud of your dad, Shea. He wore his security uniform and told the gate agent that the Elders had ordered our banishment. His love for his family was stronger than his obedience to the Elders. Of course, we came back for Maya. They expected him to return without me, so they locked me up and I imagine they did the same to him."

Sister Grace clears her throat. "I'll go check Solitary Confinement for Brother Aidan."

I tell her how to feel her way to Door 5 in the darkness. "I'll be right back." She uses a key card and disappears from the room out into the dark hallway.

"Mother, I want to apologize for the way I was acting—"

"There's no need, Shea. You've become the young woman I always knew you'd become. I always loved you, Shea, no matter how angry we were. A mother's love for her children is pure and unconditional."

"Mother, I'm pretty sure I'm pregnant," I say, tears forming in my eyes.

"Oh, Shea." Her cold hands grasp mine and she scoots down from the table she was strapped to. When she reaches the ground, she throws her arms around me and squeezes me to her, rocks me. "You don't have to have it. We'll get out of here and—"

"I want to keep it, Mother. I do understand a mother's love because I feel it for this child."

I'm disappointed when she pulls away, an unreadable look in her eyes. Her words are quiet and purposeful. "Shea, when I was younger than Maya is now, I was raped and gave the child up for adoption. It was before they were aborting teenagers' babies. I love that child and hope someday he—"

A key card in the slot.

I whirl around, stepping in front of Mother, my gun pointed at the door. Sister Grace appears and I drop the gun to my side, letting my breath out in a little gust, catching it again. She pulls the door closed behind her. "He's in Solitary, but he's in bad shape."

"My poor Aidan. What have they done to him?" Mother asks, stepping toward Sister Grace.

"They've been torturing him, trying to find out where you left Sister Shea." She drops her gaze to the floor. "His feet are a mess. He can't walk."

Mother stifles a sob with a hand clapped over her mouth. She sniffs a couple of times and then squares her shoulders. "We'll get him out of there first. We'll take him to the RV and make him as comfortable as we can. And we'll get those bastards, girls. Then we'll find Maya and Julian and get out of here. Who's left?"

"Brothers Christian, James, Eli, Thomas, and Nathanael," I say, extending a finger of my hand as I name each one. "But we don't have any way to restrain them. Mother, I want to take them alive."

"Why?" Mother asks, her eyebrows up.

"Killing them one by one isn't big enough for what they did to me. Or to Jace. For what they did to all of us."

"Well, it's your call. But remember, I saw the results of what they did to you. I want them dead."

"Leave it to me," I say, my hand on her forearm. "For now, we need restraints."

"I think I have just the thing. You have key cards to all of the rooms?"

"We think so," Sister Grace says, handing her a key.

"We can find what we need next door in the Pharmacy. Come on, girls." Mother scans the card to exit. Sister Grace takes hold of the handle. She opens the door a gap and listens for movement before pushing the door open and nodding us through.

I exit, the .44 held out in front of me, and Mother follows. Mother scans the card in Door 2 and locates the adjacent light switch. The room lights up, revealing shelves of clear bottles filled with pills, silver medical tools, medical dressings in white packaging. "This ought to take care of them, but only for an hour or two." She stuffs a handful of capped syringes in a pocket of her white lab coat.

"Bring enough for all of the Elders. How do you know if it will be one hour or two?" I ask.

She adds more syringes to her pocket. "You don't. It depends on the Elder's weight and metabolism." She crams more than a dozen small vials of clear liquid into her other jacket pocket.

"Here, Mother, you take the gun," I say, handing it to her.

She pops the cylinder open and checks it. "It's only got two bullets." I look at her and she raises her eyebrows and snaps the cylinder closed. I reach into the strapwork and pull the hunting knife from my pack. Sister Grace scans us out, checking the hallway again before moving aside for Mother and me to pass.

I hold the knife in my left hand and pass my knuckles along the wall as I lead Mother by the hand to the inky blackness of the north wall, Sister Grace behind us. I count twenty-nine steps across the hall and feel my way to Door 5. There's a glow coming from the hallway to the northeast.

Sister Grace opens Door 5.

A man is screaming inside that room. Daddy?

Mother pushes me aside with the gun held out in front of her and I run ahead of her. The twins are sitting on low stools, their backs to me. They're torturing my dad. Their bodies block my view, but a blowtorch and various hand tools lie on the floor beside them. They tortured me too. Rage fills me and I want to stab them again and again, but that would be the easy way out for them.

They don't hear us come up behind them.

Dad quiets to sobbing, his teary eyes wide, giving us away. The twins jump up and swivel to face us, their faces etched with disbelief. One holds a bloody box cutter that he swipes at me, missing.

Mother elbows me aside and cocks the gun.

I bump her arm up as she fires; the bullet sparks against the wall above us and zings past us, clicking off the walls and floor, landing harmlessly without hitting anyone. I wrestle the gun from her grasp. One bullet left.

One twin runs toward the back wall of Solitary Confinement. Sister Grace pulls her bowstring back and sends an arrow whizzing into his heel. He crashes to the ground, yowling, sliding a few feet on the rock floor.

The other one, the one Mother would've shot first, cowers in front of us, tears and snot streaming down his face, his lips downturned and quaking. "Please," he says, his hands up.

"Were you there? Did you breed me?" I ask.

"Y-yes. God—"

I slam him in the side of the head with the butt of the gun and he falls to the ground at our feet, unconscious. Sister Grace squats down and takes his key card.

"Leave it to me, Mother. Now, please inject them. We have to keep moving. There are three more Elders loose out there. Only one to two hours after these two injections before we need to be out of here."

"Help me, Helen," Dad says, his voice deep and wet.

"Oh, Aidan. I'm so sorry." She rushes to him. "Did all of the Elders torture you?"

"Just these two," he sobs. "I haven't seen the other Elders since they locked me in here."

"You may be safer in here than anyplace we try to hide you, then," she tells him, not looking in his eyes. "I'm going to give you a half-dose of the injection to let you sleep while we deal with this, Aidan. I'll give you something for the pain and treat the wounds when we get these sons-of-bitches taken care of. It won't be long. I promise."

She cups his pallid face in her hands and kisses his quivering lips, long and gentle. Then she prepares a syringe, flicking an air bubble out with two taps of her middle finger. "I love you, Aidan. Everything's going to be fine when we get out of here."

"I love you, dear." He lies back and closes his eyes. Mother finds a vein in his arm and injects him. His arms fall to his sides and his face twitches into peacefulness.

Mother turns and gives a shot to the twin nearest us. Her skirt moves from in front of Dad's feet. My toes curl up and my stomach roils. His feet are red and puffy, slashed and burned. The fresh cuts are bleeding. The burn blisters ooze and there are black holes where his small toes should be. Three other toenails have been removed. A wave of nausea and searing hatred passes through me.

When we reach the other twin he makes a feeble attempt to get away from us, looking over his shoulder at us and sobbing, scrabbling with his hands. A pair of needle-nose pliers lay beside him. Mother takes hold of the arrow in his heel and twists it and he screams.

"Were you there, too?" I ask when he pauses for breath. "Did you rape me?"

He nods, shivering. Sister Grace yanks the arrow from his heel and he yelps. She wipes the blood on his white pants and places the arrow in her quiver. The twin lets Mother inject him and he falls unconscious.

I pocket his key card. Our eyes meet over the gun as I hand it back to Mother.

"The countdown begins," I say.

38

We make a hasty check and find no one else in Solitary Confinement or Security. Then we slide down the glowing hallway, weapons at the ready. The warm light grows brighter as we near the entrance to the northeast section—the door Julian had gone through the night he escorted me back to Detention from my recon of the north wing. He was working that night. This hallway must lead to the Purity Room.

The flickering light diminishes, like a candle flame that's going out.

We reach the door. It's ajar. Sister Grace's face glimmers as she peeps through the crack.

She lowers her head to us and speaks in a low voice. "It's the Purity Room. Someone's in there with the entrance door propped open. He's burning something in the incinerator. I only see one man, and his back's toward us. It's dark except for the light of the fire."

"I'll go in first," Mother says.

Sister Grace pushes the door open. The fire is brighter now, roaring, throwing heat into the hallway. Mother and Sister Grace slip into the room and I follow.

The man closes the incinerator with a clank. The roaring

diminishes and the light of the fire is gone, leaving us in the dark. We stop walking. Fear starts tickling at my scalp.

He opens it up again and the flames leap forward as he throws something in.

Mother runs up behind him and places the gun to his head. He slams the door shut with a metallic bang and we're thrown into darkness again.

The click of the hammer being pulled. The stifled roar of the fire. The smell of ammonia.

"Hold it right there." I throw my pack off and dig out my headlamp. Switching it on, I move into the warmth in front of the man. Mother's expression is curiously detached.

My light shines off the man's white face and yellow teeth, his too-black hair, making him squint.

Brother Eli stands with his hands up, pissing down his leg. He's the one that burned me in my harrowing dreams. Phantom pain burns my forearms.

"Please. I didn't want to do it. God said we had to do it."

"Do what? Tell us what you did," Mother says.

"It wasn't just me, it was all of us. We ... bred you, Sister Shea."

"You raped me." My voice is as rough as the rock wall inside Daeios. "Give me your key card." He digs in his back pocket and places it in my hand. I pass the headlamp to Sister Grace and take the gun from Mother, pressing it against the crown of his head. My hands shake.

"Don't—" he says, then drops to my feet in his own urine. Mother tosses the used syringe into the darkness.

I flash the headlamp around the room. The incinerator is constructed from red brick and has two black steel doors, one larger than the other. Red rock walls to the east, white human-made walls to the west.

I move into the hallway and scan the walls. The headlamp beam passes over something silver along the white wall. I approach it and see that it's a stainless steel elevator door. No button to call the elevator, just a scanner with no light. I reach into my pocket for a key card.

A brilliant flash of light comes down the hallway from the south. I extinguish my headlamp and pocket the key. The light is dull now, facing another direction. Beneath my feet I feel a vibration, its sound masked by the roar of flames from the incinerator.

The beam of light comes straight at us again, then turns to the west.

Someone's driving down the ramp into Daeios.

39

Sister Grace grunts and her feet scuff on the ground as she runs in the direction of the driveway. Brother Christian and Brother James returning to Daeios?

"Stay here," I tell Mother, handing her the headlamp and the gun. "We'll meet you here when we're done with them." I sprint off before she can say anything.

The headlights face us at the bottom of the ramp. Sister Grace jinks into the shadows of the west wall of the hallway and I follow her.

The car turns toward the tunnel that leads to D section. They must not have seen us. But they'll see the stopped RV, with Brother Michael tied up on the ground. A clear warning that we're here.

We can see better as we near the tunnel because of the light emanating from within. Sister Grace runs to the wall where the southeast section meets the tunnel and peeks around the corner. She turns her head over her shoulder as I reach her. "It's a black town car with tinted windows. I can't tell if there's anyone inside besides the driver." She looks around the corner again and reports to me. "The car is heading to the RV with its brakes on. Barely moving."

"When the car stops, we go, try to catch them as they're exiting the vehicle."

She nods once and turns back to look around the corner. She takes off down the tunnel. I'm right behind her.

The driver has his hand on the open door, his foot on the ground. No movement from the passenger side.

As the driver leans to the left to push himself out of the car seat, a display of brassy blond hair. Brother James. He bit my shoulder in my nightmare and I smelled the reek of his spicy cologne. I quash a gag.

Sister Grace has an arrow ready, her bowstring pulled back, as she dashes to the driver's side of the car. I run to the passenger side, my knife in position to hold the blade across someone's throat.

Brother James steps out of the car, not taking his eyes off the RV. The arrow is making a red dimple in his neck before he realizes we're here. He sucks in a deep breath and holds his hands up at shoulder height.

I open the passenger side door. There's no one else in the car.

"Brother James, my seed-bearer," Sister Grace hisses. "What a joke."

"Is that what this is about?" His face is brazen, haughty. "You didn't see what you thought you saw, little girl."

"It's about what you did to me." I step in front of him.

His face shows astonishment. He had no idea I was here. But his smirk returns in an instant. "Sister Shea. Our special breeder. I didn't have any problem having sex with you." He chuckles. "When I saw the fight in your eyes ... well. That's all it took."

Sister Grace's knuckles turn white on the hand that holds the bow. Her breath is coming out a slow, deep pant. I don't know if I can keep her from killing him.

"Sister Grace." I don't know if she can hear me; she doesn't even blink. The slow movement of her chest, the flaring of her nostrils. "Leave it to me, Sister Grace."

She holds her posture, her muscles taut. Her lips jerk and then she licks them. The knife feels prickly in my hand.

"Girls! I've got him." Mother hurries up behind Brother James, handing the gun and the headlamp to me. She pulls serum from a vial with a syringe. Sister Grace doesn't move. Mother plunges the needle into his neck. He slumps to the ground, unconscious, disappointing that savage part of me. I stuff his key card in my pocket.

"Brother Michael, Mother," I say. "Inject him while we're here."

He tries to squirm away from her, tries to plead through the tape, but I hold him still while she gives him the shot. "I want them all to have injections."

"Alright. Can I ask why?" Mother asks, counting the syringes and vials to double check that she has enough.

"Because I want them out for now. I need them awake at the end."

The three of us stand facing each other, silent.

Sister Grace breaks the pause. "The north section next?" She places the arrow in the quiver again and the bow on her shoulder.

Mother has her forearms wrapped against her abdomen. "You've already looked everywhere else?" She points the question at me first, then at Sister Grace.

"Yep," we say in unison.

Mother begins, "Then—"

"Hello, Brothers and Sisters of Daeios!" booms through hidden speakers and echoes around us. Brother Christian is on the stage in the Gathering Area.

40

I hand the gun to Mother and stow the headlamp and we race to the east wall of D section and continue most of the way through C. Mother lags behind but not by much. We stop just outside the Gathering Area to regroup. Breathe.

"I know you're out there, Sister Shea. Come in with your hands up and I won't hurt you."

I don't think he knows there are three of us. One of us will get him. I turn to the others and ask the question with my eyes.

Mother nods. Sister Grace blinks her agreement and readies herself at the right side of the doorway.

I sprint across the entrance, throwing a glance over my shoulder into the Gathering Area. Brother Christian stands on the stage, a gun pointing up at the ceiling, his elbow bent.

My knees threaten to give out at the sight of him. A memory of the vicious leader of my rape slapping lubricant on his penis and grabbing my ass. Pulling me to him on the breeding table. The white walls sway around me. I press my shoulder against the wall next to me to keep my balance.

Mother walks into the Gathering Area, her gun held steady in front of her. "Put down the gun, Brother Christian. I've seen you shoot. You'll have a better chance without it." She strolls toward him, the skirt of her gown swaying to and fro as she advances. Sister Grace moves through the doorway and stays to the wall on the right. Brother Christian points the gun at her. He turns and, undecided, swings the gun back toward Mother.

Unnoticed, I slink down the hallway toward Medical. The north section hallway outside Medical goes right into the Gathering Area.

"I'll bet, Brother Christian, that this arrow can reach you before you can pull the trigger on that gun," Sister Grace says, her voice overflowing with malice.

I peer around the doorway. Brother Christian is aiming his gun at Sister Grace. Both she and Mother are approaching him. He stands near the steps, stage left, and points the gun back and forth between the two. His back is to me. "Don't come any closer," he says to them, a catch in his voice.

I rush up the other stairs, grabbing hold of his silver hair and pulling him back toward me as I press the hunting knife to his throat. His gun clatters to the stage.

"God will punish you for this," he rasps.

I want to finish him. To slice his throat open, get his hot blood on my hands, watch it pump onto the floor, the light draining from his eyes. "Mother."

"He's yours, Shea. Take him," she says, her weight shifting, her voice black with hatred.

"Kill him," Sister Grace says. A glint of bright eyes, the animal's.

"You can't do it." Brother Christian has a note of victory in his thick voice. "God has stayed your hand."

"I have stayed my hand. Tell me what you did to me. Say it." I speak at normal volume, my mouth close enough so he should be able to feel the rebound of my voice off his eardrum.

"I gave you my seed," he says, a loud hiss directed up at me.

I pull the knife so tight to his throat that he squeaks. "Mother. The serum."

She passes her gun to Sister Grace. Gets a syringe ready. Glides up the steps.

"How dare you hurt my child, Brother Christian? I hope you rot in hell." With brute force, she stabs the syringe into his neck by his shoulder. I let him go and he collapses onto the stage. All three of us watch until he is still.

"We're sure that's all of them?" Mother asks.

I pick up the handgun and take his key card and hand them to Sister Grace. She stuffs the gun inside the survival pack and the key card in her pocket. I run the names through my head twice. "That's all twelve. Thank you so much for helping me, both of you." I give them quick hugs. We have to hurry.

I instruct Mother on where to find the other Elders so she can inject those who haven't been dosed with the knockout serum yet. "Then it's time to fetch Dad, Maya, and Julian, and get out of here."

"The Daeiosians, Shea. We need to find them and let them out, too."

"I know, Mother. Maya and Julian are probably with them. We'll need them to show us how to get through the blast doors, anyway."

"I'll sedate the other Elders while you girls move Aidan. Take him to Medical where I can tend to him. He'll need morphine for the ride to the hospital. There are gurneys up against the back wall, use those to transport him. Bring some towels. Don't leave your dad until I return."

"We won't, Mother." I hand her a key card. She takes up her skirts and runs lightly toward the Activity Area.

41

How strange it is for Daeios to be so silent and tranquil. What a relief to be safe in here for the first time since we arrived in May. Sister Grace has her bow on her shoulder and I have the .44 Magnum and my hunting knife in the strapwork on my daypack.

By the time we wander around in the dark north sector with the headlamp, retrieve several white fluffy towels and the gurney from Medical, and wheel it to Solitary Confinement, Mother is jogging toward us through the Gathering Area. I dash to her and light our way back to Door 5.

"Helen! Shea!" Dad cries in shuddering, happy sobs when he sees us. Although the twins aren't yet moving, the knockout serum already wore off on Dad, who is a shadow of the man he once was. Mother runs into his arms and I witness the gentle love that lies between them. I hug Dad when it's my turn as Sister Grace stands awkwardly by. We Donovans get ourselves together and I introduce Dad and Sister Grace to each other, forgetting that Sister Grace was the first to see Dad.

"Aidan, we've taken care of the Elders. Now we've got to get everyone out of here. Have you heard anything that might tell us where to look for Maya and Julian and the Daeiosians?"

"No, they only interrogate me. How am I going to get out of here? I can't walk." The suffering in his voice stings me.

"We'll go to Medical and I'll collect some morphine. Then I'll see what I can do for your wounds, Aidan. I can at least make you more comfortable for the ride home. The girls can find everyone else."

He gives her a painful smile and nods, scowling at his damaged, size 14 feet. Sister Grace and I move the stools and torture devices out of the way.

Dad lets out a shaky breath before trying to stand on the towels Mother has lain on the ground to cushion his feet from the hard rock floor. She and I act as his crutches and support his weight as much as we can as we transfer him from the seat in his cell to the gurney. He howls deep in his throat, his teeth clenched when he first stands on his tender, inflamed feet. Breath explodes from his chest. He lies on the gurney with his eyes closed and lips trembling.

"Aidan, I'm so sorry," Mother says, gripping his hand and dabbing the sweat from his brow with a towel. She bends over and gives him a kiss on the lips.

"I feel better already, dear," he says, his voice shaking, trying for a smile but failing.

We help Mother wheel Dad into Medical. I leave the heavy gun with her, and a key card. I give him a kiss on the cheek and try not to look at his mangled feet before Sister Grace and I leave to look for the others.

"There's an elevator door in the northeast section. We need to check it out too. We don't have much time before the Elders start regaining consciousness. Let's split up."

"I've got the north wing, Sister Shea. Two more doors on this side. Twenty-nine Sister Shea-sized steps across. Two more rooms that we haven't looked into on that side of the wing. You go see where the elevator leads; I'll handle roaming around in the dark."

As we stand in the light of the Gathering Area, I pull myself up to give her a hug. "I couldn't have done this without you, Sister Grace. Thank you for changing your mind."

"We're going home." She almost crushes me in her strong grasp and I withdraw from her arms to get my wind back. Her eyes are shiny with tears.

"Do you want the headlamp?" I hold it out to her.

She runs a fingertip under each eye to remove the dampness. "Nope, I've got this. See you in a few." She beams as she pulls out a key card and disappears into the darkness near Door 3.

I stride through the Gathering Area with my daypack dangling from my left hand. Before heading into the dark hallway I pull the aluminum water bottle out of the strapwork and drink some water. They all did it. The Elders raped me, and I have their confessions. Soon I'll have my revenge. I head into the hallway that leads to the northeast section, leaving the door ajar and shining my light around until it lands on the shiny elevator doors.

What will I find up there? Will I find the Daeiosians? Will I learn more sinister secrets of Daeios?

42

As I push the elevator button, I smell stale smoke and the damp and dirt of Daeios. Is the incinerator fire still burning? I don't hear it. I board the elevator and press the *UP* button, then stuff my headlamp in my pack. The faltering fluorescent light from the elevator is intermittent, bright then dark. The doors start to ease closed.

A hand reaches inside the elevator doors and keeps them from closing.

"That was fast," I say, throwing on my pack and looking up, expecting Sister Grace.

Julian steps into the elevator, breathing hard.

"I'm glad I caught you, Shea. You weren't leaving without me, were you?" He tilts his head, Julian-style, gives me that same shy smile he gave me when he took my hand at the first Gathering.

My dear Julian is unharmed. I start to go to his arms when I see a large smear of blood on the elevator door where he touched it. I instinctively step back and pull my eyes away from the red smudge, trying to keep my breathing measured.

The strobing elevator light makes Julian's face jump out at me and then recede, making me dizzy. I lean my shoulder on the icy steel wall across from Julian to steady myself. He hits the button to close the doors and then the *UP* button, marking them both with blood.

I try to shrug off the sure knowledge that I'm trapped in here. He drew blood on my parents or my friend, maybe killed them all.

"Going up?" he asks, his face no longer elfin. The elevator jolts and starts ascending, fast, making me sick to my stomach. My fear feels like a poisonous snake slithering up my back.

Julian hits the *STOP* button, and we lurch to a standstill. It feels like my stomach slipped through my esophagus and stayed in the depths of Daeios. My blood moves through my veins, an icy sludge.

"Kiss me," Julian says as he wraps his arms around my waist, below the daypack, and pulls me in. He has a spray of blood droplets on his face, across his white shirt.

I pull away from him and hit the *START* button. The elevator starts to ascend. Julian hits the *STOP* button again. He leans in and pecks my taut, cold lips.

My breath catches in my lungs; I'm going to pass out. The bats return from their long sleep and flap around inside me, sucking up all of my oxygen, all of my blood.

I turn and push the *START* button again, standing in front of the control panel, facing it, gathering my courage and my wits. Julian can't get to my knife without a tussle. Neither can I.

Julian snickers, a horrible, evil sound. "Aren't you happy to see me?"

I turn to face him, hoping I appear calm, unknowing. His face is a total blank, his hellish eyes drilling through me, roaming inside of me.

He flashes a Cheshire Cat grin and slithers around me. Pushes the *STOP* button again. Facing me, he puts his hands on my shoulders, squeezing them, hurting me. "You seem tense. Come here, you."

He pulls me to him, pack and all, squeezing the held breath out of me. His penis is hard against my thigh. I try to wriggle from his grasp, but he holds me in place, his breath too hot on my skin. He presses his chin into my scalp as he says quietly, "They had no right to take you out of here." He ejects a loud belly laugh that presses against me and makes me recoil enough to push away from him and hit the *UP* button again. "You always wanted to get married. Let's find Brother Mark the minute we get off the elevator, shall we?" He's sporting his shy, boyish grin. My mind fights to come unhinged, to not know what I know.

"We can't get married without my family. I want them at the wedding," I say inanely, swallowing bile, my voice strangely calm as I turn to face him. The bats almost smother me, their black, hand-like wings crawling out of my throat, making my vision spotty.

"We're all family down here, Sister Shea," he says, donning the beatific look he wore while I was living in Daeios. He wasn't brainwashed by the X in the water. It was all an act.

The elevator reaches the floor above Daeios and eases to a halt. The doors don't open. Julian steps in front of the buttons so I can't press the *OPEN DOOR* button.

I can't wrap my mind around it, who he really is. I want to glare at him, to show him I'm not afraid, but my eyes fall under the blankness in his eyes.

He smiles lasciviously, his gaze wandering up and down my body. "You're looking mighty fine, Sister Shea. Those perky little breasts of yours have grown." His eyes snap up to meet mine. "I've seen enough pregnant women to know one when I see one. That baby belongs to Daeios."

I capture a primal, savage voice from deep inside and I hurl my words at him. "It's my baby."

Julian slaps me, hard, leaving me reeling. He stands back to admire his barbaric handprint on my face. "Your baby? My baby! You finally got your wish. I fucked you. Was it worth the wait?"

My knees threaten to buckle. "No. You weren't with them." My voice is small, the voice of the petrified little girl buried deep inside me. He can't have been there. I would've seen him in my nightmares. I would've heard his voice.

"Oh, yes, I was. The baby's probably mine."

My world has tilted 180 degrees. I put my hand on the elevator wall to keep from falling over. Julian presses the *DOWN* button and we start descending.

He rubs his fingernails on his shirt and then examines them. He smiles brightly and places his hand on my pregnant belly, and I throw it off. He ejaculates a chilling laugh.

I barely have control of my voice. "Why were you with the Elders?"

"You just don't get it, do you? I ordered the rape as your punishment for refusing to breed. When I came into the Breeding Room, they parted the way the Red Sea did for Moses." He grabs his crotch, holds it for a minute. "I raped you first. It may look like me, but this baby is the Chosen One. It has thirteen fathers. The Chosen One belongs to Daeios."

A stab of revulsion runs through me. The fluorescent light flashes and buzzes.

"Did you think that simple-minded Brother Christian could lead something as important as Daeios? The Elders are my twelve disciples. My sadistic little pawns. They do as I say. God works through me."

A drop of his spittle lands on my face, and I wipe it off before it burns through my skin and muscle, through my skull to stain my brain with madness.

"Unfortunately the X didn't work on you and Sister Helen, but that's okay now." He lifts my chin with his left hand and I see the blood, smell the blood on it. Oh, Mother, are you alright? "You'll never leave Daeios." He winks at me.

The elevator lands with a slight bump on the ground. I elbow Julian in the solar plexus, stomp on his instep, punch him in the neck, and knee him in the groin. He grunts with each impact and falls to the elevator floor, choking and wheezing, holding his crotch with both hands. I push the *OPEN DOOR* button and sprint to the entrance to the north wing. It's no longer ajar.

Willing myself to keep my fear of the dark from disabling me, I fumble with the button on my cargo pocket. My hands are shaking. I pull a key card out of my pocket and drop it. I turn to see Julian in the light of the elevator, rising, a large, bloody knife glinting in his hand. I think of my own knife, secured behind me in my daypack's strapwork. He'll be here before I can throw off my pack and tug the knife free of the mesh.

Hurry, Shea, hurry! I fumble in my pocket some more, retrieving another key card.

The elevator doors shut with a pneumatic hiss and a metallic tap, pitching me into total darkness.

I want to scream. Julian is after me. He killed Mother or Dad or Sister Grace or all of them. He's going to kill me, and my cherished baby dies with me.

I find the scanner with my fingers. I don't know which way to hold the key card in the dark. I don't know where Julian is, how fast he's moving. I can't hear him over my thrashing heart, my ragged breathing.

I scan the key, and it fails with an electronic beep cheerfully announcing my presence. I turn the card and scan again. Another beep. What if I don't get it right in time? I imagine the sharp blade at my throat, biting into my flesh and slicing me ear to ear.

I flip the card over and scan it. Just the beep. What if the card doesn't work? I turn it to the last possible position. Hold my breath. Scan it.

The latch clicks. I throw the door open, releasing my held breath. Julian grabs my ponytail and jerks me back. He shrieks with a burst of insane laughter.

He sounds oddly gentle in his nasal voice. I think I broke his nose. "My favorite part, though? Raping Maya and then slitting her throat and watching her die. She screamed like a little girl until it was just a gurgle. Of course, she was—"

No, no, no, not Maya! I turn my body, slashing my straightened arm down, connect with his arm, and he loses his grip on my hair. I push him away and sprint down the hallway and through the north section. There's no light under the door at Medical. What has he done to Mother and Dad? Where is Sister Grace?

I reach the dim light of the Gathering Area. Where do I go? The living area? The Activity Area?

I can't hear Julian. Total silence. The utter cold and emptiness of Daeios takes hold of me. My family. Sister Grace.

"Shea, I'm coming for you," Julian taunts, his strange, pinched voice echoing. His steps are loud and uneven and he's moving faster. He's limping. Step-step. Step-step. Step-step. "I'm tracking you with your phone." My hand moves instinctively up to Buzz, the bud embedded below my left ear. "I always know where everyone inside Daeios is. Your parents. Sister Grace. You." He sniffs loudly, swallows his own blood. "I always knew what everyone was doing. I have cameras everywhere."

Shit! I sprint south toward the bright light of the Activity Area. I run to the Theater and scan myself in. Making sure the door latches behind me, I flip on the light. My stomach twists when I come to the boxes in front of the closet where Julian and I spent so much time in each other's arms. It was my favorite spot in all of Daeios. Now I'd like to fill it with concrete, bury all the feelings I left in there.

I dart behind the boxes and reach for my hunting knife. But it's too big and sharp for the delicate operation I have to perform. As I sit on the floor, I take off my survival bracelet and unravel it. The tiny knife falls to the floor, and I pick it up.

"Shea-ay. I'm coming for you. Are you in the Theater? Are we going to have a little tryst?" Julian bellows from a distance, hissing the "s" in "tryst."

I open the small knife.

Drawing in a deep breath, I feel for my phone bud with my left hand. I exhale and draw in another deep breath and start cutting.

The knife resists for a beat, then the blade punctures through the skin. The pain is excruciating. I break into a feverish sweat. The blood ekes out, making my hands slick. I carve an X over the bud and try to pull the phone out with my slippery fingers. It's not loose enough.

I make an incision on the side of the bud, where it feels like the bottom of it is implanted. It's still not coming out. Hurry, Shea.

Sliding the blade in underneath the bud, I stifle a scream and pry up with the tip. The blade breaks. But the bud starts to loosen, partially poking out. I pinch it with my fingers, and it slides out in my hand, a bloody mess. Dime-sized, it resembles a thick watch battery underneath all the blood. The wound aches, throbbing with each beat of my hammering heart, stinging from the salt in my sweat.

"Oh, Shea, I'm so glad you're not letting this come between us."

He sounds far away. Can he see the Theater door yet?

"I'm getting ready for you," I call out as tantalizingly as I can, smearing the blood on my hands on a black costume jacket. I may as well act when I'm in the Theater. "Give me a minute, will you?"

"Okay. I'll wait here and count to ten, just for fun, and then I'm coming in. One."

This is a game to him. Pulling the duct tape from my pack, I place a small piece on a key card so I'll know which way it scans in the dark. I shove the tape back in the pack, fold the top of the pack over, not cinching it. I pull the knife from the strapwork and put the pack on. The key card goes in my left cargo pocket, away from the others.

"Two."

I run to the boxes in front of the room where we ... ugh. I lay down the hunting knife and move them aside.

"Three."

I open the door and rush to our "bed," where I bury the phone bud and the tiny broken knife between layers of red velvet stage curtains. I loosen the light bulb so he can't turn the light on.

"Four." He's getting closer.

Pushing the lock in on the doorknob, I pull it closed. Picking up the hunting knife, I venture out to peek around the corner at the entrance door. Julian's face isn't showing in the window yet.

"Five."

He's still down the hallway. Can he see the door from where he is? Is he coming from the east or the north? I edge along the wall toward the door, as quickly as I can, moving sideways.

"Six."

I reach the door, crouch down in front of it, poking my head up just long enough to see if Julian's in sight of the door. He's not.

I scan the key card and let myself out as he says "Seven." I hope it covered the sound of the door opening. I let myself out, leaving the door ajar so he can meet me for our "tryst."

"Eight." His grating voice is much louder now.

I scurry down the hallway in the direction of the Gathering Area, stealthy as a cat, hoping I don't run right into him.

"Nine." He's coming from the east. I sprint for the opening to the Gathering Area.

"Ten. Ready or not, here I come."

I stop and back up against the wall so my movement doesn't catch his eye. He hobbles into the Theater from the east sector. The door slams shut behind him. He didn't see me. I've bought a few minutes. I think of my family and Sister Grace. Are they all dead? I try to shove the burning tears back into my eyes with my bloody fingers. It doesn't work. I swipe them away.

Julian shouts maniacally at me for locking him out of "our room" and fires several shots from a gun.

Shit! Where did he get a gun? I run toward the Gathering Area, breathing hard.

Julian roars. He actually roars. My body stiffens with mind-shattering terror. Looking over my shoulder, I see him trudging down the hallway toward me, holding a handgun in front of him. "Wasn't it nice of Brother Jace to hold your gun for me? I knew I made the right decision to let him rot in the Suicide Room."

Bile rises in my throat as I remember trying to find Jace. I tried to find Julian, too.

"I put the gun—your gun—in Jace's hand," he says, like he's speaking to a toddler.

Julian killed Jace, just when he was returning to his old self. Returning to us.

They didn't cremate Jace. I imagine him lying on the bloodied white couch, the blood now black, his headless body shriveling.

Nausea eddies in my stomach. I turn my head and spit vomit on the floor as I enter the Gathering Area.

"Shea, I don't want to kill you. You're carrying the Chosen One. But that doesn't mean I won't hurt you, for the good of Daeios." Julian marches toward me down the Activity Area hallway, his limp less pronounced now. "Brother James can scramble your brains. Or put you in a coma. We'll have breeding parties whenever we want to."

I freeze, breaking into a sick, cold sweat. He said my baby belongs to Daeios. He'll keep me here and take my baby. Nausea threatens again. He fired several shots at the door to open it. How many rounds does he have left? Where should I go?

Just as I decide my chances are better in the darkness of the north wing, I hear the bang of a gun. A round slams into my calf, throwing me to the ground in the light of the Gathering Area. My hunting knife flies from my hand across the tiles, out of my reach, as I crash down, screaming, spraining my left wrist and scraping my knees.

The scan of a key card. Mother runs out of Medical with her gun in both hands, kicking the door closed behind her. "Shea?"

"Mother, it's Julian, he's coming down the hallway behind me!" I warn her.

Mother pulls the hammer back and aims at the hallway entrance, her stance solid, her arms steady. Her eyes are black with vengeance.

Julian strides in and shoots her in the forehead, a black hole opening in the center of it like a third eye. The .44 Magnum fires, but the bullet misses. He pulls the trigger of the Ruger again. Click. He tosses the empty gun.

"Mother!" I scream as she collapses to the floor. I lift myself off the ground, ignoring the agonizing throb in my calf, and stagger as fast as I can into the darkness of the north wing. I shrug away the thought of cold hands raking my body as I enter the darkness.

I'm unarmed. Mother is lying there, dead, her warmth dissipating into the coldness of Daeios. Tears stream from my eyes, blurring my vision. Blood runs down my neck, the wound throbbing, the salt in my tears stinging it.

I make my way to the inky blackness near the north wall where the light of the Gathering Area won't touch me. My right hand is out in front of me to find the wall. My mind races with what to do next, the two aspects of my bipolar confusing me. Fear of the darkness. The malignant eyes grope me, reach inside me to squeeze the air out of my lungs.

I trip over something large and yielding in the dark and slam to the floor. I hear my left wrist snap as I hit the ground with a grunt. The faint smell of death washes over me: rotting flesh and human waste. I'm next to the Suicide Room. The odor clings to my nostril hairs, making me woozy.

I crawl around on my burning knees and right hand, holding my left wrist against my body to keep it from moving. My hand lands in a cold, viscous puddle. I kneel and hold my fingers to my nose. The coppery smell of blood.

I pat around until I find the source of the blood. Lots of blood. Sister Grace's canteen. Moving my hand up, I feel for a pulse at her neck and can only find blood and sliced skin. I clap my hand over my mouth to keep from crying out.

Julian stands silhouetted where the Gathering Area meets the north wing. "I couldn't get the gun without killing her. Well, I didn't try. Shea, I want to get you the help you need for your leg. No sense in risking your life anymore. No one can help you. It's just you and me."

Daddy.

My hand lands on Sister Grace's hunting knife and I pull it from its sheath, the sound of metal scraping against tanned leather.

When I look up, Julian is gone.

I wipe my tears, quiet my breathing. Julian's feet shamble on the rock floor. Step-step. Step-step. His steps could be coming from any direction. He could be anywhere in the darkness.

A metallic sound tells me he's tracing the tip of his murderous knife across the wall, approaching me. It skids across the Pharmacy door. He can find his way in the darkness too.

"Did you know? The incinerator is a great way to make people disappear. One by one, they burn away, leaving no trace they ever existed."

My head feels like it's spinning on my neck, and I see spots. The garbage man. Human bodies are garbage to him. I choke on the bile that rises in my throat. How many Daeiosians are left?

A shuffle. He's only feet away from me.

I run toward Door 5, fear compressing my chest.

"You're such a fucking bitch. If the Chosen One wasn't so important, I'd just kill you."

Silence. I listen for the sound of the knife scraping against the wall, his footfalls, his breathing. Has he stopped moving, or is he creeping toward me? Fear engulfs me and my eyes skitter around in the darkness, searching for him. My bipolar's playing tricks on me. My head feels detached from my body.

He sniffs. He's right behind me.

I sprint away from him, my calf shrieking, and turn to face him. He sniffs again.

Pictures of their murders flash in my mind: Mother, Jace, Maya, Sister Grace. All the fury I've ever felt fills me, and I charge toward Julian, my right hand holding the knife out in front of me. I shove the knife deep into his belly, releasing a primal scream of outrage from deep in my core.

The impact knocks his knife from his hand, and we fly through the air a few feet. The light of the Gathering Area touches us. Julian lands on his back, his head pounding sickeningly on the rock floor. I land on top of him, putting weight on my broken wrist and crouching, a wild animal, not feeling any pain. The blood pumping from his stomach feels hot on my leg.

"You took too much from me," I say, my voice dusky and thick, the sting of tears behind my eyes.

As I stand, I yank Sister Grace's hunting knife from Julian's gaping stomach cavity. He draws in a sharp breath. "What about. Uncon ... ditional love?" he says, his high-pitched voice breaking with pain. The taunting grin in his voice is gone.

"That's how mothers love their children. How I love this baby."

He's silent for a moment, and I think he's gone until he says, his voice small and bewildered, "She's going to let me die." He murmurs something else, but I can't hear it.

"What is it, Julian?" I ask, my throat constricted with tears. I lean in to hear him, holding my body tense, knife ready to stab him in the throat if he reaches for me. I expect him to grab me and try to choke me, like in the movies, but he doesn't.

"I'm. Not. The only. One," he says with great effort, and he's silent.

43

I press Julian's eyelids shut, resisting the urge to press too hard. My sarcastic inner voice heckles me, asking me how I ever loved him. I thought he was my only chance for love in Daeios, which was to be my grave. Julian stroked my bruised ego by choosing me over the other women. He kept me around by promising to make love to me, to marry me. All I've ever wanted is love. I played right into his murderous hands.

This brutal death was too good for him.

Staring at Julian, I think about my baby. My child could have Y Chromo if Julian's the father. If it's a boy. He could die young, in unrelenting, mortal pain. I'll give him the best life I can until then. But please, God, don't let my child suffer. Don't take my child away from me.

I wipe the blood from the knife on Julian's sleeve and slide it into the strapwork. Locating his knife, I place it next to Sister Grace's. I don't know if Julian was referring to the Elders when he said he wasn't the only one, or to someone else I don't know about. I have to stay alert. I take his key card and place it in my shorts pocket with the other unmarked cards. My broken wrist is screeching in pain after putting my weight on it. Blood from the bullet hole in my calf has oozed down to my heel. Stickiness inside my shoe.

I limp to where Mother lies on her back, one arm contorted behind her and the other holding the worthless gun. I try not to look at the puckered hole in her forehead, but my eyes are drawn to it. Red leaks from the black hole and trickles into her hair on one side. Her eyes stare wide with shock, no blaze of strength within them. Kneeling beside her on the cold rock floor, I skim her cheek with the back of my forefinger, cup her cheek in my hand. My tears are stuck behind my eyes, burning them and making my head feel swollen.

"I'm so sorry, Mother. I had hoped you would know that Maya is okay. But she's not." A tear rolls down my cheek and lands on hers. "I was so looking forward to spending time with you, to seeing you hold your grandchild." I run the back of my hand under my nose. "I have to tell Dad. He loved you so much. I have some of your strength." I squeeze my eyes closed, my voice failing me for a moment. "Please, God, let it be enough." Leaning forward, I kiss her on the lips and close her eyes, squeezing her cold hand before getting up.

I slip the gun into the strapwork on my pack and stuff the key card she had in my cargo pocket with the others. Seeing my hunting knife, I place it with the other ones.

Grasping the sun pendant, I will it to give me strength too. Taking a long, shuddering breath, I open up Medical and switch on the light.

Dad's lying on the gurney, blinking in the glare of the overhead lighting, evidence of Mother's nursing on a tray table at his feet. His face is crumpled so that it may stay that way forever. It's blotched pink and wet with tears. He's been lying here this whole time either suspecting the worst has happened or certain that it has. He reads the truth on my face.

"Daddy?" I can barely get it out before I'm in his arms, sobbing and shaking. After a moment I pull away from him and wipe the tears from his face with my good hand. "She never even knew it happened, Dad. It was instant. She didn't suffer."

A small moan escapes his lips. He bobs his head, trying to gain control of his emotions. "H-have you found Maya and Julian yet? Where's Sister Grace?"

I shake my head, my lips pulled back into my mouth like they're trying to hide. He bows his head, his shoulders convulsing, anguish bleeding from his throat.

"I'm going to find the others now, Dad, but I wanted to make sure you're alright first."

"I'll never be alright again, Shea." He looks at me, his face wet and shattered.

"We'll do the best we can, Dad. Did Mother tell you you're going to be a grandfather?"

He gives me an almost smile, nods his head.

"I'll be back as soon as I can."

"Be careful, Princess."

"I will, Daddy." I ease the door closed behind me, leaving him locked in with my hunting knife, the only one that doesn't have blood on it.

Now to see what they did with everyone else.

44

I figure Sister Grace checked Door 3, Detention. I'm not going into Door 4. What's left of Jace is still in the Suicide Room. I walk across the hallway to Door 7, the light from my headlamp leading the way and lighting up the door to the Spa.

A chill bursts inside me and I break into a sweat. Maybe there's no sign of the Daeiosians because Julian killed them all. He made them disappear in the incinerator. Dad and I could be trapped down here with the Elders. The Elders will be conscious soon. Dad can't help me fight them. I have to hurry. Please let the Daeiosians be okay.

I scan a key card and enter, turning on the light, bringing tears to my eyes until they adjust. I switch off the headlamp and slide it on, adjusting it with my right hand until it sits evenly around my cap. The strong perfume in the air repulses me.

"Hello?" I call. No answer.

My eyes land on the mirrored door to the Breeding Room. An icy claw grips my heart, and I want to run, screaming, out of there. I see the scanner for the door, remember Sister Leah scanning me in and holding the door for me, the soft hands pushing me through. I don't think I can open that door. But open it I must.

I approach the door cautiously, picturing my reflection attacking me. I pound the side of my bloody fist, my right hand, on the mirror several times. My reflection shows how savage I look with blood smeared everywhere. It's on my face and hands. Blood from the gouge I made in my neck is seeping down my neck onto my shirt. Seeing it makes it hurt. I have Julian's blood on me. My unblinking eyes show fear.

No one answers from behind the door, but several voices, muted by the wall, call to me from the north. Someone is behind Door 6. Several someones.

I limp to exit the Spa, but the door is locked.

I turn the handle again, but it won't open.

I take a deep breath, and once my head is clear, I see the scanner, mocking me with its tiny red light.

The card scans and the lock opens. I let out a heavy, shuddering sigh. I'm okay.

Funny, I don't feel okay.

I light my way to Door 6: Unknown. My left wrist yammers as I remove my pack and lean it against the wall next to the door, the knives facing me. I pull a key from my cargo pocket. Scan it. The scanner beeps. I verify that I'm holding it in the correct position. Yes. I scan it, and it beeps.

I try another key. Just the beep. Do I need a key card I don't have? What if I can't get in and the people on the other side can't get out?

I pull another card from my pocket. Insert it in the slot. It unlocks the door.

I pull the door open, and the tangled voices come at me like a flock of small birds. I can't understand their words. The fetid air smells of unwashed bodies and human waste. I flip the light switch. No lights. My headlamp beam moves around the room as I turn my head, making me dizzy and blinding Daeiosians.

"Hello? Who's there?" a woman near the door cries above the clamor, her voice hoarse. The other voices silence.

I stand with my foot holding the door open in case I need to seize my pack and run. "It's Shea Donovan. I've come to—"

"Sister Shea! Thank God!" I know the voice. It's Sister Bethany.

She's hurrying to me in the trail of my headlamp beam, pushing her way through a crowd of people. Cries of "We're saved!" and "Praise the Lord!" and "Who's Shea Donovan?" reach me as Sister Bethany comes to me through the crowd.

I put my right hand out and she grips it in both of hers. Her hands are warm and calm, and mine are cold and shaking. She squints at me so I turn the headlamp to the side. "You need the key card that opened the door to turn on the light. Let me do it."

I hand the key card over. A moment later, the room is bathed in light and I switch my headlamp off. We stand there in front of dozens of white-clad women, blinking in the bright white room, shielding their eyes as those aboveground do from the sun. The room smells atrocious. Their white gowns are stained. The room appears to be a vault. There are closets and cupboards all around the walls, all padlocked. All white.

Sister Bethany hugs me to her, pressing against my neck wound. She still has her shiny, blonde hair. "You're covered in blood, are you alright?" she asks as she pulls away and looks at me. I bled on her neckline.

Tinkerbell shuffles to the front of the crowd, her little head shaved. "If you're looking for your family, they're not here, Sister Shea. They were never here with us. They disappeared about the same time as you did."

My baby sister and my mother are gone forever. And my brother, Jace. My eyes burn but I hold back the tears.

Daeios started with at least twice this many people. Other than children, only women stand before me, most of them bald. Their ID badges are missing—the last step in removing their individuality. Except for those with hair, only their varied facial features show that they're different. Their complexions are ashen, as if they've been drained of blood. Their only color is in their blue eyes and the remaining buns.

Did he get rid of all of our men?

"Is this ... everyone?" I ask.

"As far as we know," Sister Bethany says. "We started fighting them and they put us in here."

"Where are the Elders? They'll lock you up with us if they find you here," a woman says from somewhere in the crowd.

"We ... took care of that. I've got so much to tell you." I stand tall and square my shoulders as I say, "Brother Julian is dead. I killed him." Sister Bethany's head spins toward mine. "He's the reason for the disappearances. He's the reason for the breedings, the banishments. He gave the orders for everything the Elders did to us."

"How brave you are. I couldn't have killed him," Sister Bethany says, a shadow crossing her eyes as if she sees Julian cross over to Hell.

"Can I get everyone to the Gathering Area?" I yell above the crowd. "Go to the light." They all start shuffling to the door, slow, as always, so different from the abundant energy Sister Grace and I needed to survive. The women drag cranky children along.

Sister Bethany stands beside me. "Sister, there are three bodies out there, two in the north wing and one in the Gathering Area. Brother Christian is unconscious on the stage. Will you cover all of them in something before the children see them?" I say.

She calls to Sister Ariel and a sister I don't know to join her. They fetch several thick blankets from a pile and leave to cover the dead bodies and Brother Christian.

I'm the last to exit the room. The lights are on in the north section for the first time. I close the door to the vault, shutting in the worst of the horrible smells emanating from the overflowing portable toilet in the back corner of the room. Struggling, I wrap duct tape around my broken wrist a few times to hold it steady, leaving most of my hand and my fingers free. Picking up my pack, I shrug it on.

Sister Grace's blanketed body lies outside Door 4, the survival pack beside her. I stand over the body for a moment, and then squat, wincing as it tugs on my calf wound, and pull the top of the blanket down to reveal her face. Kneeling down next to her, I see and smell the blood that pumped from her throat, creating a large puddle on the floor. Her neck looks slashed open by giant claws.

The last traces of color have drained from her tanned face. Her eyes are wide with surprise. No longer wild, she's painfully human, lying on the floor in her own lifeblood.

I bow my head and close my eyes. Our time together was short, but she proved to be the best friend I ever had. My Spoon Sister. She gave her life for me and my family, for the Daeiosians.

"Sister Gr—" I stop myself. I should have dropped the Sister long ago. "*Grace*. Thank you, Grace," I whisper, smoothing her wispy hair off her forehead. "I used your knife to kill him." I close her opaque eyes and cover her face with the blanket.

As I stand to leave I remember to take her key cards. I have twelve cards now.

Julian didn't want me to see where *UP* leads. I'll check it before I talk to the Daeiosians. No one notices when I duck down the hallway to the northeast. Entering the hallway outside the Purity Room, I pick up the dropped key card and get on the elevator.

The elevator travels at a speed that leaves my stomach 140 feet below the ground. It stops in a few seconds. Being in an elevator with a lunatic really slowed things down.

I suck in a big breath. I push the *OPEN DOOR* button, and still, the door doesn't open. Claustrophobia envelops me, a python squeezing me around my chest.

Breathing out, my shoulders dropping, I see a key card scanner and pull a card from my pocket, inserting it into the slot. It doesn't work. I try it again. It doesn't work. I try the other key cards in my pocket until I find one that works. Only one of them had access to this room.

The doors open upon a small apartment.

45

"Hello? Is anybody here?" I call as I step off the elevator. It's toasty in here and smells like vanilla candles. A memory tries to worm its way into my heart, but I squelch it. "Hello?"

No one answers.

Everything's white: walls, carpet, furniture, and kitchen appliances. A spartan living area, kept as neat as a barracks room. White boxes in various sizes are stacked against a wall, sealed with white duct tape. A console with an array of switches. There are multiple screens, showing various views of areas in Daeios. Some Daeiosians are seating themselves in the Gathering Area, avoiding the blanketed body on the floor. Mother's body. Some are still traipsing out of the north section. No activity from any of the other cameras.

One of the knobs turns a radio on.

"—slow, homes are being rebuilt, businesses are reopening, and public services are being restored. It's been a long, painful process, but life is returning to normal for many folks in northern Arizona and southern Utah. According to—" I switch it off. We can go home. I hope our home is still standing, that it didn't get destroyed in the storms.

I push some colored buttons on the console one at a time to see what they do, watching the cameras. When I flip a red switch, all the cameras go black and I switch it back on. Many of the Daeiosians are looking up at the ceiling above them. Flipping a green switch makes the Daeiosians flinch and cover their ears. The Daeios song. I flip it off. This is where Julian watched us via the monitors. He controlled the lights and the intercoms so he could leave us in darkness and blast us with the Daeios song. So he and the Elders could torment and banish us. Make us disappear.

I hit a clear blue button, and chime, chime, chime, chime— thousands of chimes start coming from my right. Our mini-computers are in one of the boxes, and they're downloading messages. Wi-Fi.

The light pad of bare feet on the floor behind me. I whirl around toward the sound, shrugging off the pack, my hand reaching for a knife.

"Shea? Shea!"

It can't be. Can it?

Maya tumbles into my arms, laughing, and I let the pack fall at our feet. "I thought I heard your voice. I didn't know you were coming back. Julian said you and Mom and Dad went home." She's fresh from the shower and smells of lavender and freesia. Her head is shaved, which wrenches at my heart. "Did Mom and Dad come, too?" she asks, pulling back and looking behind me. "Oh," she says in disappointment, then looks back at me. "What happened to you? You're hurt."

"I'll be okay. We're going home, Maya. It's safe up there now and—"

"Shea, you know I can't go. They'll terminate my pregnancy because of my age. I know about that law. We have a doctor here to deliver our babies. And look at this place," she spins, holding her arms out. "Julian calls it the Penthouse."

"You're pregnant? Julian lived here?"

"Lives here. He's my husband. We're going to have a baby. Lots of babies." She holds her hands on her stomach and her dimples show her delight.

I clear my throat and take her hand gently in my own. "Maya ... Julian's dead. He killed—"

She sees murder in my eyes. "You killed him? I loved him! He was a man of God!" She jerks away from me, tears filling her eyes and spilling over.

"I had to, Maya. He was going to—"

"You don't need to explain anything to me." She speaks through gritted teeth, her blue eyes flashing. "You wanted to marry him, but you left. How could you be so selfish? How could you be so jealous of our happiness? Get out!"

"Maya, please, let's—" I reach for her, and she shoves me away.

"Get out!"

This is not the dear girl I know, the one with the innocent blue eyes and the face of a cherub. Her sweet face warps with anger, with hatred, making it impossibly ugly.

Is she still brainwashed?

"Maya? Julian lied to you about everything. Lied to all of us. He was never the man we thought he was. He killed Mother. Right in front of me."

"Shut up. Shut up!" she screams, her fists in tight balls. Then her face droops and she looks on the verge of collapse. "I don't want to hear any more." She's shaking, looking like she'll break apart into small, fragile pieces. She looks so young it tugs at my heart. "I knew something wasn't right when he wouldn't let me leave the apartment." She breaks into fresh sobs and I take her into my arms and hold her. It feels like she'll never let me go. We stay that way, her stubbly head rubbing against my chin, until she quiets.

When she pulls back I brush her tears away with my good hand. Her gown doesn't have a bow on it. They changed the rules again.

"Is Dad okay?" she asks, cringing, expecting the worst.

"Dad's okay. Well, the Elders hurt him, but he'll be fine once he recovers. He'll need lots of care for a while."

Her lips tremble and she drops her head to my chest and cries quietly, sniffling. I wrap my arms around her again and struggle to keep my voice calm, like Mother's. "We can leave here and go back home. The cities are rebuilding. The weather's calmed down and the earth is healing."

"But what about my baby?" she asks, her tender blue eyes huge with fear.

"Dad and I will take care of you. We won't let anything happen to you or the baby. Let's go," I say, taking hold of a strap on my pack. "I have to talk to the Daeiosians in the Gathering Area. Do you want to see them?"

She shakes her head, sniffles. "I just want to see Dad."

"Okay. He could use a good nurse. The Elders hurt his feet real bad."

"I'll do what I can," she says. "You need a nurse too." When she mentions it, my calf and wrist and the hole in my neck throb. "But, Shea, can we go through the boxes before we go down? Julian never let me touch them. Maybe some of our stuff is in them."

"Good idea. Let's see what we have. But quickly." I pull Sister Grace's knife out and slash the boxes open.

I start with the largest two boxes, the ones that are chiming intermittently now. They contain hundreds of personal mini-computers. Luckily, the charge lasts a lifetime. Now that my bud is gone, I can check my messages and make calls. If I can find my mini-computer in this mess.

We dump the mini-computer boxes and sort through the pile until we find ours. Maya squeals when she sees hers. Mine is deep purple and I spot it right away. Yes, I matched my mini-computer to my car. I hope I'll get to see Smart, that the storms didn't damage him. Or that a couple of strong teenagers didn't carry him away. But I think I've outgrown him, especially with a baby on the way. I wonder what it'll be like, living among civilization after the storms.

I jerk to my senses. We have to hurry. The Elders will be reviving soon.

Inside the next few boxes: Daeios contraband. Watches and clocks, jewelry, various methods of birth control, and wallets. How did Mother manage to keep my survival pack and her gun, and then sneak them out for me? She gave her life because she loved us. I'm going to miss you, Mother. Mom.

Inside a shoebox: confiscated ID badges. The Daeiosians will never need these again.

The last carton contains hundreds of tiny white boxes. I pull one out and open it to find a white flash drive with *Property of Daeios* stamped on it in black. I look at the tiny box again. It has a name printed on it in a fine-tipped black marker. The printing is neat and even as if it were made by a word processor: *Foster, Jebediah.*

The rows of tiny boxes are in alphabetical order. Finding the Ds I skip through them, searching for Donovan. I find Donovan, Jace, and Donovan, Shea. No boxes with flash drives for Mom, Dad, or Maya. I stuff the two boxes into my daypack. Someday I'll want to see what's on them.

"They're waiting for me, we need to get going. We need to get out of Daeios," I say, putting on my pack.

"Shea, what happened to you after your breeding? Your head's not shaved."

"I'll tell you all about it on the way home, okay?"

"Yeah. Okay." We take the elevator down. I hand her a key card and tell her to go see Dad.

I yell above the babbling crowd. "Sisters! Children! Please be seated. We need to move fast. We have lots of work to do."

I see Sister Bethany in the crowd and wave for her to join me on stage. We sit on the edge of the stage, our legs dangling, and wait for the congregation to seat themselves. Brother Christian lies under a white blanket behind us. Blood on my legs, and on my hands. Sister Bethany's muumuu is spotless, other than where I bled on it.

"Those of you in the back, can you hear me?"

They nod, so I continue. "I've come to free you from Daeios. You can—"

"I don't want to leave Daeios," an indignant Tinkerbell says in her squeaky voice. "Our pregnancies are safe here." The thought of little Tinkerbell being bred makes my heart twinge.

"Me too," all the youngest mothers say, their heads bald and no bows on their gowns. The youngest of them may still be in grade school. It sickens me. "We're safe here, from the forced abortions."

"You can't stay here. It's safe aboveground and we're all going home. We'll have to protect the young mothers so nothing happens to their babies. Homeschool them, whatever it takes. But I want you to know what happened to you." I pause before continuing, knowing how shocking this is. I clutch the pendant for strength. "The Elders and Julian drugged the water supply. They brainwashed you so you'd do as they said. When they ran out of the drug, they locked you up. God hasn't had a say in any of what happened to you down here. They used your faith in God for evil."

A low, feminine buzz starts, but it silences when I speak, my hand up to quiet them. "Please. Listen. I've been living aboveground with Sister Grace since my parents rescued me from Daeios." My throat catches, and Sister Bethany puts her arm around my waist. "The cities are rebuilding. God hasn't made it impossible to live aboveground, as the Elders led you to believe. The earth is healing. The storms come in patterns now. You can live your lives aboveground, taking shelter during the storms."

Again, they start to talk but stop when I resume speaking.

"We have to get the vehicles running and get out of here. I have key cards to all of the rooms. I need the rest of you to get all of the vehicles running once I assign other duties. Who knows how to work the blast doors and the gate out front?"

"I do," a young bald woman with a snub nose says, standing.

"I need you to show me." She approaches the stage. "Do we have any nurses or doctors here?" I continue, searching the crowd. Three women stand up. "My dad is in Medical and needs some morphine for the trip home. And could you disinfect the wounds on his feet and bandage them? Come get a key card. Take him and my sister to our RV and then help the others prepare the vehicles when you're done."

One of the women approaches me to get the card. The three of them leave the Gathering Area, going out the doorway to Medical.

Nausea curdles in my stomach. "I need help with my mother's body and Sister Grace's. We'll leave Julian. But the other two need to make the trip with us. I can't deal with it myself right now. Will someone please load them up in their RV and transport them for me? You can get gurneys from Medical to assist with moving them. And collect all the blankets and return them to Medical."

Sister Ariel stands and walks toward me, her hand out for a key card. "I'd be happy to help with that, Sister Shea. We have body bags in storage. We'll be ready to go in a jiffy." She turns to the crowd and summons three sisters to help her. They walk through the doorway to the Storehouse.

"I need four strong sisters for this next job." Women look around them, and then the two tall sisters that seated me in the Jacuzzi tub stand up and pull two other sisters with buns with them.

I hand the tall sisters key cards and tell them all where to find the Elders. "Make sure you get all twelve of them. Some of them are tied up; you need to cut them free." I hand Julian's hunting knife and Sister Grace's to the tall sisters. "Strip all of them. Drag them out of the rooms they're in and latch the doors. They've been drugged but will wake up soon, so be careful. When you're done, head to your vehicles and get ready to leave Daeios." I tell them to start with the twins. To leave Brother Christian naked on the stage once the others have left the Gathering Area.

They nod and head in the direction of the north wing.

I turn to Sister Bethany, handing her a key card. "Will you take charge of everyone else and get the vehicles running? I won't have time to fuel up our RV, will you please do that for me and make sure it starts okay? I want all vehicles running, with plenty of fuel, by the time the other ladies have completed their tasks. By the time I finish what I'm doing, we need to be out the door."

"We'll take care of it." She hops down from the stage and faces me. "You're destined for great things, Sister Shea. You and the baby you're carrying. Yes, you've got the glow of motherhood about you. Keep in touch with me, okay?" She rattles off a phone number I tuck into my brain for later.

"I will." We hug, and I wince from the shriek of pain in my neck.

She breaks the hug, her eyes, a silky blue, peering into mine. "You're more special to me than you know, Sister Shea. Goodbye." She calls for the remaining women to help her get the vehicles ready to go and they all leave as a group toward the Storehouse, taking the children with them.

I look at the young sister left standing with me. "We need a key card. I'll show you how to work the blast doors and the gate," she says.

"We need to hurry."

She runs off at a quick pace. I limp behind her to a door set underneath the driveway. I hand her a key card and she scans us in. It's a large room with a staircase leading up from the corner. That must be how Brother Christian and the security guard came out to us when we were in the void between the two sets of blast doors on the day we arrived.

She sits at a chair in front of a wide desk covered with switches. "You have these video monitors here so you can see the doors and the gate open and close. It's automated when a vehicle comes to the gate and the sensor reads that the owner of the license plate is welcome in Daeios. But entrances to vehicles that aren't registered with Daeios and exits are done manually."

"Can I open both doors and the gate at the same time? Leave them open until everyone drives out?"

"Yes, you can. You have to insert a key card here," she says, pointing to a scanner on the wall. She shows me the switches to open each door and the gate. "Should I open them now?"

"Yes, go ahead. I'll be the last one out. How do I close the doors and gate behind me?"

"There's a slot for a key card underneath an intercom out there."

"I know where the intercom is."

"You insert the key and all three exits will close at once. No buttons. Just the key."

"Okay, thanks for your help, Sister. Now go out and tell Sister Bethany to have everyone drive out as soon as their vehicle's ready. I'll bring up the rear and close it down."

"Got it," she says and races off.

Pulling the door of the room closed behind me, I hustle down the tunnel, the first car driving past me on the way to the exit. Brother Michael is lying naked against the wall, still unconscious, but no longer restrained. Brother James lies in a heap of white flesh a few feet from him. Seeing their naked bodies brings memories of my nightmares to my mind and I wrangle them down. The Elders will start waking up soon. Hurry, Shea. Hurry.

The Xanadoxalate will be locked down here with the Elders. A parade of autos drives down the tunnel toward the ramp. Toward freedom.

I lumber around the corner to the bustle of the Daeiosians getting into their vehicles, slamming doors, driving off.

I stop at WD119. Our RV is running, the Zipper attached to the back. Maya and Dad are in the RV, and Dad is sleeping on the bench seat, his large feet wrapped in white bandages. My hunting knife lies on the floor beside him. The fuel gauge registers a full tank.

"Are we leaving, Shea?" Maya asks. "The girls came by and I got their phone numbers stored in my mini-computer. I'm ready to get out of this place."

"Me too. I have to do a couple more things and then I'll drive us out of here." I place my daypack on the floor behind her seat and brush my lips against her cheek, kiss her. "I'm sorry for what's about to happen." She frowns. I take a long look at Dad and then leave the RV, limping north. Other cars and RVs are pulling out now. Sister Bethany is directing drivers so we don't have a traffic jam.

Stumbling as far as the road to the Gathering Area, I turn right. Mom has been moved, a fist-sized spot of blood where her head laid. We'll have a small ceremony for her when Dad is up to it, then bury her in the family plot.

Brother Christian is lying nude on the stage in the position of a spread-eagled Vitruvian Man.

Turning into the north wing, I stand over Julian's body for a moment. I'm shocked to see his elfin eyes staring back at me, his lips appearing pink and gentle.

There's a large, congealed puddle of blood where Sister Grace was, a giant smear. We'll have a separate ceremony for her. We can bury her in our family plot too. Or maybe I can locate her family; I can't think about that now.

I pull the survival pack to Door 3 and set it just inside the door. I dig around inside the pack to find Brother Christian's gun but can't find it. A man wails and I can't tell where it's coming from. I'm running out of time. Pulling the shovel from the survival pack, I unfold it, kicking the door to Detention closed. My left wrist hurts, but the duct tape holds it steady and my hand supports the shovel.

The twins are lying naked and colorless outside Door 5. One of them is groaning but neither moves. Hurry, Shea.

I switch on my headlamp and scuff down the hallway to the northeast section. Brother Eli lies facedown, immobile, outside the Purity Room. I have to step over him to reach the stainless steel doors.

I scan a key card to summon the elevator. The door opens immediately and I step in, pressing the blood-smeared *UP* button.

The little apartment looks like it's been ransacked. It's too bad we don't have time to get everyone's belongings back to them. The room behind Door 6 was full of storage lockers and surely held more of our possessions. We don't need them now. Freedom is enough.

I cross to the console in the corner and consult the monitors. One screen shows that the last of the vehicles are driving to the ramp that leads out of Daeios. They're leaving us behind with the Elders: an injured woman, a young girl, an unconscious man. I zoom in on Maya sitting in the passenger seat of the RV. She's looking around, watching for me. Worried.

I'm sorry, Maya, for what I'm about to put you through.

I shut the lights of Daeios down. The monitors go black except for the lights of the vehicles making their way out. Our RV still sits there, the headlights shining toward the tunnel that will take us out of Daeios. Switching on my headlamp, I scan the elevator door open.

Returning to the console, I flip the green switch. The Daeios song should be playing. I crank up the volume, run to the elevator, and ride it down.

The music gets louder as the elevator approaches the floor of Daeios. When I open the door, the music hits me like a blast of freezing air, assaulting my eardrums. Poor Maya. I hope it doesn't wake Dad up. He needs to be unconscious for the ride to the hospital.

Brother Eli no longer lies where he did only moments ago.

I race through Daeios as fast as my injured calf will take me, my headlamp beam cutting a way for me in the darkness. I'm being pursued by the wicked music, by my memories. My movements seem slow, as though I'm moving through black water. I can't hear anything but the earsplitting music, not even my own breathing, which is rushing in and out of my lungs.

Limping through the Gathering Area, I flash my light on Julian's body so as not to trip over it. Movement on the stage. Brother Christian is struggling to his feet, his white body hunched over. My fingers clench on the shovel. They're awakening. They'll come after me.

Continuing on, I round the corner toward D section, my eyes holding tight to the only lights left: our RV's lights. I hobble to the RV and climb in the driver's door, tossing the shovel on the floor next to my seat. Maya's crying and she has her hands over her ears, but her face shows relief now that I'm here.

I pull a key card from my pocket and hold it in my lips. As I turn the corner and steer into the black tunnel, something moves across the beam of the headlights.

Brother Michael, his mouth wide in a silent scream, naked and holding his palms over his ears. I swerve around him, almost running over Brother James, still in a motionless heap.

I stop in front of the Activity Area hallway and shine my headlamp down it. Brother Matthew is on his knees, his arm muscles bulging, his head on the ground, trying to cover his ears from the

Daeios song. I don't know if all of the Elders who should be in the Activity Area are still there. Other than Brother Matthew, they appear to still be unconscious. Lucky them. For a few more minutes.

A flash of movement. Brother Christian comes loping toward us, a hideous, evil scowl on his face.

I hit the gas pedal and steer the giant craft over to the towering, spiral ramp, gearing down for the ascent. Adrenaline races through my veins, but we have to crawl up the ramp. Easing up and around. The darkness swallows the edges of the narrow path. The headlight beams bounce off the walls. Mania makes me giddy. Up and around. I drive out of Daeios, leaving Brother Christian stumbling behind us.

I slam the RV into park on the other side of the gate, my whole body pulsing with nerves. Even at this distance that damn song is loud. I'd hate to be locked up with it forever.

Maya pulls her hands from her ears as I turn to jump down from the driver's door. Brother Christian is tripping up the ramp out of the darkness, the light of the outdoors shining on him.

I clutch the shovel and throw myself out of the RV. Lurching back through the blast doors, I bash Brother Christian in the face with the back side of the shovel. It stuns him and he fights for balance. I strike him in the face again and he falls on his back, writhing on the surface of the ramp.

Ignoring the pain in my calf, I sprint outside the gate. Brother Christian is getting to his knees.

I stab the key card into the slot. Nothing happens.

My heart slams inside my chest, and then both doors glide shut at once, sealing in the lurid notes of the Daeios song. Sealing in the Elders. The chain rattles and the gate clinks closed. The Elders are enclosed in total darkness, the song repeating over and over and over at top volume.

Daeios is locked down without exception.

46

My ears ringing, I jump into the driver's seat and lay the shovel by my seat as before. Dad is still sleeping, his breathing calm and even. The mirrors are no longer black. The line of vehicles leaves a rusty dust trail in the distance.

I pull a deep breath through my nose and let it ease out of my chest. "Are you ready, Copilot Maya?" I ask. My voice sounds tinny.

She runs the back of her hand under her nose and says, "Oh, yeah. Definitely."

"Seatbelts," I say. We smile at each other and buckle up.

We hold hands and take a moment to bow our heads for those we've lost: Mom and Jace, Sister Grace. I got revenge for all of them, but that doesn't ease the agony of losing them. What I feel is much stronger than grief. I pull my hand from Maya's and place it on my stomach. This new life, and Maya's baby's, will soften the pain of death.

"Shea? Let's go," Maya says, her hand on my arm.

My mind races with thoughts of my new life. For the first time ever, I'll be taking care of someone who will be wholly dependent on me. I at least have that much direction now, to be a mom. To be an aunt. To take care of Maya and Dad. To be responsible. No more squandering my life. No more partying, no more one-night stands.

And I'll never wear white again.

Daeios is still visible in the rearview mirror when I notice the sky is glistening in the sun. Tiny crystals fall to the earth and land in breathtaking, complicated shapes on the windshield. Snow?

I stop driving and roll the windows down, turn off the air conditioning. It's cool outside, and it smells fresh, not like the dirt and damp of Daeios. Maya sticks her head out her window and inhales deeply, trying to catch a snowflake with her tongue. Millions of snowflakes cascade down, the bright sun shining through them, making them sparkle like diamonds.

I touch the golden sun pendant on my chest with the miniature diamonds decorating its rays, then check its reflection in the mirror. The diamonds glint. It's winking at me. It holds Mom's strength. And mine.

I drive on through the desert. My finger skims over the sticky scab beneath my ear, and I think of Buzz. I'll get another bud and program it with his voice.

"It's 3:18, Tuesday, January sixteenth 2035? We were down there for a long time, weren't we, Shea?"

A whole new year. And a whole new life. It's been about eight months, then, but it seems a lifetime since we left home for Daeios. "Too long," I say.

"The weather calls for afternoon thunderstorms," Maya says, her eyes on her mini-computer.

But for now, it's this magical snow shower.

I toss my headlamp and cap behind me, stopping the RV once again to check my face in the rearview mirror. My eyes are ablaze, gleaming sapphires on ice. I smile as I learn that I like who I see, what I see. I love me. I have scars, but they're battle scars, and I've earned each one. I am a survivor.

I have some forbidden, but cute, freckles sprinkling my crooked nose, and my face is aglow with remembered sunshine. I even like the monobrow—it adds character. I smooth it with the fingers of my good hand. I could braid my underarm hair, but I'm okay with that, too.

I no longer fit the description of an Elite, and I'm fine with that. I don't want to be an Elite any longer, and I won't raise my child that way. I'm hopeful Maya and Dad will feel the same. The world as we knew it has changed. I hope to be a catalyst for reuniting the races, and for all whites to be on equal footing as well. No one is perfect or imperfect. There's no reason for us to remain segregated. The Human Race is God's Greatest Race.

"Shea? Can we go home now?" my sister asks, shaking me from my trance. Home. Will it be there, waiting for us?

I put the pedal to the floor, letting my hair fly loose out the window, pulling the cool, clean air through my nose and mouth. I reach over and place Maya's hand on my pregnant belly, and we both laugh with joy.

We are free.

We are boundless.

Thank you for reading DAEIOS: 140 FEET DOWN. Please kindly leave a review online at Amazon, Barnes & Noble, and/or Goodreads. Thank you.